DO

Also by André Hansson

THE JACKET TRICK

DOME

ANDRÉ HANSSON

André Hansson
2024

ISBN: 9798307543931

André Hansson
www.andrehansson.com

For my parents

Prologue: Scott

London's central dome stood tall and proud, its crown soaring impossibly high above the towering skyscrapers below. It was the pinnacle of human achievement, according to some, surpassing even the wonders our species had hurled into the dark depths of space. Constructed from composite materials that blended strength with an almost ethereal lightness, it was sturdy and unyielding, practically impervious to even the most vicious thunderstorms. It was our savior, with Mayfair and Westminster, The City and West End, Battersea and Waterloo, London Bridge and Bermondsey sprawling beneath its protective cupola—the heart of the capital itself.

As Scott Davies gazed upon the geodesic latticework and translucent panes of the dome's inner ceiling, a fleeting sense of awe mingled with a trace of melancholy. This architectural wonder was a symbol of both protection and imprisonment. A twinge of sadness brushed his heart, knowing what was to come. It was more than just a structure; it was a sanctuary for millions, soon to be disrupted by his very actions.

While not the first of its kind—that distinction went to Singapore—London Central was one of the oldest and most prominent such structures on Earth. Despite its strictly utilitarian and unadorned construction, it possessed a certain grace and allure. While the domes had their detractors, Scott agreed, at least on those days when the sun broke through the cloud cover and bathed its surface in a brilliant, effervescent glow, they were glorious. From certain angles, the London dome, in particular, was a wondrous spectacle, illuminating the city below in a dazzling light show that left all who beheld it spellbound.

Today was one of those days. Sunlight found its way through, with no rain or thunder. The rays bounced off the panes in a prism-like fashion. The dome's automated environmental controls had dampened the usual opaqueness of the topside plating and dimmed the artificial lights to let natural illumination seep through. He could watch it indefinitely, lost in its magnificence. The contrast between the typical day and today was unmistakable—overcast and rainy as the former always was. Artificial light would brighten those days, but, try as they might, the engineers still hadn't quite gotten it right. Yet for this particular wonder of human resourcefulness, the burden of carrying a belligerent sky on its shoulders was coming to an end. It's almost a shame I have to bring it down. Time to stop admiring the view.

He re-engaged his neural braid and requested a sitrep. The AI, a custom-built Lux Aeterna model, displayed a detailed holographic schematic of the dome before his eyes, highlighting structural vulnerabilities and security nodes with pinpoint accuracy. He imagined a faint buzz as the braid's AI tickled his neural pathways, the schematic unfolding on his lens with a series of confirmations in the form of soft, digital chimes, audible only to him. Over that background, green target reticles highlighted his people, while red indicated the security staff. Green for the righteous, red for the wicked. Amber highlighted the strategic points of weakness along the geodesic latticework where the charges would be placed. It was a ballet: amber and green drawing ever nearer as his team closed in on their respective targets. Easy peasy.

Scott paused for a moment, his heart now pounding in his

chest. The gravity of the mission weighed heavily on him as the colors danced, and a brief flicker of doubt clouding his thoughts. He shook his head, dispelling the unease. This was no time for second-guessing; he had a job to do.

Moving on, he assigned magenta to maintenance staff, blue to large enemy drones, and yellow to enemy squitoes (those that his sensors could pick up, anyway). The myriad of colors was dizzying. There are too many.

This was indisputably the most intricate operation he had ever overseen. He realized he was nervous, something he hadn't felt in a situation like this for...a decade? The stakes were high. Failure was not permissible. It wasn't just that Alixha would have his head on a platter if he failed, or even the prospect of imminent death right here and now. He had to succeed to prove to himself that he... What? That he could execute an operation of this magnitude? He honestly didn't know. Anyway, this was hardly the time for such introspection. But there are definitely too many colors on my overlay. The damn thing looks like a Christmas tree on steroids.

He instructed the braid to erect a proximity barrier that would remove anything non-essential within a thirty-meter radius and to alert him of anything of tactical relevance. He had people too, he reminded himself, scattered across the facility. They had their own AIs, monitoring and assessing every second on the clock. They had radios. They could call in if there was anything important to report. They had it under control. I don't have to see every little thing all the time.

As he viewed the complex overlay, a sudden rush of responsibility surged through Scott. He realized that the lives of his team—each a person with their own story and dreams—hinged on his decisions. He felt a heavy burden, a sense of protectiveness mingling with the fear of failing them. With a subtle eye movement, he confirmed the activation of the barrier. And just like that, his screen was decluttered. There. Much better.

The fact that his overlay was now clearer didn't mean he was safe. Trust the plan, he reminded himself. It is sound. Despite that mental reassurance, he couldn't shake the sensation of something crawling along his spine, as if he had a bug inside his combat suit. As an additional precaution, he launched another volley of squitos to scour every corner of the facility. From hallways to offices, from maintenance corridors to air ducts—he wanted to ensure that any possible enemy countermeasures were identified and neutralized.

These tiny drones were military-grade, he reminded himself, equipped with a vast array of sensors: audio-visual, infrared, radar, DNA spotters, motion detectors—every kind of scanner known to man. Some were passive listeners, while others could instantly deploy lethal force. They were armed with electromagnetic pulse emitters that could disrupt other drones, tasers, and even paralyzing chemical agents that could instantly incapacitate a man. Or kill him.

Alixha had really gone all out on this one. Scott had no idea how she had gotten her hands on some of this stuff. But he was as safe and equipped to carry out his mission as anyone could ever be. So relax. Trust the tools at your disposal and calmly execute the plan. Then again, the fact that these extraordinary (and massively illegal) tools were needed said something. If nothing else, it was a clear indication that the domes were among the planet's most well-defended facilities.

The planning that had gone into this operation was nothing short of astounding. The insiders who had labored intensely had not only managed to provide him and his team with all the necessary schematics, passcodes, and credentials to enable the operation, but had also bio-tagged the entire security staff so their movements could be traced, their patrol routes diverted, and their shifts rescheduled. They deserved commendation. Alixha, of course, didn't give out medals, but they deserved them nevertheless.

Scott had little information about that part of the operation, but he knew that these infiltrators had worked for more than a year. His part was just the tip of the iceberg. That tip, though, would be the most spectacular part. Still, Scott held no illusions about the importance of his contribution in the grand scheme of things.

He made his way to Operations, recently cleared by Simian and his team. The place was in disarray, a quick glance revealing fifteen bodies, two of them belonging to his team. The rest were operations staff, regular security, and two of the heavily armed paramilitary personnel stationed throughout every dome in Europe. It was a good thing Alixha had targeted London and not one of the major American domes. Across the pond, they understood the value of going overkill with firepower, but here, they didn't.

Thankfully, only a handful of live rounds had been discharged during the skirmish, with Scott's men falling victim to them. The remaining resistance had been eliminated by the e-war squitos, which unleashed electromagnetic pulses to neutralize any security bots and countermeasures in place. Then, using tasers, the human component was swiftly pacified with minimal fuss. With any luck, the other security teams, rerouted by the insiders, may not have noticed anything.

In the aftermath of the battle, the room stank of gunpowder, the acrid stench hanging heavily in the air. He knelt by one of his fallen men. The young man's face was a gruesome tableau of destruction, a single bullet having transformed him from a living, breathing being into an abstract of gore, his lifeblood and brain matter smeared grotesquely on the wall behind. Clad in a standard-issue Lux Aeterna combat suit, its fabric torn and stained with blood, the young man lay in a grotesque pose, his left leg splayed at an impossible angle. His automatic rifle lay discarded nearby, its barrel still smoking.

Scott's throat tightened, the image of the young man haunting him. He felt an unexpected surge of anger, not just at the enemy but at the circumstances that led them here, at a world that necessitated such brutal acts. He pushed the anger down, focusing on the mission. Emotions were a luxury he couldn't afford now. But as he turned his gaze away, a shadow of unease lingered. For the first time, he questioned not just the cost, but the benefit of their mission. Is this the only way? The question echoed unanswered in the caverns of his withered conscience.

Scott was no stranger to the harsh realities of combat, having seen—and inflicted—carnage more ghastly than this. Immune to the terrors of his profession, he had always faced such horrors with an iron constitution, his visage unflinching, his stomach unyielding. Yet, against expectation, this scene tugged at him, churning his stomach. The sharp, metallic tang of blood, the lingering odor of gunpowder, and the terrible spectacle of the youthful casualty—whose name he did not even know—stirred an unfamiliar sense of anxiety within him, prompting this uncharacteristic urge to turn his gaze.

This is new, he thought. His disposition dictated that he could not afford to look away; such an action was anathema to the code he adhered to, and it was paramount that he exhibited no signs of vulnerability, especially before his men. But the sight of the desecrated youth was too potent, threatening to induce vomiting. Activating his heads-up display, he hoped the diversion would help shield him from some of the gruesome visuals. Keep your eyes elsewhere, he mentally chided himself.

Pushing off the ground with grim determination, he ambled toward the observation panorama, where the spectacular aerial view of London stood in stark contrast to the scene of carnage behind him. Yes, this is better, he thought, making a herculean effort to calm himself. Breathe.

Focusing intently on the display before him, he concluded that none of the red target reticles were converging on their location. None had breached his perimeter. That was excellent news. Nevertheless, paranoia still held him firmly in its grasp. He instructed Simian to do an additional sweep of the area, using both squitos and human assets, to ensure no threats remained to spoil the party. The element of surprise was key to the success of the mission. Without it, the operation would be over in an instant.

Scott looked around again, still bothered by an incessant need to assess the situation, but carefully avoiding a glimpse of the young man without a face. The operations staff and security personnel who weren't riddled with bullets were hopefully still alive. Never kill unless you have to, even if your opponent does. Besides, bullets make noise; tasers don't. The tasers carried by their squitos were set to maximum power, a potentially lethal dose, but it was a risk he was willing to take. He couldn't afford to have any security guards wake up and interfere with their operation. A powerful stun would be sufficient to incapacitate them long enough for his team to finish their mission and leave without the need for further violence. However, his men wouldn't be as fortunate. The paramilitaries cared little about lives or making noise, so they used bullets.

Satisfied he had now thoroughly assessed the status of the mission—and calmed himself—he turned back to the west-facing observation window. Scott turned off the Operations Overlay, preferring his own display. Oxford Street lay below, bustling with shoppers and red double-decker buses, too far down to see any details without zooming in with his braid. His overlay displayed bubbles of information, such as encyclopedia entries, old photographs, and other points of interest, as he gazed over the urban landscape. There were Oxford Circus and Selfridges, Marble Arch, and Hyde Park.

Below him, the historic Regent Street was bustling with activity, pedestrians weaving between the neo-Georgian facades, while the iconic double-decker buses, electrified and emissions-free for decades, navigated the thoroughfare with advanced algorithmic precision. Unlike elsewhere, here there were no second or third levels obscuring the view. The ground level was visible from above, and conversely, the sky and inner ceiling of the dome were visible from below. It was as open and free as a dome the size of central London could be. So little had changed—all had been frozen in time. By a decades-old government decree, Central London was considered a protected landmark, with no development or additional construction allowed. All resources were earmarked for preservation and restoration. He closed all but the images.

The Marxists, Neo-Marxists, Stalinists, Guevarists, Maoists, and Leninists had all been wrong. Capitalism would never cave under its own weight. But the ruthlessness of creative destruction could be stalled, at least temporarily. That was what it was all about—the message. Making it clear to the world that things had to change. The irony of destroying the dome to accomplish that was not lost on him. But as Scott watched the crowds below, moving from one consumerist institution to the next, spending their money on frivolous things like electronics, fashion, coffees, and lunches, he couldn't help but wonder if their efforts weren't in vain. So far.

Scott didn't consider himself an enemy of capitalism, and neither did Alixha. They weren't necessarily anti-capitalist; in fact, Scott had no idea where they fell on the political spectrum, nor did he care. He simply felt a deep disdain for the dome dwellers. The Innies.

Despite his hostility toward them, Scott couldn't deny that he, too, was an Innie. The same was true for Alixha and most members of their organization. They all lived comfortably inside the domes, surrounded by wealth and security. That irony, too, was not lost on him. We're fighting the fight the Outies can't fight themselves. At least, that was how they all rationalized it.

Scott's gaze lingered on the bustling streets below, a pang of guilt washing over him. These people, oblivious to the impending chaos, went about their lives. Did they deserve what was coming? He wrestled with the moral implications, feeling a chasm open within him. Once more, he had to remind himself that he was no stranger to violence, but this… this was different.

As he continued to survey the monitors, his eyes fell upon the towering skyscrapers of The City, the banking giants that embodied everything he and his team were fighting against. He tried to envision the damage they would inflict. It was hard. No one had ever attempted to bring down an Atlas arch. Security around them was tighter than anything else on the planet, except for a fusion reactor or a military base.

Alixha had only managed to secure access and schematics for the lower midsection of the West End. The charges were carefully placed along the arch to maximize damage. Oxford Street would undoubtedly fall. Piccadilly, Trafalgar Square, and Charing Cross would also be affected, but he couldn't be sure about The City, Knightsbridge, or Buckingham Palace. Parliament had extra fortifications and would remain unscathed unless the secondary structural collapses they were hoping for materialized. According to the custom AI created for this operation by one of Alixha's genius post-human coders—a cybernetic merger between man and machine, drawing upon the strength of both—the odds of that were about five to one, according to her.

Scott used his braid's optics to zoom in, gazing at the oblivious crowds below, their casual demeanor a stark contrast to the tense postures of his team members. *Are they really so evil?* he mused as he observed the civilians go about their business, the thought unsettling him more than he cared to admit.

"Sitrep?" he asked as he walked back toward the command console. Simian confirmed that sixteen out of twenty-one charges had been placed and connected. They were making good progress. A few more minutes, and they could proceed to the execution phase.

"Leader," Simian said, his image appearing in the upper right corner of Scott's lens. "Squitos on the second level are picking up bio signs. Security staff. Untagged. That's how they avoided detection. They're heading this way."

"How many?"

"Unknown. Lots. They've drenched the place in e-war squitos, so we can't get an accurate read."

When an operation seems to go smoothly, something is about to go wrong. A truism, a piece of unsolicited advice delivered once upon a time by Alixha in a public dressing down. *Bitch.* It was long ago, but it still stung. And she was right. In any op, there are unforeseen complications. Murphy's Law is always present. And now, it seemed, they had been caught.

Scott went over to the command console. The intercom crackled to life. They were being called.

"Should I try to steer them away?" Simian asked.

There wouldn't be any point. *The jig is up.* The element of surprise was gone.

"Take the team," Scott said. "Leave two men behind to cover my exit, and then take the rest and handle it. Any means necessary." Never kill unless you have to. Well, now we do.

They exchanged a brief glance before Simian went to carry out his orders. He nodded to Scott. They both knew this was their last mission together. A minute later, gunfire erupted, echoing through the corridors. Any remaining security measures would now kick into high gear. Attack drones would overrun them within minutes.

"We're out of time," Scott said to the two men still with him. "Secure the backup exit route. Distribute the chutes."

He linked the order to arm the explosives and execute via his braid. Set a two-minute delay. He calculated that was the margin they could afford before squitos with extended military capability would discover and neutralize the charges, five of which were still not even set. But he had no other options. It was either that or nothing at all. Alixha would be displeased, but at least with the first option, she might let him live. If I make it out of here to face her in the first place.

As Scott issued the order to arm, a cold, sinking feeling settled in his stomach. The finality of the act was suddenly and surprisingly overwhelming. Lives would be forever changed, including his own. It signaled the beginning of Lux Aeterna's campaign against the world, but also the end of something; the old world had its faults but also its wonders. He took a deep breath, trying to steady his nerves. There was no turning back now. As his braid confirmed the explosives were armed, a fleeting vision of a different path, one less soaked in blood and fear, flashed through his mind. But he quickly pushed the thought away before it could congeal and fester, yet it clung to the edges of his consciousness, an uninvited specter of what could be.

The men he sent away would not survive, that much was clear. If they persisted through the encounter with the human security squad or the drones, they would undoubtedly perish in the ensuing blast. There would be no time for them to get out.

Scott heaved the parachute onto his back and made his way

toward the backup route, a maintenance shaft that led to an external air duct. This intricate network of ducts was a crucial component of the dome's environmental system, ensuring precise control of the inner climate.

The route was risky, a vertiginous drop of two thousand feet toward ground-level London, and Scott had dearly hoped that he would not have to use it. With the constraints they now faced, they had to time their escape perfectly, shooting out of the shaft mere seconds after the charges went off, with debris from the arch raining down upon them as they dropped toward the strike zone below. But they had no choice. The charges were live, and the clock was ticking. All stations reported ready. It was time to go.

Scott's tactical display revealed that Simian's men had been pushed back inside the perimeter. As he emerged from Operations, they were retreating around the corner, laying down smoke and suppressing fire to keep the security forces at bay. But Scott knew that the smoke would do little good. The security guards' braids could easily track through it, and so could the drones—unless Simian had doused them with an electromagnetic pulse. However, he doubted he had. Such pulses worked both ways, and Scott's own braid was still fully operational, indicating that there was little to no interference in the area. Whatever effect the security forces had as they approached had dissipated.

Simian locked eyes with Scott, urgency in his expression. "Go," he shouted. "We'll hold them off as long as we can." Scott nodded in understanding. "Your chutes are in Operations. Get out if you can."

Simian's men moved up to the front line, sacrificing themselves so that he could have his slim chance at survival. *Goodbye, my friend.* He overlaid the path to the shaft—thirty-four meters through a labyrinthine network of corridors. *I can make that.* In those fleeting moments, as Scott dashed toward the shaft, his mind was a whirlwind. Fear, determination, and a profound sense of loss collided within. The sounds of battle, the lives slipping away, the impending destruction—it all blurred into a surreal, nightmarish hellscape. He couldn't shake the feeling that this was the end of more than just the mission.

He ran toward the shaft, constantly monitoring the battle raging behind him through his overlay. As he sprinted, the rush of air against his skin was both cool and biting, the physical exertion and the burning in his lungs a sharp contrast to his overheated mind. His breaths came in ragged gasps, the sound of breathlessness loud in his ears amidst the distant echoes of conflict.

On his tactical display, Simian's team was being rapidly decimated, friendly target reticles disappearing from his view screen one after another as the men they represented fell. Meanwhile, combat drones were closing in on the other end of his route, threatening to cut off his escape in a matter of minutes.

Scott pressed on, racing toward the maintenance shaft, located in a secluded part of the dome's service area. He navigated the maze of corridors with practiced ease, his path illuminated by the flickering lights of the emergency system and directional guidance overlaid before him on his lens. Just as he approached the grate where the shaft was, Simian's target reticle extinguished. Now, only four green tags remained, including himself. He wasted no time, launching all the squitos he had left in his pouch and started to cut through the grate with his portable hand welder. Perhaps the additional squitos would buy him a few extra seconds.

Finally, the grate gave way, and he dove headfirst into the shaft, cutting both of his thighs on the searing hot metal as he did so. The braid registered a thirty-degree slope, and then he a free fall toward the ground below. Fuck me sideways! That's why this was always the backup route. Oh well, at least it won't be boring.

As he raced down the shaft and out into free air, Scott's mind churned with more than just tactical calculations. What are we truly achieving? The question was now a constant gnawing presence, even amidst the chaos. The clarity he once had about their cause was now shrouded in a mist of doubt, a feeling he couldn't quite shake off.

Moments later, the charges detonated, unleashing a deafening explosion that reverberated throughout the city. A shockwave rippled through the air, blowing wind in his face, and as the dome cracked, unfiltered sunlight seared his eyes. Scott plummeted, free-falling as long as possible before finally deploying his chute. As he descended toward Oxford Street, massive chunks of debris rained down around him. Dome plating, pieces of the arch structure, operations, climate control—all of it came crashing down in a cacophony of destruction, crushing buildings and people along the way.

A massive section of the Atlas arch hurtled past him as he was jerked into a slow descent, his eyes, aided by the braid's AI, scanning the debris for smaller pieces. If any of them hit the chute, it could be torn to shreds. If anything larger struck him, it wouldn't matter anyway. A moment later, he was approaching touchdown. The destruction around him was staggering—an all-encompassing devastation. And for a moment, he wondered if maybe, just maybe, Alixha wouldn't be pleased after all. But even if she was, it had nevertheless come at an unexpected, personal cost.

Scott

The campaign seems to be progressing smoothly," Scott remarked as Alixha slipped out from under the covers, her body gleaming in the dim light with post-coital sweat. And indeed, it should be no surprise. He had given it everything he had this time, every muscle, every sinew aching, now pleading for rest. The air in the room was heavy with the scent of their exertion, a musky blend of bodily fluids and the faint, metallic tang of blood from minor scratches. The dim light cast shifting shadows over Alixha's form, accentuating the sheen on her skin.

"I'll get you something to drink," she said, her lithe form gliding effortlessly toward the kitchen, her bare feet gently tip-tapping against the polished hardwood floor of the luxurious Tokyo penthouse. As Alixha moved away, Scott felt an unexpected void, a lingering hollowness that physical exertion couldn't fill. He brushed off the feeling, attributing it to fatigue, yet it clung to him, an uninvited shadow in the aftermath of their intimacy.

Watching her glide across the room, his eyes caught one of the tiny security cameras in a far, upper corner—the discreet yet unmistakable presence of her security detail, evident even in the sanctity of her penthouse. Shadowy figures patrolled the perimeter, invisible through the one-way glass that encased most of the luxurious abode. Had he switched on his tactical view, he would have picked up *squitos*, their sensors perpetually sweeping the area. Beyond these walls, a labyrinth of security measures—biometric locks, armed guards, AI-monitored systems—guarded against any external threat. In Alixha's world, opulence and fortress-like security were inseparably intertwined.

"Something with sugar and caffeine," he requested, his gaze intently fixed on the external screens that illuminated the room with news feeds from around the world. The AI was running filters in the background, carefully monitoring, sifting out, and displaying anything involving violence and death. She had that running whenever they fucked. *Whatever gets you off, I guess.* The feeds bombarded the room with a cacophony of sounds—shouts, explosions, and the relentless drone of commentary. The screens flickered with the harsh light of distant conflicts, casting a surreal, strobe-like effect across the room. The AI-curated segments depicted images of unrest in distant locales—a protest in Paris, a skirmish in the South China Sea, the aftermath of a bombing in Mumbai, and civil strife relating to an unwanted dome expansion in the south of Frankfurt—each scene meticulously driven by Alixha's machine of manipulation and propaganda, displayed here to reflect the world's descent into chaos while they made love.

As the screens bombarded his retinas, a sense of foreboding gripped him. The enormity of his next mission, a plan shrouded in secrecy even from him, loomed large in his mind. He was Alixha's chosen instrument, a fact that filled him with a mix of pride and unease. The operations he had conducted so far were but preludes to this momentous task, whatever it was going to be. He knew that what lay ahead would change the course of history, yet the details remained tantalizingly out of reach, hidden in the depths of Alixha's enigmatic mind.

Watching Alixha's handiwork strobe across the room, Scott was reminded of the colossal network operating beneath her command. She was the nexus of a sprawling web that extended its reach into governments, corporations, and underworld syndicates alike. Her commands set in motion a myriad of actions across the globe, executed by a legion of loyalists, each a cog in her grand design. The news feeds were but a surface ripple of the deep currents she stirred, a testament to the unseen but omnipotent machinery at her disposal.

It was a relatively recent phenomenon—the news feeds. In prior years, she had not been so preoccupied with death. He sometimes wondered why she didn't run it through her braid instead. *It's because she wants me to see too. It gets her off even more.* She could easily stream everything directly to his braid, but she insisted on using the external screens. A stream he could refuse, but with the screens, she was in control. Perhaps it also added something tantalizing to the ambiance of the room. There's something thrilling about experiencing things out loud and in the space in front of your eyes, rather than inside your head and on a lens. *Even if it is the sights and sounds of death.*

It didn't do anything for him, though. *Or so I'd like to believe.* Every time they indulged, he lost a few neurons. It was increasingly difficult to discern his preferences from hers amidst the sweeping sensory overload. He'd like to think that death and mayhem repulsed him. *Who wouldn't?* He pondered whether the sheer intensity of the sex overpowered everything else, enabling him to simply tune out the carnage. *One can always hope.*

Alixha was a force to be reckoned with in all conceivable domains, including the bedroom. Her sexual prowess was unparalleled, her bodily fluids a symphony of nanobots designed to infuse her partner's bloodstream with a customized cocktail of pleasure chemicals. Who could rival such a thing? The release of noradrenaline, endorphins, and oxytocin was so intense—a sensorial excess that promised to be the ultimate experience for any man. Or woman.

The potency of it all was such that his own augmentations had to work overtime to avoid premature release. The first time they had engaged in the pleasures of the flesh, he had succumbed simply by giving oral pleasure. *I've come a long way from that awkward performance.* Not that she seemed overly concerned about his pleasure, but aside from that first time, could he really complain when he too experienced the very pinnacles of ecstasy? So what if her tastes were weird, including her penchant for copulating in the presence of death on news feeds? When he climaxed, it was like a rebirth—a transcendental experience that pushed his body and mind to the point of stroking out. *No pun intended.*

Suddenly, silence fell as Alixha muted the streams. In the kitchen, the clink of ice against glass and the abrupt fizz of a soda can opening punctuated the silence of the room, a mundane soundtrack to the complex mélange of emotions playing out within Scott. "Here you go," she purred, pressing her lips against his forehead as she returned. He guzzled down the fizzy Coke, ignoring the prickly carbonation burning his throat.

"Come back to bed," he urged.

"I have to stretch. You really did a number on my back this time."

He chuckled. "Glad to be of service."

As she stretched, he admired her flawless body, genetically engineered to perfection. Every muscle superbly sculpted, every proportion precisely measured. *And flexible like a gymnast.* It was as though she were purpose-built for sex. *Aren't all humans that?* With or without the genetic tinkering? Most people with means had undergone some form of enhancement, but she was on another level.

"You know," he mused as she bent forward to touch her toes, "this magnificent view will only make me want to go another round."

Before she could reply, a knock on the door interrupted them. She darted off to grab a robe.

"Not had enough?" she taunted as she strolled over to answer the door. "For a moment there, I thought I'd broken you."

He grinned. "You almost did. So, who are we expecting?"

"Medical. It's injection day today."

"I'll be on my way, then," he said, rising from the bed.

"No, stay. I don't mind. But maybe you want to put something on."

This will be interesting.

Scott had never witnessed rejuvenation therapy before. Being somewhat of a legal gray area, this particular medical procedure was done mostly behind closed doors. But Alixha had no need for secrecy. *The perks of power.* It was mostly common knowledge that she was old, very old. Some said she was over a hundred and fifty. *When you're untouchable, you can do as you please and make no apologies.*

As the medical team set up, he quickly got dressed. They unpacked the equipment with clinical efficiency: a hospital bed, a state-of-the-art nanobot injector patch, a sleek IV stand holding bags of a translucent solution, and a monitoring device displaying a complex array of biometric data, none of which made any sense to Scott. He could have looked it up via braid, but decided he wasn't that interested. From what he heard, it wasn't a comfortable process.

Alixha gracefully skipped onto the bed, raising the adjustable head to get a good view of the wall of screens. As she adjusted her position, Scott became acutely aware of the sharp smell of antiseptic that filled the air, mingling with the sterile scent of medical equipment. The nurse's movements were precise and experienced, her hands automatic and impersonal as she prepared the IV.

Alixha deftly flipped through the streams via her braid while the nurse readied the IV. She had several outlets split across the displays, consuming them all with equal attentiveness, her eyes intensely focused, as always, when she was genuinely interested in something.

As the room fell quiet in anticipation of the treatment commencing, Scott's mind drifted into the past. For all her fame, her power, her wealth, Alixha Rahena remained an enigma. Her ascent to the top was not the swift, violent surge of a tempest, but rather the relentless, gradual erosion of a river shaping its course through stone. Alixha's story began over a century ago, as a fiery young protester against the early domes, those monolithic symbols of mankind's desperate attempt to shield itself from a ravaging climate, rather than dealing with it. Back then, her passion was for the Earth, for steering humanity in a different direction, not for power.

But as the decades unfurled, so too did her ideals morph and harden. The young revolutionary, once driven by a dream of healing the planet, found herself ensnared in the very machinations she sought to dismantle. As the domes rose, so did the oligarchs, the tech barons, their puppets in government, and amidst them, Alixha, slowly and methodically carving her niche. Her crusade against climate change was gradually eclipsed by a darker, more personal vendetta against those who wielded power—the dome owners, the corporate magnates.

With each passing year, her body defied the march of time through her treatments, but her ambitions grew colder, more calculating. The once-vibrant protester transformed into a formidable player in the high-stakes game of power. Her ideals about the environment faded into the background, replaced by a singular obsession with toppling her rivals and cementing her position. In a world dominated by feudal lords masquerading as visionaries, Alixha had become one of them, her initial rebellion a distant echo in the annals of her long life. Now, she was driven not by the desire to save the world, but to rule over the fragments of what remained, a queen in a kingdom of her own meticulous design. This, at least, was what the publicly available information said. Scott had never believed it, until recently. And he had begun to see how his own motivations had taken a similar path.

From a skilled but nondescript operations leader in the neon-drenched streets of London, Berlin, and Paris, his knack for executing minor destruction in the name of the climate movement had caught Alixha's attention. His rise was a testament to his adaptability and unwavering loyalty. Each successful mission, each display of cunning and bravery, had solidified his position as Alixha's trusted confidant. Yet, with each step up the ladder, he ventured further into a world where morality was malleable, and the stakes were inconceivably high.

Now, since his eye had caught the youth with brains splattered across the wall in Dome NE1's Operations, whatever doubt he suffered had intensified by magnitudes.

As the nurse initiated the procedure, Alixha closed her eyes and instructed the apartment AI out loud to dim the lights. She moaned softly as the nurse started the morphine drip. The nanobots were injected, and their repairing duties initiated. At the cellular level, they would rip apart and reassemble, mending damage caused by aging or injury. The procedure was known to cause psychological distress and a burning sensation throughout the body, hence the morphine. Opioid addiction was not uncommon among those who underwent such therapy.

"Rest assured, dear," Alixha said, temporarily roused from her partial coma. He couldn't quite tell if the trance was due to the endless cannonade of death and destruction emanating from the news feeds or the effect of the treatment. "I'll need you again soon enough," she gestured toward the towering wall of screens. "These petty little incidents are of no concern to you. Not anymore. You did well in London. You're my leading man now, and I'm saving you for grander things."

Scott's smile didn't quite reach his eyes. Alixha's words, meant as praise, stirred something within him. The title of "leading man" felt more like a chain than an honor, a reminder of the path he was tethered to—one that increasingly seemed to lead into darkness.

The so-called petty little incidents were just pieces in the bigger puzzle, none designed to be of pivotal importance by themselves, but simply to create an ever-growing sense of social unease and panic. *Peace and prosperity never last. Someone always gets restless, and that restlessness can be exploited.* The words of the Manifesto itself. Those grander things, like London, would be the true catalysts of change, but only once the population had been sufficiently kneaded. *What grander things, though?* It was difficult to imagine anything more momentous than blowing a hole in a dome.

Alixha silenced the blaring newscasts and gestured toward the screens, now displaying a technical diagram. "Have a look," she said. "Do you know what this is? No searches, just a genuine guess."

While no expert, it was clear it was an explosive device. Alixha winced from the pain. "You're looking at the next step, the one where your services will once again be called upon."

"So what is it?" he inquired.

"It used to be known as a MIRV. It's a nuclear device."

My God. A cold dread seized him. The gravity of what Alixha proposed struck him with surprising force, a stark deviation from what he once believed their mission was about. The line between revolutionary and monster blurred before his eyes.

He stared at it as Alixha switched from the schematic to an image of the device itself. It was an older model, he realized, and not something her science division had devised. He quickly conducted a reverse image search and discovered it was a Trident Mk V-class missile, a tactical nuclear weapon equipped with MIRV, or Multiple Independent Re-entry Vehicle. This generation of the device had been retired over four decades ago but was capable of delivering multiple strikes on disparate targets. He was now looking at one of those warheads.

His search confirmed the device had a nominal yield of fifty kilotons, approximately five times the explosive force of Hiroshima or twice that of Chennai and Faisalabad. It had been produced by the now-defunct Lockheed Martin Space Systems and had been carried by American Columbia-class nuclear submarines. Like the device itself, most, if not all, of these submarines had been mothballed or destroyed decades ago.

Obviously not all of them. How had Alixha obtained such a device, he wondered. Had she bought it on the black market? Or stolen it from a museum? Regardless, a working weapon of this kind would bring devastation unseen in decades.

Nuclear weapons were supposed to be all but gone, with only a few exceptions. The clip with Presidents Schumaker, Pinter, Zheng, Patel, Baig, and Makarov announcing the final destruction of the last operational nuclear device had become one of the most widely viewed videos in human history. The handful of remaining nukes that the world had agreed to keep were supposedly under the strict control of the United Nations, with all nuclear production facilities dismantled. It was all highly regulated and monitored by powerful AI surveillance. Obtaining a functional device was believed to be impossible. *Until now, it seems.*

"Where did you get it?" he inquired.

"Not it. Them. We have two. One to use as leverage and one to demonstrate our resolve. The engineers are developing a detonator as we speak."

If he wasn't convinced before, he certainly was now. There seemed to be nothing beyond Alixha Rahena's capabilities. *Moral capabilities, if nothing else.*

"How will it be delivered?" he asked. It was evident that the weapon couldn't be deployed via LEO. He doubted she had access to the required launch capabilities, much less a way to avoid detection should such a method be attempted. A retrofitted detonator was more probable, with the warhead maneuvered into position via drones or people. *And by people, I mean myself.*

"This device will be our defining moment, Scott. And it's all yours. This is your next mission."

Alixha winced as a second batch of nanobots entered her bloodstream. The nurse briefly inspected her to make sure everything was alright before returning to her flick or whatever game she was playing in her braid.

"A weapon like this will kill thousands, even millions," Scott declared. Alixha groaned, partially from the pain, but also with a tone of boredom in her voice.

"What's your point?"

The London dome had only resulted in the death of a few thousand people and injuries to a few thousand more. It was a symbolic act, meant to convey the message.

"Don't get squeamish on me now, Scott. A few hundred, a few million. What does it matter? Murder is murder." She arched her back in agony.

Hard to argue with that logic. But isn't there a line somewhere?

"I need you, Scott. Come over here," she stuttered. He

approached her, and she grasped his hand tightly.

"Fuck me," she ordered, tearing open his robe. "Take me while these damn bots make me young. Fuck me through the pain with that magnificent cock of yours." She disrobed and spread her legs. To his surprise, he found himself instantly erect. He glanced at the old nurse, engrossed in her stories, eyes blanked out.

"Don't worry about her," Alixha insisted. "She's used to it. Just take me." He entered her and thrust as hard as he could. As he complied with her demand, Scott's mind rebelled against the grotesque juxtaposition of pleasure and pain. Each thrust was a battle between his primal instincts and a growing disgust, not just at the act, but at himself for participating—yet at the same time, he was harder than he had ever been. On the screen wall, the newscasts kept depicting scenes of horror and mayhem while they both writhed in pleasure.

"What's wrong, Scott?" Dai asked as she and Aki settled around their table, their voices barely cutting through the thumping club music at Neon Automaton, one of Tokyo's premier night entertainment venues, featuring Japanese-style synthetic dancers, famous for their anatomically censored, smoothed-out crotches. The club pulsated with the throb of heavy bass, the air vibrating with energy. Neon lights flickered, painting the crowd in surreal hues. The dancers' movements were fluid and hypnotic, some with their artificial skin covered in dresses made of tiny reflective panes, rivaling the mirror balls' dazzling reflections of lights and colors.

"Nothing," Scott replied, fine-tuning his braid's aural implant to better filter out the surrounding cacophony, but he still had to lean in to hear what she was saying. She replied with a distrustful glare, that knowing look saying she saw right through him. They had met years ago, at a dingy Lux recruitment center tucked away in a back street in a Shanghai dome—Jiading, probably, though he couldn't quite recall. *It wasn't Central, that much I remember.* Since those humble beginnings, they had a connection, an unspoken understanding that transcended the cultural barriers often inherent to Japanese-Western relationships. She understood him, at least, even as he struggled to sometimes understand her. *The point, dummy, is that she knows when you're lying!*

Regardless, he was about to deflect again when Garrick arrived, interrupting their conversation. They rose, greeting their friend with hugs and smiles, then hovered around the table for a while, exchanging the usual pleasantries and engaging in familiar idle chit-chat.

His braid pinged, offering to further increase the noise cancellation to improve the clarity of his friends' voices against the ruckus of the club. He accepted. It had been a while since they all met, and while socializing wasn't the reason he had brought them together, he wanted to soak up every moment. While they had once been tightly knit, fighting the oppressive rule of the evil dome corporations and their government cronies, nowadays their work kept them apart. Despite this, their bond remained unbroken, closer than most.

What have you been up to? How's work? Did you go to the rally last week? Etcetera. *How wonderful!*

"We were at the movies," Dai said when asked. She and Aki indulged in a shared fascination with old cinema. It was a strictly platonic affair, they both maintained, but he had never been able to completely shake the feeling that Aki harbored a secret crush on Dai. Conversely, he was certain Dai didn't feel the same way.

"What was it this time?" Garrick asked with a wry grin, as if he were humoring them.

"Butch Cassidy and the Sundance Kid," Aki enthusiastically replied, not noticing the sly hint of sarcasm in Garrick's tone. He went on to explain how there was a new AI-rendered release that had translated the old 2D screen version into a fully immersive virtual experience. However, they opted for the original flat-screen version that played concurrently for the purists, to which Dai and Aki naturally belonged. Aki went on to recount the film's highlights, especially the ending, with great detail, spoiling it for himself and Garrick. *Not that I'm going to see it or anything.* And neither would Garrick, a fact Aki was aware of. Had he not been, he wouldn't have spoiled anything.

Scott's mind drifted, and he only caught snippets of Aki's story. Something about being under siege, injured, with the Bolivian Army waiting outside. He felt guilty for not engaging. These were his closest friends, and he cared about them. Worse, he felt guilty for luring them here under false pretenses, using their interest in the club as an excuse to ambush them, to test their reactions as he contemplated betraying Alixha. He was just about to start his pitch when Aki went into his recount of the movie. It didn't feel right to interrupt him. Eventually, Aki finished his story, and he and Garrick left for the bar to grab more drinks. He and Dai remained behind to guard their table.

Left alone, Dai immediately turned to him. "No," she said firmly. "You can't hide it from me. Something is troubling you. I can see it in your eyes, even if you try to shield them from me."

She was right. His laughter and banter had been strained, not much more than a brittle facade. Guilt gnawed at him as he contemplated divulging his burden. He feared not only for their safety but for the shattering of the camaraderie that had been their sanctuary in a world of chaos. He smiled inwardly at her astute observation. In fact, before arriving, he had placed holomurals over his lenses, designed to mask emotional reactions, but Dai had seen through them. It was experimental technology procured for him by Alixha, made available by the same team now testing the new device. At least this prototype didn't blur his vision like the previous iterations.

Device, he mused. A euphemism for a weapon capable of wiping millions of lives off the face of the earth in an instant. No one wanted to call it what it was, but to Scott, it was too sanitized a term for something so destructive.

The preceding weeks since Alixha's big reveal had been fraught with doubt. He had pondered endlessly Alixha's argument that murder was murder, regardless of the body count. Perhaps it made sense at some philosophical level, but as he mulled over her comparison of the London dome job to detonating a nuclear weapon, doubts began to surface. The two scenarios were not equivalent. The objective of the dome operation had been to strike a blow to the dome-owning class—to send a message. The destruction of property had been the primary goal, with loss of life being an unfortunate side effect. It had not been a premeditated act of violence intended to inflict harm upon innocent civilians. Conversely, deploying a device capable of reducing an entire metropolis to rubble was an entirely different matter. The intent was clear: to cause widespread death and destruction. The sheer scale of such malevolence he could scarcely fathom.

Or could I? Death is death, after all. A killer's motivations are immaterial to the deceased. They remain just as lifeless, regardless if they were the intended target or just collateral damage. Death renders such distinctions irrelevant.

He had also wrestled with the idea of involving his friends, in violation of Alixha's explicit order to restrict discussion of the device to her approved inner circle. Doing so would be reckless, the consequences dire for all parties involved. He had not yet decided to actively involve them—at this time, he only sought counsel, but that would be damaging enough.

What would she do to them if she found out? Alixha's wrath was usually swift and merciless. While he was certain of the repercussions he would face for such a transgression, his friends would be entirely blameless, their sole crime having been to become privy to restricted information—information he had bestowed upon them in casual conversation during a night out. Would she be able to find mercy somewhere deep inside that decrepit soul of hers for such a minor offense? She wouldn't.

He feared he was losing his grip on the situation. A decade ago, he would have possessed an unwavering confidence and reached a swift resolution to the dilemmas now plaguing him. *Or would I? I would've blindly followed orders, which is not the same thing as having answers.* But a shift had transpired during the London operation, a change both unexpected and troubling. The face of the young man whose skull had become a horrific mural against the Operations wall had haunted Scott's dreams. While he now managed to keep his waking thoughts in check, the night terrors lingered, persistently reminding him of the grim realities of his work. He did not understand why, but he knew he had to take action. *In one way or another.*

Aki and Garrick finally returned with their drinks. It was time to begin the conversation. Despite the incessant noise, he welcomed the club's cacophony of thumping basslines and loud voices. It would afford them a veil of privacy, shielding their dialogue from curious eavesdroppers, while their milspec braids applied noise cancellation, allowing them to clearly hear each other. *It's why he suggested the club in the first place.* Any attempted spying that did not involve ears would necessitate sophisticated tech unlikely to flourish even among Lux agents or government operators, let alone the general population.

Nevertheless, an abundance of caution was warranted. "We need a privacy shield," he said firmly before beginning. He quickly established a local braid network for their use and surrounded it with impenetrable firewalls, ensuring their communications would be shielded from most forms of electronic eavesdropping. The others, unaware of his agenda, looked perplexed. He assured them he would soon explain.

To further enhance their privacy, he distributed holomurals for each person to use over their mouths in case any potential interlopers possessed braid AIs with lip-reading capabilities—however unlikely such a scenario was. These were nifty little gadgets developed by Mossad, acquired by Lux in some underhanded deal with the Israeli state. But even with these extreme measures, there remained a nagging doubt in the back of his mind. Alixha's reach was infinite.

The club was absolutely bouncing. Tonight's show was approaching its climax, and on stage, the scantily clad synths were now prancing and gyrating in an ever racier fashion, although still outside the realm of indecency—a performance not quite burlesque, not quite a strip show. Garrick gestured toward the dancing machines. "Did we really have to come here?"

"Oh, Garrick," Dai responded with a condescending tone. "You're such an idiot. They're synths, every one of them, with no equipment below deck." She had always taken pleasure in taunting him for his peculiar and logically inconsistent beliefs. Garrick harbored a deep-seated aversion toward synths, although the reason for this antipathy remained unclear to all of them. Were they job stealers, depriving real dancers of work? Were they unnatural, an affront to God, or otherwise "unnatural" by his standards? He felt no animosity toward AI in general, as long as they did not inhabit a human facsimile. *Had the dancers been real, he probably would've moaned about exploitation of the naked human body. But wasn't the act of displaying the human body in such a manner exploitative in and of itself? Synth or otherwise?*

Garrick shifted uncomfortably in his chair, prompting Scott to divert their attention toward the matter at hand. As much as he despised the impending conversation, he preferred it over another drawn-out debate on Garrick's contradictory convictions.

"I saw the schematics for a nuclear weapon a while back," he began, cautiously testing the waters before revealing the full extent of what he knew. Dai's smile faded, having already sensed something was amiss, but Aki and Garrick remained indifferent. Obviously still preoccupied with the ever-racier gyrations of the dancing, genitalia-deprived synths, the two let his statement slip by without reaction. And why wouldn't they? In the eyes of the world, the age of nuclear terror had faded into a distant memory, a relic of a time long gone. He might as well have told them he saw a telex machine. *So, you've been to a museum. So what?* Yet, he could see the worry etched deep into Dai's eyes. He trusted her more than anyone else. He shared more with her than anyone else, and the gravity of what he said was not lost on her.

So, where am I taking this now? He still had not divulged anything crucial. If he shut up now and changed the subject, no harm would be done. But he had to tell someone, and these were his friends—the closest ones he had ever had. If he couldn't share it with them, he could share it with no one.

He sighed and spoke the words plainly, without a hint of sugarcoating or euphemism. To do so would only serve to diminish the gravity of what he had to say. "Alixha has one," he stated bluntly, "not just a schematic, but a fully functional warhead. Two, in fact."

As the words left his mouth, Scott felt as though he had plunged them all into icy waters, and they knew it. He saw the fear and shock in their eyes and cursed himself for it. This burden was his to bear, yet he had spread its shadows to those he cared about most. Aki and Garrick awoke from their spell, the realization of what he had said hitting like a ton of bricks, forcing their attention away from the vulgarities on stage. "She intends to use them," he added, to ensure there was no confusion.

The revelation hung heavy in the air, the earlier vibrancy of the club seeming to dim further behind the noise-cancellation algorithm, turning into a muted, throbbing pulse in its wake.

Silence now pervaded around the table, like a fog heavy with the weight of unspoken words. Shock or surprise did not cause the hush; no one who knew Alixha Rahena, even in passing, would be surprised that she would detonate a nuclear device should the opportunity present itself. No, they fell silent because *he* told them about it. They knew that by uttering those words, he had condemned them, making them privy to information that should have been kept secret. He could feel the weight of their collective gaze upon him, so palpable a force it threatened to crush him.

He studied their faces, his braid's analytics suite feeding him data and analysis on every muscle twitch, every dilation of the pupils, every drop of sweat forming on their foreheads. But in truth, he didn't need the aid of an AI to read the emotions writ large on their faces. Garrick was livid, eyes furious. Aki's eyes were wild, fear now etched on his face. Dai was calmer, but still concerned. It was concern for *him*, he realized, not for herself. Unlike the others, she was calm and level-headed, as she always was in the face of adversity.

He had done it. He had gone from mere speculation and abstract musing over involving them to uttering the very words that would spell their doom. The realization of what he had done was both suffocating and relieving. There was no turning back now. They had been recruited, and they knew it.

Garrick finally broke the silence. "It's not for any of us to question her strategy or her means of achieving it. Not even you, Scott," he said, his voice calm and measured but his stare piercing and unforgiving. The conversation ended there, the words hanging in the air like a dark cloud. Garrick stood up abruptly, his chair screeching against the floor so loudly it cut through both the thumping music and the noise cancellation. Aki quickly followed, his expression one of fear and uncertainty, both of them eager to escape what they had stepped into.

Dai lingered, her gaze fixed upon him as they departed the club. "What are you planning?" she asked, as the neon-lit facade of the club faded from view, replaced by the murky shadows of a Shinjuku back alley, the sounds of the city now a muted murmur in the background. The night air was cool and crisp, a stark contrast to the stifling atmosphere of the club.

While they were now away from prying eyes and ears, they kept the privacy screen up out of an abundance of caution. The stakes were too high to risk any slip-ups, and it was safer to assume that Alixha was always watching. His admission in the club had been nothing but an attempt to silence his inner turmoil, an unloading of a burden he did not wish to carry alone. *I don't know,* he confessed, his mind racing with the possible targets of Alixha's plan—major political centers like Washington, D.C., Beijing, the United Nations Headquarters in New York, or even Aegis' mighty tower in Singapore, each a symbol of the world order she sought to upend. "But there will be retaliation, from the dome owners and states alike. God only knows where that will end."

Dai nodded in agreement, her faith in him unwavering, as always. "How long have you been wrestling with this crisis of faith?" she pressed.

With the benefit of hindsight, he realized, *longer than I'd like to admit.* He believed in Lux Aeterna's cause, but the means to achieve it were not without consequences. Nuclear annihilation was a path he could not condone.

"I'm with you," she declared. "Whatever you want to do. And so are Aki and Garrick. They're just scared."

He nodded, grateful for the support of his companions. They were in it together now, whether they liked it or not.

Jarod

In the future, we won't need roads. It was a famous quote from some politician a long time ago. *Or was it from an old movie?* It was a prescient remark, whoever said it—at least as far as life inside the domes was concerned. The roads were still there, but gone were the days when citizens cruised around *en masse* in privately owned cars. Roads were now mostly the domain of pedestrians, with many having been converted into greenery, plazas, and esplanades for shopping and dining. The ones that remained were restricted to emergency vehicles, deliveries, law enforcement personnel, and other official business. Mass transit was the preferred mode of travel today, although smaller vehicles like taxis were, of course, common.

Gone, too, were the days when vehicles were human-operated. You could still, of course, operate one manually with the proper permit, and Outside, by and large, anything still goes—if venturing Outside was your thing.

It wasn't that long ago that we all drove manually. Even my father drove without the automatics. I did too, when I was young and learned to drive. Yes, the self-driving car had been a long time coming, but it was now an unmistakable reality. How ironic that when they finally arrived in force, people had mostly stopped using them.

A sense of loss flickered in Jarod's mind, mourning the relinquished thrill of control and the tactile connection with machines that had existed before the AIs. *Human-operated* was mostly an anachronism now, a relic of a past where man and machine were partners. Today, the relationship more closely resembled that of master and servant.

As a government contractor, Jarod had the option of commissioning a car and having it drive him anywhere he desired, with or without the aid of automation—whatever his preference. Not all of his colleagues were so fortunate. Even the once-mighty Legacy law enforcement agencies did not have automatic access to such luxuries. Besides, among the lower ranks, beat cops, and similar ilk, few human officers remained, and bots and drones didn't need cars—or roads, for that matter. They had other means of getting around.

Jarod sat in the back seat with Riley, who was deeply absorbed in her overlays, tracking their targets through squitos and larger surveillance drones as the car drove itself toward the Docklands at its maximum allowed speed. They were headed to the old, now-abandoned maglev maintenance hall that was once the site of the London City Airport, back in the days before the domes. With her usual diligence, Riley had the place swarming with surveillance tech, but so far, they had found nothing.

"These Outies are really putting up a fight," Wyatt said, idly fiddling behind the dashboard of the car.

Riley, temporarily distracted from her overlays, shot him an annoyed look. "You know we're not supposed to call them that."

Wyatt scoffed. "My sincere apologies. What politically correct term do you prefer? Refugees? Asylum seekers? Migrants?"

Riley's lips tightened, reflecting the silent battle between professional focus and personal irritation that Jarod had seen in her countless times before, especially during exchanges with ol'

Wyatt. Her eyes darted briefly toward the man, a flash of familiar reproach, before diving back into her digital world. Jarod didn't blame her. He, too, felt a twinge of unease at Wyatt's callousness—a reminder of the cold pragmatism survival inside the domes often demanded. With a pang of nostalgia, he recalled a world long gone where empathy wasn't a luxury—before the era of the domes, when he had been a mere child.

Riley, back on the overlays, replied with a middle finger, her eyes blank again as she continued to focus on a heads-up display only she could see. Kale, sitting in the front passenger seat across from Jarod, remained quiet as usual. Although Jarod thought he caught a subtle smile on Kale's face, he knew better than to assume anything. Kale enjoyed the banter between Riley and Wyatt, but he rarely participated.

Wyatt had a valid point, Jarod had to admit, about the migrants being unusually savvy. Normally, their surveillance tech would have picked up on the target's exact location long before they even got close. But in this case, the *Outsiders* had managed to slip past the net. *Worrisome. Drones. Squitos. Whatever you call them. What good are they if they can't locate what we send them to find?*

The migrants obviously had access to advanced countermeasures, which was rare, to say the least. Even on the Inside, such tech was hard to come by.

"Let's go manual," Wyatt said from the driver's seat. "This is taking too long. This fucking car drives like my granny."

"It's going the speed limit," Kale remarked.

"Yeah. That's the problem."

Funny how it's still called a driver's seat. Or that you can still "drive like a granny." Few grannies alive today had ever operated a car manually, and some had never been in one where that was even an option. Nowadays, nobody drove a car manually, even if they had that coveted permit to do so. Nobody wanted to, or knew how, except for hotheads like Wyatt, who still believed they could outdo the machines.

"Cut it out," Jarod said, knowing that Riley was about to interject with a snide remark. "Stay cool and focus on the task at hand."

If anyone could outdo machines, it was Wyatt. Prepped with a milspec braid, equipped with every enhancement you could imagine, he was something of a superhuman. But then again, if he were to use any of those enhancements, could it be said that he was genuinely "outdoing" a machine?

Jarod returned to the briefing. *Focus, please.* In a sense, the case was routine. A trio of illegal immigrants had taken up residence in an old industrial complex—in this case, the old maglev assembly hall, left empty when production had shifted outside of the dome network. They had gained entry with false IDs and Outsiders' work visas, or they had utilized the labyrinth of disused sewers and subway tunnels that snaked through the underground of every domed city, despite the authorities' best efforts to seal them off.

But these illegals had managed to elude detection for longer than most, which suggested they had access to some reasonably advanced tech for spoofing their exact whereabouts. The intel appeared on the job board through a city surveillance drone, as it usually did. It had initially been flagged as unconfirmed, but in Jarod's experience, the city surveillance drones were often overly cautious and flagged anything even remotely uncertain as such. It was only through Jarod's team's further investigation that they were able to confirm the presence of the migrants, if not yet their exact geolocation.

Three individuals might not seem like much, but it would bring in a tidy profit for the whole team. *Thank God for all those tunnels, false permits, and smugglers. And for the fact that Legacy law enforcement is so under-resourced.* Without them, they would all be out of a job in an age where machines did most of everything. Who needs an old combat vet in such a world? But hunting down Outsiders had been a lucrative business for Jarod and his team for over a decade. In most parts of the world, drones and other automated law enforcement tech were prohibited from engaging in that kind of work due to human rights concerns or some such bureaucratic nonsense. Jarod wasn't well-versed in the legal nuances of the matter. He just found them and brought them in. *If anyone on the team was familiar with the ins and outs of it, it would be*

Riley and Kale.

London Central fell behind as the car sped through the tunnel to Dome North East One. They took the road beneath the elevated Overground tracks, which were mostly off-limits to the public. The lower level, remnants of the old street network, had now been repurposed for emergency, police, and other official transport, so it was busier. The connecting tunnels between the domes were new, constructed to accommodate ongoing expansion efforts. Most European cities followed a similar pattern of growth and organization, except for the stubborn British insistence on driving on the left side of the road.

As traffic density decreased, the car's AI accelerated the vehicle, rushing through the tunnels toward their destination. Jarod felt a subtle shift in G-force as the vehicle accelerated—a fleeting comfort, reminiscent of a world once vibrant with human control but now mostly at the mercy of the unerring predictability of autonomic machines. The irony that the sensation he experienced stemmed from the very gears of such a machine was not lost on him.

Visitation rights to London Central remained restricted after *Lux Aeterna* had devastated much of old London, leaving the tunnels mostly empty, both at the car lane level and the Overground level. Law enforcement and their contractors had unfettered access, of course. The car broadcasted IDs and permits as it rushed along at speeds that would satisfy even Wyatt, alerting security cameras and AI sentries along the way.

They soon emerged inside North East One, where life seemed to carry on relatively unencumbered by the disaster in Central. There were no visible signs of destruction or despair, but the scars obviously lingered beneath the surface even here. Nothing had crushed the spirits of the Brits more than the dome coming down. Some said it rivaled the devastation of the great wars of the twentieth century.

The car sped past schools, recreation centers for the job-relieved, shopping streets, bot farms, and old manufacturing plants. Nothing seemed out of place. Life went on, even after a disaster.

The car's alert jolted him back to the present. "Fifteen minutes to destination," it said.

It was time to enter the right state of mind for the mission. He usually did that by immersing himself in classical music, especially the tumultuous compositions of the twentieth-century Russians or Eastern Europeans. They helped him detach from the outside world like no other form of music. He didn't know why. Perhaps it was because the dissonant intricacy kept his mind occupied, enabling him to disconnect from reality, if only momentarily.

Jarod instructed his braid to shut out all external sound. The soundproofing would further enhance the feeling of detachment from the outside world. Penderecki's second violin concerto, aptly named *Metamorphosis*, was the perfect piece for the occasion. The city was changing, and while it wasn't immediately visible right here in Dome North East One, outside the tinted windows of the car, he could feel it in his bones.

The first ominous notes rang out, filling his mind. He turned the volume up to three-quarters and closed his eyes, allowing the music to envelop him. Although the piece had accompanying visuals—concert footage, documentaries, and bubbles of trivia—he preferred to turn them off. They distracted him from the pure essence of the music.

To an outsider, it might have seemed strange to see someone sitting with their eyes closed, not following things on their overlay or gesturing with their hands to swipe and select. Jarod thought so himself when he was the outside observer, but the others on the team were familiar with his process these days and thought nothing of it. If they needed anything from him, they would tap him on the shoulder.

Jarod preferred playing music out in the open, through external speakers, rather than through the braid's aural implants. Most people didn't these days. Many didn't even have external speakers anymore, not even for their homes. He found that direct aural had a muted quality, but nobody except him and a few other eccentrics could put up with Polish twentieth-century classical composers. And playing it out loud in the car would evoke violent protests from Wyatt and Riley. Kale, on the other hand, would never say anything, even if he found it obnoxious. *Does this car even have external speakers?* A quick braid request to the car revealed it didn't.

He held a particularly vivid and cherished memory of playing Lutosławski's second cello concerto out loud in the flat. Oh, how Dana had suffered! Ten minutes in, she had become so tortured that she just screamed, overrode his control of the speakers, and wiped the piece from the library. A futile gesture, of course; he would just put it back, albeit without making the mistake of playing it out loud again.

He would never forget her comment. She said it sounded like a flock of seagulls being run through a trash compactor. Not the new wave band from the 1980s, which his braid had helpfully informed him had once existed, but the actual bird. He chuckled to himself as he recollected the incident. *That's why I love you. Comments like that.*

Jarod was well aware that most people did not appreciate the sound of a brass section and a cello locked in a loud, tumultuous argument, even though he himself relished it. *Sometimes, even I wonder why I do,* he mused. Perhaps it helped him make sense of a world that was both chaotic and unequal, one where a vast majority of people were still trapped outside the domes. It was a world where he earned his living by chasing down those who sought shelter *Inside.*

After playing the Lutosławski piece for Dana, he had resolved never again to try to convince anyone else to appreciate it. Therefore, he only played music out loud when he was alone at home, preferring direct aural at any other time.

Anyway, stop wandering off in idle thoughts! He was supposed to clear his mind, after all. He pushed the rumination aside, attempting to submerge once more in the soothing notes. But he did not get far. Just as he had refocused on the music, a news alert flashed in his peripheral vision, interrupting the choppy, dissonant notes of the violin section. To his preference, the music automatically turned down when he accessed the article.

He couldn't focus on anything while such noise directly assaulted his cochlea. The abstract revealed that one of the suspects involved in the London dome bombing, apprehended by one of the police subcontractors a few weeks ago, had been released due to a lack of evidence. The article even hinted at a wrongful arrest charge. *Another one.*

Law enforcement agencies, from Legacy to private contractors and their subcontracted specialists, had been tirelessly searching for the culprits, yet they had come up with nothing. It was common knowledge that Alixha Rahena was the mastermind behind the bombing, even before she publicly claimed responsibility. However, she remained untouchable and untraceable. The powerful always have others do their dirty work, and they have henchmen to sacrifice.

Legacy did not have adequate resources, and private enforcement in their service had every incentive to keep finding false suspects. Chasing shadows meant billable hours. Even politicians saw an opportunity to regain some of the influence they had lost to the private sector in recent decades. Legacy had no chance against these resourceful adversaries, driven by such powerful financial incentives. *I'm rambling again. And to no one but myself!*

Like everyone else, he yearned for the return of the old world. But after a year, it was evident that such a desire was nothing more than a pipe dream. Change was afoot, and it was happening now. Paranoia permeated every dome in Europe, and Legacy government, private industry, the cabals of the super-rich, as well as the common work-relieved *Ubie*, were all feeling the squeeze. Every stakeholder, big and small, was jockeying for position in the new world that was emerging. But as with all things, only those with the resources to mount a serious challenge had a chance.

With a subtle movement of the eye, Penderecki roared back to life, just in time for the percussion section to join the fray. The orderly chaos reverberated through his skull, with every beat of the concert toms wiping away a fragment of his consciousness, resetting him to the blank slate he sought before going into the mission. Hunting outsiders bore a striking resemblance to his military days, save for the conclusion, where now he would make an arrest or, in some cases, use a taser. In contrast, before, he would use a bullet.

That last part—using bullets—was a reminder of a past he tried to relegate to the deepest corners of his mind, shackled and forgotten. It was an advanced form of mental compartmentalization that he had honed over time.

Another alarm blared, jarring him out of his thoughts. This time it was a call. From Dana. Once again, Penderecki was pushed to the background as he answered. Dana's image appeared in the corner of his eye—a still image since it was only audio. He knew that she always did that when she didn't have her makeup on. *Even after all these years.* Although, he suspected it wasn't for his sake. And it wasn't vanity in the broader sense. It was probably more for potential clients on the other end of the call. Of course, she wanted to look her best when conducting business.

"Will you be home late?" Dana said.

"A last-minute alert," he replied.

"Anything dangerous? Should I worry?" Her tone of voice was tongue-in-cheek. His jobs were usually perfectly safe.

"Standard stuff, really. Just some run-of-the-mill illegals."

He didn't tell her that they had access to tech that could conceal them. He didn't like lying to her, but it was a white lie. *It's not even a lie. It's merely withholding information.*

"Well, I have to get up early tomorrow, so try to be quiet when you come back. Okay?"

"I'll do my best," he assured her before they ended the call.

The car swung into the parking lot just as he finished speaking. Dembwe's team had already closed off the perimeter and was waiting by their vehicles to brief them. The car transmitted their IDs and passed through the temporary barricades that his team had erected.

The Docklands, once a bustling hub of commerce and industry, now lay mostly silent and forlorn, except for the Isle of Dogs, where Big Finance still thrived. The maglev hall at the site of the defunct City Airport stood desolate amidst widespread decay, its once-gleaming tracks overgrown with the creepers of neglect.

The dome plating high above had turned translucent, as it often did midday when the cloud cover was broken, letting natural light seep through. The looming silhouette of the colossal building cast a shadow over its surroundings as well as over Jarod's thoughts. The site stood as a monument to human ingenuity now forsaken, as heavy industry had vacated most city domes—a concrete skeleton from when humans still played more than a bit part in industrial production.

The building had once belonged to a contractor associated with the old London City Airport, possibly a ground service provider. After the airport shut down, it became an assembly hall for maglevs for about a decade. When the dome network expanded to include East London, the maglev assembly moved to an industrial dome up north, leaving the building abandoned. His braid displayed a popup indicating there were plans to turn it into a luxury residential area, but the project was indefinitely delayed. *Making it a perfect hideout for paperless Outsiders.* He reminded himself not to use that term.

Dembwe's team had the area sealed off. Drones circled the building, but his overlay revealed gaps in coverage. It seemed that Dembwe did not have enough units available. No surprise. The old City Airport had been smaller, but it was still a vast area to cover. He accessed the grid and saw blind spots everywhere. The patches they did cover were moving around as the drones circled in a search pattern, attempting to fill the holes. *No worries. We can cover those areas ourselves.* He instructed Riley via braid to get working on that.

Jana Dembwe was a private contractor whom Jarod had worked with many times before. He always brought him in for any case where there might be trouble. His team were specialists, equipped with state-of-the-art gear Jarod's team could only dream of: reactive nano-fiber armor, weapons calibrated for non-lethal—and lethal—force alike, and full complements of every type of squito known to man. They had police-like authority and permits to use lethal force to carry out their contracts. Not many private contractors had such permissions, certainly not Jarod himself, despite representing a government agency. They were the epitome of precision, trained for every contingency and almost always a complete overkill. Jarod had never had to use Dembwe's special powers. Thankfully. Of course, he had no intention of harming any *Outsiders*, and neither did Dembwe, but they could, should the need arise.

He brought up the engagement report as they walked across the parking lot to the command station. It had been a while since he worked with Dembwe's team, so he thought it prudent to take a quick look at her recent work. Dembwe and his team were former Navy SEALs. The European market was flooded with former U.S. military personnel ever since the Second Détente. With China on more amicable terms with the West and Russia facing challenges, the American military had seen a rise in individuals seeking alternative ventures to apply their skills.

The list of Dembwe's engagements appeared on his lens, hovering in front of him. *Impressive, as always.* Response times and operational efficiency were unmatched. After-action details were sparse, but it didn't matter since Jarod had seen her team in action many times and knew how effective they could be. He was well aware of Dembwe's reluctance to file proper reports.

He flipped through the pages of the engagement contract to the invoice. A hundred grand. *Damn.* That was considerably pricier than the last time around. He glanced over at his team and saw Wyatt sneering, probably observing the same thing he was. Ever since the dome had come down, premiums had skyrocketed. It was a good thing the city was paying for most of it. Nonetheless, it would take a substantial chunk out of their profits. He grimaced and swore under his breath, then authorized the transaction. *The cost of doing business, I suppose.*They walked towards the command vehicle, where Dembwe greeted them.

"What's up, dicks?" he said in his decidedly American accent. At least they'd understand each other. Jarod despised most British dialects; half the words were lost in a tirade of diphthongs. Nevertheless, the word *dicks* was loud and clear regardless of accent.

"I love it when you call us that," Jarod said.

"I'm sorry," Dembwe said. "Does it hurt your feelings? I'll call you detectives from now on."

He wouldn't.

"You know we're not actual detectives, right?" Kale quipped.

"I'm aware," Dembwe responded curtly. "Briefing in five." With that, he did an about-face and headed for command and control.

Riley turned to Wyatt and smirked. "He's as charming as ever. I hate the jarheads."

Wyatt sneered. "Is that so, sweetie? Is it the mustaches? Do they scare you?"

"Ha!" she scoffed. "Funny! Speaking of dicks, call me sweetie one more time and I'll rip yours off and feed it to you." She blew him a kiss and strutted away.

Wyatt responded in kind. "I better watch it, then," he said as she turned her back and walked toward the command vehicle. She flipped him off without looking back. Same dialogue every time between these two. Jarod told them to shut up. He typically permitted them to have their fun, but today he had grown sick of it.

"What?" Wyatt demanded sarcastically. "What'd you say? Come on! Hey, Riley, wait up." He jogged to catch up.

"This is going to be a disaster," Kale said matter-of-factly as he joined them.

"This is us," Dembwe said after they had all gathered around the holographic display in the rear of the command vehicle. He circled an area on the map in front of them. "It appears that the targets are in possession of an electromagnetic field generator, probably their last-ditch attempt to stay hidden once someone gets close. Our gear will work inside but not optimally. The closer we get to the source, the worse it'll be." He drew another circle. "Around this area, we'll be mostly blind. From then on, visual only. Got that?"

Jarod nodded on behalf of his team. Dembwe carried on. In

the end, the briefing added nothing new, but Dembwe could be a bit pedantic when it came to protocol, so Jarod let him finish uninterrupted. The man was merely fulfilling his duties as a dutiful commander by providing a briefing.

"Keep an eye out for drones," Dembwe instructed, his voice low and urgent. "Especially near the edges of the field. The closer we get to the source, their drones, if they have any, will perform just as poorly as ours."

Unless their tech is better. Unlikely, but not impossible. It's one thing to obtain EM field generators and identity spoofing software, quite another to acquire combat-ready drones or squitos. But caution is paramount. *Assume the worst and hope for the best, unless you want to end up with a bullet in your skull.*

"Remember," Dembwe said, addressing his team specifically, "restrain and detain only. These are refugees, not hostile invaders. So, tasers only. Understood?" His team murmured their agreement. Meanwhile, Wyatt whispered into Jarod's ear, "Let's hope the Outsiders show us the same courtesy, shall we?"

Ignoring Wyatt's comment, Jarod offered a solution to the drone issue. "We have a portable signal enhancer. It has a range of about thirty meters. Kale can operate it."

Upon hearing this, Kale's face drained of color, and Jarod knew precisely why. "I know you're not thrilled about fieldwork," Jarod said to Kale, his voice hushed. "But you'll be alright. Just stick with me and keep our drones flying."

Kale nodded. He preferred working remotely from Ops, alongside Riley, providing tech support. But the few occasions he had gone into the field, it had gone well.

"All set," Dembwe said. "Let's move out."

As they entered the maglev hall, a musty smell—a mix of rust, old metal, and an almost forgotten scent of industrial lubricants and dust—permeated the air. Their footsteps echoed eerily in the vast space, each sound bouncing between abandoned hardware and hollow walls. Cool, damp air brushed against their skin. The hall's cavernous space prodded the edges of Jarod's controlled composure, each echo reverberating with the ghosts of past operations, events from his active combat days now deeply buried under layers of deliberate self-control. It was a subtle yet persistent reminder of the unpredictable nature of their work and how it could turn ugly at any moment.

Dembwe's team took the lead, with one of his squad members covering their rear in case a target slipped past them. Part of Jarod questioned the need for such extraordinary precautions. These were migrants, after all. Yet, the presence of advanced tech suggested that they might be dealing with an armed group, perhaps even a terrorist cell rather than mere refugees. While it wasn't unheard of, Outies sometimes had access to technology like electromagnetic field emitters. Dembwe's firepower might be excessive, but in the post-London bomb world, overwhelming force was always the order of the day.

"Drone feeds are coming in," Dembwe announced.

Jarod brought up Dembwe's feed on his own display, allowing him to see everything Dembwe saw. Interference was already severe. He divided the screens between the surveillance squitos ahead of the team, scanning for signals that could reveal the presence of electronic devices like braids, tablets, and lenses, and the forward drone with a visual feed.

"Dark as hell in here," Dembwe remarked. "We'll have to activate the drone's floods."

The floods brightened the corridors, and through the drone's camera, Jarod spotted small arms fire damage on one of the walls, possibly caused by a rifle or pistol. The bullet holes were neatly arranged in a circular pattern, as if made by an expert marksman. He noticed something poking out of the holes as the drone drew closer. *Nails?*

"Are you seeing this?" he asked over the comms.

"Duly noted," Dembwe replied.

"What do you think that is? Target practice?"

"Could be."

His heart rate quickened. Could this be the moment?

"The squitos have finished their sweep," reported one of Dembwe's team members. "Nobody's home."

Jarod cursed under his breath. The Outies were there

somewhere. They just couldn't pick them up. That EMP field was doing its job.

"Alright," Dembwe said. "Switch to active sensors. Have the squitos ping those motherfuckers out. Hit them with everything. I want this place painted."

The *Outies'* field wasn't strong enough to withstand active sensors, but using them would reveal their own position. *If the* Outies *hadn't already spotted the point drone's light show.*

"We got something," Dembwe reported. "Active's got a hit. This way."

That was quick. But the team arrived at an unexpected dead end in one of the corridors. Jarod accessed the building schematics on his display, discovering that there was supposed to be a staircase. He relayed this information to Dembwe. "I know," he replied, tapping the wall a few times. "It's hollow."

The team quickly removed the makeshift drywall to reveal the staircase leading to a basement section, seemingly unused for ages, perhaps even when the factory was operational.

Jarod returned to the squitos' video feeds, cycling through the units in the hopes of spotting something. With the point drone's floods casting light down the staircase, his view was better than before.

"Where are those little fuckers hiding?" Wyatt grumbled.

The search was brief, with the illegals all gathered in one place, awaiting apprehension. They offered no resistance and weren't terrorists. Merely refugees seeking safety and employment *Inside.*

Nevertheless, Jarod was impressed with the Outies' efforts. They had put up a good fight, constructing a false wall and a basic yet impressive EMP device that, combined with the thick concrete walls, fooled the team's sensors. It wasn't enough, as usual. Jarod was disappointed that they didn't have to do more. The nail gun had excited him, and he had hoped that at least one of the illegals would put up a real fight. It seemed that someone was merely releasing tension or killing time by shooting nails at the wall. For all he knew, the nails had been there since the plant's operational days.

Why do I hope for violence? Boredom was the current answer, and Jarod knew it. He also knew it was wrong, perhaps even perverse, to hope for violence, no matter how slight. Many years ago, he had seen a therapist for PTSD, and the man had prescribed antidepressants and anti-anxiety medication. He'd told the therapist to go fuck himself, left, and never returned. *Real men don't need medication; they just punch a wall and suck it up.*

Dana had not liked that, of course. Not one bit. *What? I asked him politely.* He chuckled at his own joke. He had things under control. He was coping. *Yeah, am I not?* He didn't need that shit, but at the same time, he was acutely aware of the potential for past traumas to resurface regardless of the control applied, and if forceful enough, boredom would become anxiety, and eventually, something resembling panic attacks.

"Move in and secure," Dembwe ordered. "Then you can let the detectives have the scene."

That was Jarod's cue to proceed. It was time to work. Formal arrest warrants needed issuing, paperwork started, transport called for, Legacy informed, bounties collected, accounting done, and statutory reports filed. *Oh, God!* Boring stuff. Safe stuff. Enough to make him utter a religious expletive.

After it was all done, London Metro took jurisdiction. These particular illegals had constructed an EMP device, they were informed, as if they didn't already know. They were therefore within the scope of Europe's new terror laws. That meant no bounty, no compensation. A loss, in fact, since Dembwe still expected to be paid.

"Son of a bitch," Wyatt muttered and slammed the car door shut as they prepared to leave. All the way back, he ranted about how impotent Legacy was, how contractors were doing their job for them, and how they were now reaping the rewards. It was his usual rant, and it was annoying. Jarod sighed in relief after he finally let everyone off, free to go their separate ways for the day. Not that he disagreed, but the money wasn't his concern; he had other things on his mind.

"Will you be okay?" Dana asked. Jarod was so upset about the whole debacle that he had forgotten Dana had told him she was going to bed early, so he had called her to vent his frustrations.

"There will be new jobs," Jarod said. "It's not like the world is going to run out of Outsiders."

Jarod's voice was a mask of casual indifference, but beneath it simmered a cocktail of frustration and regret. Dana remained quiet, yet he could almost hear the worry she masked behind the silence, a concern he both appreciated and resented.

Jarod knew this would later lead to discussions about his job, the risks he took, and her fear of losing him in some altercation or to a mental abyss from which he could never rise. In the small hours of the night, they would deliberate his fears of being bored and the road that it might lead down, and her anger at him for hunting down Outsiders, which was in stark contrast to her own work. The conversation was a familiar marital dance of theirs and always left a bitter aftertaste. But she wasn't wrong. He often wondered about his motivations himself. *I'm sure as hell not doing it for the love of it.*

"When will you be home?" she finally asked. Jarod heard the faint rustle of bed sheets through the line, a soft, familiar sound that contrasted with the hum of the car. It was a reminder of the warmth and normalcy that awaited him, worlds apart from the operation earlier today.

"An hour, maybe. I have to return the car."

Living in the city meant no access to cars, and after returning the vehicle to Kent, he would have half an hour on a slow train followed by another fifteen minutes on the Tube. Jarod's mind wandered briefly, musing over the absurd dichotomies of his life—the relative thrill of the chase moments before versus the dull mundanity of routine. Then there was the deep love he undoubtedly felt for Dana, contrasted by the unspoken worries and his mostly unacknowledged frustration.

"There are leftovers in the fridge," she said, bringing him back to the conversation. "See you soon." And with that, the call ended. A heaviness settled in Jarod's heart as he hung up. It was no secret Dana disapproved of his work. He did too—a silent testament to the personal cost of life within the domes. UBI wasn't enough to cover the exorbitant cost of living under these marvelous protective canopies, and this was all he could get. She would get over it. She always did. It might take a day or two, but eventually, she would relax.

He consoled himself with the thought that most days were a lot less exciting than today. Exciting for her, that is. For him, however, it was just as dull as always. The issue of money would eventually be fixed. But his general lackadaisical outlook on life and his resentment toward Legacy were another matter. *I'm so bored, someone using a nail gun for a little target practice to pass the time gets me excited.*

As he strode toward the elevators leading to the third level, he felt a prickling sensation at the back of his neck. Two figures had been shadowing him, a man and a woman, keeping pace with his every step.

Adrenaline surged, mixing with anticipation and a subtle undercurrent of unease. A knot tightened in his stomach, and a slight shiver trickled down his spine. Years of rigorous training and a life lived on the brink had honed his instincts to a razor's edge. Yet, he noted a slight delay in reaction—mere fractions of a second, but enough to confirm that the predictable rhythm of his current existence had slightly blunted his edge. Now, however, the whisper of real, palpable danger stirred something within him, reawakening this dormant part of his being.

They had followed him closely to the parking lot, parked their vehicle not far from his own, on the same level of the sprawling expanse of London's largest peripheral parking lot. What were the odds that they would appear alongside him on the Northern Line, ride all the way out to Old Kennington, and now join him in the elevator? A coincidence, perhaps—this was London, after all—a city teeming with people at all hours of the day. And night.

Still, intuition nagged at him, insisting that there was something more to this than mere happenstance. If these two were indeed following him, they were doing a woefully amateurish job of it. Professionals were far too skilled to allow themselves to be so easily spotted. Unless they were decoys? Perhaps it was a sleight of hand, meant to distract him while their accomplices carried out their true mission?

He activated a surveillance squito to keep an eye on his new friends. Meanwhile, he fired up his facial recognition app, instructing it to run an algorithm on today's lens footage designed to seek out anyone who might have been tailing him for the last several hours, other than these two. On his corneal lens, in the corner of his eye, minimized so as not to obstruct his view, information flowed. The target reticle frantically jumped from one face to another, analyzing facial expressions, eye movements, body language, and electronic signatures from their devices. If anyone else was tailing him, he would soon know.

The searches came up empty. There was nothing to suggest that anyone besides these two was interested in his movements. In a last-ditch effort, he instructed the squito to approach and run facial recognition scans. It too was fruitless. They were ghosts, appearing in no databases accessible to him, but they had been on his tail since the job earlier in the day. City CCTV cameras had captured their movements on several occasions since Legacy had yanked their catch out from under them. They were certainly not experts at covering their tracks, that much was evident. *Overconfident amateurs or decoys? Or just two people heading his way who were also ghosts? No way.*

As he stepped out of the elevator, he made no attempt to blend in with the bustling crowd. The two figures had been shadowing him, a man and a woman, keeping pace with his every step as he made his way toward Walworth Level Three. But before he reached the busy high street, he veered into the Cranston Communal Garden, deliberately making sure they noticed him. Unlike the high street, the garden was usually deserted at this time of night, and tonight was no exception. He took a seat on a bench tucked around the corner from the entrance gate and reached inside his jacket, unclipping the holster of his sidearm. Jarod's movements were calm, methodical, but his heart raced. The familiar grip of his sidearm soothed him, ready for whatever might happen next.

In the garden, the ambient night lighting cast a soft glow on the meticulously maintained flora, their leaves rustling gently in the artificial breeze. The two ghosts were right behind him, sauntering rather nonchalantly through the garden gate, still making no attempt to conceal themselves.

"I'm armed," Jarod said when they spotted him.

"So are we," replied the man in an impeccable British accent, "but we have no intention of using any weapons, so please, stay calm." He gestured to Jarod, urging him to relax.

The woman, with a Russian or perhaps Ukrainian accent, added, "Please, Mr. Lima, we just want to talk." Not that her accent said much in the melting pot of ethnicities that was London.

"So talk," Jarod retorted, his gaze unwavering.

"Not here," the woman said. "We kindly ask you to come with us to discuss job offer." She omitted the "a," as many Eastern Europeans did when speaking English, her accent a melodic contrast to the distant cacophony of the city. Jarod's mind was a whirlwind of suspicion and, he had to admit, curiosity. The audacity of the approach, the unspoken threats—it was a game of chess with stakes resembling the good old days. He couldn't help feeling a begrudging respect for their boldness, even as he smirked inwardly at their assumption of control.

His surveillance squito was still working to detect any potential accomplices. Jarod wondered if these two were truly alone. With the shit day he was having, it wouldn't surprise him.

"Job offer, you say?" Jarod scoffed. "You know I operate under a Legacy law enforcement retainer, right? Which precludes me from accepting private contracts." The woman was about to respond, but Jarod rambled on. "But hey, maybe you don't? You two did such a terrible job of tailing me, I don't know what to thin k. Just starting out? Still learning the ropes? Or maybe you're just a couple of morons?"

The man's smile was calculated and smooth. "I assure you that you only noticed our presence because we allowed it. Mr. Lima, we only wish to converse. There's no need for mistrust.

And yes, we're aware of your professional undertakings."

"Right. Then why not just shoot me a message like a normal person?"

"Would you have been willing to talk if we did?" said the man.

Jarod had to concede that point. "Touché. I'm not interested, so can we wrap this up? My wife has leftovers waiting for me in the fridge."

The squito's efforts still came up nil.

"Mr. Lima, our employer insists, so I'm afraid you don't have a choice," the man said with blunt finality.

Jarod raised an eyebrow, his interest piqued. "Is that so? And who, pray tell, is this employer of yours, that can make such confident demands?"

"All will be revealed in due time."

Jarod scoffed. "You can try to make me," he said defiantly, "but first, bring a couple more guys, so it'll be an even fight."

The man smiled confidently, but the woman accompanying him remained deadly serious. Not a single facial muscle had moved throughout the entire conversation, aside from the brief moment when she spoke earlier. "They're already here," she stated simply, while casually snapping her fingers. As if on cue, Jarod's squito picked up five more signatures, all within ten meters of their location. Shadows moved in the bushes beyond the garden fence; figures appeared perched on nearby rooftops. *Stealth tech. Impressive.*

Jarod's hand moved instinctively toward his sidearm as the reticle on his retina display multiplied and locked onto five new faces. But it was too late. His AI alerted him that assault rifles were already aimed at him, even before he could draw his gun halfway out of its holster. A sudden bright light above blinded him, and dust kicked off the ground as a hovercraft descended from above. The bright lights from the vehicle cast stark, dancing shadows around them, painting the scene with a searingly bright and otherworldly glow. Jarod exhaled wearily, realizing his options had dwindled to none. "No choice, huh?" he said.

In that moment, as the hovercraft descended and the reality of his situation sank in, a weary resignation settled over Jarod. He was beaten, and he didn't like it. It had been a long day, and a wave of exhaustion suddenly hit, but still, he couldn't deny that the prospect of a new, unknown challenge was not only a potential weight on his shoulders but a prospective escape from the numbing ennui that plagued him.

"No choice, pal," the woman replied, finally speaking. As he made his way toward the hovercar, she snapped her fingers once more, and the five mercenaries vanished as quickly as they had appeared.

"Nice theatrics, by the way," he said, somewhat awestruck despite himself. "Most impressive." He relaxed into his seat as the car lifted off the ground.

"Don't worry," the woman reassured him. "We'll send flowers to your wife. She will forgive."

"Please accept my sincere apologies for the cloak-and-dagger, Mr. Lima," the elderly man said from the comfort of a plush armchair, upholstered in rich, dark leather emitting a subtle aged scent—like the man himself. The man sat cradled as if on a throne, his features partially obscured in shadow, and his voice seemed to radiate both wisdom and cunning calculation. "As you can imagine," the gentleman went on, "a man in my position must take certain precautions before engaging with a member of the general public, especially someone who carries a firearm."

Jarod felt a simmering annoyance at the theatricality, which was clearly more performance than necessity. Yet, despite his underlying skepticism, he had to admit they had successfully piqued his curiosity. Around him, the entire scene was shrouded in gloom; the room's only source of illumination was a handful of soft spotlights embedded in the ceiling. *A bit melodramatic, perhaps?* Nevertheless, it had a somewhat chilling effect. It was staged well, like in an old spy movie.

The hovercar had transported him to Central, landing atop the Primrose Tower, now exposed under a menacing sky, surrounded by the remnants of the damaged dome structure. Temporary fortifications in the form of a self-replicating tarp had been erected to protect the tower, stretching across the vast expanse of missing dome plating and latticework. While not as sturdy as the real thing, it provided adequate cover during the approach as long as the elements played nice. As a motion sickness sufferer, Jarod had always loathed flying, but this time, a smooth landing had left him untroubled.

The destruction had extended further to the east, while the west had mostly been spared. Chelsea, Kensington, Westminster, and Pimlico were all unscathed by the blast, where all the wealth and power resided. Despite the devastation brought upon the east, the towering buildings of The City had, ironically, also emerged unharmed. *Good job on hitting none of the intended targets.*

The elevator ride down had been brief, indicating to Jarod that they had arrived at a penthouse suite. As he stepped into the room, the old man rose to greet him, emerging from the shadows as he did. To his surprise, he found himself face to face with none other than Henry James Gibson—the enigmatic CEO of Aegis, billionaire owner of half the planet's domes, eccentric, and recluse. *Naturally!* The very embodiment of every cliché one had about the super-rich. While somewhat surprising, the presence of the near-mythical man injected an unexpected weight into the meeting, transforming it from mere curiosity to something potentially momentous.

Gibson had not appeared in public for over two decades, with some rumors even suggesting that he was dead, replaced by an AI or a doppelgänger for media appearances. However, Jarod, among other sane individuals, dismissed such folly as nothing but silly, conspiratorial nonsense. The old man's age escaped him, but he was undoubtedly pushing the limits of human longevity. He was well over a hundred. *Not such a challenge when you have every available genetic engineering and medical technology known to man at the snap of your fingers.*

Gibson made a sweeping hand gesture, signaling for the security detail to exit the room. In their place, a man and a woman in business attire stepped in. The combination of navy blue and white shirts never went out of style. The tie, on the other hand, seemed to come and go, and now it was apparently back in style.

"Allow me to introduce Lee Chen," Gibson said, "my Chief Operating Officer, who has graciously offered his home for this meeting. And this is Anya Pacula, my Chief Risk Officer." These associates, each a study in corporate cliché, wore expressions of practiced neutrality. Their attire, crisply tailored and impeccably styled, was a striking illustration of elite power. He eyed the newcomers with a mixture of wariness and faint amusement. Their polished appearance was a costume, a uniform donned to impress him, to convey the seriousness of the situation. For Jarod, it mainly accomplished the polar opposite. Gibson then gestured toward a third man entering the door, a tall, sinewy man with a prominent scar across his left cheek, dressed casually in jeans and an untucked shirt, in contrast to his colleagues. "This is Adriel. His role in the proceedings will become evident in due course."

Gibson gestured for his colleagues to take their seats on the sofa while he himself relaxed back into his armchair. "Please, join us," he invited Jarod, indicating the second armchair opposite the coffee table. As they settled in, a team of servers began bringing in a spread of refreshments. Adriel, meanwhile, remained near the door, leaning against the doorframe with an air of detached interest.

An array of sandwiches and pastries from all corners of the world, along with oysters, caviar, and truffles, were laid out before them. The spread of gourmet offerings filled the room with an enticing aroma—a blend of exotic spices, the briny tang of the sea, and the earthy richness of the truffles. Each dish was a miniature masterpiece, presented with an elegance that spoke of skilled hands and discerning tastes. It was an impressive display, to be sure, but Jarod was not one to be swayed by flamboyant manifestations of wealth. Rather, it elicited further resentment and possibly a tinge of cynical amusement. It was a display designed to impress, to flaunt an opulence far removed from his own reality, yet it only deepened his sense of detachment. *Or so I like to think.*

"So," he remarked, "is this how you guys normally eat in the middle of the night, or are you putting on a show?"

Chen chuckled in response. "Not impressed, Mr. Lima? We can get you anything you desire."

"I'm feeling a bit, what do you British people say, peckish? How about a burger and fries?"

"Excellent choice. I'm something of a burger aficionado myself. And for the record, none of us are British," Chen said, despite his impeccable accent. The lady, too, spoke perfect British English, so he would be forgiven for thinking they were. Gibson, on the other hand, was unmistakably American.

"Rest assured, the meat in your burger will be real, none of that lab-grown rubbish," Chen added, a hint of pride in his voice.

Gibson motioned for Chen to be silent. "I suppose you will want to know why you are here?"

"Nah, not really," Jarod replied. "I mostly just want to go home."

"Ah, a man who knows his priorities," Gibson said with a hint of amusement. The banter went on, an obvious attempt to put Jarod at ease before the big request was made. The burger arrived promptly; Jarod half-jokingly wondered if they had a robovendor hidden away somewhere. *It wouldn't be worthy of this kind of wealth.* No, the burger would be prepared by human hands, by a big entourage of attendants at Gibson's command, to fulfill his every whim whenever he wanted.

The burger looked and smelled delicious, and Jarod leaned in for a big bite. Too big—meat juices ran down his chin, and a dollop of mayo landed on the tip of his nose. "Delicious!" he exclaimed through a full mouth. And it truly was. As he bit into it, rich, savory flavors burst forth, and he felt a brief, comforting connection to the simpler pleasures he usually enjoyed. Juices and condiments mingled, gently caressing his taste buds in every direction. It was a momentary indulgence, grounding and disarming in its simplicity. It was, quite possibly, the best burger he had ever tasted, but he obviously wasn't about to admit that.

"This will go straight to my ass, though," he quipped instead. "I don't have the luxury of extensive gene therapy, so it's two hours on the treadmill for me tomorrow."

Chen and the woman, whose name escaped Jarod, looked on with a mixture of disdain and disgust as Jarod chewed and spoke with his mouth open. Gibson, however, seemed unfazed by the display. Jarod put the rest of the burger down, chewed, and swallowed. He wiped his mouth and nose on the napkin, folded it neatly, and then stood.

A restless impatience surged in Jarod as he rose. This was enough staged civility for one evening, and the experience had left him eager to escape, even as he was still reluctantly curious about what this had been all about. "Well, Gibbsy, it's been a pleasure," he said. "Thanks for the burger, but I really must be going." He pretended to check an imaginary watch on his wrist.

"Mr. Lima, please," Gibson replied. "Indulge an old man. Ten minutes of your time is all I ask. I believe you'll find it worthwhile."

Jarod hesitated for a few seconds, then let out a sigh of surrender. That reluctant curiosity got the better of him, the request for indulgence fully igniting that annoying spark of interest that had nagged him since the two ghosts had approached. Against his better judgment, he slowly sank back into his seat. After all, they had gone to a lot of trouble, and they were right. If they had simply called him, he would have closed the line in a flash. Perhaps it wouldn't hurt to hear them out. After all, he needed the money, especially now that Legacy had swiped his cut. "Ten minutes," he relented, settling back into his seat.

"Thank you, Mr. Lima," Gibson said with a gracious nod.

"So, what can I do for you?" Jarod inquired.

Gibson's smile was enigmatic. "He'll do just fine, won't he?" he said to the others, as if Jarod were not in the room. The others nodded in assent. Jarod motioned for them to get on with it. Ms. Pacula leaned forward, took a quick sip of her tea before setting it down—the china clinking surprisingly loud. "We want you to catch a killer."

The London dome bomber. That, I had not anticipated. A surge of unease rumbled in Jarod's gut when he considered it, yet the unease mingled with a palpable, adrenaline-fueled thrill. The weight of such a task was not lost on him; it was a high-stakes game where the world would be watching.

The super-rich targeting corporate adversaries wasn't unheard of, but they usually had their own operatives for such tasks. Involving independent contractors like himself was generally ill-advised, and it was always done with the utmost discretion. But this... This was on a whole different level. It was too significant to be kept under wraps. Not only was it risky for him, but it posed a risk for everyone involved.

Aegis itself stood to suffer unimaginable consequences if it became known that they were taking the law into their own hands. There were bound to be complications with other players, each with their own competing interests—Legacy law enforcement and intelligence, bounty hunters, and perhaps even other corporations. The chances of this ending well were slim. *But then again, there's the money. And the opportunity to do something worthwhile, for a change.* Despite his reservations, a part of him couldn't help but feel invigorated by the challenge. *This is exactly what I've been looking for.*

The goons deposited Jarod back at the Cranston Communal Garden where they had snatched him and handed him the remaining half of the burger in a takeaway box. Jarod considered throwing it away; after all, he didn't typically eat meat from animals. Out of principle, he told himself, but equally because he couldn't afford it. *But, what the hell? The animal was already dead. Might as well not let it go to waste.*

He rested on the same bench where the two goons had ambushed him and finished the food. The background hum of nightlife in Dome SE2 served as a faint backdrop to his thoughts, a constant reminder of the artificial safety those canopies provided. The stark contrast between intact SE2 and the tarped Central he had just come from was palpable.

The burger in his hand, now slightly cold, still emitted a tempting aroma of grilled meat and spices. The garden, bathed in softer light to simulate nighttime, was as serene as before the goons swooped in with their hovercraft, although there were visible marks where the thrusters had kicked against the ground.

In a back corner of his mind, his braid worked overtime analyzing every moment of the conversation with Gibson and his associates. A translucent window at the edge of his field of view, almost imperceptible unless he focused on it, was a gentle reminder of the constant flow of data being analyzed. The AI scrutinized every word, every tremble in their voices, every facial expression, and every gesture they made for indications of deception. He found none. They had been truthful, and the AI consequently concluded that there was no reason to turn down the job based on suspicion of deception.

Jarod's mind raced alongside the braid's analysis, absorbing every detail. The lack of deception detected did little to quell his skepticism. Trust was not something easily afforded in his line of work, and yet, the proposition tugged at something deeper within him—that desire for a purpose. *To do something good, for a change.*

Even the account of why they needed him specifically checked out. Legacy had Aegis under the microscope, with every one of their operatives under suspicion for numerous acts of terror against European domes owned by Aegis's competitors. They needed someone discreet, someone who could find and eliminate the culprits of the London attack undetected, and someone with no obvious ties to them. But Jarod had his doubts, regardless of what the analytics told him.

However, their motives aligned with his own. Gibson wasn't simply seeking retribution; he genuinely wanted justice to be served, and he understood that a world destabilized by violence would benefit no one. Legacy's impotence had allowed terror to run rampant, and now others had to take action. Fight fire with fire, as they say. Regardless, Gibson was no angel, and accepting the job would surely be making a deal with the devil. The thought of engaging with the likes of Gibson certainly left a sour taste in Jarod's mouth—a bitter acknowledgment of the moral compromises his life had come to entail. But the allure of justice, however twisted the path, was a siren call he found hard to ignore.

The flattery regarding his professionalism he took with a grain of salt. *Showed exceptional skill with the Outside refugees earlier today, my ass!* If he had, they wouldn't be bordering on destitution now. However, the extent of their knowledge of his past puzzled and worried him. Had they obtained access to his old military service record? Those were supposed to be sealed.

The realization that his past was an open book to Gibson ignited a flicker of paranoia in Jarod. It was a reminder of his own vulnerability, his life a chess piece on a board controlled by those more powerful. It was hardly surprising. Nothing is truly beyond the reach of people like Gibson, who have virtually unlimited resources at their disposal, and nothing is confidential—at least, not when it pertains to others besides themselves.

Hunting terrorists was an entirely different thing from hunting refugees. Killing terrorists, different still. Those skills were rusty, and that concerned him deeply. It had been a long time since he had taken a life, and over the years, he had regrown the conscience of a regular man, despite the diagnosis of that therapist he barely saw in bygone years. He wondered how the team would take it. After all, he had accepted the job without consulting them. Time would tell.

Exhausted, he climbed into bed at 3:30 a.m. Dana stirred as he tugged some of the covers away from her side. "You okay?" she asked.

"Shhh," he replied, planting a tender kiss on her forehead. "Everything's alright."

She snuggled up to him, her arm draped over his chest, and promptly drifted back to sleep.

Slipping into bed beside Dana, Jarod was enveloped by a sense of normalcy, a stark contrast to the day's events. Her warmth was a haven, her presence a reminder of what he stood to lose. But while the comfort helped calm his thoughts, he still lay there beside her all night, staring sleeplessly at the ceiling.

Dana

Dana awoke to the earthy aroma of freshly brewed coffee wafting through the air. Or was it the gurgling sound of the filter machine percolating? Half-asleep, she reached over to the right side of the bed. Empty. She felt a brief moment of loneliness in her half-awake state as her hand met the cool, empty sheets beside her, but in the very next moment, her brain realized Jarod was just in the next room. *Well, I slept in. Again!* Despite their pledge to make the most of their weekends, she and Jarod consistently found themselves languishing away under the covers, but today it seemed Jarod had better success with this elusive promise than she did.

Now baking under the thick blankets, she kicked them aside and dangled her sock-clad foot over the edge while firing up her braid. A crisp eighteen degrees Celsius greeted her as the display blinked awake before her eyes. *London. Even under the domes, it's too cold in the winter and too hot in the summer.* Never mind half of Central having been ripped away and replaced with a tarp. It made no difference. "Twenty-one degrees," she commanded the apartment AI, then brought up the time. Eleven-thirty. *That settles it.*

"Curtains," she commanded, and with a soft whir, the room flooded with the muted glow of another glorious dome-encased morning. Almost noon was a bit too long, even for a weekend with no obligations or plans. But she *loooove*d sleeping in. So much. The allure of another half an hour under the covers, floating in that intangible realm between consciousness and slumber, almost always overpowered her. What difference would another thirty minutes make now? The morning was gone, so why not indulge? A sigh escaped her lips, a mix of resignation and rebellion against the day's obligations. The comfort of denial, wrapped in the soft embrace of her blankets, was too tempting to resist.

She pulled the covers back over herself, turned on her side, and scooted over to Jarod's side of the bed. The lingering scent of him left on the sheets comforted her, and when alone in bed, she often slept on his side. Just as she began to slip away, the creak of the bedroom door brought her back.

"You finally awake, honey?" the voice softly said. The surprise in his voice pulled a reluctant smile from her lips, a warmth spreading in her chest at the sight of him, despite the fact he woke her.

Damn. He brought coffee, at least. The comforting scent preceded him as he settled beside her, the cup's steam curling gently in the air. He leaned in and gave her a soft kiss on the forehead.

"Come back to bed," she murmured, pulling him closer.

"You know what time it is, right?" Jarod responded, raising an eyebrow in her direction.

She nodded yes but kept pulling him in. Jarod grinned, immediately getting that certain look in his eyes.

"No," she said, playfully warding him off with a raised hand. "Not that. Just cuddle."

"Really?" he teased, a mischievous smile spreading across his lips.

"For now. I need to wake up a bit first."

"Hmm," he said playfully. "Don't you think me getting back

in bed will accomplish the exact opposite of 'waking up a bit'?" He put his hand down the covers, playfully trying to cup one of her breasts.

"Shut up," Dana said with a chuckle, swatting at his arm.

"Fine, you win," he said, pretend-rolling his eyes. He nestled in and drew her close. "Did you turn on the aircon?"

"Yes," she confirmed.

"Hmm."

Dana nestled closer, seeking the comforting heat of his body, a silent plea for protection from the world outside their cocoon of blankets. "I know, the bill. But it's freezing," she explained. A quiet sigh escaped her lips as she thought about the financial tightrope they seemed to have to balance.

He said nothing, just held her tightly. She knew he wasn't concerned about the bill—that was more her thing. Heating an apartment in London remained expensive, even under the engineered environment of the domes. It wasn't necessarily the same elsewhere, even with similar environmental circumstances. *The tarp certainly doesn't help.* But the tarp couldn't be blamed; it merely exacerbated a preexisting problem. The matter was not technical in nature, but rather one of corporate greed, courtesy of Aegis, and red tape caused by the leasing agreement with the city. It had been a persistent issue for as long as she could remember. Whenever they increased the heat beyond the dome's ambient temperature, the bill would soar.

"I don't want to do anything today," she whispered into the quiet of the room, her words muffled against his chest. "Let's just mope around in our jammies, drink coffee, and forget about the world. Order takeout, watch a movie, just the two of us." A simple plan, a cocoon of their own making, a rebellion against the day's demands. *Yes, that's what I need.*

Jarod nodded. Convincing him to do nothing had never been difficult, at least not in their free time. *'Nothing is something,'* he would say; it was one of their running inside jokes. *We deserve it. We both work hard.*

"Yeah, let's do that," he agreed, his voice increasingly drowsy as he began to doze off. *I might as well get some shut-eye too, then.*

But as Jarod's breathing deepened into the steady rhythm of sleep, Dana felt the stir of restlessness. She was now wide awake, realizing to her disappointment that the moment for dozing off had passed. The coffee was still steaming on the nightstand, the lure of caffeine ever more tantalizing. *It would be a shame to let it go to waste.* It was a luxury to have two conflicting needs such as this—sleep, even as noon approached, or coffee. *Oh, well. We can always make another pot later.*

Just as she slipped back into sleep's gentle abyss, the incessant beeping of her braid jolted her back, each beep a discordant note clawing her towards wakefulness. She had accidentally left privacy mode off, and an incoming work call was now demanding her attention. In her drowsy stupor, the beeping blared like a foghorn, loudly echoing inside her skull. The ident said it was Tatum, her boss. *Hell, no!* She muted the audio and hid the notification on her lens. However, a few minutes later, when she was yet again dozing off, another notification appeared, this time in the form of a text with the headline *'Urgent.'*

Her heart sank at the persistent intrusion, ruing their perfect moment. It was a reminder of the ever-present demand of their careers, that voluntary slavery she wished they could both forget.

Clients. Always crying wolf, she thought as disappointment graduated to annoyance. *What was it this time? An unfiled report no one actually reads? A meeting needing to be rescheduled? Something an AI could do? Whatever it is, it absolutely cannot wait until Monday! Screw it. I'm not answering.*

She refused to succumb—it was her day off, and her job was hardly in jeopardy at this point. They needed her. But then there was always the one time in a hundred when something truly important comes through, and neglecting it would be disastrous. She decided she'd risk it, especially now that Jarod was once again engaged, this time working a lucrative private gig (although he swore he wasn't doing it for the money, whatever it was).

She snuggled up closer, nuzzling the side of his neck behind his ear, where his scent was the most potent. *I love you. You have many good qualities, but this is the real reason I slept with you all those years ago.*

Jarod had already begun snoring. She had always envied his ability to switch off and fall asleep the second his head hit the pillow. *What is it with men that allows them to do that? Are they better at compartmentalizing? Setting aside whatever troubles them to focus on the task at hand?* She could have done with such a talent in her career, especially during the early years when she was all full of clout and consumed by ambition, seeking to make a name for herself. Perhaps it would have saved her from filling countless Somnolen prescriptions.

She minimized the notification on her lens, fully intending to deal with it later. Much later. These days, quality time between the two of them had become a rarity, both of them embroiled in busy jobs neither of them liked to afford a cramped third-level rental on the south side, where the fourth and fifth levels obscure the scant artificial light from the dome.

Now you're being unfair. The second level is worse. She pondered the ironic social hierarchy London had become. Ground level was considered prestigious and high-class, retaining its old-world charm and cultural significance (despite being artificially lit outside the historical parts). So were the top levels, due to the natural light they enjoyed on those days when the clouds decided to part. Meanwhile, the mid-levels, deprived of both qualities, were where the common people lived. And paid exorbitant rents for the privilege. *At least they live Inside. Ha!*

Now fully awake from her ruminations, that coffee on the nightstand seemed ever more alluring. Alas, it would be tepid now, and what waited on the plate in the kitchen would taste acidic and bitter. She gently roused Jarod, now in a deep, noisy slumber. He murmured and swatted her hand away. *Typical!* Before, she preferred to snooze, and suddenly, the roles were reversed! *Unfair!* She was ready for the morning now, ready for conversation, for planning their day. For breakfast. Maybe she would do that thing where she says "hmm" increasingly louder until he wakes up, and then pretend he woke up by himself? *Or maybe just rudely shake him?*

In the end, she decided to let him sleep and carefully jimmied out of his embrace. He never napped for long, anyway. *I'll get up, put on a fresh brew, and maybe the smell of coffee will wake him.*

This morning had not gone according to plan, but she could live with that. After all, she was the one who slept in and then pulled him back into bed. Besides, some alone time in the morning—or midday, as it were—wasn't all bad.

In their cramped prefab living quarters, where every inch counted, the ingenious reconfigurability of their living space was a true godsend. Most of the kitchenette was still firmly stowed inside the wall, leaving the nook comparably roomy with only a narrow high table and two chairs. Jarod had opted to only bring out the coffee maker—a wise decision, for the sink was full of the dirty dishes left by last night's indulgences—an unsightly blemish on an otherwise neatly kept abode brought on by their celebration of Jarod's new engagement. The dishes would have to be dealt with eventually, by hand, as their washer unit was on the fritz. *Eventually* being the operative word!

The quiet of the morning offered her solitude, a moment to reflect on what was important in life, and doing dishes by hand wasn't it! "Send another reminder to the landlord to come fix it," she commanded the apartment AI. "A stern one, please." Their custodian was the neglectful kind, and this would be the third note she sent. While she could take matters into her own hands and call, she had no inclination to deal with the polite yet arrogant Aegis customer service AI in person. *'Good day, Mrs. Lima and welcome to Aegis. Your call may be recorded for quality assurance purposes. How may I help you today? If you are calling about a contractual matter or rent payments, please select one. If you are calling about subletting your unit, please select—'* Blah, blah, blah. No, thanks. Better to have AI battle AI until a repairman stood at the door. A repairman who, ironically, would be a human. For manual labor, flesh and blood robots are still cheaper. Only white-collar jobs got axed in the big AI crunch.

She turned on the news and cast the feed to the wall screen, sometimes preferring that to the omnipresent intrusion of her lens. Even shifting the image to the periphery or increasing its transparency often irked her. Archaic, perhaps—she was told the younger generation didn't even use external screens anymore, preferring to live their lives entirely engrossed in their braids and the virtual worlds they rendered—but to her, it was a deliberate choice that anchored her in the physical world. Nevertheless, with this particular issue, she planned to remain obstinate. Once on the wall, she dialed in the United Nations National Development Program. *The CNN for nutcases like me.*

The UN DomeEX Program at long last reported that Poland now had over half of its citizens living under the protective cover of a dome, a momentous milestone few could claim to have passed. Most of these were wealthy Western countries located in North America, the European Union, along with a few select Asian nations. Poland, which had remained stagnant at forty-nine percent for an extended period, had, with the inauguration of Szczecin South, pushed past that arbitrarily set threshold and joined the majors in the big boy club. She couldn't help but feel a sense of pride, having been the one to negotiate the conditions for citizen relocation for that project.

Humans have a peculiar affinity for numbers like that. One hundred, fifty. They are nice, even numbers. However, these numerical values hold little significance for those still vulnerable to the rapid and aggressive deterioration of the Earth's climate.

Leaning back in the high chair, sipping her coffee, with a satisfied smile gracing her lips, she double-checked that her AI had dutifully saved this crucial information in her journal. *I'll never fully trust machines. I'm just too old.* This skepticism wasn't just about the reliability of technology but a deeper, more instinctual wariness about ceding control. To Dana, it was akin to navigating a ship with an invisible crew—efficient, yes, but intensely unsettling. The weight of her reliance on such technology pressed invisibly upon her, the invisible hand guiding her actions.

The notes she took were not so much a journal, she guessed, as a scrapbook, a collection of snippets that could prove useful in her work. She had trained her AI to pick up on the right kind of information and retrieve it when needed, whether in a negotiation, for a report, or just in conversation. The AI would chime in with a popup or internal dialogue whenever it was appropriate, and it worked like a charm. These days it was automated to perfection, and normally, she wouldn't feel the need to double-check her AI's work, but this was different. This was special, and she wanted to be certain that everything was in order.

As the caffeine worked its way into her system, she pondered the size of that raw data file. *These days, undoubtedly measured in terabytes.* Naturally, the AI could provide this information at a simple request, but she preferred not to know. It would be a reminder of the countless hours she spent working, and she couldn't bear to face that reality. Dana's gaze lingered on the screen, dreamy nostalgia briefly seizing her as she let her eyes lose focus. She couldn't shake the feeling of being a solitary lighthouse in the vast, impersonal expanse of her job. Each success, like the negotiation for Poland, was a lonely peak in an otherwise relentless grind. She felt proud, of course, but also sad, reminded of the sacrifices she'd made at the altar of career.

Snapping out of it, she returned her attention to the DomeEX cast, but halfway through it, she got bored. She also realized that in watching it, she was doing what she had promised not to (as well as contravening the recommendations for leisure time from her Aegis-mandated emotional health app). Nonetheless, she brought up her messages, displaying them on her lens. A sigh escaped her as they tsunamied across her field of view, a concession to the inescapable pull of responsibilities, a tether she despised yet felt was important and ultimately rewarding—not only to her, but to the people she advocated for. It was a balancing act as intricate as it was exhausting.

Well, she was in work mode now. Aegis certainly wouldn't mind. *Funny how employers actually expect the exact opposite of what their personnel policy advocates.* It was only a matter of time before she relented, anyway, and that urgent message she had been putting off niggled at her.

Starting from the top, she could already tell most of it was your typical office tripe. She hastily scrolled through the subject lines. Something had again gone wrong with her expense claim—she'd let the braid AI handle that. Her performance review was up in a few weeks. Beyond these matters of administrative minutia, there was the usual array of annoying requests from colleagues and a slew of invitations to paid seminars on the intricacies of dome architecture, negotiation strategies, and the social science of Insiders versus Outsiders.

[Hurry up and register! Only a few seats left!]

All of these could safely be ignored, but the top five— all from her boss—would, alas, require attention. The very ones her depersonalized AI assistant advised her against responding to outside of office hours. Sometimes, she wished she had given that bitch a real name so she could properly curse it. *Or him? Her?* But she didn't fancy being one of those people who developed an emotional attachment to their braid. Not that she really believed it would happen to her, but then again, neither did anyone else until it did. It starts with something innocuous, like a name, or adorning the AI with an image—a likeness of an attractive celebrity, a former high school sweetheart, or a deceased loved one. Next, you acquire a custom personality add-on, then an AR skin for projection on your lens, or, if you can afford it, a full-blown physical one to download into, and voilà! You've got yourself an unhealthy emotional dependency and a lifetime of therapy to look forward to. Braids are machines, and so they shall remain.

With her eyes, she indicated ever so slightly that she wished to scroll back up to the top of the inbox. An almost involuntary movement that her braid had no trouble interpreting. To her, it was as if it read her mind, but obviously, as good as they were, AIs had not progressed that far. The uppermost message, the fifth one in total and the third one marked urgent, was written in all caps.

[URGENT: ACTION REQUIRED!!!]

Three exclamation points? Only girls use them like that. But there was no tiny little heart dotting the 'i's. She opened it. It was brief: "Negotiations with the Citizen Council broke down!! Need you in now!!!"

Well, what do you know? This one actually was urgent.

As she was about to return the call, tired yawns began emanating from the bedroom. Jarod ambled into the kitchen clad in his indoor jeans, sans underwear—exactly how she liked it. He crept up from behind, wrapping his arms around her as she perched over the high counter, her hands clasping her cup of fresh brew. The warmth of his embrace was soothing, abating the annoyance that now stalked her—a reminder that even though her work had intruded on their morning, there was a life outside it.

"Finally up, sleeping beauty," he quipped, planting a kiss atop her head.

"Look who's talking," she countered.

"Hey, unfair. You lured me back into bed and then slunk away like a thief in the night."

Jarod poured himself a cup and sat opposite her. The retractable high counter was undoubtedly one of the kitchenette's best features. Its slim frame allowed them to sit closely, with their legs touching beneath the surface. It was snug and intimate. She was glad they invested in that option, expensive as it was.

"So, what's on the agenda for today?" Jarod inquired.

She filled him in on the great emergency.

"Hmm, sounds like something that can wait until Monday," he remarked.

She nodded, knowing full well that in a perfect world, it would have. But in reality, you were a slave to self-serving tyrants incapable of perceiving any perspective other than their own.

"Blow it off," Jarod suggested. "Another contract will come along eventually."

She couldn't tell if he was being sincere or not. While it was true that she had amassed enough knowledge and reputation over the years to effortlessly walk into, say, seven out of ten job interviews, it was too late to back out now. She was invested in the destiny of Niederrad's residents and their aspirations to be incorporated under Frankfurt's dome structure. She had to see it through.

Unlike Tatum, her imbecile of a boss and a self-centered narcissist of unfathomable magnitude, she had a conscience. *Sometimes, I wish I didn't. Life would be much simpler.*

Jarod understood her predicament all too well, though he was typically shackled to government narcissists rather than their corporate counterparts.

"Might as well," he concluded. "I'm meeting my contact later today, anyway."

She wasn't thrilled about his latest gig. He couldn't talk about it, which wasn't out of the ordinary in his line of work, but there was something different this time. Something in his demeanor and tone when discussing it triggered her inner alarm system. For a fleeting moment, she entertained the ludicrous idea of having her braid analyze his speech patterns to see if he was lying, but, of course, she couldn't do that. Trust is a precarious commodity in any relationship, the temptation to pry ever-present. He had given his word that he was in no danger, and she would just have to take him at his word. Besides, such applications were authorized only during formal, minuted negotiations, and even then, only under extremely rare circumstances.

"I'll hit the showers then," she declared, banishing all thoughts of doubt and suspicion.

As she rose, he sauntered over and placed his hands on her hips, casually sliding them down towards her behind. "Are you sure we don't have time for a quickie?"

She grinned and smooched him. "Screw Tatum Drake," she proclaimed.

"Who?"

"Why, my ass of a boss, of course."

"Really? I'd much rather screw you," he replied with a smirk.

She playfully slapped him as he yanked her toward the bedroom. She tugged him toward the bathroom instead. "In the shower. Two birds with one stone."

"Works for me," he agreed, and off they went.

Before she could even leave the flat, another notification popped up in the corner of her vision. It displayed a bullet-train ticket and a brief message from Tatum, apologizing for the inconvenience and stating, "I need you on the ground in Frankfurt." *Well, at least he's sorry.* She felt that familiar twist in her gut, that mix of resignation and annoyance. It wasn't just the sudden change of plans that irked her; it was the underlying assumption that her time was his to do with as he pleased. *He's not sorry at all, is he? He's British. They always apologize, but seldom mean it. Sorry, sorry, sorry!*

There was another file attached, complete with a detailed briefing courtesy of Tatum's AI. Aegis spared no expense. This AI had a soothing female voice. It didn't come across as robotic or dispassionate like most AIs. It didn't bark orders like a brusque drill sergeant, like the man who owned it. *More human than human,* as they say—it sounded like someone you could forge a connection with, even a form of fondness, if it were real.

Skimming through the instructions, at least she found them to be succinct and direct. She was to meet with Gabriel, the community's new negotiator. Apparently, Sonica, with whom she had worked side by side for months, had suffered some "unfortunate accident"—at least that was the euphemism employed by the AI. *Unfortunate accident indeed.* There were no other details. A pang of sadness hit Dana, sharper than she anticipated. Sonica had been a colleague, not a friend. Nevertheless, she made a mental note to send flowers. Or something.

Niederrad, like many of the communities outside the domes in Europe, was notorious for its web of political intrigue and less-than-stellar crime rates. Alas, the police file was sealed, so she would never know what had truly happened. And now, lo and behold, Mr. Gabriel had seen fit to reopen negotiations that had taken half a year of her life to conclude. *Bloody hell.* At least

Tari, her trusted assistant, would still be there, having also been drafted back into the mire.

As usual, Northern was packed, but it was still the fastest route to St. Pancras. She couldn't help but wonder how many of these people were Ubis, and if so, what brought them here in the first place. If they didn't have to work to earn a living, where exactly did they all need to be? *Shopping? Out for a leisurely lunch?* It was Sunday, after all.

Dana's gaze swept over the crowd with a mix of curiosity and, she reluctantly had to admit, envy. Each face told a story of freedom she seldom allowed herself to dream of—a life untethered by the demands of making a living in the expansive Inside. Somewhat amusingly, she also pondered why she hadn't applied to be work-relieved herself. To subsist solely on UBI. If she had, she would still be in the shower with Jarod. They could effortlessly maintain their current standard of living with only one of them working. *Who cares if you can't get the latest braid upgrade whenever you want? Or go on holiday? All the best destinations are under domes, anyway. To be honest, who really needs those things?*

Her father never had a braid; he relied on a handheld device his entire life. He didn't even possess a visor, let alone something implanted in his head. They had called it a mobile phone, even long after it had become far more than just an audio communication device. "It can do the same things," he had claimed, "but without screwing around with your head."

Be thankful for what you have. Years ago, she had been fortunate to enter a field of work that was difficult to automate. Even the best artificial intelligences couldn't broker deals with the desperate and disenfranchised—people of flesh and blood, with complex and genuine emotions at the forefront of the discourse. People capable of ambition, empathy, and regret. People who loved, hated, and feared. Artificial Intelligence alone couldn't yet reliably pick up on the subtle nuances of deceit, but she had proven quite adept at that, albeit with man and machine joining forces. So, *be grateful, as the saying goes, that you still have a job. Maybe, you belong to the last generation who will.*

Dana took a moment, letting the weight of her role sink in. It wasn't just about making ends meet or navigating the treacherous waters of politics and power. It was about connecting, truly connecting, with others on a level no AI could mimic. A sense of pride swelled within her, a reminder of why she endured the grind.

Her stop was coming up. The journey from Elephant to St. Pancras would take as long as the trip from there to Frankfurt. The Eurostar bullet train would take thirty-three minutes, the overground bullet from Paris to Frankfurt Hauptbahnhof an additional twenty, with two short stops along the way. Then the S-Bahn to Frankfurt Konstablerwache would take another ten. Throw in some extra time for changing trains and walking to the Frankfurt field office, and she'd have approximately an hour-long commute, excluding the thirty-five minutes on the Northern. The longest time for the shortest distance. "Oldest underground in the world, my ass," she muttered to herself. *They say that as if it's a good thing.*

She alighted and headed for the Eurostar bullet, grabbing a sandwich en route since only vending machines would be available on the train. *Fantastic. This will be my breakfast from now on.*

She had never been much of a breakfast eater. Some coffee, a banana, a shower, a quick makeup application, and off she went. Typically, she grabbed something on the way to the office, but with this commute, that was no longer an option. She loathed the bullet trains. Yes, they were speedy, but the jarring acceleration always left her feeling queasy, so cramming something down beforehand was her only option.

She had better get used to it because she'd most likely be dealing with it for another six months. According to the brief, Mr. Gabriel, unlike his predecessor, refused to meet over video. He'd go into the Frankfurt dome, and that was that. He was an old-fashioned individual who insisted on negotiating face-to-face. Not even a holo or VR session would suffice.

An hour after her arrival, Tatum greeted her. In the meantime, Tari had arranged her desk. He had been there for a few days already, though strangely, Tatum had failed to mention this. While she had been on her way out, thinking the negotiations were concluded, Tari wasn't, so he must have belonged to another contractor until he was reassigned to her. She had poached him, in other words, and someone was bound to be unhappy about losing him.

"When can we expect Mr. Gabriel?" she inquired of Tatum as he ushered her into the top-floor conference room. Despite the fact that several taller buildings now surrounded the old Deutsche Bank skyscraper in Frankfurt's city center—and the newly initiated level construction partly obstructed the downward view of the old town—the building still boasted a stunning vista.

"He won't be joining us," Tatum replied.

He transmitted a file to her braid and instructed her to open it—a 3D headshot, reasonably current, along with biographical details, a negotiation tactics profile, and a list of known cases (the last two of which, as it turned out, were blank). Otherwise, the contents were standard fare.

"Have your AI work through it. This one could be tricky," he directed.

"Why?"

"No doubt you noticed there was no prior case history? That's not because we haven't been able to dig anything up. It's because there are none."

Unconventional, for sure, but not unprecedented. If he was a beginner, he would be young. Gabriel, however, was decidedly middle-aged.

"He's not a professional," she deduced.

"Good girl," Tatum replied in that condescending tone she despised. Heat flushed Dana's cheeks, anger simmering just beneath the surface. She was no one's "good girl," least of all Tatum's. Yet she swallowed her retort, knowing this wasn't the time for prideful battles.

"They've hired someone outside the profession? That seems incredibly foolish," she stated matter-of-factly.

Tatum shook his head. "They didn't hire anyone. Gabriel is a true amateur. He's just one of the locals from the Niederrad Council. But don't be fooled by that. This one's going to be tough."

Well, shit.

In Niederrad, there was no official council or *Amt*—or whatever the Germans called it. There was no structure, no formal bureaucracy, just a loose network of individuals acting as a sort of central authority—apparently including this Gabriel character, whom she had never heard of before. The closest comparison she could draw was to the favelas of Brazil, a quasi-feudal system of governance that went largely unnoticed by the authorities. Of course, in the age of sprawling dome constructions, the Germans were spread thin, and Niederrad, like many other areas *Outside*, was a low priority. They likely assumed that once the area was officially incorporated, the *Inside* government would deal with it.

Meanwhile, the ragtag leaders of Niederrad had rejected the negotiated deal and opted to represent themselves. A first for her, and, as far as she knew, for anyone. Dome expansions had always been brokered by contracted professionals—whether independent, government, or corporate. But never before had anyone operated entirely outside the system. Up until a few moments ago, she wouldn't have even considered such a possibility.

"So, what does this mean? His negotiating skills should be rudimentary at best?"

Her braid pinged with some intriguing findings from the biography section of the profile. Not much was known, of course, since Mr. Gabriel operated outside the system. However, drone footage had captured a skirmish of some sort involving firearms and physical violence. The caption read *Internal Altercation, Niederrad,* and dated back two years. Gabriel's face was visible in an image clear enough for facial recognition. His exact role was unclear—he might have been just a passerby—but it was noteworthy, nonetheless.

"Don't underestimate him," Tatum cautioned. "He may lack formal skills, but he has something you pros don't: passion. Conviction on an emotional level. This is his home. His heart and soul belong to it. Can you say the same? Can your AI guide you through a negotiating landscape driven by that kind of emotion?" His voice took on a sharper edge, frustration creeping in. "He already... uh... threw us... what's that American phrase? Threw us a curveball?"

Dana nodded in confirmation as Tatum led her toward the southern panorama, where the outer dome wall towered above them, built on the old levees of the River Main. The proximity was much closer than what she was used to in London, a city far larger than Frankfurt. Though Frankfurt had grown significantly over the last few decades, it still lagged behind in size.

The wall screens displayed a stunning, sunny day. "If we shut down the screens," Tatum noted, picking up on her distracted gaze, "just beyond that wall is Niederrad, west of the Sachsenhausen dome. Exposed and vulnerable, its inhabitants suffer through the elements—heat, cold, winds, rain, and thunderstorms. Their buildings are crumbling, and no one's there to fix them. We're doing this for them, though they might not always see it that way. Expansion is crucial. They need it."

No need for the sales pitch, Tatum. I've heard it all before. So have they.

Dana couldn't help but feel a twinge of sympathy for those living Outside, a stark reminder of the divides their world had cemented in the wake of the climate's devastation. Divides she was complicit in, for better or worse.

Tatum sighed. "Sometimes, I envy the Asian countries. No negotiations, no civil rights. They just uproot, relocate, and expand. It's so clean, so simple."

She understood his point but remained a firm believer in rights and due process.

"So, what was his genius move, then?" she asked.

"What?"

"The curveball?" she reminded him.

"Oh, right. He changed the negotiation site," Tatum explained. "You'll have to venture outside the dome to meet them. Pretty clever, isn't it? Most people would throw their own grandmother under a bullet train just to set foot inside one of the domes, yet he's dragging us out there. It's brilliant. He knows we want this as much as they do, maybe even more."

Dana raised an eyebrow. "I see."

"So, good luck," Tatum continued. "You'll leave tomorrow with Tari by your side and a GSG team at your disposal. It's the German equivalent of... what do you call it... SWAT."

Outside? SWAT? That was certainly a stark contrast to the usual monotony of her assignments, which mostly involved offices, conference rooms, and prompting AIs to handle things. This wasn't just another negotiation; it was a venture into the unknown, possibly fraught with danger. *Real* physical danger. *A test of true grit, I suppose.* She felt a surprising rush of adrenaline at the thought, albeit mixed with undeniable apprehension.

A knock on the conference room door interrupted their discussion. Tatum instructed the visitor to enter. Tari and a man in tactical police gear stepped inside. The man introduced himself as Stefan Brett.

"We need to brief you, Mrs. Lima," Brett stated in a nearly flawless American accent. "Please follow me."

"Good luck," Tatum said as Brett escorted her out of the room.

"Jeez, thanks," she muttered under her breath. There was a bitter edge to her words, she realized—a reflection of her unease, though laced with sarcasm. Fieldwork. *Everyone's dream. At least she'd be able to charge more.*

...according to current DomeEX data, there are 187 urban domes worldwide. Among these, 94 are wholly or partially owned by private enterprises, either through direct ownership or via government or UN subsidy schemes. Most of these privately owned domes are located in Europe, North America, Oceania, and Japan. Meanwhile, all wholly state-owned domes are found in Asia, primarily in China and Russia. Furthermore, an additional 17 domes are privately owned by high-net-worth individuals who have...

...the construction time required for an urban dome capable of covering a densely populated area of one million people has significantly decreased over the years. In 2042, when Singapore began constructing the world's first urban dome, the average construction time was 21 years. However, by 2100, this is projected to have decreased to just seven. Despite this impressive reduction, it is anticipated that it will still take another century before half of the global population resides...

...based on current models and projections, it is estimated that approximately 4.2 billion individuals will still be adversely affected by the impacts of climate change by the end of the century [...] large Hamiltonian-sized mega-arcologies have been proposed, but they are not currently feasible...

...since its establishment in 2071, the United Nations DomeEX program has funded the construction of 21 urban domes in Africa and Southeast Asia. These initiatives, wholly or partially financed by the program, underscore its commitment to supporting sustainable development in regions vulnerable to the effects of climate change...

...ownership of private urban domes is largely concentrated in the hands of three major corporations: Aegis, Michau Holdings, and Fukujima. Aegis, the largest player, controls a substantial 58% of the market. This concentration highlights the significant role corporate entities play in the development...

...the year 2071. Aegis, the largest owner of urban domes, was subsequently hit with antitrust litigation. This case is still ongoing and serves as a reminder of the potential consequences of market concentration in the ownership and operation of...

...adjusted for inflation, the federal governments of the United States and the European Union have provided subsidies amounting to USD 17.6 trillion towards the construction of urban domes since the 2060s. Of this amount, only 2.2% has been directed to the UN DomeEX fund, falling far short of the targets agreed upon in international agreements. These findings highlight the need for increased...

...a partial list of countries and their respective percentages of the world's urban populations living under domes: Cayman (100%), Singapore (100%), Liechtenstein (100%), Luxembourg (91%), Dubai (89%), Netherlands (87%), Sweden (88%), Japan (87%), Norway (81%), Denmark (77%), Canada (76%), The City-State of Greater London (69%), Finland (61%), Germany (60.5%), Switzerland (59%), EU (average) (57%), Czech Republic (56%), Italy (53%), India (49%), Poland (49%), United States (44%), Spain (41%), China (estimated) (41%), Brazil (36%), Wales (33%), Hungary (34%), Bulgaria (31%), Russia (estimated) (23%), Argentina (13%), Indonesia (12%), Nigeria (12%), Myanmar (0%), Bangladesh (0%), Venezuela (0%), and Honduras (0%). For data on rural populations, please refer to...

...city of Øresund. It constitutes a rare example of an urban dome network that spans across national borders, covering central Copenhagen in Denmark, as well as the cities of Malmö, Landskrona, and Lund in Sweden, serving as a unique testament to the possibilities of cross-border collaboration...

...while geodesic or tensegrity constructions remain the most prevalent form of urban domes, accounting for a substantial 91% of all dome structures worldwide, only 9% of domes rely on tent-based construction techniques. While tents offer a quicker and more cost-effective solution, they are often viewed as less durable and require higher maintenance costs over time, which has contributed to their comparatively limited usage in development...

...individuals living outside urban domes in wealthy Western countries may choose to do so for a variety of reasons, ranging from personal preference to financial considerations. However, in poorer regions of the world...

...prior to the widespread construction of urban domes, underground tunnel systems often served as a refuge for individuals living Outside. Despite the emergence of the domes, these tunnel systems still exist in many urban areas, with an estimated global population of [...] a significant portion of these underground refuges have been abandoned, particularly in Western countries where the construction of domes and environmental reinforcement programs for Outside areas have rendered them...

...in the United States, the Reese Act (Stat. 2613, 18 U.S.C. § 3953), enacted in January 2049, and the EU's GRAR (2071/658), require corporations involved in urban dome construction to establish procedures for resident advocacy within their corporate structure. [...] The Senior Management and Certification Regime (SM&CR) mandates that a senior manager on the payroll must act as an advocate for residents in all urban dome construction projects, including expansion initiatives. [...] The role of resident advocacy is frequently outsourced to independent contractors and viewed as a "checkbox exercise" by the corporations themselves, with limited consideration given to the...

Aea

"Stop fidgeting around," Kaliyah chided, her voice exasperated as they cut through the dry and eroded dirt path connecting their school and the once-thriving Eli-Lucht Park. "It looks ridiculous when you swipe around with your arms like that. Not to mention the glasses."

The air was thick with the electrified scent of dry earth, and small dust clouds swirled off the path as they trod—a reminder of the park's better days, now lost to the wrath of Earth's climate.

"Visor," Aea corrected while adjusting the transparency of the government visa information page she was poring over, letting the surroundings bleed through more. "Not glasses," she emphasized, even though they looked like it. Glasses with embedded AR screens, in lieu of braids, which Outies like her could scarcely afford.

To the north, the dome of Frankfurt Central towered, a rising tidal wave that had never broken, made of geodesic latticework and translucent panels. Before her, the path ahead was now clearly visible through the visor screens, allowing her to continue her research without the risk of tripping.

Kaliyah brushed aside the distinction with a careless wave. "Yeah, whatever, four-eyes," she quipped, delivering a playful punch to Aea's shoulder. But the blow landed a little too hard, sending a sharp jolt of pain shooting down Aea's arm to her thumb.

"Ow!" Aea cried, wincing as she clutched her shoulder. "That really hurt!"

Kaliyah stuck out her tongue teasingly. "Heulmeier!"

Unfamiliar with the German insult, Aea looked to her friend for an explanation. "What does that mean?" she asked.

"You should know. You are one!"

Aea grinned, realizing she'd be foolish to expect a straight answer. She used her visor to look it up. *Crybaby*, it said in bright blue text hovering before her eyes. "Takes one to know one," she teased back. Behind them, the sounds of schoolyard chatter faded, replaced by the rustling leaves in the strengthening wind. A storm was coming, and soon.

Merde! That's the best comeback you have?

Kaliyah let out a light-hearted chuckle, but Aea wasn't ready to let the matter go. "At least my visor lets me see augmentations in 3D," she retorted. "You and your pathetic handhelds."

A smirk tugged at Aea's lips as she rubbed her sore shoulder, the numbness gradually subsiding. Jema, deciding to join the conversation, added her own disdain for handhelds. "Scheiß Handys," she muttered, then turned her attention to Aea. "Was glotzt du denn so, baby?" she asked with a gesture.

Kaliyah punched Jema in the arm. "Speak English!" she insisted.

"I *said* 'baby,'" Jema replied. "That's English, last time I checked. Besides, you're supposed to be learning German, so... you know, get with it!"

The three of them came from different places. Kaliyah, with her jet-black hair and almond-shaped eyes, was from Malaysia. Jema, with her pale complexion and thick accent, was born and raised in Bulgaria. Aea, the daughter of a French mother—dead since she was a child—and an Algerian father, had found herself transplanted to Germany at a young age. English was the only language they fully shared, despite Jema's constant harping that they should all speak German.

The blame for their rusty German, perhaps, lay not with the girls but with the decaying educational system outside the dome network. *Sure, blame the teachers. Classic.* In truth, they all spoke decent German—except maybe Kaliyah—but they simply preferred English.

Jema turned her attention back to Aea, still expecting an answer.

"I'm looking at visitor visas," Aea replied.

"Again?" Jema asked.

Yes, again. Like any other Outie teenager, Aea was consumed by the desire to break free from the shackles of her dreary life and seek out a place where the lights shone brighter, the shopping was endless, and the storms were mere nightmares. She dreamed of a place where she would no longer be beholden to her obnoxious dad and the drudgery of school—a place where she would be the master of her own destiny, free to do as she pleased. All of this and more awaited her, she was convinced, on the *Inside.*

In just a few short months, she would turn eighteen, granting her the freedom to apply for a visitor visa to Frankfurt Center without her dad's consent. Aea's spirits swelled with the idea of freedom, her mind adrift in the vibrant city lights of the Inside. Each thought of escape from the dreary existence of Niederrad was a mix of joy and disappointment. To her continued dismay, the cost remained beyond her meager means. *One day, I will go there.*

Visas, permits, *Papieren*, *Erlaubnis*, *Genehmigung*—the German language had many words describing the red tape involved in obtaining permission to visit the Inside. But even if one managed to navigate the byzantine process of securing one, the daunting challenge of affording the exorbitant prices on the illustrious Zeil or cozy Goethe Strasse, Frankfurt's luxury shopping streets, remained.

I love my visor, but I sure wouldn't mind having a braid! Perhaps more than anything else, she desired that. With a braid, the universe could be hers—both the tangible and intangible. A braid granted access: to food and security, to travel, to jobs, and to fantasy worlds beyond imagination. The advanced AI of a braid could even navigate red tape impossible for a mere human, including the convoluted visa application process. It granted freedom, and without one, the escape she sought would remain out of reach. But for an Outie like Aea, such indulgences were entirely unattainable. Outside the dome, these marvelous machines were hard to come by, even if one could afford it. Black markets may peddle illicit knock-offs, but installing one of those was a great way to get lobotomized.

At least, that's what happens if you ask my dad. She sighed. To Aea, a braid was more than just a piece of tech; it was the key to a world where she wasn't confined to the harsh realities of her circumstances—a beacon of hope in an existence mired in restrictions. She strongly suspected that the warnings about black-market copies were nothing more than urban legends concocted to keep children in line. After all, every parent seemed to have their own horror story to share. Like the one about the white van that pulls up, offers candy, and then kidnaps the unsuspecting child to harvest their organs. Nevertheless, even if the risks were overstated, it was a moot point. The fact remained that black-market braids came with a hefty price tag far beyond Aea's means.

So, rather than dreaming endlessly about a braid, Aea clung to her trusty old head-mounted display as one of her most treasured possessions. It lacked the advanced features of a proper braid, such as the ability to detect minute eye movements to facilitate navigation or sophisticated AI capabilities. In fact, it didn't even have basic learning functions. But despite those limitations, it was still superior to a handheld device—or a handy, as the Germans called them. *Some people here don't even have those.*

Aea couldn't help but chuckle to herself as she recalled a boy once informing her that "a handy" had a very different connotation in English—particularly British English. Nevertheless, in German, a *handy* was simply a colloquial term for a handheld mobile device.

"Let's continue," Jema suggested.

Right. She had momentarily forgotten. Just before ignoring her friends in favor of another deep dive into the thrilling world of government visa applications, they had been discussing the other thing young girls wanted—perhaps even more than an illustrious, wealthy life of shopping and the gleaming neon lights of the *Inside.*

Boys.

Aea minimized the government page and returned to the yearbook to find the boy Jema claimed had shown interest in her. With her trusty visor's basic algorithmic capabilities, Aea could filter through pictures of her fellow students based on a few simple parameters far faster than her friends' handheld devices could manage.

This is exactly what I need. Boys are here, they're available, even attainable for a poor Outie girl like me. Good little Aea! Concentrate on what's realistic. Within seconds, her visor had identified a few potential matches, and she began scrolling through the selection using simple hand gestures.

"It looks like you're swatting insects that aren't there," Kaliyah said, again referring to her arm movements as she navigated menus only visible to her.

"The only ones bugging me are the two of you." Ha! A better comeback this time. However, neither Kaliyah nor Jema reacted. *No sense of humor.*

"Is this him?" Aea asked, transferring the image to their handys.

"Mmm," Kaliyah murmured, eyeing hers closely. They were both twisting their devices at all kinds of angles. *What's that supposed to accomplish? Would the boy become handsomer if you held your screen diagonally?*

"Yeah," Jema said. "That's him." Kaliyah agreed.

Aea took a closer look. *He is sort of cute, I guess, but not really my type.*

"I don't know what he sees in you with your goggles and fly-swatting," Jema teased. She wasn't a natural like Kali, mostly just repeating teases she'd heard before.

Kaliyah reassured her, "Oh, Jema, don't be jealous. We'll find you a boy of your own someday. Not one this hot, though."

Jema made a face.

"She can have him," Aea quipped. "He's not my thing." She removed the visor and slipped it back into her purse. "Come on," she said, pulling both her friends along. "Curfew's in a few hours, and the storm front is closing in."

They had set out toward Jema's place, where they had agreed to tackle today's homework. The air, ever heavier with the scent of impending rain, was a pleasant contrast to the usual dryness. She knew what it meant when the weather was like this, but that didn't prevent her from enjoying parts of it. There were other, more disconcerting elements. The sky, increasingly a brooding canvas of grays, seemed to press down on Aea, the beginnings of a headache rising from her neck.

Usually, they gathered at Aea's place—her apartment being more spacious than Jema's—but Jema's offered more privacy. Aea shared a room with her sister, whose presence was a constant annoyance, not for the homework, but for the gossiping session that invariably followed. Today's workload was light, so they anticipated having ample time to indulge in banter. Perhaps they could carry on their discussion about boys, or any other topic that caught their fancy.

Jema lived in The Crescent, an old climate refugee camp sandwiched between the south of Frankfurt—Niederrad and Sachsenhausen—and the abandoned, half-built city dome of Neu-Isenburg. It was a hodgepodge of structures, originally patched together from various scrap and salvage. It wasn't quite a shanty, but not exactly a settlement either. The term *settlement* felt too official and imposing, implying a sense of permanence that didn't quite fit. And while *shanty* seemed appropriate, it conveyed an impression of flimsiness that was no longer accurate. The German government had invested massively in fortifying these structures, making them more resilient against the increasingly violent weather patterns that plagued the region.

These days, almost all major cities in the affluent world had such dwellings, crammed along the perimeter of the domes' frontiers or further out beyond the boundaries of the Outie parts of the city—like here in Frankfurt, where only the central and northern areas were domed. At least, that's what Frau Gehrling taught them in class. *I've never been anywhere else, so what do I really know?*

Climate refugee camps are exactly what they sound like: a refuge for people who had fled hardship—droughts, extreme heat, cold, storms, unemployment, famine, or war. The name *The Crescent* had been derived from its half-moon-like shape. In earlier days, the lights emanating from the shanties had created the illusion of a crescent moon when viewed from above, and it had been prominently featured as such in drone footage on the news at the time. As the settlement grew and evolved into a more permanent residence, it lost that form, now resembling more of a shapeless blob. However, the name persisted. The settlement, like many others, lacked official recognition under German law, but the government poured resources into its protection—albeit temporarily—while waiting for the dome to expand or for the population to be relocated *Inside.*

While The Crescent was home to Jema, Aea and Kaliyah were fortunate to reside in actual Frankfurt, in the area known as Niederrad. It wasn't the greatest place, but it was much better than living in a shanty. Aea, along with her dad and her sister Tabayah, even had a real apartment. To themselves, like the Innies. Only outside.

As they hurried toward The Crescent, Kaliyah and Jema bickered about the boy Aea had already forgotten, debating which of them he would choose to go out with. The idea that he might not be interested didn't seem to cross their minds.

They were now approaching Eli-Lucht Park, which was mostly a field—sometimes dry, sometimes sodden—a barren land with meager patches of sad green here and there. The trees, shrubs, and planted flower beds had been swept away by countless thunderstorms and floods long ago, then dried by heat waves in an endless cycle. Where greenery once thrived, only the toughest weeds claimed dominion now, their roots clinging to cracks in the parched earth. It was a mere shadow of its former self. Aea had never seen the park in its prime, but she had seen pictures of it in school.

In the distance, she heard a commotion—the voices of an irate crowd. As they crossed Niederräder Landstraße, over the dry field, the noise grew increasingly louder. Ahead, the horde gathered at the field's east end, numbering in the hundreds and growing by the minute, with people flowing in from the side streets surrounding the park. Aea could see a speaker perched atop a makeshift stage, his amplified voice barely audible over the deafening roar of agitated voices. *Obviously politics. Probably about the dome expansion.* Everything was these days. The air buzzed with a charged energy, a mix of anticipation and anxiety, as the crowd's collective voice rose and fell like the tide against a levee.

"The only thing that makes people this excited is either football or injustice." Her father always said that. She wasn't entirely sure what this was about, but she had a pretty good idea it was about the dome. Ever since the disappearance of that other lady, and the installation of Jairre Gabriel, people had suddenly gone from content to discontent. Not that she understood why. Nothing had changed since a few weeks ago, yet people had changed their opinion. What was the word Frau Gehrling used in class? *Agitprop.* Yes, that was it. It was an old Russian word, apparently, from the long-gone Soviet days. Gabriel was an agitator, a propagandist. Frau Gehrling didn't approve of him, that much was clear. She said he was someone who could skillfully sway people into thinking like himself.

While probably right, Aea wasn't sure she cared. Politics held little interest for her, and she liked to stay out of people's business, though she had to admit she sometimes felt a twinge of guilt for her lack of engagement. She was perfectly aware she should have an opinion, perhaps even desired one, but she just wasn't sure what it should be. Politics is subjective, at least according to Frau Gehrling, but she knew one thing—engaging in it was the exact polar opposite of staying out of other people's business.

Determined not to engage, she proposed a detour, to walk around the park, but Kaliyah and Jema were beyond themselves, already consumed by the energy of the agitated crowd. *Why wouldn't they be?* Aea's own curiosity was no less piqued, despite her usual disinterest in politics. The raw energy of the crowd was infectious, contrasting sharply with the monotony of daily life here. But beneath the intrigue, there was also apprehension, a wariness of the tumult such fervor could unleash.

Despite being located *Outside*, with all the challenges that brought, Niederrad was typically mundane. The word *ghetto* had been tossed around, especially by Innies, and by Frau Gehrling in one of her lectures, but nevertheless, it was mostly peaceful—a refuge for the destitute, the jobless. But not for Ubies. Frau Gehrling made a specific point of distinguishing between being unemployed and being a Ubie. According to her, Ubies were not jobless, but rather work-relieved—liberated from the toils of labor. No, Ubies were the imaginative people—the artists, the innovators, the entrepreneurs—who devoted their time to enriching society. Unemployed people were compelled to work. They just didn't have jobs. Ubies lived Inside, mostly. The unemployed did not.

Her father didn't agree with such a rosy definition of a Ubie. It was one of his favorite complaints, sitting on the living room couch, glued to the streamer. To him, they were not liberated at all, but unemployable, welfare-dependent laggards who had been forever replaced by AI and robots. Useless people to be pitied, not envied.

Niederrad, like most places outside, was a haven for the downtrodden and unwanted. The unfortunate ones who found themselves on the wrong side of a dome frontier. In the media, it was often associated with crime and violence, but Aea had never witnessed anything serious firsthand. It was her home, and while it had its faults, she appreciated it. She didn't understand the science behind the extreme weather, but she knew it hadn't always been that way. Back when Dad was young and Mom was still alive. Nonetheless, she was content in Niederrad. *I know it can be a lot worse, that's for sure!* She had never seen the inside of a dome, except in movies, in ads, or elsewhere on the net—all of which Frau Gehrling maintained were exaggerated.

As they pushed through the crowd toward the front, Aea could see the stage and the figure standing on it more clearly. It was Gabriel. She recognized his face from the news. He was shorter than she had anticipated but full of energy. As he spoke into the headset, he gestured wildly, almost bouncing with excitement, and the crowd followed in unison. He was an agitator, as Frau Gehrling had said—that much was clear. She had shown historical footage of others for comparison—Hitler, Stalin, Putin, Trump, and Bosworth. But she did not show Martin Luther King, Lech Wałęsa, or Greta Thunberg! Frau Gehrling had taught them about skepticism, and Aea knew that was important, but she still didn't know who to trust. Were all agitators bad? Was Gabriel evil because he sought better living conditions for *Outies?* Was it the way he went about it? She didn't know.

The roar of the crowd drowned out everything, making it difficult to hear what Gabriel was saying. She caught bits about relocation, new living quarters inside, jobs, and Ubie stipends for those who qualified. It all sounded fantastic, but at the same time, he spoke about everything they knew being destroyed, paved over by the construction. His words were incendiary, the crowd's fervor explosive. Jema and Kaliyah were being pulled along in the ecstasy.

"This is so cool!" Jema yelled directly into her ear.

Aea winced at the sudden loud voice and was pulled out of her musings. *Ramblings, more like it.*

Excited, yet with a feeling of unease, they pushed toward the front. They wanted to see more. Gabriel's voice boomed through the speakers, distorted by the frenzied shouting of the crowd. The excitement was contagious—they jumped up and down with the rest, as if they were at a concert.

This is bad.

It most definitely was. Dad preferred she come straight home after school—weather alerts could come quickly, and the storms would hit without mercy. She had a bit of leeway to go to the store or grab a snack at the cafe, as long as she stayed out of trouble. Well, *this* is trouble! She was pretty sure being here, in this ferocious crowd, was not covered by any exceptions. Still, the thrill of being a little rebellious was hard to resist.

A group of young boys clamored up on the stage, rallying around Gabriel and adding to the already frenzied atmosphere. They were her age, with the possible exception of one. His stubble and tattooed arms betrayed a maturity the others didn't have, yet he remained boyishly handsome. Tanned, with kind eyes and confidently athletic—unlike anyone she had ever seen before. As he swaggered to center stage, she wondered what it would be like to be so cool and carefree. Gabriel handed the boy a confetti gun, and as he repeatedly fired it into the air, his muscles flexing from the recoil, Aea couldn't help but feel a flutter in her stomach. The moment was ephemeral, a supercharged connection against the backdrop of the gathering storm, which she had, at this moment, completely banished from her mind.

Now she finally joined the others, jumping and shouting, and the boy noticed. For a moment, their eyes met, and he flashed a smile before winking and departing the stage. A jolt of excitement surged through her, her breath stopping for a moment. In that fleeting second, amidst the chaos, silent communication passed between the two of them—a spark setting her heart aflutter with possibilities. *Oh, wow!*

Kaliyah and Jema gawked at the brief exchange. For a moment, all three froze, exchanging a triumphant glance. A giggle slipped out of her—an unguarded moment of carefree joy between friends. An older boy—the thrill of it! Aea beamed with excitement as the trio resumed jumping and dancing amidst the now-dispersing crowd. The storm was rapidly approaching, and Gabriel urged everyone to seek refuge before it hit, imploring support in his negotiations with the *Innies.*

The boy lingered in Aea's mind as they weaved through the crowd toward their homes and the waiting storm shelters. "Now that's someone I can imagine as a boyfriend," Aea exclaimed. Kaliyah and Jema erupted in giggly hysteria as they jiggled past a particularly immobile group of rally attendees.

The wind howled, and rain whipped their faces, signaling the imminent arrival of the storm. Anxiety nibbled at the edges of Aea's resolve, the looming winds a reminder of their ever-present vulnerability. The rush to safety, while a familiar drill, was always tinged with a sense of urgency, and this time it was perhaps deepened by the day's unexpected events and the lingering thrill of what might have been.

Aea wondered if Dad had picked up the new power bank. *If not, there won't be any homework tonight.* The tunnels were too dim to read without backlighting, and her visor was almost drained. *Time to hurry up!* They pushed past the remaining stragglers, keen to reach their designated shelters before the storm unleashed its full fury.

Daemon was his name—the cute young man who blasted confetti over the crowd at Gabriel's gathering. He spelled it with an *a* and an *e*, just like Aea. *Surely, that means something!* He had moved in from Offenbach a fortnight ago and was nineteen, going on twenty. While not a school kid anymore, he was unquestionably the new kid in town. With his stubble and slender but muscular build, Aea had to once again conclude that he embodied everything the boys at school didn't. He was just—*adorable!* And at this very moment, he was sauntering toward Aea in the hallway. Her heart skipped a beat, an electrical charge coursing through her body. The hallway seemed to narrow as she focused on the ever-dwindling space between them. Each of his footsteps seemed to echo in time with the thunder of her quickening heartbeat. Then embarrassment hit, full-on. *Like a shy little high school girl,* she thought. *Which is exactly what I am, so why should I be embarrassed?*

"Uh-oh," Kaliyah remarked. "Here goes."

Jema began running her fingers through her hair and straightening out her bra. "What are you doing?" Kaliyah asked, with a bemused look. "He's not here for you."

"Shut up!" Jema retorted.

Although this was exactly what Aea wanted, she instinctively moved behind her open locker door, attempting to conceal herself. Shyness overwhelmed her, completely eclipsing her usual confident self. *Silly! It's not like he can't see you!* The logical part of her mind scolded her for thinking she could hide when, in fact, she wanted nothing more than to be seen. In the days since that brief, but fateful gaze at the rally, she had rehearsed in her head what to say if he ever approached her, but now, faced with the opportunity, she found herself not remembering a single word. He knocked playfully on the other side of the locker, Aea's heart now fluttering with excitement.

"Hallo, jemand da?" Daemon said.

Aea peeked out from behind her locker, still unsure of what to say. She focused on the cool metal of the locker against her palm, it seemingly having a calming effect. Behind her, Kaliyah and Jema giggled mischievously.

"Uhmm—" Aea stammered. *Shit! Do I reply in German? He doesn't seem German. He has an accent. What was it? French? Turkish? Oh...!*

"Ich... Uhm..." she began, peeking out from behind the locker. The sight of Daemon up close made the butterflies in her stomach go nuts. She was about to try to speak again, but Daemon interrupted her.

"Relax," Daemon reassured her with a warm, disarming smile, cutting through her apprehension like a ray of sunlight through a dark, gray rain cloud. He was taller than she had imagined, his dark skin flawless, and that stubble even manlier up close. "I saw you just came out of class, so I thought I'd take the opportunity to practice my language skills. But that's more or less all I know, I promise."

Aea stood frozen, searching for words that refused to come.

She was blushing, and she could feel Kaliyah's and Jema's curious gazes boring into her neck. Daemon shrugged, his tone lighthearted. "Uhmm," he said, smiling, "I think this is the part where you say something?"

Now she was blushing too. She felt warmth creep up her cheeks—a vulnerability she wasn't used to showing, making her feel exposed, yet excited and hopeful for what would come next.

"Uhmm... yeah..." Aea managed, her voice faltering. "German is lame," she blurted out, instantly regretting it. *Oh, God! I ruined the moment. I really need to work on my banter.* But Daemon chuckled, seemingly amused. "You're right. German is lame."

She exhaled, relieved that he laughed and, apparently, found her imperfections endearing. The three girls looked at each other and joined in the laughter, and for a moment, Aea completely forgot her nerves. "You're lame," Kaliyah teased, playfully poking Aea in the back.

"Go away," Aea said, turning to shoo the two girls off.

"Okay, okay," Jema said with a grin. "Have fun! Don't do anything I wouldn't do!"

As they strolled down the hallway toward the exit, Aea realized she still had Home Ec before the day would be over. She hesitated for a moment, unsure of what to do. Her mind raced as she weighed her responsibilities against the idea of spending more time with the boy. The thought of breaking the rules for him made her feel both excited and guilty. Daemon stopped, glancing at her, wondering what was wrong. *Ah, to hell with it,* she thought. *Skipping one class can't hurt.* Hopefully, the school wouldn't notify her dad. *I think they only do that after a few warnings, anyway.*

This was all new to her. She was actually contemplating cutting class for a boy. *Me! Aeona Lamonte! Of all people?* She mulled it over for a few more seconds, weighing the pros and cons. *Well, I'm doing it!*

"Where do you live?" Daemon asked, snapping her out of it.

She spun into an out-of-control, overly detailed answer about the street where their shabby high-rise was located, nearby landmarks, and how to get there. She kept talking, and talking, and talking—until Daemon had to interrupt her. "I was thinking I'd walk you home. What do you say? I'll carry your books."

The prospect of spending more time with Daemon, of him wanting to walk her home, was enticing, but also underpinned by a certain danger. For her, it was uncharted territory. Her bumbling nervousness made a brief reappearance. "But we don't have any books," she said, genuinely perplexed for a second at the suggestion he'd carry them. *Idiot! Of course, we don't have any books!*

Daemon chortled. "It's just an expression, you know. Haven't you seen old movies? But I'll carry your handy if you want."

"I don't have one of those either. Visor girl here. I just don't have it on right now, as you can see."

"Visor, huh? Ooh-la-la," Daemon teased, grinning widely. "Watch out, rich girl here!"

Aea laughed. It was said in jest; she understood that. It was true that visors were rare outside, but she certainly wasn't rich. "Not rich," she protested, "but yes, you can walk me home."

There was a lightness to his banter that seemed to cut right through her defenses. "It's a date, then," he said with a wink. "Come on, let's go. Before they catch me here."

Probably a good idea. She was pretty sure that if Daemon was caught on school premises, she'd be stuck all afternoon explaining it to the principal. Best to skedaddle.

"So, what did you think?" Daemon asked as they left the school, a playful glint in his eye.

"About what?" Aea feigned ignorance, though she was reasonably sure what he was asking about.

"You know! The rally," he said, nudging her tauntingly with his elbow.

She giggled, trying to maintain a cool detachment. "I'm not saying."

"Oh, come on!" Daemon protested. "At least tell me the confetti gun was cool. It was my idea."

It *was* cool, of course, but she wasn't about to tell him that.

Keep them at a distance, let them chase you for a bit. Wasn't that the general advice in these situations? *And above all, don't go all googly-eyed whenever they're around. I'm not doing a very good job of following that advice, though, am I?*

"Tell me," she said, changing the subject. "Are you with Gabriel? I mean, are you part of his gang or something?"

"Gang?" he chuckled. "We're not a gang!"

Party? Crew? Movement? She struggled to find the right word. Daemon didn't correct her. Instead, he just nodded as they crossed the field where the rally had taken place a few days ago. "Yeah, I'm with him," he said. "Sort of. I like what he's saying. The outside may be shit, but it's *our* shit, you know? At least here we're free and not slaves to the super-rich or... you know, fucking job-stealing AIs, or whatever."

She nodded, unsure if she agreed or not. But she liked that he fought for Outies. It made him... what? *Gorgeous!* She smiled to herself.

Traces of confetti still lingered, the storm having carried it far beyond the rally site and into the surrounding streets and high-rises. It wasn't like the Outside had public services to clean things up—at least not very often, anyway. That would change when they expanded the dome, or so they were told. That was one promise the Innies made.

"I'm sure the Innies aren't slaves," Aea said.

Daemon laughed. "They are. They just don't know it."

As they crossed the former park, now wasteland, into the streets lined with high-rises, Daemon poked her playfully. "These yours?" he joked, pointing to a burnt-out building nearby. Aea found it amusing how anything could have time to burn when it always rained. Those particular apartment blocks had been abandoned for years—as long as she could remember. In Niederrad, nothing ever got fixed. Every time she walked past, she wondered where the people who used to live there were now. Forcibly relocated to one of the outer settlements? One of the shanties? Mercifully taken into the dome where they had been given meaningful lives? Put on UBI? She hoped for the latter, but who really believed such a silly thing?

"So, do you agree with him then?" Aea asked. "With Gabriel?"

His answer was immediate and unequivocal. "Damn right. Like I said, this place may not be worth shit, but it's *our* shit."

Curious. She had never really seen it that way before. She had always assumed that living within the safety of the domes was the better choice. After all, everyone always said the domes would keep expanding until everyone lived inside. It had never occurred to her that someone might not want to.

"Don't you agree?" he asked, his eyes drilling into hers.

Unsure for a second, she hesitated. She had always been told the Outside would eventually become a barren wasteland, a place where death was the only certainty. Not tomorrow, not next year. Not in the next ten years. But eventually, it would come. Frau Gehrling had explained the catastrophic effects of the runaway greenhouse effect, but she also knew some people didn't share that belief. She guessed Daemon was one of them. "I don't know," she said finally, hoping that he would have the good sense not to press the issue further. *I so don't want to spoil this with a political debate.* They were having such a great time. She breathed a sigh of relief when he decided to change the subject.

"You close by?" he asked.

Close call! She nodded, indicating she lived just around the corner, in the tall one towering over the low-rises, on the fourth floor. Although she had avoided a potential political argument, thoughts about the realities of living Outside continued to linger. She knew she was lucky, luckier than most. Her dad had a job. An Innie job, even. Not that she understood what he did—it was something about AI compliance monitoring, or some such boring nonsense. All she knew was that his stupid work visa didn't allow him to take anyone with him. Specifically not her!

She had noticed they had things that others didn't, such as storm shutters over their windows. Theirs were real—ones that required actual currency to install—unlike the flimsy wooden planks many used to board up their windows for each storm. Their shutters could be opened and closed at will, allowing sunlight to stream in on good days, while many simply left their makeshift barriers up permanently. On days like today, when the rain wasn't pouring down and the winds weren't tearing the world apart, such luxuries made all the difference. It was the difference between life and depression. Between light and gloom. Literally.

They lived in a neighborhood that was policed, though she wasn't sure by whom. Her dad said they weren't the German government, but that they were fair enough. That they were people who believed in trade and free markets. Who believed such things were preferable to violence and theft. Most of the time, anyway.

They always had food. Always. *It's not like the Outside is a warzone, or anything!* Some were even well off—rich enough to rival the Innies. Her family wasn't, of course, but they could still count themselves among the fortunate ones. She certainly had it better than Jema out in the shanties. *Probably even Kaliyah.* Nevertheless, she understood their relative fortune was built on a fragile foundation, one that would eventually be ripped away.

They cut through the old playground, now abandoned due to the danger posed by hurricanes. Although some of the sturdier playground equipment, such as the slide and merry-go-round, remained intact, the risk of sudden storms meant that most parents didn't want their children playing outside.

"I sort of feel like I don't want this to end," Daemon confessed, pulling her out of her musings.

She felt the same. "We could take another lap around the block," she suggested. "Check out the burnt-out high-rises again. I mean, who wouldn't want to do that?"

He smiled.

Better. Not great, but better. My sarcasm is back, at least.

Anything was preferable to the bumbling mess from back at the lockers. She was slowly gaining confidence in his presence. *I must really like this boy.* She was never caught tongue-tied like this. She was always snappy with her replies, always sarcastic. Her dad didn't like it one bit and always made sure she knew. He was always tired from hours spent in line at the dome checkpoint, commuting to and from work, and had no patience for sarcasm.

"So, are we taking another lap?" she asked. "Or should I go up?"

Daemon smirked. "I have a better idea. Come on." He grabbed her hand and pulled her along. "I'll show you something. It's a bit of a walk from here, down by the Main levee, but I'll have you back home in two hours or so."

She hesitated. There was something about the way he said it, making it sound like an adventure, the prospect of which was almost overwhelmingly alluring at this point. But it would piss Dad off to no end. The area around the school and their section may be decently safe, but just like any child of reasonable Outie parents, she was told to never stray too far away. On the other hand, the boy's confidence and spontaneity were infectious, drawing her in. Irresistible, in the end. *And Dad will only be mad if he finds out.*

Screw it. She was being swept off her feet in a manner she didn't recognize. It was too powerful a feeling to resist, so she allowed herself to be swept. Feeling a bit woozy, she pressed Daemon's hand as they made their way down Deutschordernstraße, en route to the riverfront, to whatever exhilarating thing awaited her.

"Is this where you bring all your girls?" she quipped, gazing at the entrance to the old subterranean maintenance tunnel that ran beneath the Main. Daemon chortled, his laughter echoing off the damp walls of the tunnel entrance. The air was filled with a musty scent of gravel and the lingering odor of stale groundwater. "I mean, you sure know how to woo a girl," she teased. "An old dome maintenance tunnel is just the place where a lady wants to be taken on a first date."

"So this *is* a date?" Daemon said, grinning mischievously while jabbing her playfully in the side.

"Oh, I don't think so," she answered, her tone wry. "Especially since you brought me to this place. Besides, weren't all of these supposed to be sealed?"

"They mostly are," Daemon said. "But this tunnel is special. It has something no other tunnel has. Come on, I'll show you."

Without waiting for a response, he grabbed her hand and led her into the tunnel. Alarm bells went off—venturing into one of these could only spell trouble—but his boyish confidence and eagerness were infectious. She had to admit, the prospect of venturing into an off-limits tunnel held a certain allure, a kind of childish call to adventure. After about twenty meters, he stopped and grabbed a pair of flashlights hanging neatly on the wall. The click of the flashlights pierced the silence, their beams cutting through the darkness like swords. The air was cooler down here, the mustiness more pronounced. She felt a slight chill rush over her as she took a deeper breath.

"I'll lead," he said in an exaggerated heroic tone, handing her one. "It gets dark where we're going."

Taking the light from him, their hands briefly touched, sending a current through her. The prospect of danger, however silly—she didn't really think there was any actual threat down the dank tunnel—kindled a spirit of camaraderie. No, something beyond that. She wasn't sure exactly what kind of connection she felt, but something was budding. Daemon led her all the way to the wall that separated the dome from the outside, or so he claimed. How was she supposed to know?

"Ta-dah!" he said, gesturing to it as if unveiling a grand spectacle.

Her light flickered over the concrete expanse before them, revealing the rough texture of the wall, the uneven ground beneath their feet, and the occasional tendril of moisture running toward the floor.

"Well, color me impressed," she jested, her sarcastic talents continually recovering from the initial googly-eyed crush by the lockers. "A wall. What's next? A hole in the ground? A pile of gravel? A bit of asphalt, maybe?"

He clarified that this was not the main attraction of the tour—he simply wanted to emphasize that they were now under the dome, past the frontier and the checkpoints. It was just an opening act to set the tone. He guided her through a long, winding maze of corridors until they arrived at a broader passageway. Before she could fire off another broadside of sarcastic remarks, he emphasized that this, too, was not the tour's *pièce de résistance*. Just another stop.

"This access tunnel was used by the machines that built the dome's underground structure back when it was new," he explained. "It leads all the way through Niederrad, down south of the city. It actually passes very close to where you live. Some of the tunnels even go right up to the high-rises and connect to their basement storm shelters."

She knew exactly what he was talking about. One of the tunnels connected to her high-rise, right there in the basement. She and the other kids used to play in there when she was little, until one of them got lost in the maze. The authorities had the door permanently padlocked after that. She was about to enthusiastically share this fact with Daemon, but she changed her mind at the last moment. *Better not.* A mental image of the boy showing up through that door unannounced, as unlikely as that was, played out in front of her eyes like a movie. *Oh, no!* If she was going to date this one, she needed control, to be prepared for the introductions that would inevitably follow. She had to know what to say to Dad, how to explain herself. She couldn't risk any surprise visits—through the front door, or otherwise.

"We've got it all mapped out," Daemon boasted. "Nobody else can find shit down here. Not the City Council. Not the Innies. But we can."

Her mind raced. *We?* Who were *we*? And what was mapped out, and for what purpose? The statement implied secrecy and defiance. Maybe even rebellion. She wanted to know more, but somehow she got the feeling it was not a good idea to ask.

"Come on," he urged, grabbing her hand again and pulling her along before she could think too much about it or object. The darkness leaned in closer around them, the flashlight beams seeming to thin as they went deeper in. A few turns, a few more corridors. Aea now realized if she lost him down here, she would never find her way back out, with or without a flashlight. That should scare her, but it didn't. For some reason, she trusted this boy, who held her hand so tightly, who was obviously involved in things he shouldn't be. But that was part of the attraction. *What's he going to do? Lock me up? Kill me? Recruit me to Gabriel's cause? Oh, God. That would be the worst of all!*

For all she knew, maybe he was taking her to Gabriel's secret headquarters, where they were all scheming to defeat the Innies and their kind offer to expand the dome.

"Here," he declared as they reached the opening of a wide cement pipe, the flashlight beam dancing around the rim of the entrance.

Aea scoffed. "Oh great, a pipe. The one thing I didn't think of."

"We have to go through," he said, his tone matter-of-fact. "You up for it?"

Once again, despite her misgivings, she found herself agreeing. After all, what was she going to do? Turn back? The entrance to the pipe stood as a threshold, not only to a restricted part of the dome, but to understanding more about this boy and his world, and she wanted to know. It was a leap of trust to follow, surely, but one she just had to take. He led her in. The pipe was just big enough to crouch in. She wouldn't have to crawl, and her clothes wouldn't get dirty. *One less thing to explain when I get home.* The place was neat, the raked gravel on the ground suggested the pipe was being maintained and used. *Maintained and used for what?*

As she navigated the cramped space, she tried to wrap her thoughts around the purpose of such a thing. Something fishy was clearly going on. The reality of their clandestine journey settled in, a cocktail of adrenaline and increasing concern fueling her steps.

"See the metal door there?" Daemon asked, pointing his light toward the remainder of the concrete pipe. "That's the tunnel exit."

"A door!" she fake-gasped. "Well, now I will definitely, for sure, sleep with you." A sarcastic response, of course, but inside, her skepticism and worry were slowly giving way to genuine curiosity. There was obviously something behind that steel slab.

Daemon chuckled. "A door," he said, "that leads to a back alley behind an abandoned café. Inside the dome. It's unguarded, forgotten, and out of the way of prying eyes in a poor neighborhood nobody ever goes to. No cameras, no drones."

She stared at the steely surface of the door, speechless. Daemon chuckled again. "What? No sly remark?"

Yep. You got me. I did not expect that.

"Can we go?" she asked, exuberantly skipping alongside Daemon as they started back. "Oh, please, please, please!" But to her dismay, he explained that it was impossible. Anyone without a braid or a separate ID spoofer would be caught by dome surveillance—whether by drones, legacy police, or whatever private enforcement was active in the area. One step on a crowded street, and she'd be in interrogation for a few days, then banned from entering legally. *Well, that's a disappointment,* she thought, the exhilaration she had felt so strongly just a second ago fizzling out like a flat tire. Her dreams of seeing the Inside would have to wait, alas. *Just as well. I'm late home as it is!*

"What's it like in there?" she asked, swallowing her disappointment.

"Most would say better than here, I guess. Cleaner, richer, but the domes aren't that great, you know. There's still slum. There's still poverty. Not as bad as here, but it isn't the utopia they say it is."

Utopia. Another big word Frau Gehrling had cautioned them about.

"Listen," Daemon said, his tone suddenly serious. "You can't tell anyone about this. Okay?"

"Why not?" she asked, but he refused to explain, saying only that he would get in trouble if anyone found out he had told her. *Somehow I get the feeling I would be too.* A chill crept up her spine, the realization that something secretive and potentially dangerous was going on down here. Something illegal, even? It was yet another reminder that she didn't know much about this boy.

"Why did you show me?" she asked, genuinely curious.

He hesitated before replying. "I don't know. I guess I wanted to show you something special."

"You wanted to impress me?" she asked, a smile spreading across her face.

"I guess," he admitted with just a hint of shy embarrassment. The confession, simple yet vulnerable, sparked a warmth in her. It was a glimpse into the person he was—his intentions and interest in her, rather than the shadowy business of the tunnel. They continued their walk back to the outside, leaving the mystery of the manhole and the world beyond it behind for now.

Daylight washed over her face as they emerged from the tunnels. She squinted and raised an arm, shielding herself from the sudden brightness, and in the blurry distance, she saw another boy approach as they ascended the ramp to the street beyond. The harsh transition from the dim tunnel to the glaring sunlight disoriented her momentarily, making the approaching figures seem like ominous shadows emerging from a mirage.

"Shit," Daemon said, grabbing her arm. Two other boys joined, forming a line blocking their path. Her pulse quickened, a thin sheet of sweat forming on her brow in the immediately hotter outside air. They looked to be Daemon's age, maybe even a few years older. Tension knotted in Aea's stomach at the sight of the figures blocking their path, a sudden shift from innocent adventure to the prospect of real peril. Daemon's protective stance, though reassuring, underscored the seriousness of the confrontation they faced.

"What's wrong?" she asked.

Daemon shushed her. "Stay here," he instructed, before marching toward the group of boys. They began talking, but Aea struggled to hear them over the wind rustling in her ears, despite the levees lining the ramp and the tunnel entrance shielding them. The boys were only a few meters away, yet she only managed to pick up every other word.

"What's this, Daemon? You know... not supposed to... without... off the books... running... side business?" The middle boy, the obvious leader, was gesturing wildly. Irate and belligerent, he shoved Daemon, nearly causing him to lose his balance, but Daemon impressively regained his footing and retaliated. The other two responded, all three jumping Daemon, viciously pummeling him.

As the argument turned physical, fear and adrenaline surged through Aea. The violence unfolding before her was starkly foreign, a real-world intrusion abruptly ending their fleeting escapade. She screamed. Her immediate instinct was to come to Daemon's aid, but while her mind was willing, her body was paralyzed, rooted to the ground. *Don't just stand there like a dumb cow!* If she did get her feet going, what was she going to do? The big boys would toss her aside like a leaf in the wind.

For now, Daemon was holding his own, but it wouldn't last. He landed a few punches on the leader, and the underlings seemed lost and unsure of themselves without the big guy to give them orders. A momentary reprieve, she realized. *He's not going to make it alone against all three!* Caught between the urge to intervene and the instinct to flee, Aea's mind raced. The realization that she could lose Daemon—someone who had just shared a piece of his world with her, someone who she had—like it or not—developed a fondness for—galvanized her resolve, pushing her past the inertia of shock.

She snapped out of it and started scanning the ramp for a weapon, her eyes settling on the loose rocks lining the sides of the ramp, at the bottom of the levees. Determination finally overpowered hesitation, the decision to act pushing her forward. In that moment, she was driven not by logic or fear for her own safety, but by a raw need to protect, to do something—anything—that could alter the dire outcome she saw before her eyes. She zeroed in on one of the bigger stones, grabbed it, and lunged toward the fight. Her fingers wrapped tightly around the rough surface of the stone, feeling its weight in her trembling hand.

At first, she considered throwing it, but her lack of athletic ability would surely cause her to miss. Instead, she held onto it like a bludgeon and swung it in her hand. She aimed for the big guy, but he saw it coming, and she missed. *Damn!* Time seemed to slow down as she watched her makeshift weapon glide past him until it smashed into the face of one of the underlings, who didn't have time to get away. She couldn't even recall which one. It didn't matter. The boy fell to the ground, lifeless, blood oozing from the side of his head, turning the dirty ground red.

For a heartbeat, a stunned silence enveloped the scene, the immediate aftermath of her action crashing down on her with brutal clarity. It was a moment of profound shock, the gravity of the situation leaving her breathless. She had hurt someone. Maybe killed someone. Never in her worst nightmare had she thought she'd do something like this.

Daemon took advantage of the momentary distraction, freeing himself from the grasp of the other two boys. "Come on," he yelled to Aea as he crawled back to his feet. "Back in the tunnel!" He grabbed her hand, and they fled, not even looking back to see if the boys took up pursuit. Adrenaline surged through her veins, propelling her forward as they dashed back to the tunnel. Their frantic escape was a blur, Aea's mind numb to everything but the instinct to follow the boy back into the dark.

"Do you have company?" her dad shouted from the living room, the sound of his voice sending a jolt of panic through her. Her heart raced as she navigated the familiar yet suddenly alien hallway of their apartment. *Of course he's home. Today of all days.* The sound of game shows on the living room screen added a layer of normalcy to a situation that was anything but. Her father usually worked late, almost every day, relentlessly grinding to provide for her and her sister. She felt a twinge of guilt for being annoyed that, for once, he had been able to leave early.

"Just a friend from school," Aea hollered back—a lie. She quickened her pace as they snuck past, hoping to avoid any awkward conversations or lectures, leading Daemon, bleeding from a cracked eyebrow, through the hallway to her and her sister's room. As they stealthily navigated the hallway, the significance of Daemon's presence in her personal space began to fully dawn on her. The realization that she was about to cross a threshold she hadn't considered before sparked both excitement and apprehension. The hallway smelled like a mix of musty earth from the tunnels, lingering in her nostrils, of sweat, and Daemon's cologne—a reminder of what they had just narrowly escaped.

They had followed the tunnels almost all the way home and exited through a shelter adjacent to Aea's high-rise, where the door leading to the tunnels wasn't padlocked from the other side. *Control,* she mused, as they tiptoed through the hallway. Over when and how Daemon visited was clearly out the window!

She had ripped off the sleeve of her blouse to form a makeshift bandage and pressed it tightly against Daemon's gushing eyebrow. The metallic tang of blood filled the air between them as she leaned in to get a better view, mixing with the familiar scent of the lavender deodorizer she used to keep the dank out of their room.

Her mind raced back to the incident outside the tunnels. Aea couldn't believe she had actually hit one of the boys with a rock. The sound of the impact and the sight of the boy's body slumping over like a ragdoll was still vivid in her mind. *Dad will be thrilled when he finds out I ruined my shirt. Shirts don't grow on trees,* that's what he'd say. *Or, we're not made of money.* She had also learned how difficult it was to tear off a sleeve. It had taken all her strength to rip it, and she had had to use a sharp pebble to help cut the fabric. *The movies do not portray this realistically!*

No one intercepted them as they snuck past. They were in the clear. As Aea settled Daemon on her bed, she tried to recall if she and her dad had ever had the talk about bringing boys to the room. Sure, the birds and the bees talk had taken place—they discussed such matters rather openly—but bringing boys home was not the same as making out behind the school gym. *It's not like I ever actually have boys over, so why should I remember?*

Had they neglected that particular conversation and failed to pass by unnoticed, they could be in trouble. Although her dad did not ordinarily interfere in her social life, they might have to have that talk now, in some form or other. Only now, she would not only be bringing a boy, but a wounded one. And not just any boy, but an older one. *Such boys are trouble! That's what he'd say.*

Focusing on his wound, she felt a strange mix of resolve, regret, and nausea at the sight of the soaked blouse sleeve. The act of caring for him made her warm inside, a burgeoning bond she would never have anticipated just a few hours earlier, while at the same time being terrified her father would walk in on them. In fact, her attention was so fixated on stemming the crimson flow of blood—now increasingly seeping through the scrunched-up fabric—and the prospect of her father bursting in with questions, that she failed to consider Tabayh, the nosiest little sister the world had ever seen. Without warning, the young girl appeared, peeking around the doorframe like an inquisitive little squirrel.

"Dad says you can't have boys in the room," she blurted out. "It's—" Then her eyes widened as she saw the blood, the torn shirt, and the smears of soil over Daemon's face.

"It's okay," Aea said, her voice calm, almost dismissive. "He just busted an eyebrow. It looks worse than it is."

Tabayh's mouth opened, immediately ready to tattle. "I'm telling Dad," she said, and started off.

Panic coursed through Aea's veins as she lunged forward, just barely grabbing hold of the girl's pajama sleeve. "No!" Aea yelled. "You can't tell Dad." Meanwhile, blood from Daemon's wound kept soaking through the fabric, now also trickling onto the linen. The boy was getting woozy, slowly appearing to lose consciousness.

"All my desserts for a month," Aea pleaded, turning back to face Tabayh.

The young girl's expression was pensive, as if contemplating a crucial business deal. "A year," she countered.

Aea smirked. "A whole year, huh? That seems a bit too much. How about a month?"

Tabayh shook her head adamantly. "Uh-uh. A year."

"Come on. A month is more than fair."

The girl wouldn't budge.

She's a master negotiator. "Okay. Two months," Aea offered.

Tabayh tilted her head, once more appearing thoughtful. "Okay. I won't tell," she finally agreed, "but I want to help." Relief washed over Aea, her breath releasing in a whoosh that seemed too loud. *Looks like I've gained an ally.* Naturally. What stirs a child's imagination more than anything else? Perhaps even more than a never-ending supply of sweet treats? To be a part of her elder sister's adventures, of course.

Aea recognized this fact, nodding in agreement. "Alright then, I need you to get the first aid kit and towels from the bathroom. The gray ones. Dad won't notice those are gone."

Tabayh beamed with pride, eager to lend a hand, and darted off.

Aea couldn't help but feel a sense of pride—albeit mixed with desperation—in the aftermath of their sibling negotiation. Trading sweets for silence was hardly the right thing to do, but under the circumstances, she felt she could justify it.

Once she returned, Aea turned to Daemon, giving him a stern look. "Who were they?" she asked while carefully wrapping gauze around his head, over his cracked eyebrow. Daemon averted his gaze.

"Hmm?" she said, grabbing him by the chin and turning his face toward her, forcing him to meet her stare.

He sighed. "Look, it's better if you don't know."

Aea's voice took a sharp tone. "Oh no. You got us into this mess, now tell me. I had to run ten thousand meters through a maze of dark, smelly tunnels to get away from those creeps. *Sag schon! Ich hab's verdient zu wissen!*" Well, maybe it wasn't ten thousand meters, but he knows what I mean!

He smirked. "Oh-oh, she's speaking German. You know a girl is serious when she breaks out the German." He gently nudged her, then drew her close, wrapping his arm around her shoulder and pecking her cheek.

"Eww, gross!" Tabayh exclaimed. "I'm telling Dad you made out with a boy."

Daemon playfully grabbed Tabayh and flung her onto the

bed, tickling her until she begged him to stop. Laughter filled the room, a stark contrast to the tension and fear that had dominated moments before, the sound bouncing off the walls and infusing the space with a fleeting sense of joy. *Normal sounds of play,* she thought. *Good. That'll keep Dad from getting suspicious.*

"I thought we had a deal," Aea reminded her.

"Oh, right," Tabayh said. "*Ich hab's vergessen.*"

It was no secret Tabayh was the most linguistically gifted in their family. She had been only two when they migrated from Algeria and spoke French, English, and German, switching effortlessly between them. Of that, Aea had always been jealous, although she took pride in being the most proficient in English.

"Run along," Aea instructed her. "I'll come play with you later when Daemon has gone home."

"Promise?"

"I swear on my life."

"Cross your heart and hope to die?" Tabayh persisted.

"Scram, you little maggot, before Daemon tickles you again," Aea warned, joking. With a growl, Daemon pretended to lunge at Tabayh, causing her to giggle hysterically as she fled the room.

"Speaking of which," Daemon began, turning to face Aea, "I should probably be going."

"Not until you tell me who those guys were," Aea insisted.

He approached her and placed his hands on her hips. She shivered instantly as she felt his touch, biting her lower lip. *Oh no! Did I just do that? So much for playing it cool.*

Once more, she was paralyzed. An image of a deer caught in the headlights of a car popped into her mind for some reason, although she had never witnessed such a scene in real life. In truth, she had only ridden in a driverless taxi a few times, which had never collided with anything. Nevertheless, she had seen such an image many times, though she wasn't sure where. Probably from a movie, or something. From the era when people drove everywhere they went, during the time when everyone was an Outie.

Daemon drew her in close, their bodies almost touching. Slowly, unbearably slowly, he inched closer. The charged atmosphere as Daemon drew closer was palpable, a flood of anticipation and desire. Aea's heart raced, caught in the gravity of the moment, each second stretching into eternity. She could feel his breath on her, and just when their lips were about to meet, he stopped himself.

"No," he said. "We'll wait for a better moment."

Aea couldn't believe it. She had been so ready. *Soooo ready!* This one has a lot of self-restraint! This would only make her want him more, of that she was sure.

"Don't worry about those guys," Daemon reassured her. "Let's just say they're guys I used to run with. But we're done now. That's why they are the way they are."

Aea nodded. It wasn't the most detailed explanation, but she supposed it would do for now. Besides, the almost-kiss had weakened her resolve, probably just like the boy had intended.

"It's a good field dressing," Daemon complimented her, gently patting the gauze over his eye.

"You think so? It's my first."

After sneaking him back out and saying their goodbyes, Aea turned around to find Tabayh waiting for her in the hallway. "I like him," she said. "Is he your boyfriend?" Aea shushed her and quickly led her back to their room.

"I don't know," she replied. *Is he? Oh God, I hope he is!*

Might as well go talk to Dad. Try to explain who the boy was. Try as she might, there was no way all of this transpired without him noticing. The apartment wasn't that big, and he was bound to ask sooner or later. She reckoned she might as well be proactive and tell him a compelling tale on her own terms rather than being caught off guard. Not that he was that attentive—always preoccupied with work—but if he ever was, it would be now.

She realized she needed to ponder this. A great story doesn't just materialize out of thin air. She needed to be prepared, with answers ready for every eventuality. *And what about the bloodstains!*

There was no evidence he'd seen anything. Perhaps she could wait until tomorrow? She decided she could and instead headed to their room to play with Tabayh, as she had promised. But first, she had to do something about the bloody towels and change the linen. She left for the bathroom to soak the towels, and all the while, she dreamt about the boy with whom she had just had the craziest adventure.

Jarod

"So, is everything crystal clear?" Adriel inquired, eyebrow raised as they strolled along South Bank. London was lovely this early evening, the dome's still intact inner plating projecting sunny weather, and the ever-shrinking, self-replicating tarp made translucent, allowing natural illumination to permeate. Outside, the skies were overcast, and the amalgamation of artificial sun and the dreary gray hues of the clouds created a unique ambiance that made it feel more like dawn than dusk. *The color of television, tuned to a dead channel?*

Jarod nodded affirmatively to Adriel's question, but he couldn't help finding it somewhat amusing how everything had to be spoken in code, despite the deployment of the latest generation black market privacy screens. Jarod couldn't suppress a smirk at the absurdity of using such codes amidst all the high-tech secrecy—a game not just played against their adversaries but against paranoia itself. Their conversation was already as safe as it was going to be, but he supposed one could never be cautious enough when undertaking such brazenly illegal activities.

Adriel had just finished his briefing on how the operation would be funded. The massive amounts of cash required for the operation had to be camouflaged as "security fees" for dome maintenance and refurbishment initiatives. *I can almost hear the clink of virtual coins as they flow into this thing.* The hefty price tags associated with such construction endeavors would readily account for the transfers now being orchestrated.

These so-called security fees would effortlessly vanish into the matryoshka doll that was Aegis's balance sheet, providing a convenient explanation for the ongoing money transfers. Given the inevitable complications and unforeseeable snags that plague large-scale construction initiatives, these plausible delays would justify prolonging their fictitious "security" work. And if such explanations wore thin, fresh projects would emerge, further requiring the continuation of their "expert" services.

The complexity of laundering money through construction projects sparked a reluctant admiration in Jarod. The ingenuity, and irony, of using the facade of building civilization to conceal the tearing down of others was darkly humorous at its best. Make no mistake, hunting down the London bombers may be just, but the way proposed was not 'civil' in any sense of the word.

A scent of burnt coffee mixed with roasted almonds from a nearby bankside vendor reached his olfactory receptors, momentarily interrupting his train of thought with a reminder that he hadn't had any caffeine since that morning. He made a mental note to revisit that vendor as soon as he was done with Adriel.

Over the decades, Aegis might have evolved to wield powers akin to those of a state, but even so, it could not do whatever it pleased, and laundering money was the least of their concerns. They could not act with complete impunity and simply assassinate their enemies, real or perceived, for doing so would still invite swift and deadly retaliation from the political and legal domains. Legacy might be impotent, but it could still bite when it chose to.

Ensuring privacy was therefore paramount, and every precaution had to be taken. In the event an intruder was able to breach their firewall, they would hear a carefully constructed sham conversation, generated by Adriel's AI. The subjects discussed could be anything, from the banal grumblings of a disgruntled employee complaining about their imbecile boss to a casual conversation about last night's football game. *Or soccer game, as I would call it,* much to the disdain of the Brits. Any topic one would expect two middle-aged men to chat about on a leisurely evening stroll along South Bank. The themes were selected independently by the AI, translated in real-time, without any delay noticeable to human ears. It was as bulletproof as anything could get, yet their actual words still had to be hidden in code. Hence, "assassinations" became "security work," and their bounties, "security fees."

As they approached Frederick's Wharf, the majestic City scrapers loomed ahead on the north side, these once-ruined structures now restored to their former glory—a symbol of the City's resilience, its ability to rise and rebuild anew, much to the dismay of the terrorists who had tried to bring them down.

The sound of the Thames, captive, with its water flow controlled by the dome's intricate climate control system, lapping against the embankment, blended with the clamor of city life. While the tarp did a good enough job shutting out the elements, a slight smell of moisture on concrete lingered—something that could never have been experienced here had the vicious terrorist act not occurred.

Seeing the City scrapers, Jarod was struck by a sense of resilience, the architectural defiance a testament to humanity's stubborn persistence. Yet the sight also stirred a somber reflection on the futility of violence as a means of change—the scars of terrorism a wound on the city's face that no amount of construction could fully heal. And yet, he was here, planning with Adriel, about to embark on the very same quest.

"You've killed before," Adriel said, rather bluntly. It was a statement, not a question, and Jarod's heart skipped a beat at its utterance. It was a bridge he often crossed in another life, one he was loath to revisit. Yet here he was, accepting the mission.

Jarod responded with a wry smile. "Is that a question or a statement?"

Adriel chuckled. "You have a way about you, Jarod. A singular wit, if you will."

A statement, then.

Jarod's military service records were meant to be locked away, he reminded himself, hidden in the U.S. military's most convoluted bureaucratic labyrinths and under the strictest security protocols. Yet, someone like Gibson, with his bottomless bank account and endless access to decryption specialists, could have anything he desired.

"It's been a while, but I've heard it's like riding a bike," he replied.

Adriel's smile was forced, his amusement surely feigned. "As I said, a singular wit."

They parted briefly to let a family pass on the now-narrowing boardwalk. The esplanade was teeming with people, dinner time fast approaching.

It was refreshing to work with a pro like Adriel, who understood the value of hiding in plain sight. The bank's buzz was a cacophony of life, the smells of street food mingling with the laughter of children and parents alike, the din masking their presence. It was here, amid the chaos of normalcy, that they found their cloak—not behind physical walls but in the open, under the watchful eyes of the world. *And yet, we still bathe everything in electronic interference and code. One can never be too careful, I guess.*

For many, the reflex to sneak and hide runs deep. After all, it worked well for most of human history. But nowadays, with cameras and microphones being ubiquitous, there are no places left to hide. Everyone and their dog has them—not just the rich and mighty. Even your wife, your neighbor, your child—everyone is listening, watching. And all of them are hooked up to the Net, ripe for savvy crypto specialists to hack. Especially Inside. On every street corner, in every shop or restaurant, even in the most desolate of back alleys. So, hiding in plain sight and appearing unremarkable, then adding the electronics—that had become the sweet spot.

"Take a look," Adriel said as he transmitted the target

profiles along with the key to view them. Jarod quickly gestured for the summaries to be displayed on his lens. A flicker of light, barely perceptible, and the information was there before his eyes, superimposed on the vivid reality of the bustling wharf. It took only a few seconds for his AI to decode the file once it had received the key, which was sent separately. Jarod scrolled through them briefly.

Primary Targets:

[Scott Davies]
Role: Operational Team Leader
Sex: Male
Location: Unknown
Notes: Ex-military. Genetic and cybernetic enhancements unconfirmed. [Click to expand]

[Nyal Bahno]
Role: Surveillance and Reconnaissance
Sex: Male
Location: Unknown
Notes: Ex-military. Genetic and cybernetic enhancements unconfirmed. [Click to expand]

[Gayul Tyers]
Role: Weapons and Tactics
Sex: Male
Location: Unknown
Notes: Ex-military. Bomb-maker. Likely designed and made the explosive device used in the London Dome operation. Genetic and cybernetic enhancements unconfirmed. [Click to expand]

[Bertrand Siscal]
Role: Finance
Sex: Male
Location: Unknown
Notes: Civilian. Genetic enhancements confirmed—cognitive.

No cybernetic enhancements. Goes by nickname "Fiscal Siscal." [Click to expand]

[Megan Russell]
Role: Strategy
Sex: Female
Location: Unknown
Notes: Former Legacy Law Enforcement. Genetic enhancements confirmed—non-relevant (cosmetic). Cybernetic enhancements confirmed. Likely responsible for design of operational plan in London Dome operation. [Click to expand]

Secondary Target:

[Alixha Rahena]
Role: Leader of Lux Aeterna
Sex: Female
Location: Unknown
Notes: Civilian. Genetic and cybernetic enhancements confirmed—cognitive, musculoskeletal—others unconfirmed. [Click to expand]

"Rahena?" Jarod said skeptically.

"We know Scott Davies carried out the operation. He was caught by Aegis backup facility cameras parachuting away from the site. We also strongly suspect he is intimately connected to Rahena."

"So you share Legacy's hypothesis that Lux Aeterna was behind it?"

Adriel remained silent, but Jarod knew the answer. Legacy had been pursuing Rahena for decades without success. While the connection to her had not been formally established, everyone agreed she was responsible. Rahena had a vast network, and she was one of the few capable of pulling off something as audacious as a dome bombing. And among the few who wanted to.

"Don't worry about Rahena," Adriel said calmly, as if anticipating his concerns. "You won't get to her, and we don't expect you to. If the opportunity does present itself, take the shot. We'll triple your fee upon proof of death. If not, well, you'll still get paid what we agreed. You have nothing to lose."

Yeah, except our lives. His thoughts briefly drifted to the many urban legends surrounding Rahena. Depending on their veracity, the stakes could be much higher than he realized. The mention of Rahena certainly was a cold splash of reality—anxiety-inducing, to say the least, and a reminder of the deep waters they were about to navigate. But at the core of that unease, there was also determination—a firm belief that he would do the world good if he could rid it of these people. *Perhaps it's not fear that unsettles me, but the lines I'm prepared to cross?*

"Davies is the grand prize here," Adriel continued. "He's Rahena's new star. The London job was only the beginning for him, and getting rid of him will save countless lives."

Jarod nodded and instructed his AI to start analyzing the files more thoroughly.

It probably didn't matter if Rahena was tied to the bombing or not. Aegis, like Legacy, had their own reasons for wanting her eliminated. But Jarod knew better than to pry too deeply. The rich and powerful played dangerous games, and getting too involved could be lethal. It was best to pick the crumbs from their table and avoid the rest. *Isn't that exactly what I'm doing, though? Getting involved in their games? Or is this picking the crumbs? I can't tell anymore.*

The AI's scan of the files was quick, partly because there wasn't much there. "If you're wondering why they're a bit thin on information, it's because we don't have it," Adriel said, again as if he read Jarod's mind. "This is where you come in. Your surveillance counterparts, what are their names—"

"Riley and Kale."

"Right. They have a reputation for finding needles in haystacks, have they not?" Adriel gave him a pat on the shoulder. "Why do you think we need you? We can't dig too deeply without risking setting off alarms."

"But I can?" Jarod replied, sarcastically.

Adriel gave him a wry smile and turned away, looking towards one of the little restaurants at the entrance to the wharf. "I'm hungry. Why don't we eat?"

Kale and Riley had quickly confirmed Davies's connection to Rahena and Lux Aeterna, but not much else. Jarod sighed as he scanned the updated file while the car drove him toward the safe house north of London that Adriel had set up. A ripple of frustration washed over him as he digested the sparse details in the file. The connection between Davies and Rahena was a tangible thread, yet it dangled frustratingly out of reach, taunting him with the complexity of the web they were about to untangle. He could already see how difficult it would be to track Davies down.

He was last seen in central Tokyo. Jarod's gaze lingered on the photo of Davies, the pixels forming the face of a man caught between worlds. He was young—good-looking, but with the aged eyes of someone who had seen too much. He was the ex-military type who couldn't quite fit into civilian society's dull existence after his service ended, the kind of man who needed a cause to fight for, a justification for his existence that was bigger than himself. Jarod couldn't help but feel a sense of kinship with the younger man. While the file was thin, Jarod still got the sense that Scott was a mirror reflecting his own past struggles. He appeared to be a man, much like himself, ensnared by a need for purpose beyond the mundane, tempered by the harsh realities of life. A man perhaps led astray by idealism gone rampant. *I'll practically be chasing myself. Minus the crow's feet, and the fact that I'm the good guy.*

Jarod felt it was a real pity that an individual like Scott had found himself in such an unsuitable environment. He could have made exceptional use of a man of his caliber on his squad. However, he doubted that chasing down Outies would quench whatever thirst for meaning a man like Scott harbored within, after enduring years in high-intensity combat zones. *I don't find chasing Outies all that satisfactory myself.* Scott also had a blood thirst—the kind that compels one to seek out individuals like Alixha Rahena. The sort that makes one vulnerable to that kind of message, those anti-civilization tropes that propel so many toward political extremes, be it left or right.

The car pulled up to the private dome, nestled discreetly in the northern reaches of London. The transition from Inside, through the urban jungle of steady decay in Outie London, to the countryside always amazed Jarod. It wasn't often he got to make such a trip. Disparate worlds in close proximity, but not even close to similar. Here they had their hideout, away from prying eyes, safe from intruders behind a checkpoint guarded by private security. Here, the air was different, as was the silence, punctuated by the subtle sounds of nature that were all but forgotten Inside.

As he neared the checkpoint, he had his braid transmit his credentials, and the airlock let him through. Jarod felt an odd mix of anticipation and isolation. The exclusivity of their location underscored the gravity of their mission—its importance to their employer.

The dome contained only a few detached houses, leaving an open view of the surroundings. Beyond their new base, visible through the permanently translucent inner plating, an agricultural dome of epic proportions loomed, dominating the landscape like a colossal tidal wave about to crash down on everything in its path. In comparison, their humble parabola appeared positively minuscule. The sight of the mammoth agri-dome instilled a sense of awe and insignificance, a stark reminder of humanity's relentless pursuit of progress and its ability to overcome obstacles, even those of its own making. It reminded him of the diminutive role individual agency played in the grand scheme of things.

Securing such a secluded residence was a testament to Aegis's willingness to spend money on the operation—these private domes didn't come cheap. Being accessible by car only, away from the interdome bullet train network, further accentuated its exclusivity. Self-driving vehicles without proper authorization would run into a software block, rendering them unable to even approach. Driving manually or walking was the only way to gain entry. As one would expect, the dome was further fortified with an arsenal of advanced security measures, overseen by a sophisticated AI, ensuring they would be able to work undisturbed.

The sun was now setting behind the outer edge of the agricultural dome, casting a cascade of gleaming light off its outer plating and a dusky hue across the rest of the landscape. The car's windshield automatically changed tint, mitigating the glare in Jarod's eyes. In the distance, the agricultural dome's floodlights and beacons had been activated, their radiance piercing the twilight, warning air traffic that ventured too close to the potentially hazardous structure, often poorly visible in clouds and mist. It seemed redundant now, with short-haul commercial air travel all but extinct in most civilized nations boasting a bullet train network.

Well, air travel isn't all dead. But is anyone flying here? People still took to the skies, zipping across LEO in hypersonic screamers to destinations beyond the convenient reach of bullet trains, but this dome was situated far from any commercial airline routes, making it an unlikely flyby for casual or business travelers. Perhaps private flights or military operations? Drones wouldn't need visual markers in the form of beacons. But agri-domes were critical infrastructure and prime targets for various factions and powers. Too important to leave exclusively to automated patrols. Humans were here too, keeping a watchful eye on the skies. And they liked their beacons.

The driveway to the house loomed ahead, marking another tangible shift from the superstructures of the London city-domes to the more personal touch of a home. The lights from the windows cut through the dimming night sky, promising warmth and a semblance of normalcy in a world that would soon be anything but. Had it not been for the subtle latticework of the tiny dome occasionally gleaming just above the rooftops, one might have thought the old world still existed.

As he made his way up the driveway, there was yet another security checkpoint. *I guess you can't be too cautious.* A uniformed

Aegis security officer stepped out to greet him. *Human security. Color me impressed.*

Human security was a rarity these days—after all, why pay a premium for something a bot can do much cheaper? Most security issues in a typical residential dome, private or otherwise, could be dealt with using pre-programmed algorithms and standardized protocols. It was those situations that required creativity, intuition, and quick thinking—those unpredictable elements that couldn't be accounted for in an error tree or process map, however complex—that necessitated the presence of human security. Such situations rarely occurred in domestic settings, nor would they here. Aegis, it seemed, had spared no expense when it came to safeguarding their newly acquired asset.

Once more, he transmitted his credentials and was granted passage, the car gliding through the checkpoint and up the driveway. As he approached the house, the aroma of home cooking wafted toward him, rich and inviting, a stark contrast to the sterile air of the tiny dome. *Right on cue.* It wrapped around him like a welcome embrace, making his stomach rumble in reminder that he hadn't eaten anything substantial since yesterday, when Adriel had treated him at Fredrick's Warf. *Not counting that vile robovendor sandwich at Waterloo.* British-style sandwiches always tasted like soggy newspaper, devoid of any discernible flavor or seasoning. *How do the Brits manage to make every sandwich taste the same, regardless of what's in it?*

Some of Wyatt's good old-fashioned operation-prep home cooking was just what he needed—the tantalizing scent a balm on his frayed nerves. The promise of a hearty meal was a luxury in his life, and already on the driveway, the aroma was enough to make his mouth water. He drew in a deep breath, catching a whiff of that sizzling steak—Wyatt's specialty. He could practically taste it already. *There better be enough fries—or chips, as the locals call them.*

He closed the files and put his lens into sleep mode, ready to enjoy some much-needed downtime. Adriel had been right about Alixha—she was a formidable adversary and virtually untouchable. Going after her would be reckless, and he knew he couldn't afford unnecessary risks. Protecting his crew came first, even if it meant leaving behind the obscene amounts of money her head would bring. Riley and Kale would not mind steering clear of that temptation, but Wyatt? He would. Recklessness was not an option, not when the stakes were this high. *If Wyatt brings it up, I'll simply have to dissuade him of the notion.*

The food was exquisite, the meat cooked to perfection. It was the real deal too, not the synthetic facsimile. And by *real*, that meant sourced from a live animal, not the lab-grown stuff. *Well, formerly live animal*, Wyatt had been careful to emphasize. He had even splurged on some premium American ribeye cuts, flown in by Screamer all the way from across the pond. It must have cost a fortune given the exorbitant insurance premiums associated with direct imports these days. And so it would be until the transatlantic bullet tunnel was completed in a decade or so. Until then, Europeans couldn't expect reasonable prices on American goods, and vice versa.

He briefly wondered how Wyatt could afford such a luxury. *Am I paying him too much?* They made decent money doing Legacy's work, but not enough to justify this kind of extravagance. It was better not to ask. *Just enjoy not hearing him complain, for once, about having to eat synth.* And it was equally satisfying to not have to hear Riley taunt him about pretending to taste the difference between real and synthetic. Although, he had to admit, it was usually pretty entertaining banter.

Instead, Wyatt prattled on about the operation, but Riley, true to form, was unfazed by the change of topic. She excelled at busting his chops and was ready to strike at any utterance from his mouth. This time, though, she took a somewhat serious and genuinely skeptical tone.

"I'd kill those bastards for free," Wyatt proclaimed. "Getting paid is just gravy on top."

"I'm sure you would," Riley replied. "It's not that I don't think they should be held accountable for what they did, but I'd be a lot more comfortable if the kill order came from Legacy, with all the proper permissions in place, and not this mystery employer."

Jarod observed the shift in the room's atmosphere, tension clouding the table. Wyatt's jaw tightened, the vein on his forehead becoming prominent, while Riley fixed him with a sour gaze and a slight frown. True to his agreement with Adriel, Wyatt hadn't revealed their employer's identity to the team. It wouldn't be a problem. They were loyal soldiers who would carry out their work without question. Some mealtime tension wouldn't change that. *It's not that hard to figure out who the 'mystery employer' is, anyway.*

Wyatt scoffed at Riley's comment. "So it's okay to kill people as long as the government says so? I seem to recall you whining about the death penalty in the US."

"Shut up."

And so forth.

Jarod decided not to intervene, letting them hash it out. The operation was a murky affair, morally speaking, and it was better for them to air their grievances over dinner than out in the field, where hesitation could prove fatal.

Kale sat quietly, chewing his steak, ranch dressing smeared across his plate in a messy swirl. He was always the quiet one, but when he spoke, it was often worth listening to. Jarod observed him closely, having known him for years. He could see something brewing in his eyes, something he was building up to with each bite.

As Wyatt and Riley continued their pointless political debate, which had now drifted far from the actual moral dilemma of their current mission, Kale finally spoke up. "What would we have said about a job like this ten years ago?" he asked, raising his voice slightly to be heard over the chatter and clanking silverware. The group fell silent, even Jarod, who stared down at his plate. Jarod watched Kale, noticing the pensive furrow forming on his brow, a stark contrast to his usual stoic silence. Kale had a strong moral compass, and it was no surprise he questioned the course Jarod had chosen for them. Just that he did it out loud.

Kale continued, "Or what would we have said even yesterday? Think about it for a minute. We're not those people. We're not assassins."

Jarod felt a chill run through him, the truth in Kale's words cutting deeper than he expected. *He's right.* In the past, the group had always stayed within the bounds of the law, operating only under Legacy permissions and refusing to work with private interests. They weren't vigilantes, revolutionaries, or mercenaries for hire. But now, they had crossed that line.

"This is the next step on the slippery slope we've been on for a while now," Kale went on, his voice increasingly frustrated.

"Back down to the hellhole we were all in after China. After Kazakhstan. We were supposed to be done with that."

With that, Kale stood up, thanked Wyatt for the meal, and headed off to his bunk, leaving the others silent at the dinner table. Jarod knew he could scarcely justify their current path, but he also knew they had no choice. Their bank accounts were almost drained after the botched operation at the old city airport, and Legacy was now less willing to outsource to private enforcers. It was easy to be picky in theory, but in practice, when faced with harsh economic realities, it's hard to maintain lofty ideals.

Silence followed Kale's departure, each member staring at their plates. Jarod sat there, the remnants of the meal in front of him, now having lost its appeal.

"Was it something I said?" Wyatt quipped.

"Shut up, moron," Riley snapped, slamming her chair as she left the room after Kale.

Jarod quietly put down his knife and fork, wiped his lips on the napkin, and got up to leave. His movements were mechanical, his mind already elsewhere.

"I was just trying to lighten the mood," Wyatt called after him as he walked down the hall to his room. "Get some sleep, Wyatt," Jarod said. "I want prep done by 0800 tomorrow. Tactical up and running two hours before that. Let the others know. I'll meet you here."

Wyatt groaned. "You know, contrary to what Kale thinks, we're not actually in the forces anymore. Things don't have to be done that early in the morning!"

"Yeah, yeah. Just get it done, okay." Jarod quickly grabbed his bag from the bed and slipped out the back. He had ten hours to see Dana one last time before the battlefield would once again claim him. Powering up his braid, he sent her a message before heading off. Despite the display of dissent at the dinner table, Jarod wasn't worried. They were all good soldiers—they would come around eventually. They always did.

"Nggh!" she said as she pushed him away, cheeks flushed and out of breath from the effort. Her eyes sparkled in the dimly lit bedroom, not only with post-coital bliss but also with frustration. The cool night air, courtesy of the apartment's air conditioner, and the warmth of their bodies balanced each other out nicely. "Too sensitive," she said, taking a few deep breaths and fanning herself with the palm of her hand. "You're on fire tonight. It's been a while since you ravished me like this. What's going on?"

He smiled, his male ego stroked—literally and figuratively—but he sensed a note of sarcasm in her voice. Or was it concern? He noticed a shift in her gaze, from teasing to probing, searching his face for whatever truth he was trying to hide. Either way, she knew something was up.

Like any man, he put in extra effort on special occasions, especially when they wouldn't see each other for months. He was engaged in a new op, and they'd be off the grid entirely due to the dangerous nature of the work. It was a necessary precaution to keep them both safe. They wouldn't even be able to enjoy the luxury of a voice call.

He knew that Dana would disapprove of the job he had taken. He had transformed himself back into what was essentially a professional killer. She wasn't aware of his violent history—most of it, anyway—or the dangerous work that lay ahead. And he was dragging his team into the swamp with him, something that would undoubtedly upset her.

So it was a guilt fuck, plain and simple. That's where the passion came from. He felt guilty for putting himself—and possibly her—in harm's way and for lying about his past. A heavy weight settled on his chest at the thought. The guilt gnawed, feeding his fears and insecurities. He pulled her closer, hoping that the warmth of her touch could melt it away. Over the years, he had almost come to terms with these things, but now it all came rushing back. He tried to mask the onslaught, but he could never fool her when something was bothering him. She noticed right away that his smile had disappeared. Her hand reached out, touching his arm gently, a silent question hanging between them. In that touch, Jarod felt the depth of her concern, her innate ability to sense his turmoil. Her intimate knowledge of his inner workings was both a comfort and a curse.

"Come on, what is it?" she asked. The shift in Dana's posture, from relaxed to attentive, was subtle yet significant. Her fingers paused in their absent-minded tracing of lines in his palm, her touch now purposeful, seeking. The room seemed to hold its breath, waiting for Jarod's response. They briefly launched into their usual "It's nothing" and "No, really, what is it?" exchange—something they always did when one of them was troubled. He had never understood why they did that, since it never made the uncomfortable conversation go away. *I suppose it gives me time to get my lies in order.*

"The job I've taken on," he finally admitted, this time opting to be at least partially truthful, "may be less than completely ethical in nature."

Her expression softened, shifting from disappointment to fear, finally settling into support. "I see," she said, her tone reflecting the change in the room's atmosphere. The earlier tension slowly dissolved into shared understanding. She didn't press for details; she knew he wouldn't be able to discuss it, but she grasped the gravity of his confession, the weight of the choices he had made. They'd had these kinds of discussions before, and they would have them again. *I hope.*

"What can you tell me?" she asked. "Maybe I can help?"

"Not much. This one I have to deal with alone." He told her what he could, hoping to leave enough hints for her to piece together the big picture. He knew she would. She was the smartest person he had ever known, and she understood the dangers of his job, even under normal circumstances. She knew he risked his life, more or less, with every job. But she also knew they were calculated risks.

"It feels like the world is falling apart," she said after a moment of silence. Her voice carried a subtle tremble, a vulnerability she rarely showed. "The dome being bombed, the crackdowns, the loss of civil liberties. People can't live in peace for too long. Sooner or later, someone gets impatient."

He smiled. "You basically just quoted Alixha Rahena," he said.

She laughed. "I guess I did, didn't I?"

Rahena's *Manifesto of Light* might be wrong about many things, but maybe she was onto something with that quote. The uneasy truce between Legacy and the super-wealthy private interests had worked for a long time. *Sort of.* It had led to the creation of the domes, which had set humanity on a path toward redemption from its past ignorance. But there had been a price to pay for that peace and stability.

"There are some things you don't know about my past," he said after she again asked what was on his mind. "From my days in the military. It makes me suitable for some types of jobs that involve, well... it's better if you don't know any details."

He could see the concern in her eyes, but he also sensed that she had always known. The nightmares, the mood swings—it wasn't hard to put the pieces together. A few years after they had met, she stopped asking him about it, not out of resignation, he now realized, but because she understood. She didn't know the details, but she knew enough. She understood then, and she understood now. He could see it on her face. She didn't necessarily approve, of course—no one with that much goodness in their heart would ever condone the type of work he did. But she'll forgive me. For what I'm about to do. For what I am. She loved him, and he loved her for it.

"I trust you," she said, giving him a reassuring smile. "Just promise that you'll come back to me."

"I promise," he replied, pulling her close.

Dana

Try not to be intimidated by the protesters, Mrs. Lima," the task force lieutenant reassured her as they proceeded down the corridor between the construction site for the temporarily halted Frankfurt dome expansion project and the barrier holding the protesters at bay. Above, the morning sky simmered with heat and humidity just shy of a wet-bulb heat wave. The concrete beneath her feet radiated the day's accumulated heat, and the air carried the distinct odor of dust and metal. It wasn't quite the oppressive embrace of the full-blown scorchers plaguing The Meds or North Africa, but the air was thick enough to make her wish for the relief of shade or even a single breeze. *Or for doing an about-face and marching right back through the checkpoint into the dome. Never mind the damn field office.*

Dana felt a flash of annoyance at his attempt to downplay the protesters' potential threat. The reassurance did nothing for her, as the tight knot of anxiety nestled in her stomach indicated. *They look pretty bitey to me.*

She struggled to remember his name; there had been too

many lately. Brett, was it? They had met back at the briefing.

"Please, don't call me that," she said, smiling to soften the rebuke. "It makes me feel like I'm a thousand years old."

"Roger that, Mrs. Lima," he replied in a distinctly West Coast American accent, with a hint of German coming through. He returned the smile. "What would you like us to call you?"

A moment of levity. The man had gentle eyes and projected comfort, yet the returning smile did little to ease the undercurrent of electrical tension running through her. The German intonation was subtle, almost imperceptible. Had they encountered each other under different circumstances, she doubted she would have even detected it, but now everything was on edge, all her senses on high alert. "Dana is fine," she told him. He didn't offer his own first name in return. *Brett it is, then. Or would it be Lieutenant?*

This was her first time with a police escort. She had initially resisted the idea, but now that she experienced the protests firsthand, she understood why Tatum had insisted—and was glad that he had. The barricade separating them from the shouting, chanting crowd looked awfully fragile. The winds were relatively calm today, and the rain light, which had attracted a decent number of protesters. So far, everything had remained relatively peaceful. Nevertheless, she couldn't shake the feeling that it could turn violent at any moment.

A sudden rush of adrenaline coursed through her as she watched the crowd beyond the barrier. Their voices—a cacophony of anger and passion—reached her ears as a unified roar, the individual words indistinguishable, but the sentiment crystal clear. The sun glinted off makeshift signs and banners, reinforcing that message. They cast long shadows that danced across the pavement as the crowd swayed. Yes, these people disliked the domes and Aegis. They disliked her as a representative of both. And despite the current calm, her mind raced with worst-case scenarios, struggling to quell the instinct to flee and seek the safety of the field office.

She moved closer to Tarique. Not that he could offer much protection if the group suddenly turned hostile. *Scrawny little Tari.*

Talented and loyal, but even more scared than I am. If anything happened, *she* would be the one protecting *him.* As she moved closer, her instinct to flee surrendered to one of protection. The irony of seeking comfort in fragile Tarique's familiar presence, knowing she'd be the one sheltering him, underscored the surreal nature of their situation. Surely, it makes more sense to stick to Brett or one of the other officers, no? Yet, being close to someone she knew gave her a sense of calm.

Why did I agree to this? Was it because Tatum insisted on having someone—a person, not a drone—inspect the site, and she just happened to be there, Outside? Was it a power trip for him, to show he could get her to do what he wanted, even if inspecting a compromised dome construction site wasn't part of her job description? Perhaps both those reasons were part of it, but that wasn't the whole story. Even if Tatum hadn't told her to do it, she might have insisted. Her interest, though, likely had more to do with the crowd than the site. She needed to understand what drove Gabriel and the people he represented. Drone footage only provided so much. It wasn't the same as setting foot on actual soil, taking in the scene with your own eyes, and seeing the truth unspoiled by a distant camera. She'd always been hands-on in that way. *A little danger comes with the territory.*

"The site is coming up," Brett said.

Dana activated her braid and scanned the expanse of halted machinery and unfinished latticework—the skeletal beginnings of what was meant to be a new haven for the people here. Within a few seconds, Tatum's image appeared in the upper left corner of her field of view. She'd been instructed to bring him in for the inspection, so she transferred her lens view to his. From that point on, he would see exactly what she saw.

She found it extraordinary how public opinion could shift so drastically in just a few weeks. One change in leadership, and suddenly there were protests, blockades, and the destruction of property.

"Hmm," Tatum remarked as the images came through. "The damage doesn't look that extensive. Mostly some light vandalism, as far as I can see."

Dana agreed, but knew that appearances could be deceiving. One of the two AI caterpillars had been hacked and killed, and such internal damage wouldn't be visible from an external inspection. It would take considerable effort from the tech team to fix that kind of hack. Another machine, one of the smaller tunnel-boring excavators, was simply missing, as if it had driven off on its own. They had no clue where it had gone. The construction hadn't even properly begun, and it had already ground to a near standstill.

"So, do we really think Gabriel is behind this?" Tatum asked.

"It's possible," she replied. "But if he is, he has more resources at his disposal than we initially thought."

If it was him, she suspected it was a ploy to bring the company back to the negotiating table, buying more time before Aegis closed the window, leaving them with nothing. However, it might just as easily be the work of one of the many criminal organizations operating in the area, though most of them seemed too small to pull off something like this. Regardless, they would soon have an opportunity to question him about it.

"He'll deny it, of course," Tatum said.

"Most likely," she agreed. "But we have to remember, this meeting isn't an interrogation. It's a negotiation. If we can address Gabriel's concerns and get him to—"

"I agree," Tatum interrupted. "Don't press the issue just yet. We need proof. Conduct the session according to plan. I trust your instincts on this, but if you haven't convinced him by close of business next Friday, we push ahead with the construction and deal with the legal fallout when we get there. Make sure he understands that."

"I will."

"But, uh," Tatum hesitated, "don't say it like that, obviously."

"Obviously," she echoed, slightly annoyed by the implication that she didn't know how to do her job.

"I mean, be subtle about it," he clarified.

"Of course," she said, keeping an even tone.

"You understand what I mean, right?"

"I do."

"Good," he said, and switched off, making it clear the discussion was over.

Prick.

If the company forged ahead with construction without Gabriel's signature, they'd be tied up in legal battles for the next decade. Even so, that would still be more cost-effective than a lengthy delay or, worse, abandoning the project altogether. *It's just the way things work.* And if either of those outcomes materialized, it would surely be the last contract they ever gave her. Maybe the last contract anyone would, with her reputation permanently tarnished.

"You want a sitrep now?" Brett asked.

"A what?"

"A situation report," he clarified.

Right. I gotta learn the lingo.

She instructed him to proceed, and he gave an exhaustive rundown of the site's security breaches, both physical and network-related. Most of it was beyond her understanding; she wasn't exactly a tech whiz.

"Don't worry," Brett reassured her. "Neither am I. I'm just a cop reading aloud from the tech guys' findings." He continued. "We've deployed extra drones to patrol the perimeter, and the tech gurus have fortified network security. I'm not confident it'll be enough, though, given that some of the gear used to hack the AI was top-of-the-line. But we'll also add human resources in case the drones get compromised. It won't be any easier the second time around, at least."

"So you think there'll be a second time?" Dana asked.

"Yes, Mrs. Lima. I mean, Dana. My apologies."

Brett signaled for the party to head back up the ramp toward the construction headquarters. Dana now had a scant two hours to prepare before her session with Gabriel and his team. The circumstances weren't ideal, but they would have to suffice. She'd had time during the journey from London to prepare, but somewhat regrettably, she had squandered the hours before departure in the company of Jarod. *Wait a minute! How can I regret that? Who knows when I'll see you again, my love. I miss you already.*

The cacophony of the crowd grew more boisterous as they advanced toward the construction site headquarters. Brett and the two officers stayed in flanking formation, safeguarding her and Tari against the increasingly tumultuous mob. Up ahead, on their right, the construction site gave way to an expanse of unoccupied grassland. To their left stood the makeshift five-story building that served as the site headquarters, housing administrative offices and lodging for human workers. Beyond that, the roof of the mechanized bot farm, where all the autonomous construction machinery was stabled when not in use, was just visible. Further beyond loomed the towering east side of the Frankfurt-Sachsenhausen dome.

The headquarters grew larger in the distance, though at an agonizingly slow pace. They still had several hundred yards to cover, and in that time, anything could happen. *Keep calm. We're closing in. The distance is just an illusion.*

Out of the corner of her eye, she saw Brett and the officers, all of them alert and focused. No doubt their braid's tactical AIs were scanning the crowd, performing real-time threat assessments as they moved, but that knowledge failed to soothe her nerves.

As they approached the building, the crowd began to thin out, and she allowed herself a small measure of relief. Tari seemed to relax as well, but the trio of law enforcement officers remained laser-focused. Despite her momentary calm, she couldn't help but wonder how long it would take for the drones to reach them if the crowd were to become—Become what? *Let's be optimistic and say agitated.*

If they were in real danger—if Brett and his discomfortingly small contingent of officers were to be overrun—how long before the cavalry arrived? A minute? Thirty seconds? A lot can happen in thirty seconds.

Then a loud bang shattered the air, the sudden noise causing her to jump. Her heart raced as she frantically scanned the area, trying to peek past the bulky police officers between her and the barricades. She couldn't see much, but enough to witness the picketers behind the barrier scatter. And further behind them, a massive wall of hooded, black-clad individuals, armed with rocks, sticks, bats, and perhaps even axes and Molotov cocktails, seemed to materialize out of thin air. It was like a tsunami receding from the shore, only to return as an overwhelming, all-encompassing wave.

The sight of the crowd triggered a visceral fear, but Brett and the officers sprang into action with remarkable speed, reacting almost as though they had seen the attack coming before it happened. Instantly, their forearm armor unfolded into riot shields, deflecting the sudden onslaught of rocks.

"Get down," Brett shouted, pulling Dana and Tari close with his free arm. The three officers quickly crouched around them, forming a makeshift shelter just in time to deflect a Molotov cocktail. Flames erupted all around, the heat licking at her skin and adding to the searing sun above. The air filled with the acrid scent of burning plastic. She watched in both awe and panic as Brett calmly extinguished the blaze on his exposed boot with his free hand, never once relinquishing control of the riot shield protecting them.

"Tear gas," Brett said, his voice calm and deliberate. The two other officers reacted instantly, reaching around the makeshift shelter and firing their launchers. Dana heard two sharp thumps as the canisters ejected, dispersing a choking cloud of gas. Amid the chaos, she found herself wondering where the launchers had been concealed. The officers' armor was a bit bulky, but not excessively so. She had seen no indication of any substantial weaponry besides their sidearms, and she had observed no hint of any shielding until it had been deployed, as though it had spontaneously grown out of the armor. *Must be expensive stuff.*

"Drones are inbound," one of the officers announced. "ETA, twenty seconds. Crowd dispersal protocol."

Brett nodded firmly. "Understood. Cover us. Non-lethal ordnance only," he instructed the two officers. Addressing Dana and Tari, he continued, "We're going to move toward the building, away from the gas. Stay low and behind the shield. Okay?"

Dana nodded in affirmation. Turning to Tari, who seemed petrified, almost frozen, she asked, "Are you okay?" Tari nodded hesitantly.

"Okay, let's move," Brett ordered, initiating their advance. The shield unfurled even further, while the other two officers took up positions at the back, providing cover fire as they tried to disperse the crowd. Dana and Tari remained behind the shield, evading the barrage of rocks that pelted the armor.

"Don't worry," Brett reassured them, knocking on the inside of the shield. "This baby can withstand a shotgun blast at point-blank range. A few rocks aren't gonna get through."

Yeah, not through, but what about whatever slips by it? Or over it. Or underneath it?

The shield had impressive coverage, no doubt about it, especially for something that was virtually non-existent a few seconds ago, but she could see there were gaps. As they moved, their footsteps echoed off the pavement, hurried yet determined, the calming rhythm of escape in her ears. Her breath shortened into sharp gasps in the heat, each inhale tasting of smoke, tear gas, and fear. Despite the cover and their progress, she couldn't help but think a second Molotov cocktail hitting closer to the ground in front of them could have a very different outcome than the first.

The crouched march toward the building was a surreal procession, each step a battle against overwhelming fear and the physical barrier of debris that littered their path. Brett's reassurance about the shield's durability was a small comfort. Finally, after what felt like an eternity, she heard the whine of drone motors overhead, followed by the unmistakable rat-a-tat-tat of automatic gunfire, yelling, and running feet. Looking up, careful not to trip as they pressed on, she counted at least ten drones, in addition to the ones that had already flown past them.

The hammering of rocks against the shield subsided quickly after that, and one of the officers soon signaled that they were out of danger. Brett retracted his shield back into his forearm armor, revealing an area ablaze from the Molotov cocktails, with smoke from the tear gas canisters still lingering in the air. But the crowd was gone, every last one of them. The silence that followed the drones' intervention was almost as shocking as the violence had been—a sudden void where noise and fury had reigned. The smell of smoke and tear gas stung, a bitter reminder of the confrontation, as they made their way to the safety of the building. In the end, a few rock-throwing radicals were no match for a contingent of armed attack drones.

"Alright, let's move," Brett said firmly. "Let's get inside before anything else happens." He gave Dana and Tari a gentle push, urging them toward the building at a brisk pace.

Well, this wasn't exactly what I signed up for. I should ask for more money. She conjured up a grin, an attempt at humor in a tense situation—a coping mechanism, she surmised, tempering the realization of how close they had come to real harm. The truth was that she was terrified, her sense of security utterly shaken. On the bright side, she wouldn't have to venture outside again for the remainder of the project. There was no way the lawyers at Aegis would ever allow Tatum to pull something like this again. *One can only hope.*

The atmosphere in the makeshift conference room, crammed into a forgotten windowless corner of the construction headquarters, was now stale. At this point, the air was rank, even, with carbon dioxide and sweat after hours of fruitless debate. The rustling of the overworked aircon provided a rhythmic backdrop to the proceedings, while the harsh light of the overhead fluorescents cast creepy shadows around the room, emphasizing the weariness on everyone's faces. Dana did her best to maintain a composed demeanor as she repeatedly labored to address Gabriel's concerns. Round three of the negotiation was no more productive than round two, which had hardly advanced beyond round one. How does one reason with someone so definitively stubborn? Her mounting frustration kept pace with the ever staler atmosphere of the room.

"So what exactly is still missing, Mr. Gabriel?" she asked for what seemed like the hundredth time, doing her best to mask her frustration—each repetition of the question felt like chipping away at a brick wall. Gabriel's response continued to be less than encouraging. "So ten percent of the people of Niederrad will receive upgraded accommodations in the new arcology," he said dismissively. "So what? What do I tell the other 90 percent? And who gets upgraded and who doesn't?"

"With all due respect," Tatum interjected over the holographic link, "that's your problem. This is what baffles me about Europeans. Everything must be absolutely equal for everyone to be happy. For God's sake, can't you just—"

Dana's heart skipped a beat, apprehension coursing through her as Tatum's irritability threatened to boil over. He had been testy and impatient for the last hour, but now he was furious. Dana quickly intervened before he caused irreversible harm to the negotiations. "What Mr. Tatum means is that we don't have the resources to upgrade accommodations for one hundred thousand people. Nobody does."

The intermittent static crackle and flickering of the holographic link added a layer of distance, making Tatum's outbursts feel simultaneously intrusive and remote, the faint shimmer of his image a cold contrast to the heated debate—admittedly, one growing colder by the minute.

Tatum grunted audibly at her reply, but Gabriel and his five-man delegation remained unfazed. The others never said much, preferring Gabriel to do all the talking. Dana observed their stoic faces, disillusionment hitting her as she realized the depth of the divide. Their silence was a heavy presence in the room whenever Gabriel stopped talking. It was almost as if they were there just for show, she thought to herself. This so-called citizen council was poorly organized, and she wasn't even sure if it could be considered a council at all.

More like a ragtag band of... what? Cowboys? Is there such a thing as a German cowboy?

But the law was on their side. The people's needs and desires had to be given due consideration before any arcology construction could proceed. Tatum wasn't exactly modest about his view on that particular piece of legislation. He believed the individual who came up with it was an imbecile. In his opinion, no arcology construction meant certain death, and any deal the company offered would be superior to that. *Take it or die. I'm starting to see that point of view, to a certain extent. But I can also see theirs.*

"Why don't we table the discussions," Dana suggested. "It's been a long day, and we've covered a lot. Let's reconvene tomorrow at our usual time of 10 a.m."

The suggestion hung in the air for a moment.

"Fine by me," Tatum responded, abruptly disconnecting without another word. The click of the holographic projector cutting out marked a sad end to the session.

A mix of relief and resignation washed over Dana as Tatum's hologram flickered out, the abrupt end to the meeting leaving a bitter taste. Gabriel's handshake—formal yet devoid of warmth—was a tangible reminder of the day's futile efforts.

Dana turned to Tari, who had diligently taken notes along with the secretarial AI throughout the meeting, as required by regulation. "I'll go over these right away," he said before departing.

Exhausted, Dana made her way back to her cramped quarters and collapsed onto her bunk. She decided to take a short nap before calling Chaboney for the debriefing.

The quiet of her quarters contrasted with the day's chaos, the solitude of her borrowed space offering a momentary reprieve despite the nagging thoughts that refused to quiet. The bunk's now somewhat familiar, slightly lumpy mattress was a welcome relief for her tired body, though each contour reminded her she wasn't in her own bed, nestled closely against Jarod's chest.

She wasn't thrilled about contacting her old mentor. The fact that she still needed advice on negotiation tactics bothered her, but after the day's disappointing outcome, it was clear that she did. She set her braid to wake her in thirty minutes to ensure she didn't sleep through the rest of the day.

God, I don't think I've ever been this tired. A profound weariness enveloped Dana, deeper than mere physical exhaustion.

Thoughts of Jarod offered fleeting solace, yet his absence cast a long shadow, amplifying her sense of isolation amidst the unresolved tension of the negotiations.

Once upon a time, Dana had enjoyed visiting Frankfurt. The city wasn't as boring as its reputation suggested, but at present, all she wanted was to hop on the bullet back to London and wrap herself in Jarod's comforting embrace. Yet he wouldn't be there. He was off on his latest high-paying, yet potentially dangerous and ethically questionable, job—and now completely cut off from her. All his jobs were risky to one extent or another, but this time it felt different, and she worried about him. *It's a good thing this negotiation is difficult.*

The work kept her preoccupied. Today, she found herself thinking of Jarod only a thousand times, instead of the million times she had yesterday. Perhaps tomorrow, she'd think of him only a hundred times. *So, here's to that!* But she was exhausted, both from the negotiations and from worry.

Her train of thought slowly faded into a drowsy half-sleep. It was the kind of slumber where you drift off into Neverland, yet remain conscious of yourself and the fact that you're lying in bed. It wouldn't be long before she fell into a deep, proper sleep. She instructed her braid to set an alarm for thirty minutes. *Too tired. Half an hour won't be enough.* In her sleepy haze, she mustered just enough energy to reset it for forty-five instead, before settling back onto the pillow. Setting the clock was a negotiation itself, bargaining with herself for another few minutes before having to return to jarring reality.

However, the second her head hit the cushion, the alarm blared, startling her awake. It was as if she hadn't slept at all.

"Don't worry about it," Chaboney assured her after she caught him up on the latest. "Even the best negotiators need a hand every once in a while, including you." She had him thumbnailed in the upper right corner of her lens, his artificial presence still carrying a warmth in the air-conditioned room as she lay on her lumpy mattress. Dana felt a certain relief at his acknowledgment, acting as a balm to her bruised professional ego. Despite her extensive experience, this particular negotiation had left her feeling more out of her depth than she cared to admit.

She hadn't spoken with Marc in quite some time. She justified it by telling herself that she didn't want to disturb him in his retirement; however, deep down, she suspected she was simply being a lousy friend. *You can call too, you know!*

The silence in her head following that thought was filled with distant memories of her youth, when Chaboney had taken her under his wing and showed her the ropes. While that was true, guilt still bothered her for neglecting their friendship. Blaming respect for his retirement didn't quite cut it as an excuse.

"Marc, I'm at a loss here," she said. "They aren't budging, no matter what incentives we propose. We can't put them all in Class A homes, provide private schooling for everyone, or give everyone access to expanded healthcare. Even if Aegis were willing to pay for it—which they aren't—the infrastructure simply couldn't handle it." The room seemed to close in around her. As she spoke, she realized her voice carried a tone—one of desperation and resignation, the weight of her failure. The grim reality of her limitations, juxtaposed with Gabriel's unwavering, unreasonable demands, left her feeling there was no way to win. She shouldn't feel this way—Gabriel was the problem, not her—but she did anyway.

"Just a moment," Marc said, his expression turning blank as he accessed his braid to review documents. Watching Marc retreat into the digital realm, Dana felt a momentary disconnect, a pause in their conversation that underscored the difficulty she faced. A silent acknowledgment of the complexity of the situation. The moment stretched on, filled with the soft tapping of her fingers against her thigh. Each second Marc spent in absence amplified her anticipation for a breakthrough, even though she knew there probably wouldn't be one.

Marc had experience negotiating dome expansions in the U.S., but the European market posed new challenges. Dana had grown up believing that Americans and Europeans shared the same core values. However, she had come to realize this was not entirely true. Americans tended to accept the notion that not everyone could have everything all the time, as long as there was fair competition and a chance to move up in the world. In contrast, her experience negotiating in the EU had been more demanding. Inside the domes, everyone was better off. True, some had it better than others, but no one was worse off compared to being left outside, where death eventually awaited. *That is the general idea, at least.*

A minuscule sliver of enlightenment appeared amidst the frustration as she pondered the cultural chasm between her expectations and the reality of European negotiations. It was a bitter pill, acknowledging that her foundational beliefs about shared values were not as universal as she had thought.

However, in the baffling case of Niederrad, Germany, it was almost as if they didn't want the expansion at all, a phenomenon she had never encountered before. She simply couldn't understand why anyone would reject the opportunity to live in a safer, more prosperous, albeit somewhat unequal, environment. The allocation algorithms were supposedly fair, giving everyone an equal chance, and once inside, every opportunity to excel and move up existed. In the meantime, other types of support were made available.

Dana's mind wrestled with the paradox of resistance, her logical understanding clashing with the emotional realization that not all progress was welcomed. The notion that some might prefer the dangers of the Outside to the security of the domes was a concept that both fascinated and bewildered her.

Intrigued by the possibility of finding similar cases, Dana tasked a bot to do some digging. The results came back in less than a minute, revealing that such cases were not unheard of. There were currently forty-seven dome expansion projects underway worldwide, with twelve in Europe, twenty-three in Asia, ten in North America, and one each in South America and Africa. All of these projects faced resistance, and the vast majority had experienced some form of mass protest, with many turning violent. However, most of the negative themes expressed by the protesters focused on technicalities and other specific concerns.

People protested when their homes were demolished to make way for support structures or levees in coastal areas, or when they were forcibly moved. Some protested a perceived injustice in the wealth conversion algorithm when translating outside affluence levels to inside. Others protested the addition of various types of infrastructure, such as skyways, vertical farming facilities, or construction outside their balconies, which ruined the view. Still others protested the choice of the construction site itself, questioning why the DomeEX AI algorithm seemed to prioritize wealthy areas such as London and New York, rather than poorer, more exposed places like Dhaka, where dome construction had not even begun.

I sometimes wonder about that last one myself. The breadth of resistance unearthed by the bot's search sparked a complex cocktail of emotions in Dana. There was validation in knowing Frankfurt was not an isolated case, yet the prevalence of dissent cast a shadow over her mission, adding layers of doubt to an already tangled web of challenges.

Millions of people had already been displaced by eroding coastlines and frequent flooding, and while the influence of money and power seemed the obvious factors behind such outcomes, DomeEX representatives insisted their allocation algorithm was as fair as it could be. They referred to their famous—and controversial—claim that it took into account the good of humanity as a whole when recommending construction sites, rather than just focusing on current hotspots. The human race was in a battle for its very survival, and in that struggle, not everyone could be saved. Nevertheless, conspiracy theories abounded, and protests often erupted. Dana didn't give much credence to grand conspiracies, but she had to admit that the DomeEX algorithm seemed to prioritize material assets over people, which primarily favored the wealthy population centers of the West.

In twelve percent of cases, however, reports indicated resistance to the inclusion itself—not because of technicalities or perceived injustice, but because people simply preferred to live outside. Most of these cases had occurred in Republican-controlled areas of the United States, where dome expansion was seen as a limitation on personal freedom. Frankfurt, however, was the first European city where this sentiment had presented itself in a significant way.

The bot also returned results on the world's 211 new dome construction projects, including the 22 facilitated by the UN DomeEX program, and all associated expansions. Dana set aside that summary for now but instructed her braid to log a reminder, as it suggested that similar instances of resistance had been reported there.

"Your enigmatic Mr. Gabriel," Marc said, his baritone voice interrupting her train of thought, "isn't concerned about the distribution of wealth. I believe this is about autonomy."

You read my mind. His words of confirmation seemed to shift the energy of the room, reigniting her resolve. The room itself suddenly seemed brighter in the dim light from her bedside lamp.

"Look into the shadows," he continued. "Whenever there's change, there are winners and losers. You'll likely find the answer in his private interests. Perhaps, in illegitimate ones."

A surge of hope—a potential avenue for investigation that promised answers, yet hinted at murky depths and moral ambiguity she didn't necessarily want to explore. But it was a sound idea, hampered somewhat by the fact that she had already tasked both Tarique and her braid AI with such a mission, and they had found nothing. While Gabriel was a successful businessman, no illegal financial ties, no secret dealings could be traced back to him.

"Then you must go deeper," Marc urged. "It is there somewhere."

She understood what he was hinting at. To truly uncover Gabriel's secrets would require stealth tracers—the kind of digital bloodhounds that could track a mouse fart across the net. But such tools came with complex legal implications that couldn't be ignored. She'd have to clear it with Tatum. He'd have to clear it with Legal, and in turn, they'd have to clear it with the external lawyers, and finally, they'd have to clear it with the regulator. The bureaucracy alone would take days, if not weeks, to navigate.

The decision to deploy stealth tracers also carried a burden—a deliberate step into a gray area that blurred the lines between due diligence and invasion of privacy. And after all that, the answer might very well be no. Tatum would likely skip the permissions, the egotistical sociopath that he was. He always did what he wanted, damn the consequences. And he had Aegis' full support, though the board would never admit it.

Do I have a choice? With hardened resolve, driven by both curiosity and the necessity of the job, she decided she didn't. But the unease she felt was definitely real. Gabriel was obviously a crook, and if she proceeded, who was she really hurting? Certainly not the people of Niederrad.

With a subtle eye movement, she authorized the tracers to commence, the confirmation on the lens hovering above her head. If the tracers worked through the night, they might yet uncover something of use. The Outside wasn't known for its immaculate data integrity, but nonetheless, it might be worthwhile, so she sent her request through the network. Encrypted, naturally. It didn't take more than a few minutes for Tatum to greenlight the operation. So fast, he probably didn't even bother with the company lawyers. There wouldn't have been enough time. *Predictable. I do work for a greedy mega-corporation, after all.* Their logic tracked; the loss they'd suffer from failing to secure a final agreement and delaying construction would be far greater than any regulatory fine—including the legal expenses for fighting it in court for a decade.

As the negotiations resumed the following day, it was evident that Chaboney's suspicions were right on the money. The tracers' efforts had yielded nothing, and it was clear that more laborious, manual digging would be necessary if they were going to find anything. They simply didn't have the time, but to further test their theory, she dangled increasingly enticing incentives before Gabriel—offers that far exceeded any bounds of rational economic viability—but he remained obstinate, to a point where any person would reasonably be labeled insane.

The tension in the room remained unchanged. A sense of futility enveloped Dana as the negotiations went on, each rebuffed offer and unreasonable demand from Gabriel reinforcing the impasse. But in that futility, there was also hope. She knew his game now.

The delegation kept adding outlandish demands, and after again conferring with Chaboney, they reached a shared and final conclusion: Gabriel had never intended to allow the construction to proceed. The madcap requests were merely a stalling tactic, intended to delay the project's realization indefinitely. *Now, the only question is why?*

...in terms of Gross Domestic Product (GDP) per capita, the median level of wealth *Inside* is estimated to be 2.8 times greater than that of the *Outside* in the West. It is projected that this number will increase to 3.6 over the next fifty years. However, in developing regions, the same figure rises to as much as 11 times. When comparing the typical *Outside* in West Africa to the *Inside* regions of Europe or North America, the difference increases to over 40…

...for several centuries, human society has had the resources to provide wealth beyond the threshold of abject poverty for all individuals, yet this has not been achieved. The reasons for this are plentiful and have been subject to extensive debate. Numerous solutions to the problem of distributive justice have been proposed, from Aristotle to Rousseau, from Locke to Marx, from Rawls to Nozick, and from Sen to Dworkin. In real politics, capitalism, socialism, Leninism, social-democratic welfare states, supply-side economics, full employment, and other concepts have been implemented to varying degrees, and none have been successful in achieving...

...a new life awaits you in one of California's City Domes—a chance to begin again in the golden land of opportunity and adventure. Join the California State City Dome Lottery today! Why wait in the UN domeex Relocation Program when you can... [Skip Ad in 10s]...

...total population is in decline, with most developing countries now also exhibiting birth rates below the replacement rate. Nevertheless...

...of the world's 8.7 billion people, approximately two billion individuals still live below the United Nations' absolute poverty line, while another five billion live in close proximity to it...

...the Scandinavians appeared to have found a promising solution during the latter half of the twentieth century. However, in the end, even they were unsuccessful. The concept of domes offers a similar promise to these past ideologies. Once the necessary structures have been extended to include everyone, a utopia will emerge with an abundance of shelter, sustenance, artificial intelligence, and robots for all—the latter two even freeing humanity from the toils of labor. Nevertheless, the domes, like all other attempts, will fall short. The provision of wealth for all in human societies remains an elusive...

...despite leveraging the immense computational power of quantum computers and artificial intelligence, no mechanism has been developed to achieve a more equitable distribution of wealth...

...with reference to the Schumacher AI trial runs conducted in the 2050s, it was observed that when the AI was tasked with finding a wealth distribution that would result in favorable outcomes for all—without resorting to the tyrannical removal of individual free will and choice—it failed. This outcome reinforces the notion that finding a solution to wealth distribution that is agreeable to all remains...

...the emergence of domes has added another layer of complexity to the challenge of achieving an equitable distribution of wealth. Despite the implementation of domes, Gini coefficients continue to move in the wrong direction, albeit not as significantly as...

...all measures of wealth, including GDP, HDI, Gini, GNH, and GGDP, consistently indicate a trend toward greater inequality. Life expectancy continues to rise in the developed world, with individuals living increasingly longer Inside compared to Outside regions. The developing world, regardless of how its borders are delineated, is no longer narrowing the gap with...

...Outside residents are experiencing limited access to advanced medical treatments, such as genetic enhancements to the immune system, resulting in a widening gap in life expectancy with the *Inside*... [...] "On paper, Outside residents have access," remarks Dr. Plimton, "but in reality, gaining entry to the *Inside* often requires a permit, even in the West, and the process is financially costly and involves overcoming considerable bureaucratic hurdles." Dr. Plimton proceeds to elaborate...

...The concept of neo-feudalism, although admittedly a controversial term, is being used to describe the concentration of vast wealth in the hands of a privileged few, primarily fueled by the exponential expansion of the tech sector and dome-owning corporations...

...although the emergence of domes has not contributed to a more equitable world, the combination of private ownership and government control has resulted in a degree of hegemonic stability...

...more than half of the world's city domes are encumbered by surrounding migration settlements that initially began as climate refugee camps...

...refugee settlements have become permanent and have taken on the characteristics of urban slums...

...in the wake of the "Great Collapse." From the 2060s onward, climate-related migration has overwhelmed existing infrastructure for handling and settling refugees. Informal settlements, often referred to as "shanties" in colloquial language, vary in size, ranging from large settlements like The Bronx in New York to smaller ones such as The Crescent, south of Frankfurt am Main, now encircling many major Western city domes. These settlements have emerged in different ways, with some developing around frontiers in areas that were previously non-urbanized, such as the outskirts of Oresund and the aforementioned Frankfurt am Main, while others have arisen within pre-existing urbanized areas that were excluded from dome construction, such as The Bronx and the pre-existing favelas of Rio de Janeiro...

...on average, the cost of general insurance for any activity or type of property is approximately three times higher on the *Outside* compared to the *Inside*. For certain types of housing and commercial real estate properties, insurance costs can be up to six times higher. In some cases, such properties on the *Outside* are simply deemed uninsurable...

Aea

Aea and Daemon strolled hand-in-hand along the viewpoint at Construction Site One. To the west, the Sachsenhausen dome towered, yet it was overshadowed by the dominating presence of Central to the north. Below them, demolition bots and auto-excavators lay silent, suspended in the interim of negotiations with the Innie official. The view was spectacular, and Aea couldn't help but be reminded of her deep-seated desire to escape Niederrad for the domes—a yearning that had lain dormant since that fateful glance at Gabriel's rally. The air was tinged with the metallic scent of construction, mingling with the earthy aroma of disturbed soil as the auto-excavators dug deeper into the foundation. The existing domes of Frankfurt loomed like giants, their surfaces reflecting the sun's rays in a bubbly pattern across the landscape.

Seeing the majesty of the domes spread over the horizon stirred a sense of awe and longing. The view rekindled it all—the glamorous life *Inside*, contrasted sharply with the dreary *Outie* existence. But above all, it reminded her of her obligation to fulfill her parents' aspirations. They had emigrated from Algeria when Aea was just a child, with Tabayah yet to be born, navigating hazardous routes through a Greek refugee camp, then France, and finally settling in Germany's Niederrad. The journey had claimed her mother's life. They had not endured such hardships to end up with their faces pressed against the glass, longing for a life just out of reach. That was the real reason she obsessively scoured those government visa applications on her visor. The allure and glitz of life *Inside*, which she acknowledged she might have romanticized, played a part in her desire, but it wasn't the heart of it.

Their hands were growing clammy in the sweltering heat wave. The sun's fervor enveloped them in a vicious embrace, and the air shimmered above the cracked pavement. *Probably a bad idea to be out on a day like this*, she thought. But there had been no official warnings issued. Their intertwined fingers were an act of defiance against the oppressive heat, and neither Daemon nor Aea had wanted to let go, even for a minute, since he had collected her from the dilapidated old playground outside her apartment complex—the smaller, less visible one at the back of the building, in view only from one apartment window. Aea had strategically chosen this location to minimize the chances of her father catching them together. A shiver crawled along her spine—a rebellious thrill at defying expectations, at choosing her own path. What she and Daemon had was theirs, and theirs alone, and the world beyond them should stay out. It wasn't just innocent teenage rebellion; it was her first step toward independence, her first steps out of the shadow cast by others' desires for her.

Her dad had not been thrilled with the news that she was dating an older boy, but Aea didn't care, and he was too busy to do anything about it. Nevertheless, the back playground served as the best choice. Aea had been the goody-two-shoes girl for too long, and it was high time she indulged in a bit of rebellion. Nothing too excessive, of course! *It's not like I'm doing drugs or anything. Just a boy, one who just happens to be slightly older. Was that so terrible? He's one to talk. Dad's older than mom was. Besides, I'm almost eighteen anyway.*

It was surely a more adventurous form of defiance than

hanging with Jema and Kaliyah outside the Neu Isenburg perimeter, sneaking cigarettes and chugging light beer while flinging rocks at the never-completed dome structure. As much as Aea cherished her time with her girlfriends, she had grown tired of that routine, and secretly frolicking with a boy was a far more exhilarating experience—even if it only amounted to holding hands. *If I want to be a rebel so much, why am I sneaking around? Why not just show it to her face?* She had no good answer to that question.

It was admittedly rather juvenile to hold hands, Aea conceded to herself, but then again, she was still in high school, so she supposed it was okay. Daemon was almost twenty, so for him, high school was in the past, but he too didn't seem to mind—as long as no one saw. He was a boy, after all, and therefore sensitive to "girly" emotional stuff. He would only release her hand briefly when he thought he spotted one of his friends, but as soon as that threat disappeared, his hand quickly found hers once more. *Guys do cutesy-wootsy things all the time as long as their pals aren't around. And as long as they think they're gonna get some!* One might think a twenty-year-old would have a more developed sense of maturity, but alas, that was not the case.

"Just look at those things," Daemon said as they crested the ridge overlooking the construction site, his voice hushed in awe, eyes fixed on the enormous demolition bots. They were currently in a powered-down state, waiting silently for the negotiations to conclude before they would steamroll half of Niederrad to make way for the dome's support structure. *They will evacuate whoever lives there first, obviously!* While such dislocation sounded awfully harsh, she was pretty sure those people would receive upgraded living spaces in the dome as compensation for the loss of their *Outie* homes. At that moment, a curious blend of hope and guilt washed over her. She sympathized with those evicted, but surely the prospect of a new beginning was something to look forward to? Despite the complexities of the situation, Aea herself could hardly contain her excitement. It would be some time yet, but eventually, she would have the opportunity to venture inside the dome—and eventually live inside it. *Maybe sooner, if Daemon can one day deliver on his hidden manhole.*

Either way, she couldn't wait, eager to experience all the wonders of dome life that her father had talked about. Daemon, on the other hand, was less enthusiastic as usual. They had been bickering about the politics of domes lately. They had fought, broken up, and gotten back together a few times already because of it, and eventually, they had simply agreed to avoid the topic altogether.

As they strolled along Site Two, the part of the dome wall that would face in the direction of the airport, they marveled at the deserted site's tranquility. The dormant machines were like sleeping giants, waiting to awaken and transform the landscape. It was oddly peaceful, a respite from the tumultuous negotiations and protests taking place at the Sachsenhausen-facing site they had strolled past a few days ago. The silence here was profound, in a way, with only light wind blowing over the dormant machinery breaking the calm. It was almost... the word escaped her momentarily. Frau Gerhling had mentioned it in class. *Post-apocalyptic! That's it! A post-apocalyptic landscape.*

She remembered it because Frau Gerhling had insisted that they read several books with a dystopian theme. Aea had picked *Brave New World* at first but lost interest after only a few pages—the language was old-fashioned and difficult to comprehend. There were others, like the one with a year for a title, and the German one by the Pausewang woman, which was set near here. In the end, she had settled for the latter. *None of those have giant construction robots in them, though.*

Frau Gerhling didn't let them watch Hollywood movies. Those had robots, and other cool stuff, so obviously such films were not part of the curriculum. However, it wasn't difficult to get one's hands on old movies.

A car appeared on the horizon, coming down the dirt path toward them. "Who do you think that is?" Aea asked. "Site security?"

Daemon squinted in the direction of the oncoming vehicle while she scanned their surroundings, wondering if they had inadvertently trespassed onto the enclosure. But that shouldn't be possible if the security personnel had done their job.

"Don't worry," Daemon reassured her. "We'll be fine."

Unless they're highwaymen. Aea had heard rumors about such outlaws, but she had never actually encountered any. Law enforcement was scarce in some *Outie* parts, and every adult she knew had warned her and the other children about these dangerous marauders at some point. She was fairly certain they were a myth—a boogeyman created to scare kids straight, like witches in the past or the pedophiles in vans tempting children with candy. Well, they probably existed somewhere, but in reality, they were far less of a threat than her mother had made them out to be when she was younger.

"There they are," Daemon said, confidence returning to his voice. "Right on time. I'd recognize that shitty old Opel anywhere. It's Ameer and Cali." Upon uttering his friends' names, he quickly released Aea's hand—not like he was preparing for a fight as he had in the tunnels, but rather, like when he believed he'd caught sight of one of his buddies—like he was embarrassed. *His crew,* as he calls them. She was dismayed at the prospect of being interrupted—she had hoped to spend the day alone, reveling in each other's company. *But I suppose I have to meet his friends sooner or later. Might as well be now.*

She had not had the pleasure of a proper introduction to Daemon's friends yet, though she had seen them, and they had exchanged a few words outside of school when he came to pick her up, but that was it. She hadn't properly introduced him to Jema and Kali either. *I guess our relationship isn't at that point just yet.* The Opel screeched to a halt in front of them, kicking up a cloud of dust, disturbing the serene display. *But maybe it'll change right now?*

As the old combustion engine unwound, it gave way to the gritty cracking of gravel under the tires, and the air suddenly smelled of exhaust fumes. *This thing must be half a century old,* she mused. The guy on the passenger side rolled down the window and stuck out his head, snickering at the sight of them.

"Aw, isn't this cute," he jeered. "Remember, if you're going to do it, don't forget to slap a raincoat on it!" He and the driver both burst into laughter.

"Fuck off, Cali," Daemon snapped back. "When was the last time you were with a girl?" The jab seemed to strike a nerve, but only momentarily.

"I was with your mom last night," he quipped with a smirk, earning a middle finger reply. *Boys! Always so insecure.*

Ameer emerged from the driver's side of the Opel. "Hey, the protests at Sachsenhausen are heating up," he announced. "Are we going or what? I heard the Innie lady went outside. She's there right now, at the other end of the site."

Aea could see a smirk form on Daemon's face. *Oh, so this is why we came out here today,* she thought. *He intended to go and wants to drag me along.*

At first, she felt ambushed, but also found herself strangely enticed by the idea and decided to come along. That they shouldn't was a given. Nobody needed to tell her that those demonstrations could be dangerous. But how dangerous? The news warned of potential violence, but as long as they kept a safe distance, they'd probably be okay. Daemon's look was one of determination—he clearly intended to go, and she either went along or went home. In the end, she decided to go and climbed in, parking herself on the worn faux leather of the backseat. The car's interior reeked of sweat and anticipation despite the windows being rolled down. The AC was busted, of course.

"Are we sure we want to do this?" Ameer said as he revved the engine. "Gabriel told us to stay away."

"Just go," Cali said abruptly, clearly indicating that the decision was already made. Ameer grunted and drove them off.

They parked their car some distance away, near the soaring old Leonardo Hotel skyscraper that stood across from the Südfriedhof cemetery on Darmstädter. The building had been abandoned for as long as she could remember, and over time the relentless pounding of storms had reduced it to a creepy, haunted house. It was now one of those places that parents cautioned their children to avoid—warnings that, of course, made it only more alluring to daring youngsters. Among these adolescent adventurers, rumors circulated about the ghosts of former guests roaming the halls. *But that's just silly kid's stuff.*

The hotel and surrounding buildings bore the marks of decay, the once-grand facade now marred by the scars of angry weather and graffiti. As they passed the skyscraper, she felt a rush of nostalgia, the building's tall shadow a ghostly marker of childhood bravado and fears. Aea herself had scaled the fence guarding the property countless times when she was a little girl, playing ghost hunter or urban warrior inside the abandoned structure. It was eerie, no doubt, but she had never encountered any otherworldly beings. No real ones, anyway. What she and her friends had done, however, was climb the long stairs to the upper floors, daring each other to listen to the harrowing sounds of hurricanes battering the outer walls. They'd take care to steer clear of the paneless windows to avoid being caught by the fierce gusts of wind, but even so, it was frightening enough.

But those games were distant memories now. Childish antics. As they grew older, the building became a place to loiter, smoke, drink, and engage in romantic escapades. However, that was long ago as well. These days, Aea, Jema, and Kali preferred the Neu Isenburg dome as their rendezvous spot, being located farther away from watchful adult eyes.

As they approached the protest site, the commotion was already in full swing, the air vibrating with the energy of the crowd. As they stepped out of the car, a cacophony of shouts and chants reached their ears. The air reeked of sweat and asphalt, the anticipation and anger radiating. It took some maneuvering, but they managed to worm their way through the crowd and reach the barricades. Ameer and Cali—with a C, mind you, not to be confused with her friend Kaliyah—had been truthful. There was indeed the Innie lady.

It was obvious she wasn't from the outside. The way she dressed was a dead giveaway. *Nobody from here wears clothes like that.* Not that Outies were dirty or unkempt, but there was a certain neatness to her attire, a tidiness that set her apart. It was hard to articulate exactly what it was, but there was something about her that was just... different.

The woman's attire was something straight out of the movies: a silky jacket, pantsuit style, and elegant shoes. She was beautiful and had put on makeup. Sure, plenty of people on the outside wear makeup too, but it was as if she shone a bit brighter than anyone from here. *And the police escort is a dead giveaway!* Only those on their way to jail get such treatment on this side of the dome wall. Glancing over at Daemon and his friends, she could see they were mesmerized by the lady.

The Innie official moved with an elegance that seemed to slice through the dense air, her attire a sharp contrast to the drab, utilitarian, heat wave-appropriate clothes of the protesters. The sunlight caught on her silky jacket, making her appear like a beacon amidst the chaos. As she passed by, right on the other side of the barricade, Aea could've sworn she caught a waft of the lady's perfume, a blend of jasmine and something unidentifiable. Aea felt an unsettling mix of admiration and resentment billow inside. The Innie woman's elegance, so clearly at odds with the dried husk of the Outside, baking in the heat wave, sparked an unexpected twinge of envy. But the look in Daemon's eyes unsettled her more. It was a look she had not seen before—one of fire and brimstone. *I wonder what their obsession is all about?* she thought. The Innie lady was, of course, negotiating in direct opposition to Gabriel and the Council, and Daemon worked for him. That was all she knew. *She's clearly a big deal with all that security.*

Given the ongoing protests, it wasn't entirely surprising that the Innie woman had an escort. Nonetheless, Aea couldn't help but feel that if the tables were turned and Gabriel, or any other Outie, were to visit the dome—protests or not—they wouldn't receive the same level of protection. Or perhaps they would, but the escort would be there to safeguard the interests of the Innies, not the Outie. To the Innies, those from beyond the checkpoint were, more often than not, viewed as dangerous savages. *Just like we think they are all stuck up and arrogant.*

Elites. That was the word Frau Gerhling had used in social studies. The topic of dome expansion had been extensively discussed, along with the issue of stereotypes. Frau Gerhling had explained how it was a common human tendency to demonize those who were different. She had emphasized that most Innies were just like them—ordinary people who happened to be fortunate enough to live in the right place when the domes were built.

"Only three cops," Daemon remarked, pointing to the Innie lady and her entourage.

Cali snickered. "Idiots. We could probably take them."

"Don't worry," Daemon said sarcastically. "They have all the firepower they need. You just can't see it."

He probably means drones. Her heart raced at the thought, the anticipation of conflict suddenly palpable in the air. Heat wave or not, today the winds were relatively calm. Drones would be able to fly.

The dome lady and the police were apparently done with whatever they were doing and quickly pivoted on their heels, making their way back up the dirt path to the construction headquarters.

Just as the quartet began their protesting, Aea was jolted by a loud bang, followed by a bellowing scream in a foreign language, distorted as if shouted through a bullhorn. It wasn't any language she had heard before—not French or German, and certainly not English. Suddenly, a group of masked protesters dressed in black descended upon the railing separating the picketers from the Innie woman and her police entourage. The people in the front row smoothly dispersed, almost as if it had all been rehearsed. The police officers reacted promptly, riot shields deploying in an instant, as if they had appeared out of thin air, in anticipation of an incoming volley of rocks from the attackers. Someone hurled a Molotov cocktail that collided with the shields and ignited the area, setting it ablaze.

The explosion of the Molotov cocktail filled the air with the acrid smell of burning chemicals. The flames added to the ambient temperature as a wave of immense heat washed over her. Time seemed to warp, the moment stretching into an eternity as the fire erupted, casting a hellish glow over the faces around her. Aea's breath hitched, terror rooting her feet to the ground. The screams and cries of the crowd, the clatter of riot shields, and the crackle of fire melded into chaos, disorienting and terrifying in its ferocity. Beside her, Daemon was transformed—the sweet boy she had gotten to know seemed consumed by the fury of the moment, his eyes full of anger.

Daemon's voice cut through the chaos. "Come on, let's go!" he yelled, pulling Aea along with him as they sprinted toward the barricades. She tried to protest, but it was too late. Daemon was already lost in the fray, scooping up loose rocks along the way and hurling them at the oversized shields protecting the dome lady and her entourage.

He released his grip on Aea as he approached the barricades, unleashing a barrage of rocks, sticks, and anything he could find along the railing. Cali followed suit. Meanwhile, Ameer and Aea hung back, choosing to stay in the background at a safe distance. She was a bit taken aback by how rapidly and thoroughly Daemon had been consumed by rage, as if a switch had been flipped, and he had been turned on.

The police retaliated by opening fire with rubber bullets, or at least that's what it appeared to be. People in the crowd were undoubtedly struck, but they didn't seem to be seriously wounded. Some cried out in agony, others stumbled, and a few tumbled over. However, some of them got back on their feet and continued to hurl projectiles. The law enforcement officers were vastly outnumbered, and a few rounds from non-lethal riot guns would not be enough to quell the disturbance.

As the air filled with the whine of drone motors, punctuated by the smatter of gunfire, Aea's fear morphed into desperation. The sight of Daemon, now a stranger driven by hatred, clashed with the memory of his touch from just hours before. She found herself unconsciously taking a step back, acutely aware of what was about to happen. Everyone not blinded by rage knew it too. It didn't take long for the drones to swoop in and rain down hell on the attackers with an entirely different level of firepower. The drones were incredibly precise, accurately targeting vulnerable areas like knees and shoulders—areas most humans would struggle to hit, even with AI aiming assists, particularly when dealing with a moving target. Not a single bullet was wasted. Within a minute, the area was cleared.

As the crowd dispersed, Aea noticed that Daemon had been hit and was now lying prone on the ground, writhing in pain. She screamed, and Cali turned back, trying to drag him to safety. Despite Ameer's attempts to restrain her, Aea broke free and ran toward Daemon. However, she too was struck, the bullet hitting her in the thigh, causing her to tumble and hit her forehead on the gravel. Dazed, she looked up to see Cali still struggling to drag Daemon away, while the drones closed in on them from above.

You can tell only guys live here. The unmistakable stench of masculine funk permeated the apartment. The air was thick with the stale odor of unwashed bodies and old food, a pungent reminder of the apartment's neglect. Sunlight streamed through the sheer curtains covering the windows, casting beams of light on the chaos within. Aea wasted no time in flinging open every available window, hoping to at least partially dissipate the noxious fumes, clearly built up for weeks, if not months. Stuff was strewn everywhere—from dirty dishes and underwear to empty food packages and beer cans. Still reeling from the events at the protest, she robotically began clearing things away, keeping busy to manage the shock.

As they had limped back from the protest, Daemon had mentioned that this was one of Gabriel's apartments, which they "borrowed" or rented, or something of the sort. Aea didn't bother to inquire further. *The damned apartment should be the last thing on my mind*, she thought as she slumped down on the living room couch.

"I want to kill those fuckers," Cali growled, limping back and forth through the living room, in front of the wallscreen.

"Arschloch. Connards." *A high school dropout, but he can swear in multiple languages.*

The news of the drone attack was slowly filtering in, but to the boys' disappointment, it was relegated to a mere footnote at the end of the newscast, dismissed as a minor event. "Minor event! Tell that to my arm. Those bastards deserve to die," Cali seethed. His voice was raw, his anger unmistakable in the tight space of the living room. The flickering light from the wallscreen cast his face in stark relief, shadows playing over his features as he paced, limping slightly.

Aea retrieved a bag of frozen peas from the freezer and held it to Daemon's injured shoulder, then grabbed a towel filled with ice cubes for her own thigh. "Maybe you should ice too, Cali? There's another pack left in the freezer," she suggested.

Cali scoffed. "Fuck you. Ice is for weaklings."

"Hey!" Daemon reprimanded him. "Don't talk to her like that."

The tension in the apartment was like static, charged with anger, fear, and something new. They were upset about the police intervening, about being hit—that was understandable. But Aea felt a chill, not from her injuries, which were light, and not from the shocking experience at the construction site, but from witnessing Daemon's transformation at the scene. How a switch had flipped and turned him into something she never, in her wildest dreams, thought he was. Even now, after they had all cooled down somewhat, he was not the same. His defense of her from Cali was appreciated, but the force, the anger in his voice was still there, and it scared her.

"Why not?" Cali snapped. "Why are we even bringing her along? Is she part of our crew now or something?"

Daemon, his gaze fixed intently on Cali, did not flinch.

"She's slowing us down," Cali persisted, his eyes equally unflinching. Aea wondered if this was some kind of male dominance display, a contest of wills between two alpha males. *Boys and their macho bullshit!*

Daemon leaned in close, his words almost a whisper as he spoke into Aea's ear, but still making sure Cali heard him.

"Don't worry," he assured her. "He doesn't mean it. He's just angry." It took a moment, but Cali's eyes finally dropped to the floor. He punched the wall in frustration before sitting down, finally quiet.

Ameer had remained silent since the attack, his eyes now fixed on the news playing in the background. He was perched on the opposite end of the couch from Cali, knees tucked up against his chest. He had stayed away during the attack, managing to avoid getting hit by one of the rubber bullets. But Cali had been relentless in his taunts, goading him for being a coward. Aea couldn't help but wonder why Ameer didn't stand up for himself. In her eyes, he wasn't a coward; he was the only one who had kept his wits about him during the chaos. He had stayed back—exactly what they all should have done.

To an outsider, it might have seemed like bullying, with Cali pushing the timid Ameer around. But Aea knew better. Or so she hoped. It was just good-natured ribbing, she told herself—a bit rough around the edges, perhaps, but ultimately harmless. She was confident that, when it really mattered, Cali would have their backs, Ameer included. And Ameer was just scared, as anyone would be in a situation like this. *I certainly am.* Cali was too, albeit he expressed it through anger.

While Cali and Daemon discussed their next move, Aea tended to Daemon's injured shoulder. It was clear, at this point, that the two of them were unsure what their course of action would be. Ameer finally spoke up. "Maybe we should let Gabriel handle this. He knows what he's doing."

Cali scoffed at the suggestion. "Gabriel just talks. He never takes any action," he spat out. In a sudden, threatening motion, Cali grabbed Daemon by the collar of his jacket, pulling him close. Aea recoiled, feeling intimidated by the display of aggression. Daemon, however, remained stoic, steadily meeting Cali's wild gaze.

"We need to take steps," Cali insisted. "We're protecting our homes here. This is our territory, not the Innies'."

Daemon seemed to take a moment to consider Cali's words before calmly removing himself from Cali's grasp. "Yeah," he finally agreed. "We do need to take steps."

Aea had a sinking feeling in her stomach as Daemon echoed Cali's sentiment, her skin prickling with fear. The realization hit her with the force of a physical blow: the boy she thought she knew was morphing into someone unrecognizable, someone capable of violence, right before her eyes.

Daemon shoved Aea away, casting aside the pack of frozen peas in the process. He stood up, moving his arm around as if to check if it was still attached. Aea remained silent, too frightened to offer any words of encouragement or sympathy. The anger Daemon displayed had left her terrified. It was a side of him she had never seen before.

"Wait here," he ordered before disappearing into the bedroom. Aea could hear him moving heavy objects, perhaps the bed or a bookshelf. After a few minutes, he emerged, carrying a duffel bag, which he set down in the center of the room. He unzipped it with a grunt, wincing as he did so. He reached for his shoulder, grimacing in pain.

"Gabriel gave this to me," he said, gesturing to the bag. "For safekeeping in case all hell breaks loose."

Aea leaned in for a closer look. The duffel bag's contents glittered ominously under the apartment's harsh fluorescent lights, the metal of the guns cold and impersonal. The smell of oil and metal filled Aea's nostrils as she peered into the bag. She saw a shotgun, a few handguns, two military-looking rifles, and several boxes of bullets. *My God.* The sight of the weapons laid bare before her was, in that moment, a terrible confirmation of her worst fears. Aea's throat tightened, the words of protest she wanted to utter dying before even leaving her mouth. She was in shock and didn't know how to react. She didn't know much about guns, but she was pretty sure they were always bad news.

Daemon's movements were careful, almost reverent, as he handled the weapons, the soft clatter of metal on metal echoing in the charged atmosphere. He clearly knew his way around weapons—another shock to Aea's system. She opened her mouth to speak, but her words were drowned out by Cali's sudden outburst of joy and fury.

"We're gonna kill that Innie bitch!" he yelled, reaching for one of the military rifles.

Daemon swatted his arm away before he could grab it. "Nobody touch anything," he commanded.

Cali looked both disappointed and angry, but he didn't argue with Daemon. Daemon zipped up the bag of weapons and declared, "I'll distribute the weapons when the time comes." He disappeared back into his bedroom, dumping the bag of weapons, and then returned.

Daemon sat down, wincing as he reapplied the now soggy, increasingly room-temperature bag of peas to his sore shoulder. "We're not going to kill anyone," he stated firmly, his voice carrying an undercurrent of something unsteady, something almost deranged. "We're going to snatch her. And then we'll exchange her for what we want."

Cali nodded eagerly in agreement. The room spun around Aea as they discussed. She couldn't believe what she was hearing. To kidnap, to bargain with a life. *They must be joking. Yes, that's it! Has to be.* But as her gaze fixed on Daemon, searching for the boy she thought she knew, she couldn't find him.

"But how?" Ameer asked. "How do we even get to someone like that? You saw the firepower they had."

Daemon grinned confidently. "I know a way."

Scott

The roar of jet engines overhead was constant, a rumbling cacophony that drowned out softer sounds and lent a sense of impermanence to their gathering. The occasional whiff of jet fuel wafted down when older, non-sustainable fuel planes glided past, mingling with the earthy scent of the grass beneath their feet—a stark reminder of the world that buzzed relentlessly above them.

Staying directly beneath the flight path of the incoming airliners offered some protection against prying drones—legal ones, at the very least. However, Alixha, of course, wouldn't be deterred by any such prohibition. She did as she pleased and usually got away with it. Scott also knew that plenty of other organizations would disregard the rules too, from Alixha's competitors to government-backed private security firms operating off the books. They were hardly safe, just slightly less exposed.

Despite the fierce expansion of bullet trains over the last few decades, Japan, being surrounded by water, still had a few airports remaining in operation. Narita was one of these. But still, most industry experts predicted a rapid decline of the aviation industry here, as in many other parts of the world. They had made these predictions for years, arguing that the opening of the Sino-Japanese ocean tunnel would be the final nail in the coffin, but, so far, they had been proven wrong. *Kind of like the Twentieth Century predictions that the end of crude oil was always just a decade away.*

With rush hour in full swing, and the weather relatively calm, there was a constant stream of planes landing. It was time to proceed.

"This used to be a golf course, I think," Dai remarked, grabbing Scott's hand. Her voice held a subtle note of nostalgia, barely audible above the din of traffic and planes. The field around them, with its patchy grass and the remnants of sand traps, spoke of leisurely days long gone, from when unpredictable weather allowed for lengthier activities beyond the dome frontier. *Or maybe I'm just imagining it?* His braid confirmed Dai's statement and added that the unevenly grown grass was genetically modified for optimal carbon capture, a remnant from the days when humanity still had not given up on saving the Outside. *An interesting tidbit of information, I guess.* Either way, the golf course had now been repurposed for their clandestine meeting.

"Hmm," Scott said absentmindedly, preoccupied with the security arrangements, repeatedly double-checking braid encryption protocols to ensure their privacy, and then checking them again. And then again for good measure. Lines of code rolled over his lens, individual lines of instruction flickering as the AI vetted them. Faint clicks and soft chimes from his audio implant, mingling with the distant hum of the airport and the roar of engines, provided confirmation as the work progressed. When done, he turned his attention to Aki, doing the same to ensure redundancy, busting his chops for not working quickly enough.

"It's almost done," Aki reassured him. "Will you relax?" Aki's reassurance came with an easy smile, but Scott noted the slight tension in his shoulders—a telltale sign of the pressure they were all under. Aki's usual relaxed demeanor was frayed at the edges, their task casting a shadow even on his usually unflappable spirit.

Yeah, well... That's the thing, isn't it? I can't relax. Since receiving the order to deploy the nuke, Scott had been in an intense state of anxiety. *And paranoia. And depression? And delusion? What else you got? Every mental disorder ever diagnosed. I'm basically wrecked.*

Garrick gave him a sour look, undoubtedly to once more remind him of his displeasure with the situation. The look was more than just displeasure; it was one of frustration, concern, and fear. Scott knew Garrick well, and the subtle signs didn't escape him: the tightened jaw, the hard set of his eyes. The cold gaze pierced like a shard of ice. It spoke volumes about the deep bonds of brotherhood and the complex layers of loyalty that tethered them. Or, at least, had tethered them in the past. Garrick was only here out of loyalty to a friend, it seemed. *Or is it for the love of a friend?* They had years of friendship—of having each other's backs in the field and in life—but a righteous cause can be overpowering. *Can loyalty to a cause really trump the love for a friend? Or is it fear that's doing the trumping today?*

Scott pushed his concerns aside and focused on the task at hand. As he refocused, a surge of adrenaline momentarily overpowered the cocktail of emotions brewing inside him. The anxiety and paranoia were pushed to the background, replaced by the immediate need for action. Yet, the undercurrent of fear and doubt remained, a relentless whisper in the depths of his mind.

He ordered all squitos he had in the field to sound off, but only eight out of twelve reported back. The wind had caught a few of them. It was a decent day to be outside—for a human—but for small and delicate devices like the squitos, even a slight breeze could be problematic. Despite their advanced motor functions and predictive AIs, they were still vulnerable to rapid changes in environmental conditions. Today was borderline for them, even in the relatively calm winds. He launched another four to cover the gap. *At least I don't have to account for the cost anymore.* Hiding the expense from the Lux accountants was the least of his worries if Alixha got even the slightest wind of their activities. *Slightest wind. Haha. Pun intended. Sometimes I crack myself up.*

Thankfully, they didn't have to set up deflector grids to thwart satellites from spying on them. The trees in the area provided enough cover, at least against traditional cameras. However, more advanced sensors had different capabilities, and their greatest cover was the fact that no one knew they were there.

"We should've stayed inside," Garrick grumbled.

"Stop moping," Dai retorted. "It was getting too hot in there. Lux is like the fucking STASI."

"What's the STASI?" Aki asked. Aki knew his electronics. History, not so much.

The right spot had fewer people and therefore fewer prying eyes, ears, and spy gear to worry about. However, there were also downsides to consider. Masking their IDs at the checkpoint was no easy task. Unless you're Aki. They still had to contend with patrol drones, of course, and outside, satellites had a clear view of the terrain, and land-based vehicles like quads were capable of traversing almost any terrain with ease. Fortunately, they were far enough away from a dome perimeter to avoid most of those threats. Nonetheless, with Alixha, one could not afford to let their guard down.

"Okay," Aki announced. "I think we're good now."

Scott saw the disagreement brewing in Garrick's eyes, another silent challenge to the plan. He was about to interrupt, but Dai was faster. "Not a word," she snapped, grabbing his ear and squeezing it hard. "You've been complaining since we left Shinjuku. We're all aware of the risks, and we're in this together. Do you understand?"

Dai's sudden shift from calm to anger caught Scott off guard. Her outburst, though brief, was a stark reminder of the tension simmering just below the surface among them all. Her hand gripping Garrick's ear was not just a physical assertion of authority but a manifestation of the stress they were all feeling, a pressure valve releasing some of the pent-up emotions in a brief, intense flash. Scott watched Dai's outburst with a mix of admiration and concern. Her loyalty was both a comfort and a source of guilt. He knew the risks they were all taking, the immense danger they faced, and it pained him to see his friends—his family in arms—drawn into this maelstrom, a direct result of his decisions.

Garrick groaned in agony. "Alright, alright." She released him, and her demeanor quickly shifted from anger to her typical composed and collected state, like a mask slipping back into place. She had always been patient to a fault, but when her patience wore out, all hell could break loose. Aki appeared petrified, as if he were the next target. His eyes widened, momentarily paralyzed by the sudden display of anger from a friend usually so calm and collected. It was a crack in the facade of their tightly knit group, a possible glimpse of what might lie ahead. Dai then turned to Scott, smiling wryly. *Thank you.*

She had been a tether to sanity in these last few weeks. Without her, he would surely have been lost in chaos and despair. The comfort of her warm body, the solace of their conversations late into the night, had kept him anchored to reality.

"Okay," Dai said, her voice steadfast, taking charge without hesitation when she saw Scott falter. "Scott needs us." They were here for him, she declared, their loyalty and love unwavering. These were not mere acquaintances or casual companions, but true friends who had stood by him for as long as he could remember. They were his staunch allies, ready to stand with him no matter what. Yet even as they declared their unshakable support, guilt gnawed at him. For they were risking everything for him, in the face of an unforgivable crime—treason. The prospect of unmerciful retribution lurked, a constant reminder of the price of their loyalty. He was leading them down a path that could well end in their deaths.

Dai laid down the fundamentals of the plan. She spoke about the nuclear weapon and Alixha's intentions for it. The others stood in reverent silence, their eyes fixed on Dai as she relayed the intricate details of their strategy to neutralize it. As she spoke, the severity of the risk seemed to settle over the group like a heavy winter cloak. Scott felt the weight of their gazes, the unspoken questions and fears reflected in their eyes. The enormity of their task loomed over them, and he felt a strong urge to call the whole thing off. Yet, amid the apprehension, there was a flicker of resolve kindling within him, fueled by the unwavering support of his comrades. They all knew the consequences if they withdrew.

As Dai's exposition concluded, a heavy stillness hung in the air, with all eyes now trained upon him, waiting for him to pick up where she left off. "Right," he began, pausing for a moment to collect his thoughts. In that brief moment, his mind betrayed him, but he swiftly regained his composure and proceeded to outline the roles each of them would play in the plan. Garrick's task was to provide access, Aki's responsibility was to encrypt the detonators to render them useless, and Dai's role would be to coordinate their efforts. *Or, more importantly, she will keep me from falling apart.*

"I'm meeting with Alixha tonight," he finished, his tone tense but resolute. "I will change the detonation codes then. After that, we'll meet at the designated rendezvous point."

As he mentioned Alixha, the burgeoning knot in Scott's stomach tightened further. Facing her while planning deception—right there in the very heart of the spider's lair—sent a shiver down his spine. The margin for error was nonexistent, but they were committed to a path with no return.

"How likely is it that they will be able to break the new codes?" Garrick asked. *Good question.*

He pondered it for a moment, aware that the encryption on these last-gen nuclear devices was formidable, even by today's advanced standards. "I cannot say for certain," he replied, taking care not to let his voice falter, "but I am confident that it is highly improbable. These devices were built to withstand even the most aggressive attacks. Even a modern military-grade codebreaker AI would struggle to crack them."

"But it's not beyond possibility," Aki interjected with a note of frustration. "There are no guarantees."

Garrick pressed on. "Can they hot-wire the device without the launch codes? I mean, physically open it up and jury-rig a detonator or something?"

Aki sighed. "Again, not beyond the realm of possibility, but these newer devices are built like tanks, both hardware- and software-wise. They are fortified with specialized protections designed to prevent such tampering, unlike the old Soviet-era Cold War devices."

Aki spoke the truth. Following the catastrophic India-Pakistan exchange and the close call in Washington, D.C.—events that had transpired long before any of them had been born—the world had, with unprecedented resolve, managed to lock away its nuclear devices. Eventually, most of them had been dismantled, a feat celebrated as one of the UN's most significant triumphs and an exemplar of international cooperation. The polar opposite of humanity's response to global warming, where the world spectacularly failed—at least until those crucial tipping points were reached. *Maybe we've done a bit better since then, after it was too late.* Either way, there would be very few people on the planet capable of something like jury-rigging a last-gen nuke. Only an AI could possibly get past such advanced encryption, and to succeed, one would have to bypass the AI's Asimov-Brin routines. *Which, arguably, are even more tamper-proof.*

But nothing is bulletproof. Alixha may wield resources matched by few, but without the detonator and the codes, they would be screwed. *Of that, I am certain. Almost certain.*

"Why not simply destroy or take the devices?" Garrick persisted. Scott had considered both options at length; however, neither was a viable solution. Disabling or destroying the devices was an intricate—and hazardous—task, requiring skills none of them possessed. And that was assuming they could even get to them in the first place. Alixha had taken no chances, and the level of security surrounding the devices was nothing short of absurd. *It's not like she keeps them in her penthouse closet or anything.* Even Scott didn't have access to the physical devices, at least not until Alixha granted it to him.

Nonetheless, he did have access to the remote detonators, and Aki could change the detonation codes, rendering the devices inert. After that, they could dispose of them. They were physical objects, diminutive in size, that could be easily stolen.

He needed the devices to carry out the mission, and therefore, they were presently within his security profile. The techs needed to train him on how to use them, and Garrick could provide access now without drawing undue suspicion. It wasn't an ideal situation, but it was their best shot at success. *Certainly better than doing nothing at all.*

Garrick said nothing, now apparently satisfied with the explanations provided. *Satisfied is a strong word, but at least he's shut up about it.* With deft and precise eye movements, Scott relayed the details of the plan to the group via the braid network. The information had barely disseminated when the proximity alert sounded, jolting them all into a state of high alert.

"It's a drone," Aki said, her voice crisp with urgency.

The sudden alert sent a jolt of panic through Scott. His heart pounded in his chest, a rapid drumbeat echoing the thousand thoughts that immediately flooded his mind. He cursed under his breath, scanning the skies with his tactical overlay. The presence of the drone was an unforeseen complication, a reminder of their vulnerability in a high-stakes game of shadows. *So much for placing ourselves in Narita's flight path.* They activated all the dormant squitos in the area, throwing them into search mode, and Aki was already working on deploying countermeasures. *How did we miss it?* There was a slim chance that the drone had stumbled upon them by coincidence and hadn't managed to capture any critical information. Alternatively, perhaps it wasn't capable of real-time information feeds. *Yeah, right. Keep telling yourself that.*

"We have to take it out," Garrick grumbled, his tone more one of complaint than anything else. And more a statement of the obvious than a strategic suggestion. "This thing will screw us over."

Of course, we have to take it out! Without hesitation, the team mobilized their arsenal of squitos, braid tacticals, and visual overlay-guided scans to locate the drone's position in the sky.

It didn't take them long to zero in on its coordinates once they knew it was there. Scott wasted no time in giving the order to attack, and the squitos quickly swarmed the drone, unleashing a powerful electromagnetic pulse that fried its electronics.

The team's immediate reaction was an exercise in precision and urgency. Scott saw the determination in each of their movements, proving that a shared resolve still transcended individual fear. Dai's quick commands, Garrick's focused scanning of the surroundings, and Aki's rapid deployment of countermeasures were all manifestations of their collective will to overcome obstacles when faced. It filled him with much-needed confidence that they could pull this off, after all.

The drone put up a good fight, but eventually, it was no match for their combined firepower. Not even the toughest military drones could withstand such an onslaught, and it plummeted to the ground about a hundred meters away from them. The downed drone hit the soil with a barely audible, dull thud, its metallic chassis clattering against rocks and dirt.

"Let's move," Scott said tersely, already striding toward the crash site. They needed to ascertain one thing more than anything else: whose drone was it? The mere thought that it was Alixha's was enough to make their blood run cold. They could only pray it was just some random, unaffiliated craft.

As they approached, the smell of burnt electronics hung in the air, a sharp, acrid scent that sharply contrasted with the natural earthiness of the Outside. Upon reaching the crash site, Aki conducted a swift database search based on the drone's visual markings, but it yielded no conclusive results. The model was relatively unsophisticated—a simple quadcopter frame with a basic sensor array—and certainly not one used by law enforcement or the military. *A civilian model. Maybe a privateer's scout drone?* Though their defense grid had detected the drone almost instantaneously, enough time had still passed for critical information to be transmitted to whoever was controlling it. *At the very least, they would have our location. Probably some biometrics too. Possibly to identify us.*

It was impossible to know whose drone it was. It could be bounty hunters. It could be civilians flying drones for recreational purposes, as far as they knew. Or it could be the work of someone with more nefarious intentions who had anticipated their advanced security measures and deduced that an unsophisticated drone might slip through undetected. *That might border on paranoia, but it's better to err on the side of caution.* Their lives were at stake, he reminded himself. While it would have been atypical, the drone could still be Alixha's.

"Great," Garrick exclaimed. "We're fucked before we've even begun."

Scott felt a surge of frustration at Garrick's words, yet he couldn't deny the truth in them. The uncertainty of the drone's origin and purpose cast a dark cloud over an already precarious situation. Despite his best efforts to maintain a facade of control, the seeds of doubt were sown—seeds that could easily fester and grow into fear and paranoia.

"Relax," Aki replied. "Don't be so negative. I'll do what I can here and conduct a more thorough search when I have access to more processing power."

"This changes nothing," Dai said, level-headed and optimistic as always. "It's unlikely they—whoever they are—managed to find out anything important. There's no reason for concern at this point. I suggest we're still a go."

Scott considered her words for a moment. She was right. There was no need to abort just yet. The drone's logs didn't show any transmissions, though the damaged chip made it impossible to rule that out completely. They conducted a quick search on the Net and found no active arrest warrants or bounties on them in public databases. At least not yet. Aki would do a more thorough sweep of the Net's proper underbelly once they got back. Alixha's security could never be underestimated, but Scott believed they were still in the clear.

"Yeah," he said. "We're still a go. All we have to do now is wait for the right opportunity to strike."

"Why are you so stiff?" Alixha asked as her nimble fingers worked their way through his tense shoulders in a hypnotic rhythm. Each stroke left a tingling sensation—a mix of pressure and warmth resonating through to his very core. "I'm the one going on stage, not you."

They both sat facing the mirror, her behind him on the bed. Alixha had a certain taste for intimacy post-treatment, although not always with him. He didn't know why today was his turn. Their previous escapade had been an exception, preferring his company in between applications. He had no knowledge of her other flings, nor was he interested in them.

"I didn't think you had stage fright?" he said.

Her thumb drilled into a particularly active trigger point in perfect synchronization with the end of his sentence, almost as if she perceived his comment as an insult and was now administering the penalty. The sudden, sharp pain from her thumb pressing into his muscle caught Scott off guard, sending a jolt of both discomfort and curious pleasure through him. A rather feeble moan escaped his lips.

"I don't," she stated firmly.

Don't what? Scott's mind briefly fogged under the relentless pressure of her digit digging deep into his flesh, her words almost lost in the literal dizzying haze of pleasure-pain. It was as if she were squeezing the blood out of his brain, each pressure point like a faucet that could be easily turned on or off with a bit of force.

"But I suppose I am still only human," she continued, delving deeper into his knotted muscle.

What? Right. The stage fright thing.

"Well, mostly human," she added with a little giggle, cutting off any potential reply from him. Her giggle was a light, almost musical chirp that seemed incongruous with the forcefulness of the massage. It echoed slightly in the spacious room, filled with soft, ambient lighting that cast gentle shadows across their figures in the mirror. At that moment, the rough massage relaxed, allowing him a clear thought. Her casual remark about her humanity—or lack thereof—made him both smile and shiver. It was a stark reminder of the enigmatic nature of the woman behind him, a being who defied easy categorization, straddling the line between human and something other.

"How much time do we have?" he managed. The air around them was charged with a palpable tension, a mixture of anticipation and the faint, almost imperceptible scent of Alixha's recent treatments—a clinical, sterile aroma that contrasted with the natural smell of her skin, drenched in post-coital sweat.

"An hour until we need to get ready. More than enough time," she replied with a sultry tone.

Enough time for what? Oh, right! He wasn't sure if he could endure much more of this, yet he couldn't rule out the possibility that a second round of lovemaking awaited him after the kneading. With her, it was uncertain if he had any choice in the matter.

Her hands were large for a woman, with long, slender, yet strong fingers. Her thumbs pressed into his shoulder blade trigger points with such force that it was almost unbearable. Almost. It was as if she knew precisely how much pressure to apply before crossing the threshold into actual discomfort.

As he gazed at her hands through the mirror once more, they appeared even more immense, their movements exaggerated. The sight was mesmerizing—her skin smooth, movements precise as she traced the muscles on his back. Rumors abounded that she had undergone more than mere longevity treatments, that she had integrated other modifications. Some whispered that she had spliced male DNA into her genetic makeup. He pondered the rationale behind such an alteration. *To capitalize on advantageous traits of the opposite sex?* Traits such as the testosterone-driven aggression found in a small subset of males at the extreme ends of most species. When combined with feminine intuition and thoughtfulness, could she then capture the best of both worlds? There were also rumors that she had incorporated animal DNA into her genetic makeup. He wondered what purpose such a modification could serve. *Stealth, agility, and the cunning of a large feline?*

It was hard to detect what specific traits she might have acquired from these treatments, be they physical or personal. Could her large hands be attributed to these alterations? Or the gleaming eyes? In a sense, she was gender fluid, even species fluid. *Regardless, she is breathtakingly beautiful. Today, perhaps even more than usual.* He wondered if it was the result of her most recent treatment, or if his imagination was simply running wild. Whatever one may say about gene engineering, it indisputably worked. She looked no older than fifty, an age far removed from her rumored century and a half.

There was something else in those radiant eyes too—an intangible quality, both irresistibly alluring and subtly terrifying. You had to be in close proximity to Alixha Rahena to discern these attributes, and those who had been there were either trusted lieutenants, lovers, or corpses. *I find myself a combination of the first two, and I pray the last one remains hypothetical.*

The final rumor floating around was that she had infused her genetic makeup with DNA from the latest burgeoning species that had taken root on Earth—the artificial one. Her braid was rumored to be uniquely advanced, housing a previously unseen supercomputer with a genuinely Turing Test-passing AI. If this was accurate, it would be the sole such device in existence. And she wielded its awesome computing power in her campaign to revolutionize the world. Her predictive modeling was almost never incorrect, and when it was, the margin of error was negligible.

While these were all rumors, Scott wouldn't be surprised if they proved to be true. He wouldn't put any of it past her capabilities. She was certainly willing to take the necessary risks and push the boundaries, including the legal ones. *The expression post-human is thrown around a lot these days, but if anyone actually is, it's Alixha.*

Once again, she hit a tender spot, throwing him out of his contemplative daze. He suppressed a groan in a desperate attempt to not show weakness. She seemed to notice his reserve.

"You seem quiet today," she observed.

"I'm just a bit tired," he replied, not entirely untruthfully.

She began to run her fingers through his hair, a gentle contrast to the earlier rough massage. She turned him around to face her and caressed his cheek with the back of her hand. "You are so beautiful," she said. Her fingers traveled from his neck to his head, running through his hair. The touch was soothing, almost lulling, accompanied by the faint sound of their relaxed breathing in tandem with the faint hum of the aircon. "I don't know what I'd do if I lost you, Scott."

Her words were soft yet laden with underlying subtleties. He felt a mixture of flattery, fear, and a deep, unnerving sense of being ensnared in something beyond his control. Her affection, genuine or not, was certainly a double-edged sword—both comfort and threat.

"You don't have to worry," he reassured her. "I'm yours."

"Are you really?" she questioned, drawing close to him and planting a soft kiss on his lips while simultaneously easing up on the massage. "Make sure it stays that way."

Her long, powerful fingers wrapped around his throat, partially cutting off his supply of oxygen. Scott's pulse quickened, a throbbing sensation against her fingers, and a rush of warmth as blood rushed to his face. The sudden, assertive grip was a stark contrast to the rough but tender massage—a physical manifestation of the power she wielded over him, which he had to admit was both exhilarating and frightening. As she parted her robe and pulled him in, blood rushed also to his groin. She kissed him again, the touch of her lips a blend of softness and assertion, leaving no doubt who was the predator and who was the prey. Her taste lingered, a mix of femininity and something indeterminate, her scent an almost primal and wholly intoxicating aroma—perhaps an after-effect of her treatments. As her lips withdrew, her eyes locked onto his. Then, she pushed his face down toward her waiting sex.

"Listen to them," Alixha whispered as they stood in the wings of Tokyo's New National Theater, waiting for her cue to take the stage while Osawa delivered his introduction speech. The air backstage was thick with the scent of anticipation, a mix of sweat and the metallic tang of the vast electronic equipment hidden from view behind a set of heavy, wine-colored curtains.

The low hum of the machinery merged with the distant roar of the crowd, creating a palpable tension that buzzed in Scott's ears.

Like the auditorium, the backstage wing was densely overcrowded as they were flanked by an imposing phalanx of Alixha's bodyguards. Their stern faces were etched with the gravity of their duty, their eyes scanning lenses with tactical information only they could see. Above them, the mechanical whir of nimble, diminutive attack drones suitable for indoor operation stood ready if all else failed—a countermeasure of last resort should the crowd get any ideas. These drones, no larger than a human palm, hovered with eerie grace, their matte black exteriors absorbing the scant light, making them nearly invisible against the darkened ceiling.

Out in the auditorium, cameras and squitoes blended seamlessly with the ambient buzz of the theater, observing—unobtrusive to the untrained eye, yet omniscient. Despite the vehement protests of her security chief, Alixha had chosen to appear in person for this occasion, a rare and calculated risk that underscored the gravity of her message.

On the screen behind him, the reel of revolutionary greatest hits played—a carefully curated selection of images designed to stir the troops, repeated over and over to drive the message home. It was a message of triumph, a grand parade of clips showcasing Lux Aeterna's global operations, much like the propaganda Alixha broadcasted in her private sanctuary. The message also invoked pride in the revolutionary lineage, connecting present-day rebels to their forefathers, all while promising a brighter future. Much of it was fabricated, but the enthusiastic crowd seemed unaware or too elated to care. The screen flickered with vibrant colors, each image saturated with the zeal of the movement. The images ranged from triumphant scenes of rallies in iconic global locations to death and mighty military destruction, each frame meticulously chosen to evoke a tapestry of defiance and hope. The colors were deliberately oversaturated, making the reds more fiery, as if to burn the images into the viewer's memory. In the background, the faint hum of the electronics provided a rhythmic counterpart to

Osawa's words, a subtle yet constant reminder of the orchestrated, machine-like nature of this event.

But this orchestration was not mere visuals; it was masterfully written by the science division, containing subtle, neuro-subliminal messages to amplify the desired reactions in the audience. Scott remained skeptical about this aspect, silently questioning the scientific veracity behind these neuro-subliminal techniques. *Is the euphoria a product of genuine belief or a manufactured response?* In the end, it didn't matter; the outcome spoke for itself. The energy in the auditorium was positively electric, and the rally had yet to hit its climax. Scott could feel the fervor pulsating through the crowd, a tingling across his skin giving him goosebumps. The heat from the tightly packed bodies in the auditorium wafted toward them, even back here, carrying with it the mixed aromas of exhilaration and adrenaline-fueled zeal. He had to admit the scent was intoxicating.

He caught glimpses of faces illuminated by the screen, their expressions a blend of awe, anger, and fanatic devotion. The crowd had turned into a single entity, breathing and pulsating in unison with Osawa's rhythm. Standing in the wings, a mere observer, he felt a twinge of unease amidst this sea of unbridled passion. *What would it be like out there?* he mused. *No wonder it's overwhelming.*

Alixha ordered Scott to disable his braid noise filters, insisting he experience the raw power of the frenzied crowd in its entirety. Scott complied, but he wasn't sure if it was even necessary. Even with the filters, the roar of the mob was deafening. And with the filters off, the crowd's clamor penetrated his eardrums like a sledgehammer, obliterating Oz's words at the podium. The filters, typically designed to block out background noise and capture every syllable of human speech with impeccable precision, were inadequate for this level of pandemonium.

The majority of the attendees were locals, but with the Tokyo dome being one of the most open in the world, the audience comprised people from across the global community, all swept up in the same revolutionary fervor. Anyone who had heard their message and had the means to travel was present. However, Scott found it ironic that the very people who would benefit the most from the rebellion—the impoverished, the Outies—were mostly absent, lacking the resources to travel. The people present were people of some wealth—Innies, with access to bullet trains and screamers. *The upper, lower-middle class.* And the rich.

Oz droned on. The speech was in Japanese, rendering it mostly incomprehensible to Scott. Turning off the noise filter also disabled the translator. *After all these years, I still don't speak enough Japanese.* He wanted to hear what was being said, so he reactivated them both, but it didn't help. From their position behind the stage, little could be discerned through the cacophony.

"...Under the yoke of corporate fascism... serving only the billionaire class, while we subsist on crumbs... deliberately misdirected the efforts to combat climate change..."

It was a hodgepodge of messages—anything to drive unity to the cause and increase membership. Oz's message was a medley of themes aimed at galvanizing unity and boosting membership. He was an exceptional Communications Director, possessing impressive charisma and ferocious zeal. But in this context, he was still just a warm-up act. *Historically, he would've been called the Director of Propaganda or some such title.* However, in the current world order of corporate kleptocracy, he was a "director," donning the jargon from the dictionary of corporate bullshit.

As Osawa's voice crescendoed, the crowd's reaction intensified. Faces that were once contemplative now blazed with conviction. Each word from Oz's mouth seemed to strike a chord, resonating with the gathered masses. As he approached the end of his speech—the end of the warm-up—even those who had initially seemed indifferent were caught up in the tide of passion.

All great artists utilized a warm-up act, someone to rile up the crowd, someone to simultaneously raise and lower expectations as required, but never as great as the main act itself. Enter Alixha Rahena. And Alixha Rahena was the greatest main act of them all. Hitler, Castro, Stalin, and even Powell could not compare. Although, with the exception of perhaps Powell, none of them had access to subliminal neuro-stimulating imagery or ultrasound technology, deliberately designed to provoke precise emotional responses that advanced their cause. *So in a sense, she's cheating. If such things actually work, that is.*

The impoverished, the marginalized, and even the middle class were easy prey, lacking access to the hyper-advanced braids that could shield or caution against such manipulation. Scott looked on as the crowd absorbed Oz's words. In the dim light, the faces in the crowd seemed to glow, lit by a fervent inner fire as well as the stroboscopic effect of the *atrocities greatest hits* playing on the screens. The sharp tang of sweat had now turned into an acrid scent of ozone as the air filters struggled.

As Oz spoke, each mention of oppression or injustice was met with shouts of agreement, each promise of liberation with sparks of hope. He saw clenched jaws and fists, eyes that shone with tears of both rage and determination. Each word resonated deeply with their own stories, their own struggles, wrapped in an emotional tapestry woven from threads of pain, hope, and desperate desire for change. They had all been chosen for this very reason. Yes, it had never been easier to incite the masses than it was now. All it took was a willingness to break the law, evade enforcement agencies, and possibly a connection to the elusive black markets where the necessary tools could be acquired. *Considering that Alixha's various corporations produced some of these tools, she could acquire them wholesale.*

"...the unholy collusion between the ultra-rich and the legacy government, with the aim of oppressing and subjugating us—" Oz raged, riling up the crowd further.

I'm all for revolution, but if there's nothing better with which to replace the old regime... Scott glanced over at Alixha, who was still basking in the afterglow of her treatment. She lived for these moments when she could exercise direct control. *For the greater good. The ends justify the means and other such clichés.*

Scott believed that Alixha was mostly sincere in her convictions, but ultimately, her dedication was driven by something deeply personal. Deliverance for everyone was merely a byproduct. The people in the audience had come to be liberated from whatever they believed was troubling them—poverty, the climate, real or imagined injustices of every kind, or foolhardy conspiracies. But he had increasingly become convinced that for Alixha, it was power—the desire to control the world and everyone in it. *But why am I here?* He pondered it for a minute but couldn't find an answer. *But I do understand that if she's motivated by power, she's no different than Henry James Gibson, or any other of the world's power brokers.*

The crowd erupted in applause as Oz continued to fan the flames of their outrage. The atmosphere inside the premises of the New National Theater, now abandoned on the bottom level of the Tokyo East Central One dome, was feverish, seething with hatred. The theater's once-grand architecture, now dulled and worn by time, vibrated with the force of the crowd's reactions.

"...strike at the heart of the establishment..."

"...deliver justice to the people of the world..."

"...rid us of the burden of poverty and oppression..."

"...rescue us from climate death..."

New generation. Same old crap.

Scott surveyed the crowd, noting how the angry expressions slowly transformed into hopeful gazes as Oz's speech progressed. He was almost too effective. Almost. To the uninitiated, it might seem like Oz was upstaging Alixha, but that was far from the truth. It was all part of the plan, and it was perfect.

Once upon a time, Scott himself had been one of the faces in a crowd like this, captivated by the message, reinvigorated by the prospect of change, and enlightened by the promise of dignity. Dai, Garrick, and Aki had been there too. It felt like a lifetime and a half ago now.

Back then, Alixha's methods had been distinctly different. The violent component had been a relatively new addition; the ultra-violent component was newer still. From cyber attacks, to destruction of property, to assassinations, and eventually, to mass murder—none of it had been part of the manifesto he had subscribed to. Nevertheless, he had been instrumental in devising these tactics. *May God forgive me.*

Alixha had again posed the question to him the previous night before they retired to bed: What was the difference between murdering one individual, a few thousand, several hundred thousand, or even millions? *Murder is murder... The number is irrelevant. If the cause is just.*

This time too, he had been unable to come up with a satisfactory answer. "It's the next logical step," she had declared. London had been the beginning, but it was far from the end.

If we're going to sabotage Alixha's operations, we have to disappear. Remaining within the organization and trying to cover their tracks, no matter how thoroughly, would be suicide. Running wasn't much better, but it seemed somewhat less like certain death. Regardless, their lives as they knew them were over, and the ball was already rolling. *We're guilty of conspiracy to commit. Even if we stop now.*

Oz's speech finally concluded, and he began his signature oration that would culminate in the introduction of Alixha: their leader, their judge and executioner, their god. It was the same spiel every time, followed by a surge of audiovisual cues designed to trigger the release of every positive neurochemical in the brain—endorphins, oxytocin, noradrenaline, serotonin. All of them. The effects were temporary, but by the time they subsided, Alixha had you.

As Oz uttered his final words, the atmosphere reached a fever pitch. The crowd's energy seemed to condense into an unstoppable force, a monster waiting to be unleashed. Scott could see it in the way bodies leaned forward, eyes fixed on the stage, every muscle in the room tensed in anticipation. When Oz uttered Alixha's name, the dam burst. The crowd's cheer was not just a sound; it was a physical wave that washed over everything, filled with adoration, desperation, and an almost religious fervor. Scott felt it pass through him, a tide of collective emotion that was both awe-inspiring and terrifying.

Alixha took the stage, but before doing so, she glanced back at him. The moment was brief, but long enough for him to notice something new in her eyes—a resolute glare, as if she wanted to remind him of something. *What? That she owns me as much as she owns them?* The introduction music began to pound, and the chanting of her name grew louder, turning into unabashed worship. Alixha smiled and strode onto the stage.

In the dark confines of Alixha's luxury penthouse suite, Tokyo's clamorous, neon-draped tapestry barely penetrated the isolated room. Scott lay ensconced in the warm embrace of the bed. Beside him, Alixha lay in repose, her breathing a shallow, soft counterpoint to the silence. Her arm rested over his chest, its weight both comforting and surprisingly heavy, straining his breathing. The curtains were open the way she preferred them, the ethereal flickering of the city outside casting unearthly shadows on the bedroom walls. Sleepless, he observed their never-ending dance, and like the turmoil inside him, the mega-city beyond the glass panes couldn't be silenced.

Tomorrow was to be the day of reckoning—the moment when their meticulously laid plans to extricate the codes would unfurl, irrevocably severing his allegiance to Lux Aeterna. This suite had been a prison, the woman beside him his warden, and he was glad to rid both from his existence. But this place had also been a haven, a sanctuary from the machinations of the revolution he had championed. The warden could be sweet, vulnerable, and loving when she wanted, and somewhat unsurprisingly, he found he would miss it. He would miss Lux—the camaraderie, the intoxication from rushes of adrenaline, the profound sense of purpose, the belonging amidst the chaos. Despite its descent into the maelstrom of extremism, Lux had been integral to his identity.

Alixha would hurt the most. His relationship with her was an intricate weave of emotion, sown from love, respect, and now, from threads of betrayal. She loved him too, he was sure of it. *Although, who knows if it isn't all an illusion created via genetically enhanced pheromone and oxytocin releases, designed specifically to ensnare me in such a trap?* Her love was twisted and possessive, but it was love nonetheless. In the hallways of his heart and mind, he had reciprocated with an equally convoluted affection, but stark reality remained. That affection, that love, was a luxury rendered moot against the backdrop of impending destruction that threatened millions. *If her manipulations are real, they are imperfect. Here I am, breaking free. Alixha might be powerful in ways no one else is, but she is still only human.*

As the night stretched on, he wrestled with the gravity of his decision—the betrayal, the abandonment of what had been his *raison d'être* for most of his adult life, and the sleeplessness. But the longer he lay awake, the stronger his resolve became, and eventually, a peace coalesced amidst the chaos. His path was chosen, his fate sealed. There was no turning back, and he didn't want to.

Come morning, he slid out of bed and dressed while Alixha still slumbered. Before exiting the suite, he ventured back to the bedroom, standing in the doorway for a few seconds. "Goodbye," he whispered, then disappeared.

Jarod

God, I hate flying, Jarod thought, having been jolted awake by a bout of turbulence. His breath staggered as the plane juddered, sank, and recovered, the mighty Boeing transatlantic screamer being tossed around like a small Cessna. Each sensation of falling wasn't just fear of flying; it was a trigger, dragging him back to Taiwan's unpredictable combat zones, where the ground could shift underfoot without warning as traps were sprung, or as Chinese combat drones bathed the land in hellfire. The panic gripping him was familiar, and he knew how to fight it, to steady his breathing, to remind himself that it was just a flight, however uncomfortable. That war was long since over.

From the overhead nozzle, cold air blasted, drying his eyes, but at least it mitigated the odor of recycled breath and passenger anxiety. It wasn't just him who disliked flying these days. The cold suddenly overwhelmed him, his skin pricking with goosebumps, an aftereffect of the slumber as much as the aircon. He roused himself, deciding it was time to get to work.

With a subtle flick of his eyes, he brought up the time on his augmented reality display, the digits hovering before him in the lower right corner of his lens. The artificial luminescence flickered momentarily before setting, a translucent ghost dancing across his vision. At three minutes to eight in the evening, Jarod concluded a full hour and fifteen minutes of delay had been inflicted upon them, the damned screamer having been caught in a holding pattern over Kennedy while waiting for the capricious weather to abate enough for a safe landing. They had tracked their first target to New York: Lux's finance guy, Bertrand Siscal. Or "Fiscal Siscal," as he was sometimes, somewhat humorously, referred to. Funny, but not *haha* funny.

The screamer shuddered violently as it careened into another sharp turn, the sudden motion threatening to have Jarod void his stomach contents. Now awake, he could control the fear, but the nausea he could do little about. *The descents are the worst.* Takeoffs were a mere blip on the radar; the cruise, just grazing low Earth orbit, was a momentary thrill. But the descents? Oh boy, the descents. They were the stuff of nightmares. The nausea crept up on him without fail, the queasiness and convulsive spasms of his stomach always keeping him on the brink of retching, his hands desperately clutching the sick bag. There were drugs for motion sickness, of course, but somehow he always managed to forget to bring some. *I wish I had one of those fancy braids with a built-in medical.*

And as much as he hated flying, there was no other option. The transatlantic bullet tunnel was still years away from completion—at least a decade, by most estimations. One could take the long way around, traversing over Alaska, but it took too long. And let's not forget the bureaucratic tangle of checks and documentation to pass through Russia. To make matters worse, a large portion of the Trans-Siberian bullet still relied on outdated slow-train technology, hindering the journey considerably. *Space elevators. Now, there's my salvation!*

The concept was certainly intriguing, and he found himself ruminating on the possibilities as the screamer took another lap. Jarod imagined the silky smooth ascent, the gradual fade of Earth's blues into the black, starlit tapestry of space, a quiet so profound it drowned everything. In his mind, the stark silence of the vacuum seemed a soothing balm to his nerves, a stark departure from the incessant drone of the screamer's engines and the whooshing of the aircon. *Mmm. It actually helps.*

But not by much, so he returned to his braid. He had skimmed the in-flight article about it while in LEO, during the smooth part of the ride. Alas, he couldn't read during turbulent descents, so he powered off his lens and focused on keeping his stomach in check. *Unless I want to regurgitate my dinner.*

The completion of the Singapore and Quito space elevators, which would serve Asia and the Americas respectively, was imminent. But the third one, planned for Central Africa to cater to the needs of Europe and Africa, was an entirely different matter. Africa was, in essence, a development black hole, and getting anything done there was a veritable nightmare. Nonetheless, according to the article, once all three were operational, transit between the elevators through orbit, followed by the use of existing transcontinental bullet train infrastructure, would be the wave of the future. *Still sounds like science fiction to me, but maybe it could work.*

A spark of hope spread warmly across his chest as he imagined a future without flying. The idea of stepping onto an elevator and ascending to the stars stirred a sense of awe and longing. *An expensive way to combat aerophobia and motion sickness, but I'll take it!*

The article listed a plethora of issues, though, many of them not engineering-related. The authors particularly went on at length about the political instability plaguing Central Africa, implying that it made the project a non-starter from the outset. But if that issue could be resolved, or if the elevator could be built in a more secure location, like a sea-based installation off the coast, the authors would cautiously embrace the possibility of success. The engineering behind such contraptions was well beyond Jarod's comprehension, but he figured if a civilization could build massive city domes and an ocean-spanning bullet tunnel under the Atlantic, something like space elevators couldn't be too far behind.

The writer's emphasis on the importance of quickly solving these problems intrigued—and worried—him. As Earth's environment grew increasingly unstable, conventional space launches would become prohibitively expensive and difficult in a matter of decades, effectively trapping humanity in its cradle. *There are already permanent scientific research stations on the Moon, Mars, and Ganymede, so I suppose mankind has already left the cradle, but these outposts would quickly die without a continuous supply chain from Earth.* Perhaps in a few decades, their situation would improve. But for now, the space launch industry was in a state of decline, much like the airline industry before it. Bullet trains had made conventional airliners obsolete, and space elevators would do the same to rockets. At least, that's what the article claimed.

The infrastructure required for this transformation also needed to be in place long before it became a necessity, further accelerating the timeline. Building a space elevator, transcontinental bullet train tracks, or a city dome in a location that resembled Venus more than Earth would undoubtedly be challenging. Yet, there were still people who refused to accept the reality of climate change—people who maintained that the planet was not warming, despite the overwhelming evidence all around them. Social change was always difficult, especially when it was as fundamentally disruptive as what was currently unfolding. But for Jarod, the advent of space elevators and the trans-Atlantic bullet tunnel could not come soon enough. He was eager to bid farewell to air travel forever. Unfortunately, flying was still the best option for those traveling from Europe to the East Coast. And for working-class people like him, that also meant flying coach.

He glanced over at his team, who, unlike himself, seemed unperturbed by the turbulence and the delay. The dim cabin lights cast long shadows over their faces, creating a display of calm amidst the choppiness. In the quiet moments that followed, Jarod felt a pang of envy at his team's apparent indifference to the discomforts of modern air travel. Their ability to focus, to remain undisturbed, spoke of inner reserves he wished he could tap into. Wyatt was even snoozing, having slept through most of the flight. Riley and Kale were engrossed in their files, studying invisible holographic displays on their lenses, covering the operating theater in meticulous detail, preparing for every possible eventuality they might face. Wyatt's rhythmic snoring, clearly audible over the faint hum of the screamer's electric engines, and Kale and Riley's focused silence, were all oddly comforting in their normalcy. They were good people, resilient in a way he sometimes begrudgingly admired.

The turbulence had abated for now, giving him a respite from the worst of the nausea. Confident he could read for a while, he opened Siscal's file. He had already studied it extensively, but he needed a distraction from the interminable holding pattern they were stuck in, and there was no harm in taking another look.

The text scrolled silently before his eyes, revealing the depths of human malice hidden behind the facade of normal life. Siscal's face, captured in various surveillance footage, was just one among many, yet it bore the weight of countless atrocities. He was a slippery player, appearing on every terrorist sanctions list in existence. He was a master of the "hiding in plain sight" strategy, always adopting new identities to avoid detection. He now went under the moniker *Madoff*, apparently a reference to a notorious con man from the 20th century who had pulled off one of the largest Ponzi schemes in history. The information pop-up on his display made Jarod smile a little.

Everything about Fiscal Siscal was shrouded in layers of misinformation, smoke screens, and detours. Kale had to dig deep to uncover that Madoff was, in fact, Siscal; the Madoff identity had been expertly crafted and was virtually airtight. His illegal financing activities were all but untraceable. However, it was all inconsequential. They weren't there to bring him to justice, nor were they there to gather evidence that would hold up in court. *We only need to know one thing. Where they are.*

Fiscal Siscal was not their top priority; Scott was. He was the ringleader, the one their employer sought to eliminate, and his death would send the clearest message to their rivals—to Alixha Rahena. But finding him had proven challenging. Kale and Riley had managed to confirm that he was likely somewhere in Tokyo, but given that Lux Aeterna had its headquarters there, that was hardly an impressive achievement. They had run parallel queries on the other targets, and eventually, the information they gathered led them to Siscal, so they had pursued him instead.

Jarod ran through everything again, and then once more before the plane finally broke out of the holding pattern and began its descent. It was not a moment too soon. The turbulence was back with a vengeance, and Jarod once again had a death grip on his airsick bag. If they didn't make it all the way down this time, he would have to use it.

Maybe I'm old school, but there really is no substitute for actual eyes on the target. On his right lens, Jarod had a 180-degree view of the scene. Next to it, semi-translucent picture-in-picture captures from an impressive array of surveillance feeds—ranging from city security cameras to private drones—all expertly hacked by Kale. The faint hum of data streams flowing through servers filled the room, the glow from the external screens casting a pale blue light on his and Riley's focused faces. If there was a camera of value anywhere, they were plugged into it.

He deftly manipulated the screens with eye gestures, zooming in and out, tabbing back and forth. Bertrand Siscal's face cast a formidable presence in the virtual space in front of his eyes, but Jarod kept his center and left view free of any overlays. Even with all this technological wizardry at his fingertips, Jarod still preferred to trust his own eyes. *The occasional bit of zoom, maybe, but otherwise clean. Okay, so why does this guy deserve to die?*

Jarod reviewed the file on Siscal once more, making sure to always keep one eye on the target. The dossier streaming on his lens painted a picture of a man whose hands were stained with the blood of innocents, albeit indirectly. Bertrand Siscal, known in the darkest corners of the global finance world as the architect behind the funding of the London dome attack. On that day, thousands had perished, trapped under the dome's protective embrace turned prison, and the world had been thrown into chaos. But London was just the tip of the iceberg. Over the years, Siscal had meticulously orchestrated the flow of untraceable funds to Lux Aeterna, enabling a series of devastating terror attacks across the globe. Each operation, while differing in execution and target, bore the hallmark of Siscal's cold efficiency and utter disregard for human life.

Unlike the foot soldiers who carried out these attacks, Siscal never dirtied his hands with the physical act of violence. Instead, he remained shrouded in the shadows of anonymity, a ghost in the financial machine, leveraging his expertise to fuel chaos from afar. His ability to slip through the cracks of international law enforcement, always one step ahead with a new identity or hidden behind layers of financial obfuscation, made him a phantom menace. But to those who had felt the loss and despair seeded by his actions, Siscal was all too real—a man whose very existence was a threat to peace and safety.

It wasn't just the scale of his crimes that marked him for assassination; it was the calculated detachment with which he executed them. To Siscal, human lives were mere variables in his equations, collateral damage in his quest for whatever twisted ideology he served. This detachment, this inhumanity, made him not just a target, but a necessity to stop. For Jarod, and the shadowy figures that sanctioned this operation, removing Siscal from the equation was a grim duty—a necessary act to prevent future atrocities and to bring a measure of justice for the unseen victims of his financial warfare.

When Siscal entered a diner on the street corner ahead, Riley's voice crackled over the comm. "You got him?"

He confirmed.

"Told you," she taunted. Riley didn't understand his reluctance to rely solely on the augmented reality feeds. She was young, after all, born into a world where technology was seamlessly integrated into every aspect of life. Jarod, on the other hand, had grown up in a time before AR, before braids and lenses, even before wearable glasses. He had come of age with clunky, hand-held tablets or even primitive cell phones. Or *mobiles*, as the Euros called them. Words that felt archaic today, even though they were merely a continuation of the same old concept. Lessons had been learned the hard way, spending time in combat zones where electromagnetic interference rendered technological gizmos useless. In those places, the only thing one could trust was their own eyes.

It wasn't until his mid-twenties that Jarod finally installed a braid. And even now, he only used the bottom layer—the information layer. Directions, instructions, tactical data like targeting and velocities—that was all he needed. He couldn't fathom why anyone would want to overlay every little thing, completely blocking out the real world. He had seen people who replaced buildings, transport vehicles, animals, and even other human beings with fantasy elements, like alien worlds from some popular movie or game. It all seemed so frivolous and unnecessary to him. *I prefer the real world, gray and dull as it is.*

Jarod was suddenly jolted back to reality as his tactical picked up Siscal's movement. The targeting reticle locked onto him the moment he emerged from the diner, now with a bag of muffins and a latte in addition to the Reuben sandwiches he had picked up previously at Katz's down in the Village. Apparently, the man never ate anything else for lunch, but he always saved one of the muffins for his wife to enjoy when she returned from work later in the evening. *Sweet man.*

Riley's squitos were continually keeping a discreet eye on Siscal's movements, buzzing around his head at a safe distance to avoid detection. They clung to every wall along his route, tracking him as he followed his daily routine. After dropping off his daughter at school at around eight a.m., Siscal took the same path every morning through Washington Square Park, stopping first at a place called Ned's for breakfast before arriving back at his home office at precisely 9:30 a.m. He was a man of habit, making him an easy target to track once he had been located.

"Okay, I've seen enough. I'm coming back up," Jarod announced, turning off the feeds displayed on his lens. They had set up their base of operations on the corner of Bleecker and Lafayette, in an abandoned storefront not far from Siscal/Madoff's residence. The area had once been a high-end shopping destination, but now it was shrouded in darkness, withering away under the shadow of the second-level skyway above. The lack of light had driven out anyone with the means to escape, leaving behind only the disenfranchised, the drug-addicted, and the homeless.

Most upscale areas had compensation for the loss of natural light, with artificial lighting installed when a skyway was built above. But not SoHo. *Or much of it, anyway.* It had regressed to what it was before the gentrification of the last few decades of the previous century. *Slum? Ghetto?*

Not all of SoHo was equally dreadful. Washington Square Park and the immediate surrounding areas were still charming, protected by their historical significance and the regulations that prevented the development of skyways over them. Other parts, such as where Bleecker crossed Broadway, had some artificial lighting, but where they had set up was grim and murky. *Don't forget smelly!*

The residents here wouldn't care about their activities. There were minimal cameras for an area *Inside*, making it an ideal spot for them to operate in relative peace. The windows of the old store had been boarded shut, and everything had been paid for through one of the many shell corporations set up by Aegis to mask the financial trail of their operation.

The interior of the apartment was a veritable sea of holographic screens, inundating the walls with a barrage of data: camera displays, online search bot results, maps, logs, and various other streams of information. Some underlying code, primarily for Kale's and, to some extent, Riley's eyes, all jostled for space on the screens.

Wyatt was like him—an old-school operative who knew little of the intricate tech that was their lifeblood. He might occasionally dabble in offensive squitos, but his preferred methods of killing were far more visceral—first by hand, then by firearm, and only as a last resort, by drone and AI. *That's division of labor for you.* He was currently absorbed in his daily firearms maintenance routine, leisurely chewing the end of a cigar.

"You're a cliché," Jarod remarked as he settled down next to him on the couch.

"Told you," Riley added. "And would it kill you to stop with the cigars? You're gonna get lip cancer chewing those."

"Lip cancer is a myth," Wyatt retorted without diverting his gaze from his work.

"Even if it were true, it's curable," Kale interjected.

Riley punched him in the shoulder. "You're supposed to be on my side. Besides, it's just an expression. I know lip cancer isn't a thing."

"Focus on the task at hand," Jarod reminded them.

"Don't worry," Riley reassured him. "I've programmed alerts for every possible scenario. If the guy so much as farts, we'll know. Even if it's silent but deadly."

Jarod looked at her skeptically.

"I know, I know," she sighed. "You don't trust tech. Always a pair of human eyes on the target, blah, blah, blah."

Jarod smiled. "That's the spirit. Now, patch the squito feed from inside the apartment to my braid, please."

He observed Wyatt as he meticulously cleaned his vintage Colt .45. *It may be old, but it still gets the job done,* he always boasted. There was something soothing about watching Wyatt perform this routine task. He did it with such ease, with such care and affection, as if he were tending to a child or a beloved pet. The metallic click of the Colt being reassembled was a comforting sound; it meant he was there, ready to have your back.

Jarod brought up the squito feed from inside the apartment on his lens. The tiny bug continued to buzz around, keeping a safe distance from its target. Of course, "buzzing" was just a turn of phrase—these tiny bugs were eerily quiet. *It's not called a mosquito for nothing.* With the right operator and a loadout of state-of-the-art stealth tech, only military-grade countermeasures would have any chance of detecting them. As of yet, they had found no such advanced electronic defense system in operation in or around the apartment—just standard consumer-grade gear. Jarod found that strange. Surely someone of his target's importance would be afforded better protection?

Even the most sophisticated systems were not impervious to leaving traces and drawing unwanted attention. But Siscal/Madoff was different. He preferred to operate under complete silent running, simply disappearing into the gray mass, leaving behind no suspicious electronic or digital traces. He didn't hide behind encryption or the endless rerouting of data, just an alternate identity. That was how he managed to stay off the radar. *And it's effective. To a point.*

Even Siscal/Madoff had to eat, and that meant leaving transaction records behind, either directly or indirectly. Unless he paid in cash—but most vendors, human or automated, didn't accept it—so the footprints were there somewhere. And with Kale on their side, it was only a matter of time. *The boy knows what he's doing, that's for sure.*

So, after they had located him, they studied him closely. Days had passed, and their due diligence had revealed all of his habits inside and out. He took another glance at Riley's notes from the previous day:

[Begin Notes]
7:30 am: Appears outside his apartment with his ten-year-old daughter, Evelina, and walks her to Jameson's Elementary, located three blocks down on 34th and 3rd. Takes the elevator to the level three skyway where the school is located.

8:00 am: Has breakfast at Ned's Diner, ordering two pancakes with a copious amount of syrup, four rashers of bacon, one latte, and one orange juice—the same meal every time.

8:45 am: Back at his apartment, he kisses his wife goodbye as she leaves for work at Aegis.
Addendum: Wife may be involved? /RM
Addendum: Irrelevant—not a target. /JL

8:55 am: Makes coffee.

9:00 am: Works. All work is offline.

11:30 am: Leaves apartment.

11:45 am: Ned's Diner. Lunch. Cheeseburger with fries,

deviating today without the side order of coleslaw.
Side note: How is this guy not dead already? Even with extensive geneering, this is a seriously unhealthy diet.

12:05 pm: Coffee.

12:23 pm: Leaves Ned's and returns to the apartment.

12:31 pm: Works.

3:07 pm: Coffee. Reads a printed newspaper, usually *The New York Times.*

Side note: The presence of a braided device has been confirmed, but it has not powered up since surveillance began. /JL

3:22 pm: Works.
Addendum: Often plays classical music while working. /JL

4:16 pm: Saves work on a removable drive and leaves the apartment.

4:38 pm: Delivers the removable drive at a dead drop. Locations vary according to what seems to be a random pattern. He has not repeated a location since surveillance began.

4:49 pm: Arrives at Jameson's Elementary to pick up his daughter.

5:13 pm: Returns to the apartment.

5:32 pm: Wife returns home. Family meal. No relevant discussion during the meal.

6:13 pm: Wife exercises. Target works.

10:01 pm: Gets ready for bed.

10:34 pm: Falls asleep.

[End Notes]
Notes taken by Riley Mack. AI Reference: #RM58849S

Every day was a repetition of the last, with no relevant variations found in the pattern since surveillance began. Maybe this was enough due diligence. The team was growing impatient.

Their plan was for Riley to program a squito to deliver a lethal compound while the target was asleep. It was nice and clean, with no fuss or risk, and untraceable—at least by civilian forensics. Law enforcement and family would simply assume he had died of a heart attack in his sleep.

"What do you say, Boss?" Wyatt asked. "Are we a go or what? My butt's going numb from all this sitting."

Jarod knew that there were always things you miss—little holes in the plan that were obvious in hindsight but invisible now. They all knew it, but the plan was solid and simple. The time had come to make a decision.

"Yeah, we're a go. Tonight," he said, a heavy weight settling in his stomach. Jarod's fingers tightened around the edge of the table, the texture of the worn wood comforting in his grip. The room seemed to close in as the reality of what they were about to do sobered him. It was a pivotal moment from which there would be no return.

"Squito is in position," Kale announced, a slight tension in his jaw as the screen scrolled squito telemetry reflecting across his face. Jarod felt that familiar knot tighten once more, the clinical detachment of their strategy feeling starkly alien. This was hardly the honor of battle; it was a cold execution, delivered from afar—a stark departure from the chaos and camaraderie of real combat. The silence and determined focus around him felt heavy, loaded with the gravity of what they were about to do.

The tiny mechanical smart bug lay perched atop Siscal-Madoff's bedroom bookshelf, biding its time until the moment came to deliver its payload of rapidly acting toxin.

"Are they asleep?" Jarod asked.

Surveillance had revealed that Siscal-Madoff's sleep was deep and undisturbed, almost as if he were in a coma. The infrared imagery on the screen outlined two peaceful figures in the bed. Siscal-Madoff barely moved a muscle throughout the night, and his breathing was so shallow, it was almost like death itself. Such a pattern indicated the use of medication, but despite their due diligence, they had found no traces of sleep aids in his prescription history, and his braid was dormant, unable to administer any drugs. The wife, on the other hand, was a different story altogether. She tossed and turned, woke up several times during the night to visit the bathroom or grab a glass of water from the kitchen. Her breathing was erratic, and she even snored on occasion. In an otherwise silent environment, even an advanced squito could potentially wake her if it got too close to her ear. *Good thing she's not our target.*

The operation itself was unlikely to arouse anyone from their slumber. While there might be a slight sensation as the squito's stinger pierced the skin, like its organic counterpart, it would administer an anesthetic to numb the skin. It would take a second or two to take effect, but being such a heavy sleeper, Siscal-Madoff would sleep right through it without so much as a twitch.

But just to be safe, Jarod advised Kale to avoid flying the squito over Mrs. Siscal.

Wyatt scoffed. "Yeah, try not to do that, Kale."

Without looking away from his screens, Kale instinctively raised his hand and extended his middle finger.

"Don't you have more guns to clean?" Riley quipped. "Don't worry. When we need your brawn, we'll let you know."

Good ol' 'Rile up' Riley. Always takes the bait, even when the comment isn't directed at her.

Wyatt responded by flipping her off and reclining on the

couch. "She's got a point," he mumbled. "Wake me up if the shit hits the fan." He pulled his baseball cap over his face and drifted off to sleep. *Soldiers. They can sleep on command, long after their service has ended.*

Jarod had never been able to do that, not even when he was active. He suspected Wyatt had resorted to military-grade gene editing or braid-administered medications to facilitate his ability to doze off so easily. But he considered it a personal matter and didn't pry.

"On your order," Kale said, his attention still fixed on the screens.

As Jarod gazed at the eerie infrared image of the sleeping Siscal-Madoffs on the screen, he felt a sudden pang of remorse. The image of Mrs. Siscal-Madoff waking up to find her husband dead the next morning disturbed him. His immediate instinct was to suppress it, as he had been trained long ago, but then he decided to leave it—to indulge in it, even. He wasn't sure why. Maybe after two decades of no killing, he was just rusty, but it took only a few seconds—a few seconds of dwelling in that mental lapse—and he couldn't shake it.

The stuffy air of the room seemed to thicken, making it hard to breathe. The shadows in the corners seemed deeper. This experience was new to him in a sense. Siscal-Madoff was a civilian, not a soldier. Or is he? It felt different, somehow. In the past, his targets had always been military personnel or government officials—people he could justify as being part of the enemy. But Siscal-Madoff was just a man, a husband, a father, someone who dealt with numbers, not bombs. He had no uniform, no rank, no weapons. It made the act of killing him feel more personal, more intimate. On the other hand, he arranged financing for terror acts, did he not?

Are we at war? Lux Aeterna and Alixha were certainly enemies of everything he and other peace-loving, democratic citizens held dear.

Jarod's thoughts darkened, the blurred lines between right and wrong, soldier and assassin, haunting him. This felt like betrayal—not of a country or a cause, but of himself. The identity he fought to preserve amidst his struggles seemed to slip away, replaced by the unfamiliar, uncomfortable role of an unseen killer, someone who takes the easy way out. Like Siscal himself.

The conglomerate of dome owners weren't exactly angels themselves, but at least they worked with the government instead of trying to subvert it. Back in the U.S., they would have called it a war on something, but this wasn't like the wars he had fought. It was a contest between two civilian organizations, where he was a gun for hire, contracted by one of the parties. Sure doesn't sound like war when you put it that way.

"Boss?" Riley's voice crackled through the radio, but to Jarod, it sounded distant, as if she wasn't really there with him—lost in some other plane of reality. He didn't respond, absent in his own thoughts. It seemed cowardly to have a squito sneak in and do the dirty work for him, like shooting a man in the back. Even worse, it was like shooting a man in the back from the safety of an impenetrable fortress—a fortress the victim didn't even know existed. Even a sniper in the field, no matter how well-hidden, took more of a risk than that. This is what assassins do, not soldiers.

Assassins killed in the most convenient way possible—the way that posed the least potential risk to themselves. But Jarod couldn't see himself as an assassin. He wasn't ready for that. No, if Jarod was going to take a life, he wanted to do it himself, face to face. If that man was going to die, he deserved the respect of having an actual human do the deed. *Does he not?* But it wasn't only about respect for the target; it was about respecting himself and the act of killing. It wasn't something to be taken lightly, and using a squito made it feel like a simulation—a game that shielded him from the true emotional impact of what he was doing. If he could kill in that way, what did that make him? Where would it lead him? What slippery slope was he soon to tumble down?

The questions and doubts swirled around in his mind, overwhelming him. The silence of the room, the tension of unspoken words following that internal debate, felt like a corset strapped across his chest, tightening by the second. No, he wasn't ready. If all the questions and doubts told him anything, it was that he wasn't ready. *One thing is clear, though. I deserve the unpleasantness and pain of having to look my victim in the eyes as I extinguish his life.*

Riley's voice crackled again, breaking through his thoughts, and he knew it was time to make a choice.

"Stand down." Jarod's voice cut through the tension in the room, causing both Kale and Riley to tear their gazes away from the flickering screens in front of them. To him, the words *Stand down* came as a release, though they carried the weight of impending confrontation. This choice, pulling back from the brink of impersonal violence, was a reclaiming of his own agency—a refusal to let cowardice dictate morality. The others were less enthused, but sympathetic. The initial surprise on their faces faded quickly, replaced by a calm understanding of their commander's thought process. They had worked with him long enough to know he might have a problem with their current strategy, and now that problem had materialized.

Riley turned her attention to the slumbering form of Wyatt, who was still snoring contentedly on the couch. "Looks like you're up, Wyatt," she quipped, tossing a pen in his direction. The sound of the pen clattering against the floor roused Wyatt from his sleep, causing him to fumble for his sidearm for a split second before realizing where he was. But Jarod motioned for Wyatt to stand down. "No, this one I have to do myself," he said firmly.

"Sure, boss," Wyatt shrugged nonchalantly, slipping his baseball cap back over his eyes and immediately returning to his peaceful slumber. There were no hard feelings with Wyatt. He was a professional killer, and he approached his job with detached, clinical precision. There was no personal component, and he'd refrain from killing if he could. It was simply a means to an end—something that needed to be done to achieve their objective. If Jarod wanted this one, it was fine with him.

"We'll wait until morning," Jarod said, his voice quiet but firm. Choosing a direct confrontation was Jarod's way of facing his own demons as much as his target. In some twisted way, it was an affirmation of his humanity—a refusal to hide behind the veil of technology. *Behind a cheat.* The prospect of looking Siscal-Madoff in the eye was daunting and would come at a cost, but it was necessary for preserving the fragments of the soldier's honor Jarod still clung to. "When the wife has gone to work and when he's dropped off his kid. When he's alone, I'm going in."

Jarod sat on a bench in Washington Square Park, soaking in the sounds of a jazz trio halfway through a spellbinding rendition of Monk's "Ruby, My Dear." The piano was fully acoustic, on wheels, rolled out into the park, undoubtedly with great effort, and not a soulless synthesizer. The dedication these musicians showed to their craft left him in awe. It was a stark contrast to his own profession, which involved dismantling lives rather than enriching them. *At least the drum kit can be disassembled. The piano, not so much.* In contrast, his tool of choice was a tiny AI-operated squito armed with a deadly poison, quite literally the opposite of a grand piano in every way possible. One was huge, the other diminutive. One celebrated life and brought meaning to it, and the other snuffed it out.

He allowed himself to be swept away, if only momentarily. The mellowness of the bass complemented the sharpness of the piano. The rich, skillfully delivered live music enveloped him, a temporary balm to the anxiousness bubbling beneath the surface of his controlled exterior, a fleeting escape from the task awaiting him.

Jazz had always intrigued him, but he had never found the time to delve into it fully. The combination of written elements and improvisation that made each performance unique appealed to him. Some jazz was messy, much like the Lutosławskis and Pendereckis he often listened to. The chaos that one could perceive in both genres was anything but disordered. It was music that was carefully crafted, intentional, and incredibly skilled. The composer and the performing artists were masters of their crafts, unparalleled in their expertise. In some ways, he saw the music as a metaphor for his work, his life. The meticulous planning part, if nothing else, often devolved into improvisation and apparent chaos. The same level of skill and mastery was necessary in both. Just as the jazz artist had to adapt to the unexpected, he had to be ready to do the same. *No plan ever survives contact with the enemy.*

Jarod's fingers tapped unconsciously to the rhythm of the music, now deep into complex improvisational parts he didn't recall from the recordings. The trio played in an odd time signature, and finding that beat proved beyond his capabilities, but the unpredictable nature of the melody offered a strange comfort. *Trying to find solace in the complexity of jazz in expectation of an assassination. Is that reasonable?* To compare the improvisational elements of jazz to those of killing this man? *Probably not.* In this case, the deviation from the original plan was not due to improvisation, but rather his own moral objections to the original strategy. The original plan was safe and highly likely to succeed, but he couldn't bring himself to go through with it. Instead, he opted for a riskier, unwise strategy of going in himself, despite the presence of a better alternative. His tactical AI had given the go-ahead with reservations—the likelihood of Siscal-Madoff being able to resist was low, the chances of being caught on camera manageable—but Jarod still couldn't shake the feeling that he was being foolish.

He questioned whether his decision to suggest the alternate plan made him unfit for the mission, and whether Aegis had made a mistake in contracting him. *I looked good on paper, but faced with reality, I crumble.* Was he too easily swayed by his emotions, too willing to risk everything for a sense of moral righteousness? His team followed his lead, but he could sense their doubts. Wyatt agreed with him, but that was no surprise. Riley and Kale, on the other hand, were good soldiers, following orders without complaint. But even they must have had their reservations. Jarod couldn't deny that he was taking a risk, and the consequences if things went wrong could be dire. But he couldn't bring himself to kill Siscal-Madoff in such a cowardly way. He had to do this himself, consequences be damned.

He watched a leaf spiral to the ground, its descent slow and unpredictable in the light, artificial breeze courtesy of the dome's climate system. The park's ambient sounds—the laughter of children and the chatter of a few passersby—mingled with the music, now somewhat quieter as the bassist performed his solo.Despite his misgivings about the specifics of this mission, Jarod was in agreement with his employer's overall goal. He believed that the world would be better off without the targets they were going after, and that legacy law enforcement was ill-equipped to handle the task. They were doing the right thing, but he couldn't help but now question whether he was the right person for the job.

As he gazed out at the Financial District in the distance, with the dome looming above the skyscrapers, skyways, and elevators, he couldn't help but marvel at the engineering feat the dome represented. Humanity had failed to prevent the need for the domes in the first place, but the structures themselves were engineering marvels unmatched in history. As intrusive as they were, they had saved humanity—or at least were going to. But there was still so much left to be done.

The distant skyline, situated under the dome's curving latticework and translucent panes, amber light from the setting sun seeping through the outside cloud cover, served as a stark reminder of the world's fragility. Scott had shown that with London. Jarod's gaze lingered on the engineering marvel, a testament to human ingenuity and a monument to the failures that necessitated its existence.

With the final notes of "Ruby, My Dear" caressing his ears, he surrendered himself to the sweet harmony and let his mind drift away. But his fingers, betraying his casual facade, grazed the dart gun holstered inside his jacket. A 3D-printed device, the weapon was the fruit of Kale's resourcefulness—a tool unlikely to be detected by the watchful eye of dome security unless it caught a direct glimpse of it. Though it would do the job, he wished for the familiarity of a weapon he knew better.

As the music reached its crescendo, he was roused from his

reverie by Riley's voice over the comms. He had missed Siscal/Madoff's return from his daughter's school, lost in the sweet embrace of the music. The final, lingering note of the performance left a silence that resonated across the park. The brief respite music provided had ended, pulling him back to reality.

"I'm on it," he replied, his mind already focused on the task at hand. He strode past the trio of musicians, transferring a few dollars their way as a thank you for the brief respite they had provided. His braid AI, equipped with the latest private network and rerouting algorithms courtesy of Adriel, ensured that the transaction would remain untraceable. With a partly renewed sense of purpose, he set off toward Siscal/Madoff's apartment, his dart gun ready.

Kale had already been hard at work the previous night, utilizing his skills to crack the archaic code box that guarded the entrance to the building. It was a low-tech security measure, entirely offline and therefore immune to cyberattacks, which meant that his physical presence had been required. Armed with a portable decryptor and a cable connection, he had cracked the code. All very old-school stuff.

Jarod watched from a distance, allowing Siscal/Madoff to enter the building, hand holding a cup of coffee for his wife, the donut stacked on top of it, and settle into his office to begin work. Riley kept a close eye on the surveillance footage, relaying the stream in real time to Jarod's braid.

Right on cue, Siscal/Madoff's wife departed for work, leaving him alone to do his job, and when he seemed sufficiently engrossed in his tasks, Jarod approached the building, entered the digits into the code box, and made his way inside. He ascended the stairs to the third floor, his 3D-printed dart gun at the ready. Picking the old mechanical lock to the apartment, he slipped inside as quietly as possible.

Despite Siscal's preference for blending into the urban tapestry without drawing undue attention, the security within his apartment told a different story—a stark testament to his awareness of the dangers his actions attracted. Advanced security systems, from discreetly placed biometric scanners to hidden cameras with facial recognition capabilities, had turned the apartment into a fortress of modern surveillance and defense, no doubt monitored in real time by an AI, ready to alert its owner at the slightest sign of danger, upon which countermeasures would be taken in the form of defensive squitoes. It had taken some doing, but it had all been expertly diverted through Kale's ingenuity.

His braid overlaid directions through the apartment as he made his way toward the study. The layout had been meticulously studied, cross-referenced with surveillance footage and planning board schematics. But still, he took no chances, utilizing every advantage at his disposal. *By that logic, I should've used the squito, shouldn't I?*

Siscal/Madoff was hardly a dangerous man, at least not on the surface. A soft-spoken individual with the air of a gentle soul. A good man. At least until you reach the part where he finances terrorism.

The old hardwood floors groaned and protested under Jarod's feet. The sound was too loud, too conspicuous, even against the backdrop of the classical music Siscal/Madoff had playing from the study. The strains of Elgar's *Cello Concerto in E Minor* filled the room, reverberating through Jarod's bones. He didn't need a braid to recognize the haunting melody.

As Jarod moved silently through the apartment, he observed a life not much different from his own or that of anyone else. Family photos adorned the walls, showcasing smiling faces at various stages of life—a holiday by the beach, a birthday party with a cake smeared with too much icing. A child's artwork, proudly displayed on the refrigerator, a chaotic explosion of colors with the words "For Daddy" scrawled in a child's hand. The living room was a testament to everyday family life, with toys scattered about, a half-finished puzzle on the coffee table, and a cozy throw draped over the back of a well-used sofa. It was a stark reminder that Siscal, for all the evil he had wrought, lived a life not unlike anyone else's, filled with moments of love, joy, and mundane normalcy.

"Anyone there?" Siscal/Madoff called out from the study. Jarod's grip on the dart gun tightened as he prepared himself for the confrontation. He rounded the corner, entering the room to find Siscal-Madoff standing behind his desk. The man's reaction was peculiar; he made no attempt to flee or hide, merely staring at Jarod with a resigned expression. It was as though he knew this day would come, as though he had been waiting for it.

Jarod knew full well that in their line of business, no matter what side you were playing for, this particular end was not only a possibility but an inevitability. Siscal/Madoff knew that too. Jarod saw that in his eyes.

"Spare my family, please," Siscal-Madoff pleaded.

In that brief moment, the haunting image of Mrs. Siscal or their daughter stumbling upon the lifeless body of their loved one flickered in Jarod's mind. Almost two decades of avoiding bloodshed had been for nothing. *I suppose that'll have to do.*

"I will," he said to Siscal/Madoff, his voice barely above a whisper. "I promise." He pulled the trigger.

Siscal fell to the floor with a muted thud, life draining from his eyes in a matter of seconds. The silence that followed was deafening—the silence of a life extinguished, a story ended. Both his and Siscal's. As the man's last breath faded, Jarod was left with the haunting resonance of the life he had just taken, and the cost to his own soul.

Dana

As the first glimmers of dawn crept into the room, she stirred from her slumber, ten minutes before the alarm was set to jolt her awake. The covers of the hotel bed cocooned her in a warm and fuzzy embrace, like being cuddled, but still not quite. The faint chirping of birds—kept by Frankfurt's wildlife preserve bureau, a sound not often heard within the confines of the domes—filtered through the slightly ajar window, mingling with the early morning light to gently coax her from sleep. Quite the contrast to the field office bunk bed. The thought of that field office hastily rid her of any misconstrued notion that she was at home in her bed, or on vacation at a luxurious spa, the momentary warmth and comfort rapidly traded for a pang of frustration, reminding her that a day's work awaited.

If the security incident at the construction site had led to any positive outcome, it was this: her relocation to comfy luxury accommodations overlooking the Frankfurt Messe, safe, on the Inside once more. A few days of hesitation on the part of Aegis, but eventually the corporate lawyers concerned with liability had won against the number crunchers concerned about cost. One would think springing for a hotel Inside would be an easy decision, but apparently not. So, there she was, bathing in comfort and the warmth of high thread-count bedding. That didn't mean the job was done, though. With a tremendous effort, she rolled over from her side to her back, and as she fluttered open her eyes, her lens sparked to life, projecting the alarm interface to the upper right.

[5:21 a.m.]

Whoever let morning people set the world's timetable should be shot. She realized whoever did would've been dead for centuries. *Alright, fine, whoever was responsible should be dug up and shot. Happy?* Although the phenomenon is probably more of an evolutionary trait than a person making a decision at some point. *Or broader—a cultural thing. Like the advent of agriculture, or uhm... orbital mechanics! The Earth's rotation around the sun and such.* Nevertheless, she still felt someone should be shot for it. A sigh escaped her, annoyed with herself yet amused by her own absurd early morning contemplations. *It's not a good sign that I'm speaking to myself after only being awake for... what? One minute?*

While the new digs helped, they did little for her mental fortitude. Despite her best efforts, she couldn't shake off the memories of the chaos that had transpired Outside. The image of Brett's armor, flames licking at its edges as he shielded her from Molotov cocktails, was etched on her cornea. A shiver coursed through her at the memory, as vivid as if the flames were still before her eyes. In a bid to distract herself, she sought solace in her day-to-day activities, primarily work. She delved deep into the minutiae of her job, poring over meeting minutes from negotiation sessions, submitting progress reports for Tatum—on time, for once—and even going the extra mile to send in additional ones with analysis no one had even asked for. She engaged in meaningless conversations with Tariqe over lens, hoping to keep her mind occupied with trivial matters. When not working, she jogged on the hotel treadmill, her thoughts drifting to Jarod and his mysterious new assignment. But the armor was always there, a constant presence in her dreams and waking moments. The flames still licked at its edges, a reminder of the dangers she had faced.

As another potential distraction, she had the new route to work to look forward to. A commute, as it were. An activity that most people loathed, but which suddenly held a sense of novelty and intrigue for her. It was a refreshing break from the monotony of her routine at the barracks Outside, at least for the time being.

The protesters were the catalyst for her unexpected daily commute, a series of events set in motion by their reckless actions. The security breach they had caused had sent ripples of anxiety through the contracted security firm, ultimately causing a domino effect through to Aegis, which in turn had resulted in her relocation to the hotel inside the safety of the dome. She acknowledged the necessity of these measures, of course. But it also introduced a goddamn commute! *And annoying extra security measures.*

The transit now required her to don body armor, a necessary precaution for her safety, the weight of it a jarring reminder of her altered reality. Brett and his team would arrive shortly to escort her, fitting her with the protective gear every day before they set off. They would be here in... one hour. *Coffee. I need coffee.*

She dialed up room service. "Guten Morgen, Frau Lima," a female voice said. "Was kann ich für Sie tun?" She instructed the AI to switch to English. It was a daily occurrence; the AI had a habit of reverting back to German after every interaction. While she knew enough of the language to order breakfast, she preferred to conserve her energy, especially at this hour. Real-time translation was taxing on her braid, and she needed sustenance before she could even consider it. *Thank God it speaks English! Otherwise, that would've been an annoying Catch-22.* A small chuckle at conquering the AI's linguistic stubbornness offered a fleeting respite, a minor victory amidst the morning's sluggish uphill battle.

Most hotel AIs catered to the guest's preferred language, as it was registered at check-in, but German ones were an exception, along with the French. Switching to English required a manual command, but once done, it would usually remember. *Is that a bug or a feature, one might ask?*

She ordered a continental breakfast, along with an extra pot of coffee and a bowl of mixed fruits and yogurt. Stretching her limbs, she kicked off the covers and instructed the shower to start up, directing it to provide only hot water for the first three minutes. She relished the steamy ambiance that enveloped the bathroom before stepping into the shower's warm embrace.

The Herman Messe Hotel, a luxurious five-star establishment, was located right beside the towering old pencil scraper. It boasted a breathtaking view overlooking the vast Frankfurt Messe grounds. Aegis had spared no expense in securing her lodging. *From bunk to luxury,* she mused, as she stepped out of the shower and onto the plush bath mat.

The recent incident had been an embarrassing fiasco, and they were anxious to avoid any potential lawsuits or bad press. Unfortunately, the news of the incident had already spread like viral wildfire; however, for the time being, they had managed to keep her identity concealed. *At least I get to bill the company a fancy hotel stay because of it.*

She slipped on a robe and stepped out onto the balcony. It was entirely still today, the dome's environmental algorithm having deemed today pleasant, allowing natural light to filter through the translucent walls as dawn approached. It was a small consolation on an otherwise lonely morning. She missed Jarod, who was now off the grid, completely immersed in his enigmatic mission. He promised to be in touch soon, but for now, the comfort of the hotel covers would have to suffice. Her gaze lingered on the horizon. Elegant Frankfurt, with the grandeur of an opulent Western city dome—its skyscrapers reaching for the inner ceiling—juxtaposed with old architecture and crossing monorails, mixed with a feeling of isolation. Despite the postcard beauty, it was but a reminder that he was not with her.

Her braid chimed, signaling the arrival of breakfast. She granted entry to the bot carrying the tray before retreating to the shower, hoping the coffee would still be warm by the time she finished. Anticipation for the meal bubbled within her until she recalled her order. *Dry toast and low-fat yogurt. Yay! I wish I could afford gene editing. At least the coffee will be good.*

As she ate, she perused the holographic Gantt chart hovering on her lens above the coffee table. Its colorful lines displayed the progress of all work streams, providing a comprehensive overview of the project's status.

Shit. Nearly every work stream reported good progress, except hers. A sinking feeling in her chest settled as she observed the black-and-white proof, dangling in the air on her lens, that her achievements paled in comparison to others'. A heavy cloak of unmet expectations dimmed her once unshakable confidence. She foresaw an uncomfortable conversation with Tatum in her near future. Zoning permissions, land acquisition for support structures, relocation of affected refugee settlements, and various infrastructure plans, such as airlock checkpoints and public transport—the list seemed endless, each line showing greater advancement than hers. *Fucking Gabriel. This was a done deal a few weeks ago.* She had gone from best in class to worst.

The number of rows in the chart was, if nothing else, a testament to the amount of bureaucracy involved in building a dome section, with the red tape often taking longer to clear than the construction itself. This was especially true in legal and regulatory environments as complex as Germany's—or any Western country, for that matter. She had always found the EU to be particularly sluggish, a reflection of the continent's general affluence. The richer the city, the more infrastructure to consider. And the more citizens with deep pockets, capable of hiring lawyers to contest, for whatever reason they deemed fit.

Thankfully, all the affected Innie residents had signed off, with the work stream considered closed for quite some time. That wasn't always the case; getting the signatures from the Innie population was one of the most challenging tasks, often requiring a considerable amount of time and effort. The Niederrad dome section would be separated from the rest of the Frankfurt Cluster by checkpoints, providing an added level of protection against contamination. This likely helped expedite the process of obtaining those signatures. Having worked on the Innies' stream in the past, she was relieved to be working with the Outies this time, as they were usually more appreciative. *Usually* being the operative word here.

With a deep sigh, she closed the holographic Gantt chart, resigning herself to the meager progress in her work stream. Resignation mingled with an ember of resolve as she turned her attention to her breakfast. The bowl of low-fat yogurt on the table before her seemed to call out to her, beckoning her to imbibe.

Brett and his officers arrived just as she finished her breakfast, the aroma of freshly brewed coffee still lingering as she finished the meal. She recognized Brett, of course, but had trouble recalling the names of his two colleagues. *Renny?* And the other one had something Indian or Pakistani sounding.

Admittedly, Brett had introduced them on their initial visit, but had neglected to mention their names again, and the two seldom spoke. She wished she had recorded their names on her braid, but she preferred to keep such aids off. *Better to keep your brain working.* While there were horror stories circulating in the media about the dangers of letting braids do all the work, leading to anything from Alzheimer's to plain old brain rot, she wasn't convinced of their validity. It didn't matter anyway. *In any case, I doubt I'll need to know their names. Cops aren't particularly talkative. I assume. What the hell do I know, now that I think about it?*

She realized that she didn't know many law enforcement people, aside from Jarod and his crew, who weren't exactly cops. They could be considered bounty hunters, or privateers, but Jarod disliked either term, preferring the label of law enforcement contractors. A brief moment of bittersweet sadness washed over her as she contemplated how Jarod and his crew intermingled with her current situation. Jarod, like Brett, was a man of few words, speaking only when necessary. Wyatt and Riley were the loudest of the group, constantly yapping at each other. Kale, on the other hand, was as quiet as a mouse. *So, is there a conclusion to be drawn with this comparison?* She decided there wasn't.

She had Brett and his colleagues wait in the main room while she dressed in the bathroom. After she emerged, they fitted her with the body armor, following the established routine before departing. The routine of donning armor had become a tangible reminder of the danger she faced, each clink and zip while a piece was fitted adding to her apprehension.

Their arrival had caught her off guard, leaving them behind schedule, but Brett remained relaxed about the delay. The other two officers, as usual, remained silent, gazing off into the distance like mindless bots. But she supposed they were just doing their jobs, having their braids run scenarios and scan for threats.

Initially, she had questioned the modest size of her escort, recalling the chaos that had occurred Outside. The outside air, even as it was filtered through the dome's climate control, carried a certain chill. She wasn't sure if it was the dome's way of simulating the freshness of early mornings or her imagination, the threat of unseen dangers lurking beyond the dome frontier. Nevertheless, the escort offered a semblance of security in the unpredictable world beyond the dome. Brett had assuaged her concerns when they first began their journey a week ago, stating unequivocally that three officers would be more than sufficient to keep her safe. They were Inside and surrounded by additional layers of security, but she couldn't help but feel a twinge of apprehension as she contemplated what lay beyond the dome's protective walls.

Sensing her unease, Brett was quick to reassure her. "Don't worry," he said. "Once we're outside, we'll have a direct path to the field office. No one can get close." Brett had meticulously outlined the route they would take. A *Strassenbahn* from the hotel to the checkpoint, then a priority passage through permit control and access to the VIP lane via the airlock, followed by the controlled route to the office.

The officers accompanying her all wore plain clothes, a subtle approach Brett insisted was the best. He explained to her that blending in was key, rather than drawing attention with motorcades and visibly armed escorts. Such displays gave the illusion of security, nothing more, unless you brought a small army like a president or other dignitary would. Obviously, the company wasn't going to spring for anything of the sort. Anything beyond Brett and his two human robots would have to come out of her own pocket, but the current arrangement was more than enough, she told herself. And Outside there would be a car and a somewhat larger escort. That all made sense. While Inside, in the heart of the city, under the protective shelter of the dome, the three officers would be enough. There, she would even be safe on her own. Reminding herself of this fact didn't help. Instead, fear kept nagging her. *I'm just being paranoid.*

As she rode the *Strassenbahn* towards her destination, she attempted to focus on the opening remarks she had prepared for today's session. The early morning light, dimmed as it was filtered through light clouds and translucent dome plating, cast long shadows across the pedestrian zones, painting the city in hues of gold and gray. Distracted by the city's early morning calm, she found herself ensnared in the beauty and paradox of the dome—its protection a golden cage that both comforted and confined. She quickly swatted away the thoughts, realizing she had limited time to rehearse. But when returning to the preparations, her mind refused to cooperate, still reeling from the residual anxiety of the recent attack. The presence of Brett and his team, spread out around her while trying to maintain a low profile, only served to heighten her unease.

Her attention inevitably drifted away from her notes and towards the window, where the bustling activity of the city unfolded outside. She couldn't deny that a motorcade or even a single car in Frankfurt would attract unwelcome attention. As they made their way through Münchener Strasse towards the inner city, she noted the transformation of many streets originally designed for vehicles into pedestrian zones, with only delivery vehicles permitted access. Taxis and privately owned personal transports were prohibited, a far more drastic change than she had seen in London or other Anglo cities she had visited, which still allowed personal transports outside the central domes despite their largely superior underground networks.

Deciding to fully immerse herself in the view outside, she minimized her notes and gazed out the window. The serenity of the empty streets contrasted sharply with the turmoil within her, and provided a sense of calm before the storm. *Everything here is so clean.* The pristine streets, devoid of the usual hustle and bustle, lay in silent anticipation of the day ahead, waiting for daily life to commence. She couldn't, for the life of her, fathom why anyone would resist the idea of being included in a dome of such unparalleled wealth.

Frankfurt had long been one of the wealthiest cities in Europe, even before the construction of the domes. As the first dome in Europe, it had been meticulously maintained over the decades and continued to outshine newer domes like Paris and London in every conceivable metric. It boasted a higher Gini coefficient, a higher ranking on the Human Development Index, and scored higher on the World Happiness Report. More people here lived comfortably on UBI than almost anywhere else, and there was less crime. But perhaps, she couldn't help but wonder, all this comfort came with a price. The city was riddled with cameras, checkpoints, and permits. Germans seemed to accept these intrusions with greater ease than their English-speaking peers, and maybe even more readily than the Scandies.

Expansion of the dome had primarily occurred to the north of the city and to Offenbach, with the south of the Main River being left behind in terms of growth. In that particular metric, many other cities had surpassed Frankfurt, having expanded to cover more of the exposed Outside compared to baseline. She couldn't be certain, but she suspected that German red tape might be at least partially responsible for the discrepancy.

Transitioning from the Outside to the Inside would be a profound change for anyone. It meant giving up some measure of freedom, but also offered the promise of greater safety and a higher quality of life, depending on how one defined it. She recognized that for some, freedom was synonymous with quality of life, and that was, of course, a valid perspective. She empathized with the concerns of the Outies, but the extent to which Gabriel had frustrated negotiations was still baffling.

She had been thrilled at the prospect of negotiating the expansion to Niederrad. It was long overdue, especially considering the enormous wealth accumulated in this part of the world. It was always the south of the river that seemed to be neglected, not just in Frankfurt, but also in London and other cities. *There are no banking skyscrapers south of the river.*

As they rode on the new elevated tram track above Zeil, built to reduce pressure on the old S-Bahn underground, she marveled at Frankfurt's resistance to building skyways and residential levels, allowing natural light to flood the city. While this resistance to high-rise development had helped preserve the city's beauty, it had also led to significant congestion. Nevertheless, she found it breathtaking to see Frankfurt's ground level relatively untouched, especially when compared to London, where artificial light now illuminated much of the city's surface. Protected areas, where skyways were never built, were the only exceptions. *Like the parts now ruined by the bomb.*

The sun had only just begun to rise, casting a warm orange glow, filtered by the dome, over the near-empty stretch between Hauptwache and Konstablerwache. Normally, this area was teeming with life—people shopping, dining out, and enjoying the city's offerings. But it was still early, and the shops had just opened their doors, with people not yet arriving. The quietness was surreal, as if the city was holding its breath, waiting for the day to truly begin.

Prior to embarking on this daily commute, she had never seen Zeil as empty as it was today. The bustling street had long been considered one of Europe's busiest shopping destinations, and despite the convenience of online shopping and home delivery, it remained so. The predicted death of city centers due to 3D printers and home deliveries had not come to pass. People still enjoyed leaving their homes, dining out, and indulging in food they did not have to prepare themselves. She found herself included in this group. *When was the last time me or Jarod actually cooked a meal?*

This held true for high-end shopping districts in major city centers, such as Oxford Street, Champs-Élysées, or Fifth Avenue. However, more peripheral areas were struggling to keep up and, in some cases, had already succumbed to economic decline.

The damn checkpoints, whether internal or external, slow everything down to a crawl, causing people to cluster in already busy areas. Even with priority access, they added almost an hour to any commute. *Why subject yourself to that?* She couldn't help but think of the Outies who traveled to the Inside every day for work. The sheer inconvenience of it was unimaginable, week in and week out. Although the same applied to Innies working Outside, they had the advantage of not requiring work visas. Residence IDs were usually enough, which made the process much quicker. Unfortunately, work visa requirements were a one-way street in Frankfurt, and probably most other places too. If you were an Innie working Outside, you didn't need one. *No wonder the periphery is dying, whether inside or out.*

The tram was approaching Berger Strasse, where it would turn south toward the southeast checkpoint, with a waiting car on the other side to take them to the construction field office. Brett had assured her that the exposure during the transfer from the checkpoint to the car would only last a few seconds, and there would be extra security during that time. *But, as they say, a chain is only as strong as its weakest link.* Brett couldn't guarantee that nothing would happen during those brief moments, no matter how much he reassured her. It was up to her to silence those fears, currently drowning out the rational part of her brain.

As the tram made its way toward Berger Strasse, she couldn't help but feel a sense of nostalgia. The tram's gentle hum and the rhythmic clack over the tracks provided a soothing backdrop, as familiar storefronts and street corners whisked by, each carrying a fragment of past experiences. A pang of longing struck her as she passed these familiar streets, the city's unchanged beauty a perfect example of the world she was fighting to provide for the people of Niederrad. *This is exactly what I want for them! If only they could see it. Live, and not on some flatscreen or even VR experience. Nothing compares to the real thing.* Berger Strasse had always held a special place in her heart. Unlike the rest of the city, it remained largely unchanged since before the dome was erected, enjoying cultural protection. It was a bustling hub of activity, and even at this early hour, she could imagine the street coming to life soon enough.

She pulled up the route map on her lens, and the places she had visited highlighted themselves automatically. Most of the lunches had been business affairs, where Tatum's team of lawyers and project managers had secured permissions from the Frankfurt Amt. However, some had been private, with Jarod mostly. Those were happy memories, and she yearned to revisit them, even if only in her mind. It was a bit silly, perhaps, but it gave her a sense of connection. A little fantasy island of happiness in their time apart. The chatter and clatter of dishes in the background of her braid calls with project managers, a reminder of the vibrancy and warmth that human presence brought to even the most mundane activities.

Germany was one of many countries outside the English-speaking world that introduced legislation mandating a certain percentage of retail and hospitality venues be staffed by humans, a policy aimed at preserving jobs in a world rapidly being automated. While the legislation had its detractors—mainly economists and business executives—she couldn't deny the charm of ordering her Schnitzel and having it cooked and served by a human rather than a bot or vending machine. Of course, involving humans often made things significantly more expensive, but it was a unique experience that one couldn't easily replicate with machines.

Nevertheless, despite technological advancements, many jobs remained unautomated, even Inside. In defiance of political and economic theories from a century ago, there were still many things that only humans could do, and in most places—especially Outside—flesh-and-blood workers were still the cheapest ones around. The working class was far from dead. *I am part of it, myself.*

The tram glided past Piccolomondo, an Italian establishment where some of the later meetings with the Frankfurt officials had taken place. A bot-serviced eatery instead of the extravagant human-serviced establishments of the earlier gatherings, a reflection of Aegis' penny-pinching approach toward expenses once the sale had been completed. After all, only the boring details involving lower-level government bureaucrats, people like her and her fellow project managers, were discussed there. No need to splurge on extravagant human-serviced places. *The food was still pretty good. Authentically Italian, maybe not, but still good. At least it's a step up from robovendors that print the food.*

It had been a grueling process to woo all the right people to get what the company needed, yet it paled in comparison to the difficulty of negotiating with the residents outside the dome. At times, she couldn't help but envy her Russian and Asian counterparts, who didn't have to concern themselves with the rights of the residents they encountered. *We're expanding the dome. Move out of the way, or we'll pave over your house! With you in it.*

While these counterparts may have it easier, their approach was not commensurable with the principles of individual liberty and the rule of law upheld by Western societies. The West still endeavored to preserve freedom, even in the face of the challenges posed by life within the domes. Nevertheless, citizens within the dome were constantly under watch, and true freedom was but an illusion. *Hehe. That's Jarod talking.* The London attack was a stark reminder of this reality—that the need for surveillance was ubiquitous, for the good of everyone.

She was a firm believer in the domes and the benefits they provided to mankind. There had been a price to pay, but ultimately, there had been no other choice. Mankind had only itself to blame for not doing enough when it had the chance. However, she also understood the arguments against them. She empathized with the apprehension felt by the Outies who hesitated to trade their freedom for the wealth and security of the Inside. But the clock was ticking, and although decades felt like a long time, they would come and go in the blink of an eye. The expansion of the world's domes was an inevitable fact. It was either live Inside or face eventual death.

Nonetheless, the concerns of the Outies had to be heard and addressed. She felt a sense of guilt whenever her thoughts strayed toward the harsh measures employed by some of her counterparts in other parts of the world. *Forced relocation and incarceration for those who refuse. It's not the way.*

The tram slowly made its way down Berger Strasse, inching toward Bornheim Station, and from there, it would turn south, then back east along the Main toward the checkpoint. Along the way, she noticed a handful of AI delivery vehicles transporting goods and produce to the few AI kiosks in the area. *AIs delivering to other AIs.* It was almost as if they occupied a world within a world, separated from human society. *At least they still serve humans at the end of the chain.*

Her mind couldn't help but wander toward the growing trend of people engaging in romantic relationships with bots. Some even went as far as having dinner dates with AI lovebots, complete with personality add-ons and human-like appearances. It wasn't as common as some old science fiction stories had predicted, but it existed nonetheless. *How would a dinner date with a bot that didn't eat work?* Or maybe there were super-advanced models that did? *But how's the conversation?* Would there one day be a Turing test-passing dinner date bot? The possibility was intriguing, but also slightly unsettling.

The knot in her stomach tightened as the tram slowed down at the station. She had kept herself busy until now, but seeing the checkpoint and the Outside looming made her anxious. She reminded herself that her fears were irrational and went through Brett's instructions in her head once again. The checkpoint was inside the dome, and anyone without a permit would be stopped dead. The road to the office was controlled, and there would be a car and an escort with drones. She repeated it a few times, telling herself to stay calm.

"Irrational fears," she muttered under her breath as she and her escort got off the tram. Brett walked beside her, with the two officers flanking them. The checkpoint was just around the corner.

But they never got that far. Despite Brett's assurances, the Outsiders had somehow made their way inside the dome. A cold dread seized her as the strangers' presence shattered the morning's fragile peace, the hard reality of her vulnerability crashing down around her. The group of men materialized out of nowhere, surrounding them in an instant. They were armed, and one of them pressed a hard object against her back, making her freeze. Brett's officers bristled, but weapons were already trained on them.

"Don't do anything stupid," the man holding the gun warned. "Keep walking and nobody will get hurt."

As the men closed in, their rough hands pushing and prodding, she felt a cold sweat break out across her skin. Brett tried to reassure her, his words transmitted via text directly through her braid. **[Stay calm. Alert has gone out. The dome's security system will pick them up, but there will be a delay.]**

Stay calm! Sure! She took a deep breath, trying to steady herself as they were herded toward an unknown fate. Brett urged his men to observe caution, offering her reassurance that they would not be without help. **[Men will stand down. Safest. I don't want to risk a confrontation. Let local law enforcement act at checkpoint.]**

But the young men had other plans. They led her and the others down a twisted labyrinth of empty side streets, far away from the safety of the checkpoint. Once they were out of sight and earshot of any prying eyes, the men blindfolded them and tied their hands tightly behind their backs.

As they stumbled forward, unsure of where they were headed, she could feel the cold dampness of underground tunnels surrounding her—perhaps a disused sewer or some long-forgotten maintenance tunnels under the dome. Her footsteps echoed hollowly against the ground, each step an echo in cavernous darkness.

Her suspicions were confirmed a little later when the blindfolds were removed, revealing the dark, damp surroundings of the tunnels. Disbelief and fear tangled within her as the unmistakable touch of real wind, erratic and uncontrolled compared to its artificial Inside counterpart, brushed against her skin, wrapping her in near panic. She suppressed a panicked shriek, but it did little to help—the feeling of dread had already settled over her like a heavy cloak.

The zip ties around their wrists stayed on, but at least now she could walk with more confidence, without fear of tripping over unseen obstacles in the darkness.

Drawing a deep breath, she reviewed, yet again, every minuscule detail Brett had imparted. The unspoken understanding was that, within the dome, she would be safe, with the police escort—unarmed—mostly serving to soothe her nerves. They had never formulated a contingency plan for an event such as the one that was currently unfolding.

The young men, their faces twisted into a mixture of both malice and fear, flanked the four of them as they herded them through the twisting underground tunnels. One walked in front, while two others followed behind, their hands pushing and prodding whenever they stumbled or hesitated. She looked around, trying to get her bearings in the dimly lit surroundings. It was difficult to see, and her lens had no night vision capabilities. But as they walked on, the tunnels gradually widened into large corridors, and more light seeped through. It was daylight, real daylight, not the filtered glow of artificial light within the confines of a dome. As they walked on, an eerie sound howled through the corridors—wind, real wind, not the managed and tamed winds of a dome's automatic climate control system. She knew it instantly, could feel it in her bones. *They were outside.* She couldn't help but wonder how these boys had found a way in and out of the dome, bypassing the checkpoints and security measures that were supposed to keep her safe.

Her eyes had adapted to the dim light of the tunnels now, and she looked around cautiously, trying not to provoke her captors any further. She could see Brett now, his normally calm expression replaced with a growing sense of unease and anxiety. As they walked further into the tunnels, it became abundantly clear that they were, in fact, now outside, far from the safety of the dome and its carefully orchestrated security measures. And as the reality of their situation sank in, Brett's confidence began to fade from his eyes, and hers along with it.

The other officers, realizing that they were now out in the open, away from any potential help, made their move, against the orders of their commanding officer. Brett tried to keep the situation from escalating, ordering his men to stand down and avoid confrontation, but it was too late. Panic had already set in, and one of the officers managed to break free from his zip ties and wrestle the gun away from one of their captors. A shot rang out with a deafening boom, filling the tunnels with smoke and chaos. Dana crouched down as Brett and the other officer dove for the other two boys. The free officer produced a knife from somewhere and quickly freed his colleagues, but more guns went off, and the tunnel was again ablaze with flashes of light and thunderous booms. One of the boys—the shorter one—was shot, falling over like a lifeless rag doll.

Time seemed to warp around her as the tunnel erupted into violence, each gunshot burying her deeper inside the nightmare, her screams lost amidst the cacophony. For a moment, everything spun in a dizzying blur. She wasn't sure if she'd been hit or not. All she knew was that the world had turned into a deafening, chaotic nightmare. And then she saw one of the officers dive for the taller boy's weapon, and everything again exploded into a frenzy of flashes and loud bangs. Dana crouched, buried her head into the ground, and screamed, wondering if they would ever make it out of this alive.

...the integration of artificial intelligence and robotics resulted in widespread unemployment within a few decades of the twenty-first century...

...on average, the percentage of individuals who are granted Universal Basic Income is more than twice as high inside as compared to outside...

...despite advancements in robotics technology, human labor continues to be extensively utilized for typical robot work outside. However, unemployment rates remain significantly higher...

...the utilization of new materials, energy-efficient production techniques, advanced manufacturing, and automation has resulted in substantially reduced production costs, reaching near-zero marginal costs in certain areas of the globe, resembling elements of a true post-scarcity economy. While mass unemployment has become an unfortunate reality, the necessity to earn income has significantly decreased, enabling a considerable segment of the population to maintain a comfortable standard of living despite their lack of employment...

...in contemporary times, the proportion of individuals enjoying traditional, permanent employment has notably declined. Instead, a significant percentage of the workforce has shifted toward freelance contracting and gig work in both private enterprise and government sectors...

...jobs have become obsolete, primarily due to the integration of automation. This phenomenon has affected numerous professions, such as fast food workers, factory workers of varying capacities, custodians, roadside workers, construction workers, security guards, as well as transport workers, including truck drivers, train operators, and pilots…

...automation and technological advancements have also extended to several white-collar occupations, including but not limited to accountants, insurance actuaries, risk analysts, financial analysts, administrative workers, regulatory compliance specialists, paralegals, and financial auditors. Artists have also not escaped job displacement...

...many of these jobs remain in one form or another on the Outside, where adoption of Universal Basic Income policies lags behind, but even there, automation has...

…Several countries have introduced legislation to limit the prevalence of automation, often to safeguard job opportunities. Germany and France are notable examples within the European Union, while China and the state of Victoria in Australia have also implemented similar measures. However, within the United States, such legislation has not seen substantial adoption, except in the state of California…

Aea

The knock on the door was heavy and furious, reverberating throughout the apartment, shaking its very walls. "Baby, open up!" Daemon's voice was urgent and strained, his words muffled through the wooden door but still loud enough for her to hear clearly. Aea could tell immediately something was wrong. His fists continued to hammer the door, an unyielding assault Aea was sure would alert the entire neighborhood. Her heart pounded now, fear gripping her like a cold hand around her throat. Daemon's voice, usually calm and reassuring, carried an edge of desperation she'd never heard before. It sent shivers down her spine, her mind running through every worst-case scenario.

Behind her, Tabayah's voice trembled with fear, jolted awake by the sudden interruption in their movie-streaming slumber. "What is it?" she quivered.

"Go to your room," Aea commanded as she rose from the couch. Tonight was just another night where she assumed the responsibility of babysitting, her father tied up at work. As usual, no commotion was the rule. This wasn't the sound of a raucous party, though. Aea could hear Cali too, and the panic in both their voices was unmistakable, real, and raw. Or was it just some elaborate prank, a twisted game they were playing on her? She wouldn't put it past them. *He's not that good of an actor.*

She approached the door cautiously. The banging and shouting grew louder, more frantic, until she almost expected the flimsy wood to crack and splinter under the onslaught. She hesitated for a moment, her hand hovering over the door chain, before she finally relented, unlocked it, and turned the knob. As soon as there was a crack between the doorframe and the door, Daemon threw it open with a force that almost knocked her off her feet. The door handle smashed into the porous drywall with a resounding crash, leaving a gaping hole in its wake.

Daemon burst into the room, his face a mask of fear and urgency. Sweat beaded on his forehead, his chest heaved as his powerful frame supported a man with a leg wound that was bleeding profusely. His eyes darted around, assessing, calculating, like at the protest, but this time with terror rather than anger. A shirt sleeve was tightly bound above the leg of the wounded man, saturated with blood. Despite his own injuries, Daemon appeared to be in better shape than the man he was supporting. Aea could see blood seeping from multiple wounds on Daemon's body, but she couldn't pinpoint the exact locations of his injuries.

The gruesome sight rooted her to the spot, her breath seizing for a moment as Daemon barged in. Her eyes darted across the faces, her brain trying to process the blood, the strangers, the panic. Her stomach churned with a mixture of fear, confusion, and a desperate wish that this was just a nightmare. *That's right, I must be asleep on the couch. I must be.*

Beside the injured man stood a woman that Aea recognized from the local news. She was the Innie who had been leading the negotiations for the dome, from the protest. She was clearly terrified, her eyes darting around the room as she and Cali struggled to support another man, this one clutching his side as blood poured from the wound.

"First aid kit," Daemon barked as he supported the man with

the leg wound into the hallway. The woman and Cali followed, their injured man groaning in pain with each movement.

"You alone?" Cali asked as they squeezed past Aea in the narrow hallway, his hand clutching a gun.

She nodded, her heart racing. "My sister is here," she said, gesturing toward the closed door of her sister's room.

Cali quickly helped the woman lay the man with the wound in his side on the living room couch. The man with the leg wound sat down next to him. Cali then swept through the apartment, checking each room, wild-eyed and anxious. He moved with frenetic energy, his actions swift and jerky, his wild gaze darting side to side. Every now and then, his eyes would lock onto the injured men, a flicker of something like fear passing over his features before he masked it with a grunt and a tightening of his jaw. Despite being dirty and bruised, he seemed to be mostly uninjured. At least he wasn't bleeding.

As he passed her on his way back to the living room, Cali spoke in a low, urgent voice. "Ameer didn't make it," he said, his eyes fixed on the two injured men. "But at least we got one of theirs too."

What!? Aea stood frozen, the words swirling around her, now lost in a meaningless cacophony. She heard Cali speak, saw the police officer's movements, and the woman's eyes meeting hers. Their lips moved, sounds came out, but the significance of the words slipped through her mind like sand through fingers. She was adrift in shock, her body refusing to move, her brain refusing to process. The woman said something again, a question perhaps, but it was like trying to understand a foreign language she had never heard before. Yet, when her gaze locked with the woman's, she saw a reflection of her own terror mirrored back. Her face was etched with the same shock. If she realized anything, it was perhaps that the Innie woman, too, seemed a victim in this unfolding nightmare.

As her mind slowly recovered, so came the questions. *What did Cali mean by "Ameer didn't make it"? What did he mean by "got one of theirs"?* Aea's ears rang with Cali's words. The smell of blood, stronger now with the wounded so close, filled her nostrils, a sickly sweet odor that made her stomach churn.

"What have you done?" she cried, her voice breaking with despair as she snapped out of her trance.

"Aid kit!" Daemon yelled, his grip on Aea's arm almost painful as he propelled her toward the living room. She shook herself out of her daze and sprinted to the kitchen, heart racing. As she emerged with the first aid kit, she spotted Tabayah standing in the doorway to her room, tears streaming down her face. Aea rushed past her and handed the kit to Daemon, who motioned for her to give it to the wounded man on the couch.

"Do what you promised, cop," Cali growled from the doorway, his arms crossed and his gun at the ready. "Patch us up. Then you can have a look at your cop buddy and yourself."

These men are cops? The injured man groaned as he sat up, motioning for Daemon to approach. Aea watched in horror as the man carefully removed the makeshift bandages, inspecting each wound with a practiced eye. She functioned well enough now to notice his hands were steady, his movements methodical and precise, contrasting sharply with the chaos around them. Despite the gravity of the situation, there was a kindness in his eyes, a softness that belied his firm, professional demeanor.

"Will he be okay?" she dared to ask, her voice trembling.

"Don't worry," he said, looking up at Aea. "It's not bad. Just flesh wounds, cuts. See this here? Bullet went straight through. A graze, that's all." The man's gaze was no longer kind but wary as he addressed her, his tone laden with a professional detachment that bordered on suspicion. "And you are?" he asked, his voice measured, eyes scanning her as if trying to piece together her role in the gruesome situation.

"Shut up and fix him," Cali barked.

The man ignored the order, turning his attention back to Aea, his eyes now kinder, less suspicious, perhaps noticing her fear, that her demeanor was starkly different from the others'. "I'm Brett," he said, introducing himself. "What's your name?"

"Aea," she said, her voice trembling.

"Hi, Aea." Brett worked quickly and efficiently, his hands moving with practiced ease as he bandaged Daemon's wounds.

The first aid kit lay open on the coffee table, its contents spread out in a chaotic array. Brett's hands, though steady, were smeared with blood, leaving crimson streaks on the white bandages as he worked. The sharp, antiseptic smell of the medical supplies filled the room, mingling with the metallic tang of blood.

"Is it bad?" she asked again, her voice but a whisper. Brett nodded, his voice calm and controlled. "He needs a doctor," he said. "But don't worry, we have training in field medicine. He'll be alright."

Some relief in the chaos, yet it did little to quell her fear or the nausea building at the sight of all the blood. She swallowed hard and nodded, her eyes shifting to the woman who sat on the floor beside the corner sofa, while the man they had brought in was lying on it, barely conscious and bleeding profusely. Aea couldn't help but think about how her dad would react to the bloodstains on the couch. *He doesn't look too good,* she thought, eyeing the man on it. Blood on the couch was the least of her concerns.

The woman looked okay, dirty and disheveled, her clothes stained with dirt and blood. But she seemed uninjured. Aea assumed it was the injured man's blood on her stockings. She remained silent, her eyes still frantically darting around the room.

"See?" Brett said, breaking the silence. "All bandaged up. He'll be fine." Aea breathed a sigh of relief at the news.

"And don't worry," Brett continued, smiling. "We're not here to arrest you." He shifted his gaze between Daemon, Cali, and the other injured man, as if asking permission to treat him. Cali nodded in agreement. "A deal's a deal," he said.

Brett groaned as he got up and crossed the room to the corner sofa, where the other injured man lay. The woman stood up to help, but Brett gestured for her to stay put. As Brett examined the man, the woman asked how he was.

"Not good," Brett replied. "He's lost a lot of blood, and he probably has a concussion."

The woman's gaze fell. "Will he make it?" she asked, her voice trembling. Brett didn't say anything, but the expression on his face spoke volumes.

"What's his name?" Aea asked.

Cali seemed agitated, but Daemon raised his hand, silencing him. The atmosphere in the room had shifted from panic to a tense calmness. At least nobody was shouting. That helped.

"His name is Remy," the woman said in a soft voice.

Brett gestured toward the living room doorway, prompting Aea to turn and see her sister standing there. "And who's this?" he asked.

Aea turned around and saw her sister standing just inside the room, sort of looking at her and Cali at the same time as he stood there, keeping watch. Tabayah had stopped crying and was now staring at Aea and Daemon, still somewhat bewildered by the situation. Aea rushed over and hugged her sister, feeling relieved that she was unharmed, and a little ashamed that, in the commotion, she had almost forgotten her.

"Hmm?" Brett asked again.

"It's my sister," Aea said. "Tabayah."

Brett nodded.

"Tabayah," the woman said. "What a pretty name." She rose and began slowly walking toward them. "I'm Dana," she said with a smile, probably meant to be reassuring but still carrying a trace of fear. Her eyes continued to nervously scan the room. Her clothes, rumpled and stained, spoke of the ordeal she had been through, yet she clearly attempted to project calm and a semblance of normalcy for the little girl's sake.

Brett grabbed Dana's hand as she passed. "She shouldn't be in here," he said sternly.

Dana suggested going to check out Tabayah's room, and Aea could come with them. Cali was about to protest, but Daemon intervened, "Let them go," he said. "I'm sorry we had to come here, baby. We had no choice."

Dana gestured for Aea and Tabayah to follow her out of the living room. Aea was torn between protecting her sister and her desire to know what was really going on. She felt overwhelmed by fear and uncertainty, but knew she had to keep her wits about her. It was reassuring to distance herself from the blood, strange men, and a boyfriend who wasn't himself anymore. *And his wild-eyed partner with a gun.* But as they walked down the hallway toward Aea's room, she couldn't help but feel that they were no safer there than they were in the living room.

In the relative calm of their room, Dana had succeeded in soothing Tabayah to some degree by enticing her to show her assortment of toys, and now she was showcasing her most prized playthings—mainly her Barbies. The room, normally a sanctuary of childhood innocence, had turned into a sanctuary amidst a storm. Aea absently observed Dana, knelt on the floor, her movements deliberate as she engaged with Tabayah.

The normally colorful toys seemed muted in Aea's eyes, lost in the glow of the bedside lamp. Exhausted, she was finally coming down from the razor's edge of panic and fear, allowing herself to drift. *It's not as if I have a choice,* she thought, her brain on the precipice of shutting down. *I couldn't stop slipping away even if I tried. Maybe it's a defense mechanism? Diverting my thoughts to keep me sane?*

As she observed Tabayah play, she recalled how many of her toys had been hers during her own childhood. In fact, the majority of Tabayah's possessions were hand-me-downs, from clothes to school backpacks, and even her tablet, which had become hers when Aea got her visor. *The downside of being the younger child in a poor family.*

The dolls were of the simpler, non-robotic variety, lacking any form of AI tech. They were incapable of walking, dancing, singing, or talking—mere pieces of plastic. Even though Aea had sometimes envied friends who had more, she had cherished these as a child, just as Tabayah did now. *We're not that poor,* Aea reminded herself. Her dad was gainfully employed, she reminded herself, and hence, they were relatively affluent compared to most Outies, certainly more than the unemployed, and definitely more than those in The Crescent.

Dana had a good hand with children, Aea noticed. Despite the unexpected appearance of strange men bleeding out in the apartment, Dana had managed to calm Tabayah, a feat to admire. Observing her sister at play had an equally soothing effect on her. As she came down further from the previous tumultuous state of panic and dread, she was overcome by the desire to slumber, to unplug from the responsibility of safeguarding Tabayah.

"I won't hurt her," Dana had assured. "I'm not with them. I'm a hostage, just like the police officers."

Hostage? A chill coursed along her spine at hearing the word. *What did it mean? Was she a hostage? Or am I a hostage-taker?* She loved Daemon, and he loved her. Of that, she was convinced. *He would never harm me, so I couldn't possibly be a hostage, right?* But where did that realization leave her? And Tabayah? And Dad? *Daemon, what have you done?*

Aea sat slumped against the wall beside Tabayah's bed, her gaze fixed on her sister, who seemed to be playing with a sense of comforting normalcy. Yet, fear lingered in the girl's eyes, playtime being but a mechanism to shield herself from the distressing events unfolding in the living room. She may have been exhausted, but her survival instincts were very much still in high gear, a reminder that the relative calm was treacherous—the eye of the storm, not the storm truly having blown past. So, she wasn't merely watching Tabayah play, she wasn't coming down; she was listening, hoping to glean context from the muffled voices next door. She was thinking, trying to find clues about what lay ahead.

Previously, after the drone attack, Daemon and Cali had talked about "doing something," but Aea had never thought it would amount to anything like this. Anything at all, really. Even after Daemon had brandished the firearms at their apartment, she had dismissed it as a display of male bravado and posturing, so typical of young boys trying to impress their peers. *And the girls too. Just harmless horsing around.* And when nothing happened, she had been even more sure it was just empty talk. But now, something had happened, and people were actually dead! Another lay dying, bleeding out just a thin wall away. Daemon himself was injured, his friend pacing the hallway, clutching a gun, eyes frenzied and trigger-happy.

She strained her ears, forced herself to overcome the

exhaustion. The murmurs emanating from the living room were still audible—it was a small apartment, after all. Brett was doing most of the talking. She gleaned that Remy, the other police officer, required medical attention, or he wouldn't make it. The implication was that Daemon ought to receive treatment as well, or his wound would fester and become infected. Brett implored them to relinquish their weapons, emphasizing that Cali and Daemon were in control and that he and Remy posed no threat. However, he also warned that police reinforcements would be en route, and soon the neighborhood would be crawling with them.

"Just shut up," Cali snapped in reply, unwilling to listen.

Brett kept attempting to reason with Cali. Aea couldn't discern much of what Daemon was saying, or even if he was saying anything at all. Every time Brett spoke, Cali would erupt in a tirade, ordering him to keep quiet. Brett, in turn, implored him to calm down. Brief intervals of quietude interrupted the heated exchanges. This pattern repeated itself over and over, with Brett doggedly attempting to de-escalate, and Cali bursting out, hysterically.

Their attempts at a resolution proved futile, and eventually, the clamor dissipated into a more protracted lull. The volume of their exchanges receded into a muffled drawl, no longer clearly audible. Eventually, they ceased completely. In the sudden silence, Aea noticed she was holding her breath, to the point of passing out, as she listened intently for any sign of what might come next. The absence of sound was almost more terrifying than the arguments and accusations that had filled the air moments before. *Like this was the calm before a storm.* Aea hugged her knees as she sat against the wall watching her sister play, trying to ward off the chill of fear and the sense of impending doom that loomed over the apartment.

It was clear that Daemon, Cali, and Brett had arrived at a...what was the word...*Stillstand? Stalemate? Impasse?* She was unsure of the right word in any language. Frau Gerhling had mentioned it at some point, she was sure. *I'll go with stalemate.*

The thought of her teacher imparting wisdom comforted her, reminding her of a world of normalcy, one where mundane homework assignments and boy crushes, not bleeding hostages, were her biggest concerns. However, the comfort she derived from that recollection was fleeting. Stalemates are not everlasting, and the ending to this particular one was unlikely to be happy.

...high-speed bullet trains have significantly reduced distances in large parts of the world. Nevertheless, their traffic is primarily limited to routes between domes, disconnecting the Outside from...

...while travel permits are relatively accessible, particularly in the democratic countries of the West, bureaucratic hurdles are often imposed for Outside residents...

...the proportion of air travel in the overall transportation mix has decreased by more than 50% due to the expansion of bullet train networks and the growing unpredictability of climate patterns...

...consistent with numerous DomeEx surveys, improved accessibility to the global network of high-speed trains is frequently cited as one of the most significant advantages of relocation to the Inside...

...among citizens residing in Europe and many parts of the United States, the concept of privately owned personal transports is now a remote and nearly forgotten memory. The urban city domes of Manhattan, Tokyo, Singapore, London, Paris, Berlin, Oresund Metro, Stockholm, and Oslo distinguish themselves as virtually devoid of such vehicles, while many other primarily European cities are now approaching similar levels of...

...in a surprising turn of events, Los Angeles, once considered one of the most heavily polluted cities in the world due to high levels of private road traffic, is now one of the major metropolitan domes that has made the most significant strides in addressing...

Part Two: Pursuit

Garrick

"Rise and shine, sweetheart," crackled the guard's voice over the intercom. Instantly, the dim and dank cell was awash with blinding light, as bright as the noonday sun, and the brutal furor of heavy metal music pierced the silence, jolting Garrick awake from his shallow slumber. The cell's stale air, thick with the mustiness of damp concrete and his own unwashed body, was momentarily forgotten as the light and noise assaulted his senses.

Dazed and disoriented, his heart pounding in his chest, it took him a few seconds to realize where he was. The sudden transition from darkness to blinding light, from silence to auditory assault, left him bereft of his senses, panicked. He squeezed his eyes shut, a feeble attempt to protect himself from the onslaught, his breaths coming in short, ragged gasps as he fought against the rising despair.

"It's time," the guard barked. The mechanical sound of the door's lock clacking open echoed through the room, followed by the shrill shriek of the rusty hinges as the guards forced the door aside. They had once again come to drag him to the interrogation room where another round of torment awaited.

As the guard escorted him away, the heavy metal raged on in

the cell behind him, but after a while, it faded into a muffled echo and soon it stopped, leaving Garrick in an eerie silence in the interrogation chamber. Had he been taken out of earshot of the music, or had they turned it off? He was too tired to tell.

How long had he been asleep? Not long. A few minutes at the most. He had been in detention facilities before, and he knew the drill. Deprive him of sleep with blinding lights and ear-splitting noise, allowing him only moments of dozing off before another round. Waterboarding would be next, followed by barbaric physical violence. His stomach tightened into a knot at the thought of what was to come, memories of tortures playing in his mind like a grotesque slideshow. Each method they used was designed to break him, to peel away his resolve layer by layer until nothing remained but raw, exposed vulnerability. A withered husk who'd tell them what they wanted to know.

The cold concrete floor beneath his bare feet seemed to leech the warmth from his body. The anticipation of the even colder water's suffocating embrace and the sting of fists against his face had him tensing involuntarily.

He recognized the pattern from his time with Scott in Southern China. He had stood firm then, but this time would be different. Not necessarily because he lacked the fortitude to resist, but because he simply didn't possess the information the interrogators sought. They could continue their brutal torture in perpetuity, and he would not divulge, for he did not know.

Over the years, Garrick's loyalty to Scott had waned, and it was already stretched thin like taut wire. His actions this time had snapped it. His allegiance now lay solely with Alixha, and whatever fealty he once had for Scott had evaporated. *If I only had the information they wanted, I would have willingly provided it.*

A bitter laugh threatened to bubble up from Garrick's throat at the irony of his situation. The realization that his loyalty had shifted still felt like a betrayal—not of Scott, but of the man he once was. But in the dim light of the interrogation room, such distinctions seemed trivial, overshadowed by the immediate need to survive. To escape the pain.

During the interrogation sessions, it was not only the physical discomforts that repeated, but also the questions, reverberating in the damp room over and over in a nauseating cycle: The encryption key? The whereabouts of Scott, Aki, and Dai? The encryption key? The whereabouts of Scott, Aki, and Dai? The encryption key...and so it went on. *Why don't they get it? I don't know!* By now, had he known, disorientation and pain would perhaps have overcome him, and he would not have had the strength to resist any longer. He would have spilled any secret he might have held, except the one they demanded. *One simply cannot offer information one does not have!*

As they sat him down in the bleak room, he was handed a meager meal of a glass of water and an egg salad sandwich. The guard's gruff command to eat was unnecessary; he was starving. His belly groaned as he scarfed it down. Yet, as wonderful as it was, even this repeated. It was always egg salad. To his surprise, another guard strode in with a cup of black coffee. This was a new development.

"You have a special guest today," the guard said, the announcement barely registering as he ravenously imbibed, burning his lips and mouth in the process on the steaming beverage. *I guess they want me to be alert for this special guest.*

Left alone, he savored the rest of the sandwich, sipping the coffee and water in between bites. The sandwich, though simple, was a feast for his deprived senses. The bread soft, the filling creamy—each bite a tiny rebellion against the deprivation they put him through. *At least it's not moldy.* He let the coffee's bitter aroma fill his nostrils, its steam wash warmth over his face as he brought the paper cup to his lips. The caffeine did wonders as his body greedily absorbed it, jolting him further awake.

A few minutes later, the sound of tapping heels echoed through the hallway. As the door groaned open, a woman entered. *Is it...* He had to squint to see, but it was her. Alixha.

Her sleek silhouette framed by the doorway momentarily blurred as his eyes adjusted, the light from the hallway casting her in an ominous halo. The click of her heels as she slid across to the table was like a metronome, keeping the beat of his impending torture. The steel-legged chair screeched against the concrete floor as Alixha seated herself across from him. She asked of his well-being with a veneer of congeniality, as if they were meeting for coffee on a Tuesday afternoon.

Was that a joke? Light small talk ensued, as if recent events had not transpired at all. She inquired about his girlfriend, whom he was no longer seeing, and how his favorite football team was doing, all with a smile that appeared sincere.

"Garrick is a Welsh name, isn't it?" she asked, laughing. "And yet, you're a Liverpool fan? How can that be?" She smiled at her own jest, but Garrick struggled to force one in return. He wished she would just get to the point. Her casual demeanor was obviously a ruse to lull him into a false sense of security. Or into a state of full-blown panic.

Garrick's mind raced as he tried to keep up with Alixha's seemingly innocuous questions. The absurdity of discussing football and past relationships in this context was not lost on him—his faculties were still not that shattered. Her words added an almost surreal quality to their conversation, like he was a puppet in a twisted play, his strings pulled by the woman across the table—a woman offering him a glimmer of hope which he knew she would soon snatch away. She would use their connection to her advantage. Of that, he was certain.

The effort to maintain a semblance of composure, to not let the fear and confusion show, drained him more than he cared to admit. He was tired, so very tired, of the games, the manipulation, the constant push and pull between hope and despair that Alixha now brought to new heights. Sure enough, after a few minutes of banter, she offered him her sincere apologies for the inhumane treatment he had endured, stating also that it could all end if only he would reveal what she wanted to know.

Alixha leaned in, caressing Garrick's cheek with a soft touch that was both comforting and disconcerting. After being confined to a cell for God knows how long, the sensation of human contact was overwhelming, and desperately needed. The warmth of her hand sparked a tumult of emotions he could scarcely keep in check, and for a fleeting moment, he allowed himself the luxury of that twisted human connection. The comforting sensation of being seen as more than just information to be extracted washed over him. Garrick struggled to hold back tears, but he managed to maintain his composure long enough to reply.

"I would tell you," he said, "but I genuinely don't know."

Alixha withdrew her hand, and Garrick slumped over in desperation. Whatever hope had momentarily flared was predictably lost, leaving only hollow hopelessness in its place. The walls of the interrogation room closed in on him once more. He repeated that he didn't know. He pleaded with her. He begged.

"I believe you," Alixha said, a smile spreading across her face. He met her gaze, skeptical, but still daring to hope, maybe one last time. *She believed me? Was it over?* No, of course, it wasn't. It was a tactic, another lap in the cycle of psychological trickery, one that he had been through countless times now. *Hope, then despair, repeat. Just like the Chinese had used on me long ago.*

Alixha continued, "But I have to make sure. You know that." It was a statement, not a question. Garrick nodded in agreement, for he did know.

Alixha leaned in once more and whispered in his ear. "If you don't tell me what I want to know, I will have to vivisect your braid. I will have to vacuum every byte of information out of you that way instead. You know what that means."

Once again, it was not a question, and once again, he knew. His skin crawled at the whisper, her breath warm against his ear. The intimacy of the gesture, human, comforting, but also a twisted, visceral reminder of the fate that awaited him.

"So, Garrick," she said. "I'm asking you one more time. Where *are* they?"

The silence that followed pressed upon him, now more than at any time during this ordeal. The weight of knowing he could not give her what she wanted, his heartbeat pounding in his ears, pushed him over the limit. Now, he could no longer hold back the tears.

Scott

"We have company," Dai announced over braid, as they made their way through the bustle of Kabukicho. "My tactical is picking up a large number of potentials. I've got red target reticles everywhere. My lens looks like a Jackson Pollock."

Scott's pulse quickened as he navigated the round-the-clock neon-lit streets, his senses on high alert, aided by his braid's tactical. The vibrant chaos of Kabukicho, usually a pleasant sensory feast, now felt like a maze of potential threats. Each shadow, each face in the crowd, could be an adversary, despite the tactical's best efforts. The air was thick with the buzz of electricity and the murmur of the crowd, but Scott's focus was razor-sharp, filtering through the noise for any sign of danger.

That Pollock reference was lost on Scott, but his braid jumped in, offering a brief exposé of the painter's signature style utilizing drip technique and chaotic patterns of splattered paint. An apt analogy, he thought, quickly dismissing the popup, annoyed at the intrusion. He reminded himself to adjust the pop-up algorithm as soon as they were out of danger.

Scott's own tactical feed confirmed Dai's assessment, its reticles glowing with a hellish red as they tracked potential threats amongst the throngs of people on the crowded street.

The algorithms had identified a dozen faces that could be potential agents, their movements and postures suggesting they were on the prowl. *For us.*

Again, he brought up the map, reviewing their position. Not far now. They had made arrangements to rendezvous with Treston, an old friend of Scott's, who could help them not only disappear, to leave Tokyo, but also to help them stay permanently in the shadows, safe from the far-reaching clutches of Alixha and Lux. The problem was urgent—if they didn't vanish soon, light would inevitably shine and force them out into the open. The walls would close in, and death would surely follow. *I didn't expect us to run out of luck this soon, though.* A cold dread settled in his stomach at the thought. Their very lives hung in the balance, and every second in the open was a second too long, each movement an echo on some squito scanner array, giving them away. The vibrant energy of Tokyo's nightlife around him suddenly felt oppressive. The weight of leadership bore heavily on him, each decision a razor's edge separating salvation and catastrophe.

The streets of Kabukicho, notorious for their sensory overload, both in the physical as well as the virtual world, both helped and hindered. He grimaced as his tactical display, on top of the angry target reticles, was overwhelmed by a deluge of virtual ads, flashing and pulsing with garish colors, making his eyes ache. Tokyo's net was one of the most ad-infested on the planet, and it showed. The cacophony of noise was only matched by his increasing apprehension. He adjusted the sensitivity of his blockers to scramble the ads' presence. Better. Relief came as the visual chaos dimmed, granting him respite from the overload. *Maybe this isn't the day our luck runs dry, after all.*

Treston had chosen this place for a reason—to blend in, to fool the cameras, to overwhelm the scans but it worked both ways. While such a tactic gave them an edge, it also muddied the waters, making it harder for them to sort out the threats from the noise. *The artificial lights from the level construction above also don't help.*

Despite his efforts, his lens was cluttered, the threats unclear. False positives were bound to occur, leaving them partially in the hands of chance. As his tactical applied processing power to eliminate those false positives, the picture became clearer still, the confidence level of the threat assessment rising. Now there could be no doubt. They had been made.

"Aki," he said over the comm, "you got eyes on them?" Of the three of them, Aki had the most advanced braid, capable of several times the computations of Scott and Dai's. They therefore relied on him and his superior hardware to take the brunt in coordinating their movements and sifting out the good guys from the bad.

"Affirmative," Aki replied. "I don't understand how they could get on us so quickly."

Scott had an idea, one that he didn't like to entertain. *Damn it, Garrick!*

But it was too fast. Even with the best tactical apps, it was unlikely that Alixha's stormtroopers could have tracked them down so quickly. *If you did betray us, I forgive you. I hope you didn't suffer too much, old friend.*

At least he had lasted until the operation was complete. The launch codes were safe, tucked away in the most remote and inaccessible part of the net that Aki could find. Garrick didn't know where, and neither did any of them, should they eventually be captured. Not even Aki himself knew. Even for Alixha, with her army of tech wizards, it would take a decade to locate them, and then another to unscramble the encryption.

Just because they didn't know where the codes were didn't mean they were out of danger. Alixha's shadow would loom over them for the rest of their lives, but he was damned if it was going to end already before they'd left Tokyo.

The rendezvous point provided by Treston wasn't too far off. There was hope, a fragile flame in the dark, and they still had a chance to make it.

"We can move about 80 meters closer without revealing our positions. Give or take," Aki said, transferring the route to their braids, each with a different destination.

His route was one street down, then right, then two streets down, and a left. He was to hold outside a bar on the right side of the street, opposite the brothel. The bar had a crowded atmosphere that would allow him to blend in, while the privacy-minded adult entertainment venue had electronic veils under which he could hide virtually. Their instructions were clear. Stay out of sight, keep their faces hidden from cameras, including bystanders with easily hackable consumer braids, and wait for further instructions. Dai's route was similar, but with a different target destination. *No point in making it easy for them.*

"Okay, Dai," Aki said. "Move."

Scott watched as the dot symbolizing Dai moved on the map in the upper right corner of his lens. It was his turn now, but he had to hold for a moment, his tactical display showing he wasn't clear yet. A lone reticle indicated a threat between him and his target destination. The tactical quickly projected a course that would take him around the threat, allowing him to avoid detection, but it would also take him perilously close to other hostiles. Thankfully, it also projected the current target was about to imminently round a corner and disappear from view. The best course of action remained the original route. He moved, and so did the threat. As he closed in, his heart raced, counting down the seconds until the target would turn and leave his line of sight.

Thirty seconds.

Twenty.

Ten.

And just like that, the reticle vanished, the target rounding the corner and disappearing off his path, exactly as the tactical had predicted. A wave of relief washed over him. *Glad something's going our way.* The AI had missed the mark by a mere millisecond or so. Humans may be unpredictable, but not to a degree where a high-caliber AI could no longer compensate.

He set off in a brisk walk, careful not to break into a run. Even with extensive operational experience, the default human response to stress and anxiety is to rush. Any sudden movement could draw unwanted attention, easily spotted by their pursuers' tacticals, and running in Kabukicho, even light jogging, would stick out like a sore thumb. His gaijin appearance presented another predicament, but there was little he could do about that. He could implement a mural to deceive facial recognition apps, to appear more Japanese, but they were mostly ineffective, and a good AI could spot them a mile away. *Hopefully, there are enough Euro and American tourists milling about to hide among.*

He moved at a controlled pace, trying his best to appear casual. Upon arriving at the bar, he joined the queue to order a drink. The establishment was a cramped hole-in-the-wall, with only a handful of seats inside, forcing most patrons to gather outside. The narrow street was teeming with people, plenty of faces to blend in among. When the beer came, he took a sip. If he had to stay long, he'd eventually have to figure out a way to dispose of it. Drinking all of it would be out of the question. Being inebriated, even slightly, in a situation like this was a bad idea. Pouring the beer out, little by little, in a discreet manner, was feasible, but even that behavior could be flagged by a savvy tactical AI.

The team checked in, confirming that everyone had arrived. He accessed the tactical once more, scanning for any red target reticles within his line of sight. The AI's predictive algorithm indicated that three hostiles were in close proximity, but located on adjacent streets, with no line of sight. For now, he was in the clear.

"Clear," he relayed over the comm. He briefly contemplated whether it was wiser to switch to text-based communication instead. The crowded venue was bustling with noise, making verbal exchanges relatively safe. However, just like prying eyes, there were also eavesdropping microphones everywhere. Cameras and microphones often went hand in hand, fitted on squitos and other similar tech installations. Nonetheless, his tactical indicated that there was nothing of the sort nearby at present. The confidence level was above ninety percent.

Soon after, Dai and Aki chimed in with their status updates. Aki forwarded a slightly revised path to his next objective, which for the moment seemed free of obstacles, but Scott held off until Aki gave the green light. He had appointed Aki as the director for a reason—his superior AI would provide the best guidance. Moreover, if the situation permitted, they should all make steady progress together.

The next two maneuvers proceeded without any hitches. On

the third one, they converged on the same destination. With only one more move left, they would soon reach the rendezvous point that Treston had established.

In the field, circumstances could shift in the blink of an eye. For nearly three minutes, they had a clear path, which was ample time for Aki to map out the next move and transmit it to Dai and Scott's braids. However, the tactical system abruptly recalibrated, revealing red target reticles on their lenses that hadn't been present before. The markers were drawing closer, rapidly boxing them in.

"Aki?" Dai said.

"Hold on. I'm analyzing."

The intended route that Aki had previously sent had been severed. Scott's pulse quickened, the imminent threat igniting a rush of adrenaline as both Scott's and Dai's tactical systems confirmed it. There were two alternatives, each requiring a forced entry. The first was a back-alley emergency exit leading to a novelty store's stockroom for tourists, entirely automated. The second entrance led to the rear of a ramen eatery's kitchen, staffed by humans.

"Aki!" Dai implored once more.

"Almost there."

The red reticles on Scott's lens crept closer to their hiding spot in the alleyway. The tactical analysis suggested that the incoming contacts had yet to detect them, and no squitos or larger drones patrolled overhead. But that was bound to change any moment now. In a matter of moments, give or take a fraction of a second, the first target would round the corner, transforming from a mere bracket into an armed human being. *At least, I think they will be armed.* Weapons were prohibited Inside, but the restrictions were easy enough to get around with the right tools—tools Alixha's men would possess. Her resources were practically limitless, certainly dwarfing their own and those of most others. *We could have had guns too, if we didn't have to leave in such a hurry.*

"Inconclusive," Aki finally announced. "The damn tactical doesn't know what to do."

Sometimes, there was no substitute for human intuition and

leadership. It was time for Scott to showcase that he possessed both. Doubt crept up on him, the weight of command a cloak over his shoulders. He hesitated. He had relied on AIs for the majority of his life. It had been a crutch too heavily leaned on, and he couldn't help but feel paralyzed.

"Fifteen seconds," Aki reminded him. "Make a call, boss," Aki said. "Tac says either or."

God dammit!

"Ten seconds."

"The ramen place," a new voice instructed over the communication channel. "Go now." The voice was disguised with a scrambler to avoid voiceprint identification. Whoever had infiltrated their communication frequency had some serious tools at their disposal. And balls.

"Five seconds," Aki said.

"Tress, is that—" Scott began, but the voice cut him off.

"Ramen place now," the voice repeated emphatically. "Go! We'll talk later."

With the directive clear, Scott felt a jolt of adrenaline surge through him, the immediacy of the command sparking a flicker of hope. Without further hesitation, Scott gave the order, and they burst through the kitchen door and took off running. Relief and hope gave way to disappointment as they ran. The decision had been made, but ultimately not by him. He had been put to the test and failed.

The familiar scent of ramen hit him as they burst through the kitchen. It was oddly comforting, a brief respite easing the tightness forming around his chest. The steam, the clang of pots, and the head chef shouting instructions were a stark reminder of the world they were leaving behind, one step at a time, as they plunged into this unknown, guided by a strange voice. *Odd,* he thought. None of the kitchen staff batted an eye as they forged through their place of work. It was as if they had seen it a thousand times before. *Tress, you old bastard. This better be you.*

The Treston Reeves Scott now looked at was not the same man

he had known in years past. In some strange, eerie way, everything had changed, yet it remained the same. He pulled an image from his braid memory banks for a quick comparison. The contours of Treston's face, the flow of his hair, the stature of his body, all differed from what Scott remembered, and from those recorded memories. Even his body shape had undergone a transformation. He appeared taller and more slender than before, and not merely in a "lost weight" manner. It was as if his entire body template had been reconfigured—yet only slightly—as though someone had attempted to sketch him from memory and had gotten the details slightly awry.

With a flourish of arms and a grin plastered across his face, Tress announced his transformation. "Tah-dah!" he exclaimed, as if he were a magician unveiling a spectacular illusion. Scott could barely mask his astonishment, arching his eyebrows more than he would've liked. The transformed Tress didn't seem to notice. This was a man who had quite literally shed his old skin and embraced the future, something that awaited them all. Scott's mind raced, pondering the lengths they'd have to go to stay hidden.

"It's a whole new me," Tress continued. "Like it?" His voice, too, was slightly off, though still identifiable. It was undoubtedly still him, as confirmed by a brief conversation. The acerbic wit and biting sarcasm that had once defined Treston were still present.

The ramen place in the alley had turned out to be an entry point—a front, practically—for one of Tokyo's underground sanctuaries. After they had entered the kitchen, Tress had directed them down into the basement and through a series of underground tunnels. The ramen place staff had done nothing to try to stop them or report them. They had barely even noticed them as they rushed through the premises. At the end of the tunnels, there had been an elevator where Tress had finally met them. They all took that elevator down into the deep, a descent that felt like not just a journey through space, but through time. Scott couldn't help but feel it was a physical manifestation of the departure from their old lives. *Each meter we drop adds weight to my shoulders,* he thought, *and makes the air harder to breathe.* He couldn't decide if the latter was psychological or simply the air getting staler.

As they descended, Treston proceeded to regale them with the intricate details of his metamorphosis. From his fingerprints and cornea to his retina and even his DNA, every aspect of his being had been meticulously re-sequenced, optimized to cheat AI power scans.

"And my name, of course," he added, almost as an afterthought. "I go by Bob these days. Bob Jones."

Aki raised an eyebrow at this revelation. "Bob? Jones?"

Tress, or rather Bob, flashed a wide grin. "Is there something wrong with it?"

Aki shook her head. "No, no. It's just not the name I would have chosen."

This seemed to amuse Bob, who tilted his head to one side. "Really? What name would you have picked, then?"

Aki now looked a bit bothered. "If you have the chance to completely reinvent yourself, why not go with something a bit more...I don't know? Exotic? Cooler. Like James Powers or something?"

Tress, or rather Bob, merely shrugged. "The whole point of disappearing is to actually disappear," he explained. "Bob Jones has an innocuous ring to it. Something ordinary which allows me to blend in. As a foreigner, obviously. As a gaijin. Even in Tokyo, there are Bobs and Joneses."

Scott's gaze drifted over Tress—now Bob—taking in the man's new, unremarkable exterior. The sound of his voice, slightly altered but still recognizably Tress's, echoed strangely in the tight space of the elevator, a sonic reminder of the transformation. The sterile light of the elevator cast shadows that seemed to dance around Bob's features, highlighting the uncanny valley between the man Scott knew and the stranger before him.

Scott felt a mix of admiration and sorrow, marveling at Tress's dedication, yet mourning the loss of the man he once was. To don a completely new identity, to vanish so thoroughly, spoke volumes about the price people sometimes had to pay. A sobering reminder of their own future. Curious about the statement regarding the throngs of Bobs and Joneses, he conducted a quick braid search and confirmed Tress/Bob's words. There were, in fact, several hundred people registered with the name Bob Jones in Tokyo alone. In a city with over fifty million people in its greater metro area, it wasn't hard to believe that such a name could still be relatively common.

"I'm American, and my name is Bob, like millions of others with my background," Tress/Bob continued. "You can still refer to me as Tress, though. As long as we're down here."

He sure looks like a Bob.

The ride down into the depths of the earth seemed to drag on for an eternity. *Maybe it's just slow-moving?* There was barely any sense of motion or sound, save for the faint hum of the machinery around them. After a minute or so, a braid notification flashed in the corner of Scott's lens, informing him that he had been disconnected from the net. The others nodded their confirmation as they, too, were severed from the grid. Tress explained that they were now inside what amounted to a massive Faraday cage. Nothing went in, and nothing came out.

A sense of isolation enveloped Scott as he powered down his braid, a severance from the digital world that had been an extension of his being. The virtual silence that followed was profound, as if he had stepped into a void, cut off from the world above, left to navigate this new reality with only his wits and each other.

"Those who come here often choose to permanently sever their braids anyway," Tress added, "to ensure that they are as untraceable as possible. Nothing I would recommend if you ever plan to leave. Just power them down. That's usually enough."

Usually? Scott nodded, taking in the information. The mere thought of permanently severing his braid sent chills down his spine, and powering it down, only marginally less so. But he trusted Tress/Bob and powered it down, letting himself sink into the quiet darkness of the underground.

The lift shuddered to a halt, its metallic doors parting to reveal a cavernous expanse, a colossal chamber hewn out of the surrounding bedrock. The air in the chamber was cool and dry, a stark contrast to the artificial perfection of Tokyo's domed streets they had left behind. Scott's eyes adjusted slowly to the dim light, the vastness of the chamber unfolding before them like a scene from another world. The sound of their footsteps echoed off the walls as they approached the checkpoint.

Lattice-like structures enveloped the walls and ceiling, coalescing into what Scott surmised to be the intricate design of the Faraday cage alluded to earlier. The complexities of such a system were not exactly Scott's forte, but he certainly could appreciate its sheer scale and the ingenuity of it. As he surveyed his surroundings, Scott noticed that the chamber's surface was partially clad in a peculiar metallic coating, seemingly pliant in nature. *Insulation, maybe?*

At regular intervals along the ceiling, massive ventilation fans jutted out, their mechanical hum dispersing gently across the chamber. Scott couldn't shake the notion that they had ventured beyond the confines of the dome—he doubted these gargantuan turbines were part of the dome's internal climate control system, and it seemed improbable that one could filch air conditioning from within the dome unnoticed. The fans must be drawing air from the outside. If so, the elevator had not only plunged us deep below, but also transported us laterally, traversing the barrier of the dome and venturing beyond its artificial atmosphere. *Curious. I never noticed any change in direction.*

Before them stood a barrier and checkpoint, with a warning sign sternly declaring that all weapons must be surrendered upon arrival. "This place is like an old frontier western town," Dai remarked. Aki concurred. Scott recalled they had both been to see a Western recently. *Which one was it? Mitch Cassidy and Sundance or some such thing. I doubt any old Western town was deep underground like this.*

Beyond the checkpoint, at the end of the cavernous concourse, three tunnels beckoned, teeming with people bustling to and fro. The three of them stood there, transfixed by the spectacle. "Impressive, isn't it?" Tress remarked, pointing towards the tunnels. "Welcome to Rothbard, bolthole of choice for the forlorn, the rejected, the dejected, the wretched, the tired, the poor—you name it. If you don't fit in somewhere, you fit in here."

A sense of relief washed over Scott at those words, a tangible sense of safety momentarily enveloping him. Yet, it was tinged with a melancholy realization. This was a haven for those cast aside, a society built from the remnants of the world above. It was both awe-inspiring and heartbreaking. He should feel a profound sense of connection to these people, his fellow refugees from the unforgiving light of day. *But I don't. Maybe it'll come?*

He had heard of these underground sanctuaries before but had never been entirely convinced of their existence. Could governments allow such a place to thrive right under their noses? It was hard to keep anything of this scale hidden. *They probably know but choose to look the other way. For whatever reason.* Lux had never hidden like this, even in the humble beginnings when the movement could be legitimately deemed "underground."

Tress led them up to the human-operated security station. AI and bots were shunned, apparently, potentially vulnerable to hacking as they are. *So are most humans.*

"If you're carrying a squito pouch, check it," Tress instructed. "Other electronics are permitted, but only in offline mode. They can't connect down here, anyway, as I said."

"So we're safe here?" Dai asked.

"Well," Tress replied, "one is never completely safe, but yes, here you're as safe as you can be anywhere in Tokyo."

"So what is... or was this place?" Dai asked, after security had let them through.

Tress explained that it was an abandoned sewage system from the Sixties. "It took us years to clean this shithole up," he chuckled to himself, but the others didn't join in. "It's an old internal joke we sometimes like to tell down here. But yeah, it's an old sewage network that the Japanese government never finished when the central dome was constructed. We expanded it about a decade and a half ago."

Tress motioned for them to follow him towards the left tunnel. "We'll pass through the market and grab a bite on the way to Admin. I assume you're hungry?"

They all nodded in agreement. *Oh God, yes! I'm starving.*

Tress wasn't kidding when he said they had expanded the

unfinished sewage tunnels. The place was enormous, more like caverns than tunnels. The bazaar extended the entire length of the tunnel, as far as the eye could see. There was ample space for three aisles with vendors hawking everything from groceries to scavenged topside goods—tools, kitchenwares, low-grade electronics, and anything one needed for comfortable living.

"This is the general market," Tress said. "High-end stuff is a bit harder to come by down here, but if you need anything, let me know, and I'll see what I can do. This way to the food court. There's this place that makes a spicy kebab that'll make your toes curl. Real meat too."

"Where do you get real meat down here?"

"You don't wanna know," Tress replied with a grin. "But trust me, it's great."

Yuck. Scott couldn't help but chuckle, a momentary lapse into levity in the gravity well of a crushing black hole. Yet, his laugh bore a sliver of unease, the origins of their meal underscoring the precariousness of their new existence.

"We don't ask too many questions here," Tress continued. "Policing and regulation are kept to a minimum unless it threatens the existence of Rothbard itself. This is supposed to be some sort of utopia of libertarian freedom, after all. That means, of course, that if you need anything to relax, you know, pass the time, feel a little happy for a while, you can find that too."

"Good to know," Aki said.

Scott allowed himself an inward smirk. *Aki barely even had a drink on New Year's, let alone anything more exotic. I, however, might actually go for it. Later.*

"Of course, there's no such thing as real freedom in a place like this," Tress admitted. "This is a well-oiled machine, dependent on technology to survive. When I say we keep policing to a minimum, I'm not entirely truthful. But we try to be discreet about it. So that we can at least pretend we're free, you know?" He chuckled.

Scott couldn't help but again think that Tress wasn't the same man he once knew. It wasn't just his physical appearance that had changed, but his personality and mannerisms as well. He used to be calm, collected, and formal, like a wise and learned grandfather. This jittery, almost manic version was a stranger wearing a vaguely familiar face, his jokes jarring in their incongruity. Now, he seemed more like a cocaine addict in recovery. Scott couldn't recall Tress ever making a lame joke like that. He also never used to end his sentences with "you know." The transformation was not just physical; the essence of the man had shifted, leaving Scott to wonder once more about the cost of their survival, the pieces of themselves they would lose in this process.

A rattling sound caught Scott's attention. As he turned to look back through the tunnel, he saw a new group arriving, this time using the large freight elevator. The security team was much more thorough than they had been with them.

"Trade team," Tress explained. "Can't be too careful with what they bring in." He went on to explain how a customs team scrutinized every item brought into Rothbard, subjecting everyone to the same checks as any dome—health and safety, animal control, tech sweeps, and so on. *So much for a libertarian sanctuary.* Nevertheless, the checks were reasonable since Rothbard was essentially a sealed bubble, just like a dome but without its sophisticated environmental controls.

"One virus gets loose down here," Tress said, "and we're all puking our guts out. Trust me, it's happened before." He motioned for them to move on. "Come on. I'm starving."

The kebab place was located close to the tunnel leading down to the residential zone. Scott and Dai joined Tress for a meal, but Aki had decided to retire to his assigned "residence," which, Tress explained, was more like a utility closet with a bunk bed and a hot plate. Scott had managed to score a slightly larger one for himself and Dai. "I guess we're pretty close these days," he remarked to Tress, "Closer, at least, to... you know."

"About time," Tress replied with a chuckle.

Tress was right about the food—it wasn't half bad, but it was definitely spicy. The proprietor jokingly remarked that the secret to anything tasty down here was in the sauce, to which Tress nodded in agreement. "Always in the sauce, my friends," he quipped.

He then ordered a round of shots. "The good stuff," he said,

"Absolute. It's Swedish, brought here by one of the international trade units. Savor it. Down here, luxuries like this come at a high price."

"I won't get used to it, I promise," Scott replied.

Tress changed the subject. "You have to be sure about this," he warned. "We can arrange to have anything about you changed. But, like the vodka, it comes at a price."

Disappearing off the face of the Earth was a complex problem. Scott's mind churned with the implications, the enormity of the decision weighing heavily on him. To erase his past, to become someone new, was a daunting prospect. It was not just about survival; it was about losing a part of himself, the identity he had crafted over a lifetime. *But the alternative is far worse.* Alixha's relentless pursuit left them no choice but to dissolve into shadows, to become ghosts in their own lives. The prospect filled him with a deep, existential dread, a mourning for the self that would soon cease to exist.

Getting new identities would not be enough. There were a few options, with going Outie being the simplest, but not necessarily the most pleasant in the long run. Outside, there were fewer cameras, facial recognition drones, and squitos couldn't operate with the same efficiency as on the Inside due to the weather. There would be fewer humans too, in the right places. Going Outie, however, wouldn't stop Alixha. Then there's the pesky little problem of managing the elements. It's still okay now, but what about in five years? Ten years? Twenty?

He and Dai were too young to consider a life on the Outside. They had too much life left to live before conditions would become unbearably harsh. However, staying Inside would get complicated. To be safe, they'd have to evade the nearly ubiquitous surveillance of dome security. Both humans and AI had to be fooled if they wanted to ensure that nobody would come knocking on their doors in the middle of the night. Changing papers was just the beginning of the process. Facial features, eyes, fingerprints, and anything else that could identify them had to be altered. That meant surgery. But even that was not enough. They had to rewrite the very essence of their being—their DNA. "We can fix everything here except the latter," Tress informed Scott.

Obviously, any alterations aimed at tampering with their identity were illegal. Finding facilities that had the required capabilities and people willing to do it was difficult. "We have another guy for DNA, but he's in Shanghai," Tress added.

Of course. The former Chinese province was the leading market for illegal stuff, especially anything technically complicated. Tress explained that he had ways to get them there, but it would take some time to get an appointment and make the necessary arrangements. "In the meantime, you can recover from the surgeries here and enjoy the hospitality of Rothbard. My treat," he offered.

Tress also warned that the list of potential side effects from the reinvention was long. Everything from post-operative pain to long-lasting psychological effects like body dysmorphia, schizophrenia, clinical depression, and even straight-up madness made an appearance.

"The pain," Tress said, "may be long-lasting. We're literally going to reshape the bone structure and soft tissue all the way down to your very core to make your face look like someone else's. That comes with consequences." It was manageable, he insisted, and it would get better with time, but in the medium term, they should be prepared for life on opioids.

Great. Always wanted to be a junkie. Nevertheless, all of that was better than being dead. *There is no choice.*

Tress grinned—the way the new Tress would smile before he was about to say something he found amusing. "You know, now that you're redoing yourself anyway, you might as well throw in some goodies. Whatever you want. Want to be taller? Have better muscle tone? Lose some belly fat? Want a bigger dick?"

Scott grinned back. "Set it up," he said. "But just the standard package. No pun intended."

Tress nodded. "I'll do it first thing in the morning."

Adriel

For forty-five minutes, he had paced the sterile reception at Aegis's Singapore branch office, waiting to be summoned. Finally, a bot—a tin can on wheels named Aura—called him in, politely but perfunctorily, in his native tongue of Hebrew.

"English is fine," he replied, somewhat impatiently.

The little conference room was scarcely worthy of the name. It was as though someone had squeezed it in as an afterthought, like an appendage that had outgrown its usefulness. The table was small and could barely accommodate six people. He wondered if this was an intentional snub, a subtle reminder of his place in the pecking order. *I guess the big room with the view is reserved for more important people.*

Despite his request for English, Aura persisted in addressing him in Hebrew, directing him to take a seat and enjoy the refreshments while he awaited Ms. Pacula's arrival. He couldn't help but wonder if his accent was the cause of the bot's confusion. His grasp of the English language was far from perfect, and he had always struggled to blend in with the Anglos. *Perhaps that was why Mossad dismissed me all those years ago. I was a square peg in a world of round holes. Anyway.*

The refreshments on offer seemed American-style—sparkling water, coffee, and cookies, likely of the chocolate chip or caramel variety. The aroma of freshly brewed coffee mingled with the artificial air, creating a false sense of comfort. He glanced at the cookies, their edges perfectly browned, yet despite their inviting appearance, they sat untouched—a symbol of hollow corporate hospitality that held no appeal for him. *Like the meeting itself*, he mused, chortling inwardly at his own jape. The thought of indulging in such trivial comforts while his mind was occupied with orchestrating Aegis's counter-assault on Rahena, on civilization itself, seemed pointless.

His thoughts drifted to the prospect of returning to Israel and his beloved privately owned apartment, perched above the Tel Aviv beaches—a perk of his affiliation with Aegis. The residence, though hardly palatial in size, was more spacious than most in Tel Aviv, courtesy of the corporation's sponsorship. *It may not be the biggest, but it's mine.* Had he been forced to secure it independently or rely on the scant offerings of the DomeEx program, it would have been no larger than a broom closet. Only the rich, or those who owned legacy properties, would have anything resembling a decent living space Inside.

The bot bid him farewell—this time, finally, in English—and rolled out of the room. He opted for a glass of water, refraining from the coffee. The water was, he had to admit, chilled to perfection and provided a brief respite from the caffeine jitters and acid reflux that had plagued him throughout the morning. He took a slow sip, allowing the cool liquid to calm his nerves as well as his stomach. *Heavenly and alkaline.*

Outside the dome, it was a particularly heavy, gray, and rainy day, and even though he was Inside, within the confines of the dome's carefully regulated climate, he was knackered and had a migraine. He blamed the weather for his malaise, as illogical as that was. After all, when one is encased in a bubble of technological perfection, how could weather affect you? *But it does.*

Maybe it's just psychological? But the effect was undoubtedly real. Or felt real. *Whatever.* Even so, one could surmise that in Tel Aviv, with its scorching, dry desert climate, he never suffered from migraines or had to consume excessive amounts of caffeine to combat exhaustion. Inside or Outside, it didn't matter.

Mrs. Pacula kept him waiting, leaving him to sip on the water with a burgeoning need to relieve himself. The tension in the room seemed to thicken with each passing minute, the ticking of the analog clock on the wall amplifying his growing impatience and discomfort. The water in his glass now seemed less refreshing and more a reminder of his predicament, each sip a calculation of time against his bladder's capacity.

He detested conducting business while basic bodily functions needed tending to and pondered the possibility of excusing himself to the bot assistant for a quick visit to the men's room. He ultimately abandoned the idea, fearing that if he were absent when Mrs. Pacula arrived, it would reflect poorly on him. *All of a sudden, I'm the one who's late.* The prospect of jeopardizing his position over something as mundane as a bathroom break felt ludicrous, yet here he was, weighing the risks. His stomach churned, not just from the need, but from the realization of how precarious his standing really was—how insignificant he was in the eyes of the top layer.

As he sat there, stewing in his discomfort, he pondered the purpose of the meeting. Pacula, being Aegis's Chief Risk Officer, was a prominent individual within the organization, signifying that this was no ordinary chat. He had only met her once before, during the planning stages of the London retaliation op, in Chen's private office with Lima and Gibson himself present. From this little rendezvous, there were only two possible outcomes: either he had made a grievous error and was about to be chewed out, or the mission was evolving in a way that required his expertise.

His pulse quickened at the thought, a mix of dread and anticipation churning within him. The former would be a bitter pill to swallow, but the latter was just as unpalatable. Yes, the idea of facing reprimand was humiliating, yet the possibility of being drawn deeper into the vortex of Aegis's machinations was equally daunting. It would mean more work, more risk, and more uncertainty. *Fuck.*

He cursed his luck and silently prayed that Henry James

Gibson himself would not make yet another appearance. He'd find out soon enough.

When Mrs. Pacula finally arrived, she sauntered in as if she had all the time in the world. And why wouldn't she? She was the queen, and he was merely a pawn. One does not rush to meet with a subordinate. Her presence seemed to bring with it a chilling breeze, icy confidence palpable in the way she moved. She carried herself with respect-demanding authority. Her casual demeanor towards the refreshments—a mere glance before dismissing them—underscored that she was here for business. She acknowledged him with a polite greeting, her handshake like grasping a block of ice, before proceeding to the refreshment table to pour herself a glass of water. She, too, abstained from the cookies.

"I'll be brief," she said, settling into her seat. "We're expanding the operation, and we're pleased with your work on the London mission." He nodded and forced a smile. *Okay, so I didn't screw up. More work it is, then.*

Pacula leaned forward slightly, her gaze sharpening. "Before we proceed with the briefing, tell me. How is Mr. Lima performing?"

Adriel paused, considering his words carefully. Internally, he couldn't help but chuckle at how Aegis likened Jarod and his team to their own personal *Tzadikim Nistarim*—the hidden righteous ones. The term, steeped in mystical tradition, referred to those whose virtue and righteousness protect the world, unbeknownst to the people around them. The irony of applying such a sacred concept to Jarod's operations—clandestine activities far removed from any moral high ground—was not lost on him.

But outwardly, he maintained his composure. "It's going alright," he responded succinctly, keeping those musings to himself. "They're meeting expectations."

That was, of course, partially a lie, considering Lima's mental hiccup in New York. However, the mission was completed adequately in the end, so he decided against disclosing it. Pacula nodded, seemingly satisfied with his response, and without further ado, she proceeded with her brief.

"We are targeting Alixha's cyber unit. Her online activities have resulted in significant distress for us, and we are striking back. You will receive a list of targets via braid, and two new strike teams will be at your disposal to carry out the operation. The distribution of targets between the teams is entirely up to your discretion."

She transmitted the files to his braid, adding, "Familiarize yourself with these documents and return with a plan of action. The same operating procedures used for Lima and his team should suffice. Everything must remain confidential and on a need-to-know basis. The teams should not be aware of each other's existence or operations. The fewer individuals who are privy to this mission, the less chance there is of it being compromised. Naturally, you will be generously compensated for your efforts."

Adriel concurred but expressed his desire to return home, at least for a brief period.

"I don't see an issue with that," Pacula replied, "so long as you take the requisite precautions."

Then it was over. The exchange lasted scarcely five minutes. Pacula excused herself, leaving her water unfinished. Adriel rose to see her off, and they shook hands in the hallway before Aura appeared once more.

"This way," the bot stated, leading him towards the elevators.

Pacula veered off into an adjoining corridor, leaving the lobby slightly warmer in her absence. *The ice queen literally affects the temperature around her*, he mused. As she disappeared around a corner, he felt a sudden weight lift, only to be replaced by another, heavier and more complex. The briefness of the encounter left him disoriented, the swift exchange having altered the course of his future, steering him into uncharted waters without a compass. *Surely, this is still just the beginning. If I'm lost now, just wait.*

As Adriel settled into the screamer that would take him back to Tel Aviv, he set up a security veil and began poring over the plans Pacula had sent him. The scope of the operation was massive, with more to come. Aegis wasn't content with just striking against Alixha's cyber unit. The plans hinted—if not outright stated—that Aegis was gearing up for a full-scale assault against the other dome corporations, even against Legacy itself. It was clear that Aegis had reached a breaking point, and they were ready to strike back with everything they had. Gibson was determined to fight fire with fire, to escalate the conflict into something akin to a cold war—with plenty of hot elements. The era of peace and stability that had defined life since the domes was on the brink of collapse.

A sinking feeling settled in the pit of Adriel's stomach as he contemplated the gravity of Aegis's plans. The notion of being instrumental in such a pivotal, potentially cataclysmic shift was both exhilarating and terrifying. The responsibility weighed him down, a constant reminder that his actions could tip the balance in a fragile world teetering on the edge of chaos.

The social contract that had existed between the state and the dome builders was shattered, and Adriel had a critical role to play in the ensuing chaos. And he would play that role like a good little soldier, but he couldn't help but wonder if they weren't playing right into Alixha's hands. *Stability is the enemy of revolution.* Wasn't that the core tenet of the *Manifesto of Light*? Though he couldn't recall the exact wording, it was something to that effect. *Outright war is precisely what she wants. And we're walking right into her trap.*

Jarod

The private dome housing the residence of Gayul Tyers, the weapons and explosives specialist who had constructed the London bomb—and the next target on their list—loomed before them. They approached on foot, under the cover of darkness, surveying the dome's security capabilities through night-vision filters. Through the overlay, the landscape transformed, the looming dome appearing otherworldly. The surrounding terrain, once teeming with life as farm animals grazed in times before the climate disaster, now seemed desolate, not unlike the barren expanses of Mars. *Not that I've ever been,* Jarod thought. All fauna and wildlife that once called this place home had been recreated and relocated to terraria domes.

Jarod was dismayed by the sight of the barren landscape before him. Old enough to remember a time before the domes, he was reminded of all that was lost to climate catastrophe. The withered land, illuminated by the eerie glow of his night-vision filter, was a grim premonition of life without vibrancy. Without zest. Without hope. *This is what we're fighting to prevent,* he thought, a mix of determination and sorrow tightening in his chest. Destroying the domes would mean destroying life.

Similar to the secluded dome Adriel had arranged for them in the English countryside, the structure before them was a modest residential area, consisting of only a handful of houses—all belonging to Tyers. "Her bank account must be spectacular," Wyatt remarked, as they surveyed the perimeter from their rendezvous point. *Wyatt... always with the gun metaphors.*

Indeed, Gayul Tyers' bank account would be a sight to behold, amassed through her craft as a bomb-maker. The dome's artificial lights flickered, dampened by the night-vision filter, yet still casting long, ominous shadows that danced eerily across the sterile land. The stark contrast between the luxurious glow inside and the desolate darkness outside painted a vivid picture of disparity—a gilded fortress amidst ruins.

A wave of disgust rolled over Jarod as he observed the dome's opulence. "Wealth built on ruins," he muttered under his breath, the injustice fueling a simmering anger. Over the past two decades, Tyers had left a trail of death and destruction, with countless explosive devices attributed to her. And she charged handsomely for it, allowing her to live a life of luxury few could afford. As much as he loathed her, he begrudgingly respected her cunning and ability to navigate the treacherous waters of her world. Crime was often the secret ingredient to achieving such lofty heights, and Tyers was no exception. *I suppose one could win the lottery. Or be old money.*

Jarod didn't fully subscribe to the ubiquitous public dogma paraded through media—both social and otherwise—that attaining even a modest level of wealth through diligent work was all but unachievable in the present day. The economic landscape, they said, had shifted inexorably from the dynamic mobility of the past two centuries back to the static pyramids of caste and class from the pre-Enlightenment era. The disillusionment ran deep. The academics had a term for it: *neo-feudalism*—the notion that society's hierarchy was once again locked in place, with Henry James Gibson and his ilk occupying the top, while Outies languished at the bottom, consigned there indefinitely, even after being incorporated. *But is it true?*

He had to confess he didn't know. *We might all be pawns in a system rigged against us. I cannot dismiss that.* The middle class appeared to still maintain a foothold, at least Inside. And some places Outside weren't as dreadful as people claimed—at least that was his impression. Nevertheless, he relished his return to Europe after their stint in the States. It was here he felt he truly belonged—his home of choice. *It's where Dana is.* While she may not presently be at his side, the closer he was, the better. The thought of her momentarily lifted his spirits. *She's the true beacon of hope in the gloom.* He truly believed his efforts weren't in vain, but hers were what really mattered.

Tyers, while obviously a despicable human being, at least possessed an admirable work ethic, whatever one might think of her methods. Underestimating her would be a grave error. The security measures—unseen yet palpably omnipresent—whispered threats from every shadowy corner. The flickering lights seemed to mock them as they made their approach. Each glimmer was a potential harbinger of an alarm yet to be sounded. There was a reason she had evaded capture all these years.

And, I have to admit, she does have a refined sense of aesthetics. Choosing to live in the South of France was certainly a good decision. Even Outside, though not precisely at their present locale north of Cannes, it still held an unparalleled beauty. Tomorrow, after the operation had hopefully been successfully executed, Jarod intended to spend the day touring the Riviera on Aegis's dime. *Antibes is supposed to be stunning. Completely preserved as it was before the dome. Or so, I've heard.*

Despite the scorching heatwave currently tormenting the entirety of the Mediterranean, the night was tolerable. Rain was pleasantly absent with only a slight breeze - not forceful enough to impede the drones. The squitos would be a different matter, but would play a vital role first inside the dome. He had hoped the wind would bring more respite from the scorching heat, but alas, sudden gusts felt like standing in front of business end of a hairdryer. But the physical discomfort was a small price to pay if it meant taking down another pillar of the anti-dome establishment. Jarod watched Wyatt and the others, their faces set in stone, focused on the task. "We're all carrying unseen burdens ," he reminded himself.

Wyatt holstered the last of his weapons before initiating the radio check. "All units report in," he commanded, rousing Jarod from his thoughts. Riley responded in her usual composed and detached British accent, "Read you five."

Wyatt acknowledged, "Read you five also." He would act as mission commander on this job, and Jarod was grateful to relinquish control for once. Human-to-human operations were Wyatt's forte. After Wyatt's confirmation, Dembwe's team chimed in, and Kale closed the loop.

The calm before the storm. Jarod took in the tactile feedback of gravel under his booths, the cold metal of his weapon in his hand, both tangible connections to the task before them. He felt more at ease with the job now, having successfully completed the Megan Russell operation, the second target on their list, following the challenging mental lapse with Siscal/Madoff. The apprehension he had experienced before pulling the trigger on the previous job had faded, albeit not entirely. He had been surprised by how seamlessly everything had gone. Once they had identified Russell's location, they had set up without a hitch, utilizing squitos to eliminate any unnecessary risks. And moral dilemmas. After a thorough stakeout and due diligence, Kale had moved the squito in while Russell slept, relegating her to hist Despite the scorching heatwave tormenting the entirety of the Mediterranean, the night was tolerable. Rain was pleasantly absent, with only a slight breeze—not forceful enough to impede the drones. The squitos would be another matter, but they would play a vital role inside the dome. Jarod had hoped the wind would bring more respite from the heat, but sudden gusts felt like standing in front of the business end of a hairdryer. Still, the physical discomfort was a small price to pay if it meant taking down another pillar of the anti-dome establishment.

Jarod watched Wyatt and the others, their faces set in stone, focused on the task. *We're all carrying unseen burdens,* he reminded himself.

Wyatt holstered the last of his weapons before initiating the radio check. "All units report in," he commanded, rousing Jarod from his thoughts.

Riley responded in her usual composed and detached British accent, "Read you five."

Wyatt acknowledged, "Read you five also." He would act as

mission commander on this job, and Jarod was grateful to relinquish control for once. Human-to-human operations were Wyatt's forte. After Wyatt's confirmation, Dembwe's team chimed in, and Kale closed the loop.

The calm before the storm. Jarod took in the tactile feedback of gravel under his boots, the cold metal of his weapon in his hand—both tangible connections to the task ahead. He felt more at ease with the job now, having successfully completed the Megan Russell operation, the second target on their list, following the challenging mental lapse with Siscal/Madoff. The apprehension he'd experienced before pulling the trigger on the previous job had faded, though not entirely. He had been surprised by how seamlessly everything had gone. Once they had identified Russell's location, they set up without a hitch, utilizing squitos to eliminate any unnecessary risks—and moral dilemmas. After a thorough stakeout and due diligence, Kale had moved the squito in while Russell slept, relegating her to history with a toxin injection. Two targets down, three more to go, with their corporate overlord thoroughly pleased with their progress.

When Jarod had first signed on for this job, he had partly anticipated greater challenges. In real life, villains didn't lurk in heavily fortified underwater hideaways or desolate, far-flung islands. Reality wasn't beholden to cinematic tropes. These individuals were just like any other person, mostly living unremarkable lives in ordinary surroundings. They had families, pets, sometimes mundane jobs, did grocery shopping, and took vacations like everyone else. They were protected, in a way, by Legacy's inability to build solid cases against them in court, allowing them to live freely with the rest of us. However, they weren't safe from the likes of Aegis, who were now prepared to ruthlessly do whatever it took to bring them down. They weren't safe from the likes of him.

They had yet to establish a solid lead on Davies but had enough targets to toy with in the meantime. Now the time had come for Gayel Tyers. Jarod glanced over at Dembwe and his team. *Good ol' Dembwe.* He was grateful they were there, providing additional security. *It's good to know the cavalry is here in case shit hits the fan.* Dembwe was a capable leader, but he could be quite the pain if he wasn't in charge. Convincing him to step down had been a challenge. Cloak-and-dagger maneuvers weren't his forte; he and his team excelled more at brute-force approaches. Nevertheless, their arsenal was unmatched, boasting some of the most advanced electronic warfare weaponry on the planet, as well as top-of-the-line offensive hardware, including drones, explosives, and other lethal implements. *All the good stuff.*

Approaching Tyers would require a shift in tactics from their prior jobs. As the highest-profile target on their list, besides Davies himself, she had considerably better security measures in place. Sought after worldwide by both Legacy and various private interests, she seldom left the sanctuary of her protective bubble. The security checkpoint was just the first hurdle; once inside, they would have to contend with state-of-the-art countermeasures that rendered any electronic gadget useless and then face human security on top of that. *Hence, Wyatt.*

Once inside, they would have to sweep the dome on foot while hopefully avoiding the watchful eyes of the guards. Just like with Siscal/Madoff, a bullet would be used to take her out—squitos genuinely weren't an option this time. That task would fall on Jarod's capable shoulders, while Dembwe and Wyatt provided backup. For this op, they were clad in body armor and armed with assault rifles, prepared this time for a real fight.

"All checks complete," Wyatt announced. "Are we clear to move out?"

Riley quickly confirmed the status, finding that there were no drones or guards in their path, save for their own. With this information, he, Wyatt, and Dembwe double-timed it down the hill toward the dome. Meanwhile, Dembwe's team headed toward the designated backup location, positioned closer but still out of the range of any surveillance drones or cameras.

The uneven terrain, dotted with small hills, provided ample cover as they advanced toward their target. One of these hills had been designated as their first destination, where Wyatt would take out the two guards stationed at the checkpoint with a sniper rifle. In the days leading up to the operation, Jarod had briefly deliberated over whether there was a non-lethal way to incapacitate the guards. If Tyers had been their first target, the decision might have kept him up at night, but after two successful missions, he was now firmly back on the horse. There were no more doubts. Although there were non-lethal ways to handle the situation, it was simply less risky to eliminate them. It was an easy call.

Their employer had given them carte blanche to carry out the mission however they saw fit, as long as Aegis remained sufficiently distanced. Innocent bystanders were an unfortunate reality, and while Jarod was committed to minimizing collateral damage, these guards were a different story. *Besides, they're hardly innocent.* By choosing to work for a known terrorist, the guards had made themselves fair game.

The hill was secured without complications. "Guard post outside the main entrance," Wyatt said. "As anticipated, two security guards are stationed outside the airlock, and three drones are circling. Kale, stand by for my signal."

It was imperative to neutralize all guards and drones simultaneously; otherwise, a single surviving unit could trigger an alarm. Wyatt aimed his rifle and fired while signaling Kale via braid. In response, Kale deployed electronic warfare drones, emitting a precisely targeted electromagnetic pulse that incapacitated the guarding drones, sending them crashing to the ground.

"Move. Text only from now on," Wyatt directed. The team moved in unison, rushing toward the guard post. Jarod found himself wishing he was in better physical condition, already feeling the burn in his lungs and muscles. In contrast, Dembwe and Wyatt seemed unaffected by the strain, their movements fluid and effortless.

When their work involved rounding up Outie trespassers for Legacy, their operating procedure was decidedly more hands-off. Drones did the bulk of the heavy lifting, while they hung back, waiting to swoop in and make the arrest once the target was incapacitated. Running was never a requirement, and their jobs were often sedentary affairs. If any physical involvement was needed, they would bring in contracted help, like Dembwe. *Thank the stars for genetic engineering; otherwise, I'd be a fat pig.* He would forever be grateful to the military for providing him with such enhancements. It kept him above the waterline, allowing for some neglect of his physical health. Nevertheless, as his lungs began to burn with exertion, he resolved to work out more in the future.

They moved swiftly to the airlock. Wyatt affixed decoy braids to the temples of the fallen guards, which would trick the dome's central AI into thinking the guards were still present and accounted for. With any luck, the short time between their deaths and the attachment of the decoys would be dismissed by the automated dome security AI as an insignificant glitch. These clever little pieces of technology, procured by Kale through Adriel, wouldn't fool the AI indefinitely, but they would suffice for the duration of the operation, provided everything went smoothly.

Meanwhile, Dembwe entered the access codes required to breach the dome's interior. Obtaining these had been a challenge—hidden behind every conceivable firewall and cryptogram—but Kale was unstoppable, able to locate any virtual needle in any virtual haystack. The codes worked flawlessly.

After gaining access through the inner lock, Wyatt commanded the release of squitos, which instantly switched to search-and-destroy mode, targeting any surveillance or offensive capabilities within the dome. Within seconds, the dome's interior erupted in an invisible electronic warfare front. It was their bugs against Gayul's. While she had impressive countermeasures patrolling her perimeter, theirs were superior and would ultimately win.

[We're clear.] Dembwe's text flashed across Jarod's lens, confirming the assessment on his own tactical display. Wyatt texted back: **[Everyone knows what to do. Go.]**

Dembwe headed to the upper level to secure Gayul's panic room in case she had been alerted to their presence. Jarod set off to locate the target, while Wyatt focused on his area of expertise: hunting humans.

Jarod swiftly dispatched surveillance squitos to map the sprawling residence and relay the information to his braid. The tiny drones scoured the premises, and within minutes, identified likely areas where Gayul would be found at night—all located in the south wing, except for the human staff quarters, which Jarod deemed irrelevant. He doubted Gayul would spend her nights consorting with the help.

As expected, the squitos located her within minutes, sound asleep in the master bedroom. His braid mapped out a route, displaying it on his lens. He made his way toward her without interruption, constantly monitoring the tactical overview of the squitos' progress in his peripheral vision. The parallel electronic warfare waged between their insect-sized drones steadily worked in their favor, systematically neutralizing one section of the house after another—dismantling drones, alarm sensors, microphones, and cameras. Meanwhile, Wyatt was efficiently dealing with human security officers.

[Panic room is secured.] Dembwe's message confirmed his success. He would now join Wyatt to lend a hand—if anyone was left. Jarod continued along the path his braid had provided, finally reaching the master bedroom. Just as he arrived, his braid alerted him: someone was approaching from behind.

In a split second, Jarod whirled around, weapon at the ready, only to find himself face-to-face with a child. The boy couldn't have been more than eleven or twelve years old. *Where the hell did he come from?* Their intel had not mentioned Tyers' children being present. They were supposed to be in boarding school in Paris, and the team had confirmed their whereabouts. *And yet, here he stands, right in front of me.*

Interference from the electronic warfare raging in the background had likely masked the boy's bio signs, rendering him undetectable. For a fraction of a second, Jarod and the boy stared at each other, the child in shock at the sight of an intruder in the house. The boy was about to scream, and there was no time to waste pondering how he had come to be there. Without hesitation, Jarod lunged forward, clamping his hand over the boy's mouth to silence him, while wrapping his other arm around his neck.

The child's panicked breaths came hot and rapid against Jarod's palm. His wide, terrified eyes, even in the dim hallway light, were full of shock. "Shh," Jarod hissed, tightening his grip.

"I'm sorry, kid."

A torrent of emotions overwhelmed him—guilt, fear, and desperate hope colliding as the mission's objectives clashed with the innocence struggling in his arms. *May God forgive me.* In the end, he maintained control, choking the boy until his body went limp. Jarod laid him gently on the hardwood floor, checking for a pulse and finding it. The boy was bruised, possibly with a crushed larynx, but he would live.

Jarod turned back toward the bedroom, now convinced they had made the right decision not to rely on a squito to take out Tyers. Had the drone survived the chaos of the electronic interference and encountered the boy, its AI might have viewed him as an obstacle to completing its programming—and simply eliminated him.

Thankfully, there was no sign of activity in the room. Tyers was in bed, as expected. A glass of water and a bottle of diazepam sat on the nightstand, explaining her comatose sleep. Jarod raised his firearm and fired a single shot, ending her life. Satisfied that the mission was complete, he confirmed Tyers was dead before signaling the team to begin their withdrawal.

On his way out, Jarod paused by the unconscious boy. Kneeling beside him, he placed his hand gently on the child's forehead, as if offering comfort. The silence in the hallway was deafening, broken only by Jarod's own labored breathing as he struggled to reconcile what he saw. He checked the boy's pulse once more, relieved to feel the warmth of life. "Tomorrow won't be a good day," he murmured, "but you'll make it."

With those words, Jarod rose to his feet and made his way to the rendezvous point.

As his check-in with Adriel approached, Jarod found himself once again clutching a sick bag on a screamer, this time hurtling toward Tel Aviv, Adriel's home, where their next rendezvous would be held. This time he was flying solo, with no crew to give him a hard time if his stomach gave in to the turbulence. *I guess you have to appreciate the little things.*

The flight from Nice was short—only twenty minutes—but it was customarily turbulent during the approach. At least the bumpy ride and subsequent nausea provided a momentary distraction from the recent operation. Even though the mission had been a resounding success, with yet another target checked off the list, the incident with the child weighed heavily on Jarod's mind. He had spent hours poring over the after-action report, sifting through sensor logs and analyzing recorded footage from not just his braid, but also those of Dembwe and Wyatt, all in an attempt to understand why they had failed to detect the child's presence. The data they had meticulously gathered prior to the engagement all indicated that the boy was residing with his father in Spain.

Using the full extent of his braid's AI capabilities, Jarod had combed through every byte of mission data, searching for any correlations or discrepancies that could explain how they had missed the child. Despite his best efforts, the braid yielded nothing but a single theory: the EMP generated during the squito skirmish had likely concealed the boy's bio-signs. Their intelligence had been impeccable, the AI concluded. The child was not supposed to be there. And yet, he was. It was a frustratingly unsatisfying answer, but it was the only one he had.

He knew he should leave it at that, yet the nightmares persisted. The image of the child gasping for air as Jarod choked him haunted him day and night, refusing to fade no matter how hard he tried to push it into the recesses of his mind. The doubts about the job that had always lingered now resurfaced with renewed intensity, threatening to consume him. So, for the time being, he welcomed the discomforts of air travel. *Kinetosis, I believe it's called, is great that way.* You can't focus on anything else. The hum of the screamer's engine melded with the occasional creaks in the airframe. Jarod felt the turbulence through his seat, an incessant reminder of the fragile barrier between him and death. The tang of recycled air mixed with microwaved sandwiches, cheap economy-class wine, and maybe his own fear—all a concoction that settled uneasily in his stomach. He clutched the barf bag tighter.

Jarod had no particular grievances against Israel, except for the fact that it was virtually inaccessible by bullet train or private road transport. The only way in or out was through the air. While bullet trains certainly existed, they were frequently shut down during times of regional tension—and so they were this time. The infrastructure they ran on was often targeted by the country's many enemies. Despite Israel's world-renowned defenses, the country's leadership often found it best to shut down service when conflict was imminent. For Jarod, that meant flying in.

The thought of navigating Israel's airspace, crisscrossed with invisible lines of defense and contention, left a bitter taste in his mouth. The aridity of the landscape below, visible through occasional breaks in the clouds, mirrored the dryness in his throat—a physical manifestation of his apprehension. There lay the domes of Tel Aviv and Haifa, and to the south, the Gaza Strip, bombed to dust, rebuilt, and bombed again in an endless cycle, as telling as anything about the current state of the world. *Not that I'm a believer in crackpot theories of cyclical history or anything.* But he could see how that idea might seduce some.

London certainly hadn't helped. In the aftermath of the incident, authorities across the globe had become increasingly paranoid. Police and military forces, both public and private, ramped up security measures to absurd levels. The resulting surge in arrests was staggering, with most having nothing to do with the bombing itself. Dissidents, protesters, and activists now lived in an even more dangerous world than before—as had always been the case following major terrorist attacks. History had shown this to be true time and time again, from London to D.C., from 9/11 to Munich, to India-Pakistan. Invariably, indiscriminate crackdowns were implemented, followed by indefinite detentions without due process. Israel was no exception to this pattern. *An endless cycle of violence and repression,* he mused. *One has to wonder if we're catalysts for change or just agents of the status quo.*

The plane descended onto a smaller military airfield located south of Tel Aviv. Ben Gurion Airport was off-limits for the time being, not only due to regional tensions but also because of a dangerous dust storm and severe heat wave that had rendered most commercial aircraft inoperable. Fortunately, Adriel had arranged for a car to pick Jarod up. While there were public transportation options at the airfield, he appreciated the gesture of a private ride.

The worst of the heat wave building over the Arabian Peninsula hadn't yet reached this far north, but the temperature was still sweltering. As he hurried across the tarmac to reach his ride, Jarod felt a flicker of panic. The scorching sun beat down on the back of his neck, making it difficult to breathe. *I definitely don't want to know what it's like at the epicenter of such a monstrous heat wave.* Still, he didn't complain; after all, he would soon be enjoying the luxury of air conditioning.

The relief of stepping into the air-conditioned car was bittersweet. The contrast to the oppressive heat outside was striking. As the door closed, sealing off the searing heat, he was enveloped in silence, save for the car's engine and the soft whir of the cooling system. Jarod allowed himself a moment of gratitude for the small comfort, though it was overshadowed by the unease of what lay ahead. *Sanctuary or prison?* he wondered, as the cool air worked to soothe the heat clinging to his skin. The temporary respite from the chaos outside gave him time to gather his thoughts.

The car offered refreshments, but Jarod, still battling residual nausea from the flight, declined. Focusing his attention on the road ahead helped, and the air conditioning provided additional relief. *Whatever you do, don't puke in the car.*

Once past the dome checkpoint, the ride continued along Jabotinsky Street. Though he hadn't visited in years, the city appeared mostly unchanged. He watched as overground trams moved sluggishly along the parade street, starting and stopping in sync with the congested traffic. Whether by car or tram, everything moved slowly here.

The city's heartbeat pulsed through the slow-moving traffic, punctuated by distant sounds outside the car: muted honks, the faint laughter of pedestrians, and the occasional wail of a siren—all things the presence of the dome hadn't changed. A blend of sea air, drifting in from the desalination plants along the dome's coastal frontier, mixed with the subtle fragrance of street food, filtering through the car's air system. *Not at all unpleasant,* he thought.

It puzzled him why personal vehicles were still allowed to such a high extent inside, unlike in other city domes, such as those in Europe. The Israelis seemed to have an aversion to such bans, their attitude more akin to that of their American allies. Nevertheless, the city remained as beautiful as ever. The streets teemed with cars and pedestrians alike; the latter strolled along the sidewalks, perpetually dressed in summer attire. Tel Aviv was kept hotter than any other city dome he had ever visited. *Not that I've been everywhere or anything,* he thought. He guessed it was kept warm to conserve energy—cooling a dome in a desert climate wasn't cheap, and people here were used to the heat.

He met Adriel at the beach, taking a seat on a public bench overlooking the crowded boardwalk. The area was packed with swimmers, runners, and dinner guests occupying the patios of various restaurants. Adriel had taken all the necessary precautions to ensure they wouldn't be overheard by electronic eavesdroppers.

In the distance, the levees kept the ocean at bay, with locks regulating the flow of seawater to the beaches. On the other side of the dome barrier, massive water treatment plants kept the water clean for the bathers' enjoyment. He admired coastal cities that had built their dome barriers offshore, rather than on it. Here, you could see a significant portion of the dome structure stretching along Tel Aviv Beach as far as the eye could see, unobscured by skyscrapers or skyways—a testament to the most ambitious and impressive construction in human history, these literal life preservers.

The salty breeze from the locks mingled with the warmth of a simulated sun, casting a soft glow over the faces of the beachgoers. The sound of artificial waves provided a soothing backdrop to their conversation, a natural rhythm sharply contrasting with the topic at hand. The occasional cry of seagulls, introduced and maintained by the authorities to simulate pre-dome life, punctuated the chatter of beach activity.

As a bot approached with their drinks, Adriel spoke. "Congratulations, by the way, on taking out Tyers. Very impressive. That was always going to be one of the harder ones," he said. Jarod nodded his thanks and took his gin and tonic off the tray, taking a sip. He wasn't much of a daytime drinker, but after the ride in, he needed something to take the edge off. A bit of life duller to help him relax.

"No luck with Scott?" Adriel asked, the question hanging in the air like an unspoken accusation. Jarod shook his head.

Adriel continued, "We have intel suggesting he's left Alixha and gone underground. Apparently, Alixha herself is looking for him, just like we are. Know anything about that?"

Jarod didn't. They had confirmed Scott had gone underground but didn't know he was now a target of his own organization. "I'll try to find out whatever I can," he agreed. If Alixha was also hunting him, it would certainly be prudent to dig deeper. "Does this change the mission in any way?" he asked.

"Not for the time being."

"Understood." He transmitted the information to Kale and Riley. If there was anything additional to know, they'd find out.

"Two down, four to go," Adriel remarked.

"Three to go," Jarod corrected him.

Adriel looked confused. "There's four—oh yes, I forgot. You have a new target," he said, transmitting the details over braid. Jarod quickly scanned the file. It was some cybercriminal he had never heard of.

"So that's how this is going to work then? We knock one off, and you add another to the list?"

Frustration simmered beneath the surface, a growing sense of being trapped in an endless loop of violence and retribution. The revelation of a new target—another name on what seemed like an infinite list—was the price of their involvement. *A pawn in a much larger game,* Jarod acknowledged, the realization leaving a bitter taste that even the gin couldn't mask.

"You work for Aegis now," Adriel continued. "You'll take on the targets we send you. You will, of course, be compensated handsomely for this one as well. And any future targets," he added, turning away to order food from a nearby bot. "Unless you want to withdraw from the arrangement." The last statement hung in the air, a thinly veiled threat disguised as a casual remark.

"Of course, if you do, you'll no longer enjoy our protection."

Aegis itself wasn't the threat Adriel alluded to—not yet, at least. They wouldn't risk damaging an asset until there was no other option. However, by taking this job, they had entered the game and become players, making themselves potential targets for other interested parties. Legacy law, Lux Aeterna, other bounty hunters—anything was possible. That's what Adriel meant by "enjoying their protection." Jarod was many things, but naive wasn't one of them. He knew the risks and understood the consequences of being in this game. *No choice, pal.*

With a friendly pat on the shoulder, Adriel signaled the end of their meeting. "Be careful out there," he warned as Jarod rose to leave.

Dana

"Grateful," Brett murmured, taking the glass of water from her hand and lifting it to his parched lips with a shaky hand. Dana's heart clenched at the sight of Brett's frail state—his body still recovering from injuries sustained during their abduction. But at least he would survive. Dana shuddered at the thought of being left alone with these children. Watching him struggle, she felt an instinct to protect this kind man from further harm, but also a deeply rooted fear of what would happen to all of them if he stayed incapacitated. She wouldn't be able to handle their captors without him. Daemon seemed fairly rational, but the one called Cali was something else entirely. *Kid or not, he's scary.*

The Niederrad hostage drama had now stretched into its fourth day, with no end in sight. The authorities had swiftly caught on after Dana's disappearance, but their response had not been fast enough, allowing Daemon and Cali to barricade themselves inside the Lamonte family's apartment. A hostage negotiation team, along with snipers and SWAT, had set up camp around the building, effectively cutting off any escape routes. Remy had died on day two. While Daemon had allowed medics to treat him, he refused to let them take Remy to the hospital. Despite their best efforts, Remy's injuries proved fatal, and the medics had taken his body on the third day.

The silence in the room after the medics' departure, and the look on Brett's weary face, lingered. Dana's thoughts scrambled uncontrollably with the uncertainty of their fate. Each passing day had been a torment of hope and despair. The strain of the standoff, the pressure of the encircling authorities—it was like living in a tightening noose. The weight of everyone's collective gaze—from the police outside to their captors within the apartment—was suffocating, a palpable presence that invaded every rare moment of respite they'd had. She was relieved not to have to share her prison with Remy's decomposing corpse, at least, but she couldn't shake the guilt of feeling nothing for his passing. She barely knew him, having only interacted with him and the others in passing. But she couldn't shake the feeling that someone out there would miss him.

She wrestled with that numbness, with the odd sense of grief at a distance, and the guilt-ridden acknowledgment of her detachment. *A defense mechanism,* she thought, though it offered little comfort against the dread that they might not make it out alive.

Their situation had drawn the world's attention. News outlets and social media had latched onto the drama, pulling in curious onlookers from near and far. Eventually, the crowds had grown so large that the police had to bring in reinforcements to manage them. Drones now buzzed around the building, occasionally peering through the thin curtains of the living room window.

Immediately after the police arrived, they swiftly severed all communication lines—a move Brett explained was to ensure that negotiations would go through their appointed negotiator. They also blocked all devices connected to the internet, including Dana's braid, the Lamontes' tablets, and Aea's AR visor. None of them worked. The only sources of information were either peeking through the windows or the old public television broadcasts, where updates on the situation were narrated by an indifferent AI, interspersed with emotionally charged images of the children's desperate father, pleading with the kidnappers to let his children go.

They were fortunate that the Lamontes' living room screen

still had a functioning TV receiver. Daemon kept it running around the clock, tracking the outside world through news broadcasts. Television signals were transmitted the old-fashioned way, outside the internet, and were therefore harder for the police to block. Apparently, television broadcasts were protected by different laws and required a court order to shut down. Brett said the police were undoubtedly working on obtaining such an order, but it would take some time.

The twice-daily public news broadcasts and PSAs offered little useful information. The television was mostly used for government announcements, and the news segments were minimalistic in every sense—only five minutes of automated feeds sandwiched between continuous rolls of PSAs and weather forecasts. Even Outside, everyone was connected to the Net in one way or another.

A few hours prior, the TV news had shown brief aerial footage of the dilapidated building and the growing crowds outside. The murmurs of the crowd could be heard even from within the apartment—chants and shouts mixing with the occasional blast of what sounded like foghorns and vuvuzelas. The growing mass of people had metamorphosed into yet another protest. The whir of drones buzzing outside the windows, a reminder of their spectacle-turned-prison, slowly eroded what was left of her resolve. *God, what I wouldn't do for a shower and my own bed.* Any semblance of normalcy would do at this point. The protests, a distant roar beneath the drone's hum, were both terrifying and strangely heartening—a sign that the world hadn't forgotten them.

Dana desperately wanted to catch a glimpse of the situation outside, but it wasn't possible. Cali had made that clear when he pressed the cold steel of his gun against the back of her head the last time she tried to sneak a peek out the window. He patrolled the apartment, keeping watch over everyone while Daemon negotiated with the authorities behind the closed door of the master bedroom.

Throughout the tense hours and days of their captivity, Dana and Brett had pieced together fragments of overheard conversations and observed behaviors—a jigsaw slowly forming a motif they couldn't quite complete. They knew there was a larger force at play, an orchestrator in the shadows whose motives were as obscured as the murky daylight filtering through the curtains. Daemon, Cali, and Ameer had been unknown to both Brett and herself, but Gabriel's name had been mentioned repeatedly.

The two had tried, in moments of feigned casualness or through direct questioning when courage allowed, to extract more about why they were taken. Daemon's evasions and Cali's volatile dismissals only deepened the mystery, a frustrating labyrinth with no clear exit. "Is this an escalation in the negotiations?" Dana had asked aloud at one point, her question hanging in the air—unanswered but increasingly likely.

Her speculations about Gabriel's resistance to the dome's expansion and its threat to his empire were theories cobbled together from scraps—a crawler search here, a word spoken aloud there. Yet, without concrete evidence or a direct confession from their captors, she could still only guess. She understood they were caught in the wake of two young knights' ambition, perhaps a desperate act to prove their worth to their king, but if there was a grand design, it remained just out of reach—a story half-told, waiting for its missing pieces.

Brett's condition had fluctuated over the past forty-eight hours, leaving him in and out of consciousness. On the second day, his leg had become infected, and it seemed like his chances of survival were diminishing. But Daemon had relented and allowed another team of medics in to redress his wounds and administer a healing gel patch. Slowly but surely, Brett began to regain lucidity, and he was now fully conscious. *Weak, but conscious.*

Dana felt immense relief at Brett finally regaining his strength. Although Aea and Tabayah provided welcome company, the ongoing terror required Dana to invest considerable energy in keeping them calm. The pair had retreated to Tabayah's room, attempting to remain out of the way. Over time, Dana noticed a deepening bond between Aea and Daemon, and it soon became apparent that they shared a profound and intimate connection. Despite this, it was clear that the girl was not complicit in their captivity. Like Dana, Brett, and herself, she too was a victim of the situation they were trapped in. *As are Remy, Pankash, and Tabayah.*

Dana often found herself left to entertain Tabayah while Aea spent time with Daemon. In those quiet moments, away from the chaos that had become their lives, Dana caught glimpses of Aea's true self—fragments of vulnerability that she tried to hide beneath a facade of solidarity with Daemon. It became increasingly clear to both Dana and Brett that Aea was entangled in a web she hadn't woven, her affection for Daemon exploited to anchor her to a cause she hadn't chosen. The realization dawned on them slowly, a truth pieced together through whispered conversations and shared glances of understanding. Aea, much like them, was trapped, her love twisted by Daemon's manipulation. Despite her association with their captor, empathy for Aea's plight grew within Dana, a recognition of their shared victimhood that transcended the barriers Daemon and Cali had erected.

The moments of playtime with the younger girl did not bother Dana in the slightest. In fact, it helped keep her own nerves at bay. In the stolen moments of play, whispered exchanges over hastily shared meals, Dana found herself inadvertently stepping into a role she had never known she could fill. Aea, with her guarded vulnerability and stories of a childhood cut adrift—of emigrating from Africa, of losing her mother—evoked an instinct in Dana she hadn't realized existed.

While Tabayah played, they talked. At first, about trivial things—memories of family meals, the scent of a mother's perfume, the warmth of a comforting hug—each conversation a delicate dance around the voids in their own lives. Dana, who had lived a life with no thought of motherhood, found herself drawn into a protectiveness she had only seen from afar. And Aea, so resilient under that facade of bravado, seemed to seek guidance and assurance in Dana. It was an unspoken connection, fragile as it was new, but in the shadow of their shared captivity, it felt like a silent rebellion against the hand they'd been dealt.

Every delicate moment ended sooner or later when Cali needed to blow off steam and would have an outburst. He would flail about and wave his firearm around until Daemon calmed him down. The boy appeared frightened and fatigued, like a trapped animal. There were moments, however, when he seemed more at ease, exhibiting a sense of self-control. He would strut confidently throughout the apartment, gun tucked within his jeans, knife stashed away in an ankle holster, checking to ensure that neither she nor Brett was up to any mischief. Whenever he entered a room, all chatter would cease, as if they had been up to something nefarious, but nobody ever was. *What could we possibly be up to?*

Brett grunted, now awake from another feverish slumber. Dana felt a wave of relief wash over her now that Brett was awake. Even with his diminished capacity to protect her, she felt safer with him conscious and alert.

"What's all that noise?" he asked, struggling to sit up on the couch.

"Protests," she replied, filling him in as he took a sip of water to rehydrate. Explaining the situation to Brett, she felt a renewed sense of despair at the chaos unfurling. The cacophony of dissent was a bitter reminder of the broader fractures in society, their bubble inside the apartment a microcosm of that fragmented reality. At first, the protests had been about the police presence itself. Outies naturally held a deep disdain for Innie law enforcement, and their mere presence was enough to incite anger and frustration. But over time, the protests had evolved, taking on a life of their own. They were now about anything and everything that angered the people of Niederrad. It was about the dome, the inaccessibility of the Net, the unsightly presence of The Crescent, poverty, economic injustice, freedom, and the general oppression of Outies. Inevitably, the protests attracted bandwagon jumpers, each attempting to co-opt the movement's agenda for their own purposes. The messages often appeared contradictory, such as clamoring for increased social welfare while simultaneously railing against the tax hikes necessary to fund it. The TV news had detailed as much.

"I can't access my braid," Brett said, frustration etched into his voice. "They won't shut mine down, but I'm still too weak. Or maybe it took a beating in the tunnels. I'll know as soon as

I'm strong enough to run a diagnostic."

Dana quickly fetched him some food from the supplies the medics had brought in during their last visit. Braids ran on glucose, just like any other organ in the human body, and Brett needed the fuel to regain his strength.

"As soon as they see I'm online, they'll likely try to contact me. Maybe put me to work from the inside," Brett said. Dana's stomach tightened at the thought—the prospect of Brett being roped into it rather than sitting it out while the pros handled it was a glaring testament to their vulnerability. That the authorities outside had no answers. "What does it look like outside?" he asked.

"It started out slow," she replied. "Just a few people outside the police barriers, but it's grown a lot bigger in the last day. Now there are hundreds, and what appears to be the entire Frankfurt police force."

Brett nodded thoughtfully. "Day four has begun, you said?" He took another sip of his water. "Then we don't have much time. A day, maybe two at the most. They've held off because they're children, especially because of the little one, but with the crowds growing, they're going to feel like they're losing control. Unless the negotiator makes some headway soon, they'll make a move."

His words sent a shiver down Dana's spine, the impending sense of doom suddenly crystallizing into unvarnished reality. The thought of an assault—of violence breaching what was both their prison and their sanctuary—ignited a primal fear. She played scenarios in her mind, each more terrifying than the last. Brett groaned in pain as he shifted position on the couch. "They might try to use me to talk them down," he continued. "Or they may decide it's time for the special forces to take over." The latter, Brett further explained, would be bad news for everyone involved.

As the evening wore on, Brett's condition improved noticeably, and he felt confident enough to attempt starting up his braid.

However, it soon became apparent that something was indeed amiss. The self-diagnostic routine revealed that his braid had sustained damage during the altercation in the tunnels. Although his police-issued model would eventually self-repair, by the time it was functional again, the hostage situation they were trapped in would likely have concluded. One way or another.

No, the braid was useless, and they were left with no other option but to rely on the TV broadcasts for information about the outside. The television screen, with its flickering images and crackling audio, became their only window to the world, casting a pale, artificial light that deepened the shadows in the dimly lit room and on their faces. The broadcasts were a lifeline, yet each AI-narrated newscast segment felt like a countdown, the voice from the screen a monotonous drone telling them things they already knew.

The lack of communication with the rest of the police force also dashed their hopes of negotiating from the inside. "Even if I had stayed in contact, I doubt my feeble negotiation skills would have made a difference," Brett remarked.

The very next TV broadcast brought an unsettling revelation, as the names of the parties involved in the hostage drama were finally made public. Aea was listed as a perpetrator, not a victim, the police having made the connection between her and Daemon. Brett's face contorted with worry at the implications of this development. "If they storm in, Aea will be a target," he fretted. "She'll be lucky to come out of this alive."

Dana spoke quietly, her voice laced with concern. "Killed? Surely they'll exercise some restraint? They wouldn't want unnecessary bloodshed."

Brett's response was bleak. "I don't know. After London, everyone's gone haywire. There's no interest in showing mercy or restraint anymore." Indeed, governments worldwide had made Outie crimes against Innies a particularly hot agenda item, essentially blaming Outies for London despite a clear lack of evidence. In the EU and the US, crimes against Innies perpetrated by Outies were almost automatically defined as terror events. "Even if they manage to capture the girl alive," Brett continued, "she'll be locked up in a detention center for years before she even gets to speak to a lawyer."

Their testimony, hers and Brett's, would make little difference. *If we live to testify in the first place. What are the chances of any of us just getting caught in a crossfire?*

"It's a new world since London," Brett stated matter-of-factly. "Like it or not." In any case, the poor girl's life would be irreparably damaged. Dana watched as the worry etched deeper lines in Brett's face, the glow from the television casting shadows that made them deeper still. The room seemed to grow colder with his words. Brett rose from his seat, wincing in pain. "Help me to the window. I need to assess the situation firsthand, see what we're dealing with."

She assisted him as he limped over to the window, intermittently glancing toward the bedroom door to ensure Cali remained on the other side of it. From the sounds emanating from inside the room, she could tell that he and Daemon were once again arguing. *Good. That'll keep him occupied for a minute or two.* However, Cali had not been through the apartment in a while and could emerge at any moment.

"Hurry," she whispered, guiding Brett closer to the window. He suppressed a groan as he put weight on his injured leg. Dana's heart raced at the sight of Brett's cautious shuffle, their shadows flickering on the living room wall like fleeting ghosts. It was a stark reminder of how vulnerable he was—and how little chance they had of returning to the couch undetected if Cali or Daemon appeared.

"Stay low," Brett warned. "They likely have snipers in place, and we don't want to provoke them unnecessarily."

Outside, the police base of operations was surrounded by a frenzied mob, hemmed in by a ring of riot squads. The cacophony from below rose up to them, a discordant symphony of anger, fear, and defiance that vibrated through the glass. The sight of the teeming masses, hundreds by now, illuminated by the sporadic flicker of police vehicle emergency lights, painted a surreal tableau of desperation clashing with order. Dana was surprised the noise could penetrate this high up in the building. She could easily comprehend the desperation of Cali and Daemon, trapped in the midst of a situation that had spiraled entirely out of control. *They must be terrified out of their minds.*

A rumble from the master bedroom interrupted their conversation, followed by the hushed voices of the captors. Then, only the sound of frantic pacing. They quickly retreated back to the couch and the mattress Daemon had taken from Aea's dad's' room before the captors could notice they were up and about.

"I need to stay off my leg," Brett grimaced. "It's not as bad as I thought, but I have to conserve my strength for when things inevitably go down. The healing gel should speed up my recovery, and hopefully, I'll be fit enough to move when the time comes."

"When it all goes down," Dana repeated, noting the shift in Brett's tone from "if" to "when."

"I saw three snipers placed on the surrounding rooftops," Brett continued. "There are probably more, but without my braid, I can't do any detailed scans. But they're close to moving in." He began questioning her about the layout of the apartment, any potential weapons they could use, and other pertinent details. His voice was low, each word measured, but the underlying urgency was palpable. It was like a current running beneath the surface of their entire conversation. Around her, the room seemed to shrink with the realization of the danger posed by the unseen snipers on the rooftops. The air felt heavier with unspoken fears.

She shook her head. "I haven't looked for any of that. I don't know." *I was too busy being scared out of my mind.*

As she sat there, her mind racing with the implications of her kidnapping, she couldn't help but feel overwhelmed. The fact that her abduction had become the talk of the entire city of Frankfurt—if not the world—was slowly sinking in. News traveled fast, and it was likely the story had spread far and wide by now.

In the end, it all came back to the dome expansion. For complex reasons she did not yet fully understand, the people of Niederrad wanted nothing to do with the Innies. They wanted no part of their world and were unwilling to allow them into theirs. Her kidnappers were criminals, driven to desperate measures by the fear that their way of life—their very existence—was slipping away. Others, too, shared their sentiments, albeit perhaps for less nefarious reasons. The deep-rooted animosity and distrust between Outies and Innies had created a volatile and dangerous environment, where violence and extremism seemed like the only options left. *People can be terrified of change. Even if it's for the better.*

She kept hearing Gabriel's name in the captors' internal debates and discussions with the negotiator. However, these conversations always took place behind the closed doors of the bedroom, beyond her reach. She strained to hear muffled voices through the walls, but never clearly enough to decipher any specific details. *Is he really behind this? Does it matter? We're here. At gunpoint, with the cavalry waiting outside, ready to go in, guns indiscriminately blazing.*

"One thing is for certain," she said, "the dome negotiations are over."

"Don't give up hope," Brett interjected. "I promise to help you through this. You'll be fine."

She chuckled wryly at the absurdity of her previous preoccupation with the contract negotiations. She had momentarily forgotten that her life was now in danger.

"Keep your mind busy; it will ease the tension," Brett advised.

"These people are losing everything," she murmured, her thoughts turning again to the plight of their kidnappers. "Their homes, their jobs, their planet, their lives. And now they believe we're taking what little remains. They cannot see that we are trying to save them."

Brett remained silent.

"Perhaps I am suffering from Stockholm syndrome," she mused, a wry smile on her lips. But her attempt at humor fell flat, as Brett only responded with a grave nod.

"No," he said. "You may be right."

The weight of her failure settled heavily upon her as she contemplated the disastrous consequences of her and Aegis's inability to win over the people of Niederrad. She would undoubtedly be fired, and the bulldozers would come to raze the city. But for now, survival was paramount. She had to protect herself and these children, to ensure they weren't caught in the crossfire of a hasty rescue attempt.

"There's still hope to talk them down," Brett insisted. "I may not be a negotiator, but you are."

"But I negotiate civil rights," she protested weakly. "Not hostage situations."

"It's not all that different," he countered.

She sat for a while in contemplative silence, mulling over the daunting task ahead. If the professional negotiator had failed to broker a surrender, what chance did she have?

"Listen, Brett," she began, her voice laced with urgency. "If what you say is true, and the army of evil is going to come bursting in here, guns blazing, then we need to be somewhere else when that happens. Maybe I can't convince Daemon to surrender, but maybe Aea knows of a place where we can take cover while everything goes down? At least get the two girls out of the way."

"Hide? What do you mean?"

"I don't know," she replied, her mind racing. "The building attic? The basement? A broom closet, for all I care. We just need to get them out of harm's way. It's a big building." Perhaps she couldn't help the people of Niederrad, but maybe, just maybe, she could help these particular ones.

"I guess it can't hurt to ask," Brett conceded.

With that, she rose to her feet and made her way over to Tabayah's room, where the girls were playing. She knocked on the doorframe, hoping to speak with Aea.

"Aea, can we talk?"

Journal

...the quest for structural explanations of global dynamics has evolved from the Cold War's West vs. East dichotomy, through the early twenty-first century's "Clash of Civilizations" between the West and Muslim societies, to the current contrast between traditional legacy governments and economic elites ("dome owners") against the emerging force of Lux Aeterna. This reflects the shifting focus of international relations from ideological conflicts to the rivalry between...

...Lux Aeterna, originally a relatively benign climate activism group, has evolved into a formidable challenger to the status quo. Operating with no territory to protect or expand, this powerful virtual entity opposes legacy governments and dome-owning mega-corporations, criticizing the domes as a superficial fix to climate change. They argue that such measures neglect the root causes of environmental degradation. Over time, their strategies have evolved toward increasingly aggressive tactics, including the use of violence...

...Governments, whose influence and power have arguably been in decline for decades, have seen a resurgence after the London Incident[...] Outsourced services continue to dominate, and the state, in its broadest definition, remains far from its past glory...[...]...yielding the playing field to private actors in areas of social life previously dominated by government organizations. States, constrained by the massive cost of dome construction subsidies[...] even law enforcement and certain branches of the military, previously considered unsuitable for outsourcing, are now being[...] the rise of neo-feudalism...

...187 acts of terrorism directly targeting dome structures since 2069, when the statistic became available. Most of these acts of terrorism have been classified as minor in nature...

...Dome structures are heavily fortified against external attacks, often to the point where even state-sponsored military operations would be deemed prohibitively...

...or from weaponized transports. In 2001, terrorists flew commercial airliners into two skyscrapers in Manhattan[...] deemed unlikely due to the modern defense systems in place around the dome structures...

...The London Incident demonstrated that despite the strong defenses, domes are still susceptible to attacks. However, investigations into the incident have revealed that the level of planning, organization, and complexity involved in the attack was substantial. As a result, experts consider the possibility of a similar attack in the future to...

...In the past three decades, there has been a relative sense of calm, and it could be argued that an equilibrium had been established globally, resulting in a fragile but existing peace among the world's competing interests. The London Incident has disrupted this precarious balance and shifted the momentum toward unrest[...] As Alixha Rahena famously stated, the world cannot remain peaceful for long, as someone inevitably becomes restless...

Gabriel

Have I bitten off more than I can chew?

A shiver of doubt crept up on Gabriel, a chilly reminder of the gamble he'd taken. The weight of his choices, driven by a hunger for more, left a bitter taste in his mouth—not unlike the aftertaste of too-sweet icing on an overindulgent slice of cake. The feeling had relentlessly hounded him for the past few days. The air in the penthouse felt unusually heavy, as if charged with the static of his unease. Even the usually comforting hum of the city below seemed to echo his restlessness, a constant reminder of the world teetering on the brink of change.

He could have played it safe and made do with the deal his predecessor had brokered. He could have satisfied himself with what he had, even flourished for another decade before the winds of change swept through Niederrad and reshaped it into something unrecognizable. He would have made it inside, worked out a new business plan independent of the tunnel, but he had to get greedy. He had to have the cake and eat it too. *I like cake!*

He stood before the panorama in his penthouse, gazing out over Niederrad while overlaying newscasts about the recent

Innie kidnapping on his lens. A moment of solitude enveloped Gabriel as he stood alone, the expanse of Niederrad stretching before him—a silent witness to his dominion and his doubts. The glass of the panorama window was cool to the touch, a stark contrast to the warmth of his penthouse. The city lights flickered like distant stars, a false firmament that underscored the artificiality of his domain—not unlike the domes themselves.

His heart ached with a mixture of pride and an unnameable sorrow for the city that bore his mark—a kingdom of concrete and steel, dilapidated and torn by an angry climate—that mirrored his own ambition. *It may not be much, but it's mine.*

Finding nothing new in the cast, he minimized it to get a clearer view of the world outside. Niederrad wasn't pretty; it never had been. But it was his, and he was the undisputed king here. He wanted to remain on the throne and keep his power intact. He surveyed his apartment with a sense of satisfaction. It was big, luxurious, and well-fortified against the elements. Real storm shutters, weather-fortifying plating, and AC to fight the sweltering heat waves. The marble bathroom was a work of art, and the smart electronics and AI made life convenient and comfortable. Network extenders provided connectivity on par with the inside, and the fridge was stocked with delicacies that were hard to come by on the Outside. The liquor cabinet was full of the fancy stuff, the little things that made life worth living.He uncorked a bottle of aged whiskey, its rich aroma briefly displacing the sterile air of conditioned luxury. The clink of ice in his glass sounded like a chime, a momentary distraction from the swirling thoughts that plagued him.

This apartment, the whiskey, everything, was his, purchased legitimately—a luxury few could afford, even among Innies. *Who can say that these days?* He let out a sigh, a sound that filled the spacious room with the weight of his achievements and the solitude they brought. The luxury surrounding him was as much a fortress as a prison, a testament to his success and a reminder of the obligations that left him trapped in a gilded cage, slave to his possessions like most others.

Once upon a time, home ownership had been commonplace among the middle and working classes, but that was half a century ago, before the domes. Now, space was at a premium on the Inside, and Outside dwellings were often dilapidated beyond redemption. Owning your home had become a luxury exclusive to the super-rich. Strangely enough, home ownership on the Outside was actually higher than on the Inside, one of the few metrics where Outies outdid Innies. The only problem was that most properties on the Outside were not worth owning. Once the domes arrived, the government would expropriate them, and the former owners would be shipped off to their new, shiny, and tiny government-allotted Innie living quarters.

Innie envy was a common affliction, but as he knew all too well, it was only worth it if you had been one from the start or if your former home had miraculously survived degradation at the hands of the elements. In the early days of dome expansion, things had been different. Back then, being included meant just that—you were welcomed into the new world that was being built without having to sacrifice everything you had known and loved. But that was a long time ago, before climate change and neglect had ravaged the outside.

Despite the odds, Gabriel had done well for himself. He paused, his gaze drifting from the tangible symbols of his success to the horizon beyond, a horizon that blurred the demarcation between sky and city, the latter lost in hazy humidity and heat. A swell of pride in his accomplishments battled with a gnawing worry for the future. The world outside, with its relentless challenge to his domain, seemed at once a battlefield and a reminder of the fragility of his existence. The apartment was a testament to that fact. It was a rare luxury that few could afford, no matter where you lived. The tunnel was the lifeblood of his operation, a conduit for contraband to enter and luxury to flow out. It was a simple equation, really, aside from the rather complex operation of making the business seem legitimate. It required the usual complex network of fronts, cooked books, and other deceptive miscellany to keep the authorities at bay. But it was worth it. His operation was a gold mine, not just for himself but for many others as well.

Make no mistake, despite his dominion over Niederrad, Gabriel was acutely aware of the limitations of his reign.

Niederrad, for all its loyalty and lawlessness, was a small enclave in a vast world, a microcosm where he could play king. He led the Niederrad Council, a title that lent a veneer of legitimacy to what was essentially a mob commission. Within the confines of this favela-like community, his word was law, his influence unchallenged. Yet outside the invisible borders of Niederrad, his name held little weight. The German government's presence loomed large, a constant reminder that his kingdom was more akin to a small fish in a sprawling ocean than the sovereign state he sometimes fancied it to be. In the grand scheme of things, Gabriel knew he was a minor player, significant only within the narrow confines of his immediate surroundings.

Within the borders of this modest kingdom, Gabriel liked to think of himself as a sort of Robin Hood, using his network of businesses to enrich the lives of those around him—his fellow Outies. Without him, countless people on the Outside would be considerably worse off. Of course, he had benefited more than most. *But what's so wrong with that?* Gabriel wasn't a hardened criminal, at least not in his own mind. He didn't run a mafia or anything like that. Violence was not his preferred method of doing business, although he wasn't above resorting to it if absolutely necessary. For him, it was all about the bottom line. *Contraband goes in, luxury comes out. Cash flows.*

It was a simple computation. Supply and demand, Economics 101. The Innies got to enjoy the things that were prohibited inside the domes, while the Outies got a taste of the quality of life they deserved. There was nothing inherently wrong with that, as far as Gabriel was concerned. It was a win-win situation for everyone involved. *Sure, Legacy gets screwed out of tariffs and taxes, but who cares?*

He was acutely aware that citizens' rights were the only things standing in the way of the unholy union of Legacy and Aegis paving over Niederrad. It was the only card he had to play, but it was a good one. Gabriel leveraged a seldom-invoked clause in the dome expansion regulations, stipulating that a community targeted for inclusion under a dome may bypass the official Legacy Government negotiator and conduct its own negotiations. Seizing this opportunity, he positioned himself at the forefront of the talks, effectively taking control. Yes, the expansion project would eventually be completed, and with it, the end of the tunnel and the disparity it created. Sure, the tunnel would remain, but it would no longer lead to the Outside. It would simply join Niederrad and Central, a pointless node when there would be a legitimate, non-supervised entry point. No more disparity to take advantage of.

No, the key to his success lay in incorporating The Crescent, and that required him to do exactly what he had done. The shanties of The Crescent would become the new Niederrad once the dome was erected. The tunnel was already there, a part of the old system, only it ended three hundred meters short of the new frontier. All they needed was an autoexcavator to quickly tunnel through, and they would have a direct link to The Crescent, just like they had to Niederrad before. It could be done in a day.

It had all gone according to plan up until now. The sleight of hand with the protests, the hack, the removal of the excavator from Aegis's compound, the covering of their tracks. It had been a difficult and impossibly complex operation, but they had pulled it off. Stealing a massive autoexcavator and getting away with it was a feat to admire. And now, it stood ready to start tunneling, to connect The Crescent to the new dome in the same way that Niederrad was connected to Central.

The Crescent was a market that remained largely untapped, at least until now. Despite being a shanty, it was relatively well-off. Many of its inhabitants had jobs, some of them even here in Niederrad. A fair few worked for Gabriel himself, either directly or indirectly, through one of his businesses. Some even held permits and Innie jobs. There was wealth in The Crescent—not much, but enough to create a critical mass that could generate more. Their operation could continue for another ten or fifteen years before the next scheduled expansion of the dome. By that time, Gabriel would be able to retire comfortably, having made enough money to last him a lifetime.

All they needed was to stall negotiations for another two weeks while the excavator did its job. After that, they could have a sudden change of heart and sign the deal with the Lima woman, which wasn't a bad one by any stretch of the imagination. They could step back and let the construction begin anew without having their dirty little secret revealed.

Oh, Daemon, my sweet boy. Why did you do it? The silence in the room grew oppressive, punctuated only by the distant, muffled sounds of the city. It was in these quiet moments that Gabriel's facade crumbled, laying bare the turmoil beneath. Tears threatened to breach his stoic exterior, a level of vulnerability he could only allow in private—and mostly not even then. The thought of Daemon, so full of life and now ensnared in a web of his own asinine actions, brought a pang of guilt that clenched his heart. It was a pain sharper than any physical wound, the sting of a mentor's regret for not steering a cherished protégé away from the precipice. He knew that Daemon's actions were born out of a warped sense of loyalty. The boy had only wanted to help. *I should have done more for him.* Perhaps if he had made Daemon feel less disenfranchised, as the media liked to call it when describing the plight of the Outies, he might not have turned to radicalization. Gabriel should have made sure that Daemon was more involved in the organization, in the decision-making process, and in sharing in the spoils of their operation. If he had given him a slightly bigger piece of the pie, he might have been able to keep him in line. But then again, maybe not.

Gabriel's thoughts often lingered on Daemon, the young lieutenant who had become more than just a part of his operation. In many ways, the boy was like the adoptive son he'd never had, brought together not by blood but by circumstance and shared ambition. Gabriel had seen potential in Daemon, a bright spark of loyalty and drive, and had taken him under his wing, guiding him through the complex underbelly of their world. But with that mentorship came a depth of feeling Gabriel hadn't anticipated—a fatherly affection that made Daemon's impulsive decision to help through radical means all the more disappointing.

He couldn't help but replay their last conversation, the tension palpable, as he tried to impart some wisdom, some semblance of restraint. Daemon's fervor, his unwavering belief that he was contributing to something greater, and his lack of patience pained Gabriel. It was a mirror to his own younger self, but with one crucial difference—Daemon hadn't tempered his zeal with caution. Not yet. He was too young, too hot-headed, for that kind of self-restraint. The disappointment he felt was unquestionably that of a father's—the sting of seeing a child you've nurtured make choices that could lead to their downfall. The same sting he had felt with his own children long ago, before they cut ties and headed for the domes. The love remained, unconditional and complex, a tether that Gabriel could never sever, even now as he faced the consequences of Daemon's actions.

Angry youth is something that few can control, and Gabriel understood it all too well. He had been young once too, and he had been mad as hell, just like Daemon. He had, like the boy, been prepared to do whatever it took to achieve his goals. It was merely coincidence that he hadn't acted out in a similar manner, that he had stayed the course and played it smart for the better part of his life. *Why* was a question he could not answer. Perhaps it was simply a lack of opportunity to be stupid. He had made it through those critical years, until he had matured and started thinking with his brain instead of his heart. Gabriel wished he had been able to guide Daemon down the same path. But it was too late now. The damage had been done, and they were all about to pay the price for it.

Daemon's actions had brought the world's attention to little, insignificant Niederrad, an Outie community on the border of a dome, one of a thousand just like it all over the planet. It had also turned the world's eyes on Gabriel. He had spent countless hours with the authorities disavowing any connection to the boys. He swore that they had acted on their own, despite their claims that they had acted in his name. Of course, nobody believed him. But thanks to his expensive lawyers, he had managed to avoid arrest, at least for now. Evidence still mattered, even in a post-London world. At least, it did if you had the resources to demand it.

So what was his next move? Gabriel's thoughts jumbled as he considered his dwindling options. A sense of foreboding tightened around his chest, a physical manifestation of the fear that his empire might crumble. The uncertainty of the outcome was a specter that haunted the edges of his mind, a ghost whispering of failure and loss.

He swirled the Scotch in his glass, watching the liquid catch the light from the spots above. The amber hue, rich and deep, was a brief respite for his eyes, tired from the harshness of the screens he had been staring at all morning.

Caught between a rock and a hard place, he thought. If he pulled the plug, he would likely be pulling it on his entire way of life. But if he went ahead, he risked getting caught with his hands in the cookie jar and undoing it all the same. As he stood there, in front of his panorama, holding a glass of fancy Innie Scotch, Gabriel felt the rare sensation of indecision. He had always been supremely confident in everything he had ever done. Hesitation was not part of his constitution.

A third option was to delay. Wait until the drama blew over. Surely it wouldn't last much longer. But Daemon had proven tenacious. He could drag it out further, until it all snapped. Gabriel wished he had one of those fancy tactical AI applications to help him make a decision. He promised himself that he would get one as soon as he got to the other side of this mess. *This is what I get for liking cake.*

He smiled at the metaphor. He could eat it now, throw it out, or save it for later and hope it didn't grow stale in the meantime, but one thing he knew: he needed to make a decision soon.

Aea

Mein Gott! I am so bored. A twinge of guilt pricked her conscience. *How can I feel bored in this situation?* Danger lurked just beyond the door to their room, where Daemon and Cali negotiated with the authorities, where Brett lay severely injured, and Dana held it all together. While things had settled over the last few days, they were hardly back to something even close to ordinary. She could only conclude that the human mind is a curious thing, capable of seeking distraction even in the direst of circumstances.

She sat listlessly on Tabayah's bed, her eyes fixed on the girl's dolls. At first, Aea had joined in on the playful fantasy, but as time wore on, her enthusiasm waned. She knew that she couldn't stop playing, because then Tabayah would notice and ask why. That would break the trance-like state the dolls had cast over her, reminding her that this was not a normal day. That dad was absent, and in his place were two dangerous boys—a wounded police officer and an Innie lady. *But I can probably take a little break.*

Her hand trembled slightly as she set the doll aside, its synthetic hair brushing gently against her fingers. It was both a tactile reminder of simpler times and a manifestation of the ever-present undercurrent of fear running through her. She rose from the bed, the fabric whispering a soft protest, as if reluctant to release her from the momentary escape it provided. A terror lingered in the back of her mind, shadowing even the most mundane actions. The normalcy in this room was but a facade. With a gargantuan mental effort, she shifted her train of thought before it spiraled out of control. Staring intensely at the toys around her, she almost forcibly recalled the captivating allure that playthings once held over her, a source of endless fascination when she was Tabayah's age. But she wasn't anymore. Now her attention was fixed solely on things like permits, domes, and getting the hell out of Niederrad. *Don't forget boys!* Specifically, one boy who presently occupied her dad's bedroom, conferring with the police, which had arguably led directly to their current situation.

The thought of Daemon unmercifully brought her back to reality, the distant, muffled sounds of discussion seeping through the walls. That noise represented a constant undercurrent to her spiraling thoughts, pulling her attention away from the child's play and back to the present, albeit now with a slight semblance of control. She listened intently, straining to hear any hint of a raised voice. The last thing she wanted was for Tabayah to be yanked from her comfortable world of make-believe and forced to confront the harsh reality that surrounded them. The constant shouting and chaos of the last two days had been hard on them all, and the quiet was a welcome reprieve. But Aea knew it was a fragile peace, easily shattered by the slightest disturbance. If Tabayah started crying again, she would have to be there to comfort her once more. *And who's going to comfort me?*

It was exhausting work, but she supposed this is what moms endured on a daily basis. *So, based on this experience, do I even want to be a mom?* She had never thought about it before, and why would she? After all, she was just a teenage girl, dreaming mostly of the usual things teenage girls do—travel, exploration, and adventure. She longed to venture Inside and experience the wonders it held. She imagined herself dancing in front of the mirror and sharing videos with her friends online. And, of course, boys were always on her mind. Boys and sex. *But I suppose if I think about that, I should also be thinking about becoming a mother. Someday.*

She and Daemon had shared a few intimate moments up to now, but she had been a good girl and forced him to use the contraceptive spray, just like she had been told countless times by various representatives of the adult world. The subject of motherhood had always been present, poking at her from multiple directions, yet she had proved adept at blocking it out, managing to remain emotionally indifferent to the topic. To her, pregnancy, motherhood, and family life were just information—neutral and unemotional information devoid of personal significance. She approached them with the same neutrality she had toward other topics taught in school—paying enough attention to pass exams, but swiftly disregarding them thereafter. She wasn't sure why, but perhaps the loss of her own mother at a young age played a part. The room felt colder at the thought, a chill seeping into her very core. Thoughts of her lost mother were often absent in her life, but now they charged back with full force, a physical manifestation of the loneliness she always carried below the surface.

Aea's thoughts momentarily drifted back to Daemon, that bittersweet distraction. The warmth of those stolen moments clashed with the cold reality of their situation, leaving her heart aching for something resembling normalcy. She still felt what she felt, and the events of the last few days had not changed that. But something else had changed. Tending to Tabayah's needs had a peculiar effect on her, one she couldn't quite place. It was an unsettling sensation, tinged with a strange allure. She couldn't quite put her finger on what it was, but she knew it was a powerful sensation. Nevertheless, it was evident she had bitten off more than she could chew. Dana had helped and had a good hand with children, but she was frequently occupied with Brett, the policeman, leaving the care of Tabayah to her. It was the lesser of evils, after all, compared to dealing with the mess in the living room.

Aea was grateful that Daemon had allowed the medics to treat Brett; the prognosis was good, and he would make a full recovery. Eventually. Unfortunately, the other policeman—she couldn't recall his name—had not been so fortunate. At least his body had been removed, offering some sense of closure.

Aea had assisted Dana in cleaning up the blood. Her hands had shaken as she scrubbed, each stain a stark reminder of the violence that had breached their home. The act of cleaning, so mundane and something she had done countless times before (albeit not blood), had never felt so significant. Each motion had been a desperate attempt to erase the nightmare that had unfolded. The sight of it all had elicited a range of emotions within her—feelings of helplessness, fear, and nausea. Aea had only ever seen that much blood in movies, and the reality was nothing like the fiction. *The smell! Ewh!* The living room reeked—a vile mixture of copper and iron, with a sickly undertone of something rotten. Even after they had cleaned everything up, the odor lingered. Perhaps it was just stuck in her nose. She also couldn't help but notice that the color of real blood was different from what she had seen on screen. It was deeper, almost brown in certain spots. Movie blood looked like ketchup in comparison.

The last few days had their moments of calm, and during those, Aea had found herself in front of the television, the screen flickering with an AI newscast, punctuated with the somber image of her father. His face, usually so strong and composed, was etched with worry and despair. He pleaded directly to the camera, his voice cracking. "To those who have taken my children, I beg of you, let them go. They are innocent in all this." The quote aired over and over, and she could remember the exact words. Cali frequently switched the TV off, sick of hearing it, but Daemon swiftly turned it back on. They needed the information, he said, but Aea liked to think he was driven by sympathy, the kind of heart she had seen in him in the months prior—in the tunnel, on their walks.

Watching her father break down in such a public and vulnerable way had shaken Aea to her core. Tears had welled in her eyes, not just for her own situation, but for the sheer helplessness she saw in her father. It was a moment that underscored the gravity of their predicament, making her feel even more isolated and desperate for a resolution.

Aea's heart ached not just for Tabayah, her father, and herself, but for everyone involved. She wrapped her arms around herself, a meager attempt at comfort as she navigated the emotions overcoming her. The fallen policemen probably had families that would never see them again, and Ameer, who had been so young, would leave his parents devastated with grief. She recalled he had a brother who had moved away. Perhaps to Wiesbaden? She also sympathized with Daemon and Cali. The outcome of this nightmare would not be favorable, no matter how it unfolded. She had overheard Dana and Brett expressing similar sentiments, with Dana mentioning something about Stockholm Syndrome. Had she had access to her pad or visor, she would have looked it up. It wasn't a subject Frau Gehrling had ever touched upon.

"Here," Tabayah said, offering her the Ken doll as their playtime resumed. *I guess the break is over.* Aea forced a smile, her heart not in it. The simple act of playing suddenly felt like a Herculean effort, a struggle to preserve a shred of innocence in a world that had become all too real and terrifying. It wasn't that she disliked playing with her little sister; she adored her, of course. There was a time when they played together constantly, and she relished it. But that was before, obviously. Perhaps it was just the turmoil and chaos of the situation that made it difficult to focus. She found no peace of mind to play, being preoccupied with what essentially came down to their survival. But she played with her sister for another fifteen minutes before eventually deciding it was time to resume her vigil and make her rounds.

"Can you play on your own for a little while?" Aea asked her sister with a comforting smile, hoping she wouldn't start crying at the prospect of her leaving for a few minutes. Tabayah didn't seem to be bothered, but Aea nevertheless reassured her, "I'll be right next door."

Every so often, Aea would take a walk around the apartment, checking on each room—hers and Tabayah's, the kitchen, and the living room. Dad's bedroom was mostly off-limits, but she would peek in occasionally, just to ensure everything was okay. To keep her mind occupied, she busied herself with household chores—loading the dishwasher, doing the laundry, and cleaning up. She even made sandwiches for everyone with the food brought by the outside people every once in a while. Their own provisions had long run out, a stark reminder of how quickly things stopped working when Dad wasn't around. *Must be exhausting.* This thought gave Aea a newfound appreciation for the mundane stability her father had provided, a stability she now realized was the foundation of her and Tabayah's own security and happiness.

Aea decided to make sandwiches for everyone, as it had been a while since they had eaten. She made simple ham and cheese on Bauernbrot and distributed them to the group. Brett expressed his gratitude, thanking her with a warm smile. She asked how he was feeling. "I'm better," he replied. "The gel pack is really helping."

After giving a sandwich to Dana, Aea made her way to Dad's bedroom and knocked on the door. She noticed she was breathing heavily as she prepared to face the uncertainty on the other side. It was dead quiet inside, which was unusual. Typically, she could hear one of three things—either the boys muttering to each other as they plotted their escape, communicating with the police at a loud volume, or screaming at each other in frustration. Regardless, nothing new ever seemed to come out of it. The stalemate persisted.

Out of the three noises that could be heard from the room, the shouting was the most frightening. It was usually Cali talking about killing people and shooting their way out, with Daemon attempting to calm him down, to talk him out of it. The outbursts typically lasted only a minute or so before it became silent once more—eerily silent. Aea knew that Daemon was right: forcing their way out would end in disaster, and Brett and Dana appeared to agree. She had overheard them discussing it, with Dana mentioning something about an army waiting outside. *The army of evil,* I think is what she said. While she recognized that it was likely just a turn of phrase, the presence of the words "army" and "evil" did not bode well. Before her eyes, shadows morphed into armed police in the dim light of the room.

It's been a while since they had a shouting match. Maybe they're about to surrender? Hope flickered briefly, a fragile candle in the dark torrents of her thoughts. The thought of surrender was both a wish and a fear. What would it mean for them all? For Daemon, for herself, for Tabayah? *For some of us, nothing good,* she concluded, realizing how bizarre it was to hope for change and for continued status quo simultaneously.

When there was no answer from the other side of the door, she knocked again. After a moment, Cali flung the door open halfway, revealing Daemon crouched on the side of the bed with a gun in his hand. "What?" Cali shouted.

Aea held up the plate of sandwiches, but Cali snatched them from her and slammed the door in her face. Brett, who had been standing behind her, attempted to reassure her. "It'll be alright," he said. It was a phrase he repeated often, but Aea struggled to believe it. The words were meant to comfort, but they echoed in Aea's mind, hollow and insufficient. The reality of their situation, the depth of the danger they faced, made such reassurances feel like a fragile Crescent shed in the face of a Niederrad summer storm.

"It's a good sandwich," the policeman continued.

She thanked him for the compliment. "It's just ham and cheese."

"It's delicious," Brett said.

Aea excused herself, realizing that Tabayah had been alone for a while and would likely start to worry.

Later that evening, as Aea distributed another round of sandwiches, she overheard Dana and Brett speaking in the living room. Their voices were filled with a sense of urgency, and Aea felt compelled to pause and listen before entering the room. *It's not nice to eavesdrop*, an admonishing voice said inside her head. She wasn't sure whose voice it was—perhaps Frau Gerhling again? Guilt stabbed at her briefly, quickly overshadowed by anxiety. The very fabric of morality seemed to unravel in the face of their circumstances. Eavesdropping was not something she normally did, having been taught from a young age that it was wrong. *It's ridiculous to feel guilty for something like that under these circumstances*, she thought, but her upbringing was rigorous, hardwired into her personality. After juggling those thoughts for a fraction of a second, she settled on the idea that it might be forgiven for breaking this particular rule at this particular time. *Right?*

As she listened, Aea realized that she had no clear sense of what was right or wrong in this situation. She was responsible for Tabayah's safety now, with dad holed up in a hotel room, anxiously watching the news for any updates on his daughters' situation. Aea felt a sense of obligation to find out as much as possible and make the best decisions she could.

Dana and Brett spoke in hushed tones about the police amassing outside. A black hole seemed to take shape in the pit of her stomach as she leaned closer, the gravity of their situation sinking in with each whispered word. The air felt thicker, charged with a tension that made it hard to breathe. The hallway shadows crept closer, casting the space in gloom. The soft glow from the kitchen light did little to dispel the sense of approaching darkness, and she found it hard to think beyond the immediate fear gripping her. Brett and Dana spoke about how the police would imminently storm the building, how they would shoot first and ask questions later, how the London bombing had made authorities worldwide trigger-happy and paranoid. The only reason they hadn't acted already was because of Tabayah. This revelation sent a shiver down her spine—the realization that little Tabayah, sweet, innocent, and oblivious, was the thin thread holding back a storm of violence. She was responsible for her sister, obligated to protect her, like any good big sister would. A heavy, dense mass settled on Aea's shoulders, heavier than anything she'd felt before.

The topic of discussion soon shifted to her. The police suspected her of being one of the kidnappers because of her association with Daemon, an insinuation that they doubted any explanation would alleviate. "She'll sit two years in a detention center before anyone outside will even get to talk to her case," Brett remarked from the next room. He continued to detail the ramifications, how she could lose precious years of her life or potentially her life itself in the event of a police assault. They mulled over strategies to regain control of the apartment, debating whether to convince Daemon and Cali to surrender or to attempt a takeover by force.

As she stood there, unsure of what to do next, a wave of conflicting emotions washed over her. Frozen in place, a torrent of feelings battered against her resolve—betrayal, fear, love, and a crippling indecision tangled within her, each vying for dominance. The weight of the impending decision felt unbearable. Indecision soon shifted to a powerful urge to barge into the master bedroom and reveal the sinister plan hatched by the woman and the policeman to Daemon, the boy she loved. But she knew deep down that doing so could only make things worse. If she exposed the plan, Cali might kill them all. She genuinely believed Dana and Brett when they said they wanted everyone's best, that if the police came storming in, it would end in catastrophe. And it did seem like the situation was rapidly spiraling out of control, hurtling toward an inevitable and violent conclusion.

The stress of it all made her feel sick to her stomach, and she had to sit down to collect herself. Her breathing now came in shallow gasps, a futile attempt to quell the rising panic. Each heartbeat echoed loudly in her ears. Although Brett and Dana were still discussing the situation, she couldn't bear to listen anymore. She returned to the kitchen, her hands shaking, and placed the plate of sandwiches on the counter. She reached for a bottle of water from the fridge, struggling to keep her composure. The coolness of the bottle provided respite to her clammy hands. She held it against her forehead for a second before taking a big gulp, spilling some of the water down her chin. She wiped her mouth and buried her head in her hands, feeling overwhelmed and helpless.

She composed herself and stepped back out to distribute the sandwiches. Drawing in a deep, steadying breath, Aea summoned what calm she could muster as she crossed the hallway, now seeming longer than ever. Her heart pounded, an unwelcome companion to the quiet, drumming a rhythm of both dread and resolve. It was a facade, a mask she wore, hiding the turmoil beneath—but with a practiced ease that surprised even her, the dire situation having apparently awakened unknown talents deep within her.

She made no mention of the discussions she overheard to Daemon, or to Dana and Brett, instead just focusing on the task at hand. She passed out the sandwiches with quiet determination, avoiding eye contact and keeping her thoughts to herself. Once she had finished, she retreated back to their room to check on Tabayah. The little girl was engrossed in an old coloring book, using a rainbow of colors to bring the images to life. Aea watched her sister for a moment, feeling a sense of peace wash over her. This brief respite, watching Tabayah's carefree immersion in her coloring, was a poignant contrast to the chaos outside their door. For a fleeting moment, Aea allowed herself to be anchored by this simple act of innocence, a lifeline before the coming storm.

Tabayah looked up, beaming with pride. "Look!" she exclaimed, holding up her work. "I'm coloring outside the lines on purpose!" She giggled. Aea smiled back. *My little rebel.*

Aea sank down onto the bed, her mind spinning with uncertainty. The weight of their predicament pressed down on her like an overpowering hand holding her head underwater. She felt wrapped in a suffocating blanket of fear and responsibility, every second ticking by like a countdown. The need to act, to do something, anything, burned like fire in her chest, yet she was immobilized by the sheer magnitude of their situation. She had to figure out what to do. She just had to. But she had no idea where to even begin.

Lost in her panicked thoughts, she barely registered when Dana came into the room and sat down beside her.

"Aea, can we talk?" Dana asked with a calming softness in her voice, a careful modulation that seemed to wrap around Aea. The older woman's approach was hesitant in a way that Aea thought was out of place for someone who had shown only strength and resolve thus far. As Dana sat, she gently placed a supportive arm around her. The warmth of Dana's touch was a small comfort, a human connection in the midst of disorder. The gesture was simple, yet it carried unspoken promises between them. Aea found a sense of safety that she hadn't realized she was craving. Not only salvation from the chaos on the other side of the door, but something deeper—a maternal-like warmth she remembered from long ago.

It was a reminder that she wasn't alone in this fight, that amidst the fear and uncertainty, there were still allies by her side, ready to face the unknown together.

Dana proceeded to outline the plan she had previously overheard, detailing various strategies for either convincing Daemon to surrender or hiding if the police stormed the apartment.

"We can go through the tunnels," Aea offered.

"Tunnels?"

"Yes. The basement shelter connects to the tunnels underneath Niederrad. They go all over the place, all the way to the dome, even. But the door to the shelter is padlocked."

As Aea explained, she noticed her own voice steadying, becoming more confident. *The tunnels!* She hadn't completely forgotten about them. A plan took shape, a lifeline in their desperation. Dana's response—her gaze a mixture of surprise and admiration—mirrored the trust that had silently grown between them over the last few days. It was a moment of unity, their roles blurred. They were both protectors now, her for Tabayah, and Dana for them both.

Aea couldn't help but feel a sense of pride for finally contributing to that glimmer of hope, and Dana's smile was not just one of gratitude, but of recognition—Aea had become more than just a responsibility, a liability; she was now a partner in their survival.

Dana left the room, presumably to discuss the plan with Brett. When she came back, she was beaming.

"Aea," she said, "you wouldn't happen to have a pair of bolt cutters, would you?"

Aki

The body engineering was not kind to Aki, at least not mentally. While the procedure went without complications, his mind suffered. Gazing into the mirror, he now saw a stranger staring back at him, a replica of himself, but with every detail just a little askew. *Like Treston Reeves.* The sensation was indescribable—the best he could do was a doppelgänger—someone you catch sight of, who kind of looks like you, but is not. He found no other words to convey the sense of otherness, for how does one describe a state so beyond the pale of ordinary experience? There was no lexicon to capture such an anomalous condition. He almost wished they had rearranged things properly, turned him wholly into someone else. It would have been less creepy. He reached out and touched the reflection, the glass cold against his fingertips.

"Who are you," he said aloud, his words barely a breath.

Those who had undergone similar procedures—like himself, Scott, and Dai—were few and far between. Like the three of them, most of those people were fugitives. The matter was not discussed openly, and for good reason. There were no precedents, no treatments, and no wisdom to draw upon to help alleviate the pain. The upper echelons of society had their own version of this, of course, but it wasn't the same. Their goal wasn't to disappear, but to stand out even more, to command greater attention and celebrity status. They did it by choice, not necessity. But for Dai, Scott, and himself, the changes were far more profound, a total transformation that would eventually leave them unrecognizable even to themselves. And they would be on the run, forever forced to live in the shadows, and forever remaining vigilant.

The agony wasn't in the physical discomfort—the swelling. The surgeon had scraped the bones to trigger the body's own regenerative capabilities, but that was just the prelude. In the days following the procedure, he had been reduced to a grotesque figure, deformed and discolored beyond recognition. But that was the least of his concerns. What came next was the real challenge—coming face to face with the person he had become, the physical embodiment of his new template, emerging from the depths of his former self.

In the quiet of his room, he caught himself laughing, a sound that was more a sob—at the absurdity of it all, at the grotesque comedy his life had become. *What I made it into.*

As hard as it was, the visual transformation, too, was but the tip of the iceberg—a mere symptom of the larger problem: his mind. Even his braid, the repository of his memories and identity, had been tampered with, most of it expunged and tucked away in a remote corner of his consciousness in the event that he was ever subjected to a mental probe. Akio Oichi, as he had once known himself, was all but gone, replaced by this hollow shell of a person. Yes, his brain was intact, and he retained whatever memories he could recall naturally, but after decades of integration between the natural and the artificial, his mind could no longer distinguish between the two. He felt incomplete, like a vital part of him had been excised. When he looked at himself in the mirror and couldn't access his stored braid engrams, he felt like a lifeless carcass, drained of all vitality and essence. The man staring back at him might still be his physical doppelgänger, but the person he had been was lost to the recesses of his own mind.

And this was a burden unique to him. Scott and Dai had not been forced to suffer the same invasive cleanse. It was he who had scrambled the codes to the nukes; it was he who had buried the evidence in the remotest corners of the Net. If anyone could recall where the information was hidden, it was him. And the cost of that purge had been steep—the obliteration of his most personal memories. He wondered whether the memory loss was a planned consequence or merely an unfortunate side effect of the procedure. *Had he been warned beforehand? He could not remember. Is that because I wasn't told, or because the memories of that conversation are gone too?*

Tress had warned them prior to the procedure that some struggled to adapt. *I guess I'm one of those.* A moment of bitterness overwhelmed him, the taste of it sharp on his tongue. He'd often close his eyes and trace the lines of his new face, the new contours sometimes sharp, sometimes smooth under his fingertips, but always a tactile contradiction to the memories imprinted in his nervous system. The sensation of touch was just as alien as the image in the mirror.

He resented not just the procedure but the circumstances that led him here, into this tangle of loss and transformation. As he wallowed, he noted the time. Scott and Dai would soon be there, something he did not anticipate with joy. He craved solitude and sought to avoid all contact with anyone in Rothbard, be it Tress, the locals, or even Dai and Scott. He felt anger toward them, envious that they were coping so much better than he was. He resented the fact that Scott had dragged him into this harebrained scheme in the first place. But most of all, he seethed with frustration over his lack of access to his past. He had limited recollection of his triumphs or, more importantly, his failures. And there was one failure, in particular, that he needed to hold on to: his most significant and egregious mistake—abandoning his daughter.

Little Saya. He had abandoned both his wife and daughter on the day he joined Lux Aeterna, consumed by ideology, fervor, and a burning desire to bring down the machine. He had placed his own convictions above his family, a decision he had come to regret bitterly. But by the time he realized his mistake, it was too late. Going back would have put them in danger, and even if he had, they would never have forgiven him for leaving in the first place. *And nor should they.*

For years, he had managed to suppress the pain of his loss, but as he sat there, looking at the stranger in the mirror, the enormity of his decision hit him with a force he could not reconcile. He would never lay eyes on his daughter again, and she would never see him. Even if he sought her out now, the man she met would not be him, but the individual glaring at him in the mirror. *Not that she'd recognize the real me anyway. It's been so long. She was just a child when I left.* And now, as he sat there, staring at the man in the looking glass, the realization that most of his memories of her were gone hit him like a sledgehammer.

Thus, he spent his days in solitude, venturing out into the tunnels of Rothbard to escape his thoughts. Unlike some people who preferred to talk about their problems, Aki was the brooding type, inclined to handle his troubles by retreating into himself. The early hours in Rothbard offered a semblance of peace, the dim artificial tunnel lights casting long, lonely shadows that matched his mood. He made sure to be up early, so he could avoid Scott and Dai's visits. If they dropped by while he was still in his quarters, he hid, turning off all the lights, locking the door, and making it seem like he was not there. Once alone, he would wander the tunnels, observing and experiencing new things, trying to process his emotions. It calmed him and gave him a sense of purpose, at least for the time he was out. But the desolation and melancholy always resurfaced when he returned to his quarters in the evening.

Evenings? Is there such a thing here? The unvarying sameness of his subterranean existence wore on him, undoubtedly exacerbating his already oppressive mood. The perpetual gloom of Rothbard's environmental control system provided little respite from the disorienting tedium of his days. Despite the enormity of the main tunnels, he felt claustrophobic, but the walks did help with the physical discomfort. With that thought, he instinctively caressed the medport now permanently attached to his shoulder. The device was connected to his braid, delivering precisely measured doses of morphine to soothe the pain from the physical alterations. He had toyed with the idea of overriding it, to up the dosage to levels granting relief not only from the bodily distress but also from the psychological torment. *I could probably hack it if I wanted to.*

Despite the loss of many memories, those crucial skills were still intact, a fact that he was grateful for, but he would have traded them all in a heartbeat for just one fully intact memory of Saya. And while he had seriously thought about hacking into the medport, he had so far refrained from it. The physical discomfort was tolerable, at least compared to the emotional pain, and besides, even if he did manage to create a morphine-induced rush, it would only offer a fleeting escape.

He had pondered leaving Rothbard. *Maybe that would help?* The idea of departure brought with it a rush of adrenaline, a fleeting sense of liberation that flickered through his thoughts like a ghost of his former self. *If your surroundings depress you, change it.* Wasn't that good advice? He wasn't a prisoner here, after all, and could take his chances on the surface. The procedure had certainly improved the odds, but where would he go? That question, too, he had pondered at length, and there was only one place he longed to be—with his daughter. But that was not an option. If he left, Alixha would inevitably track him down, perhaps putting his daughter in harm's way. He could not risk it. So he remained in Rothbard, wandering the corridors to distract himself from his troubles.

As time passed, the tunnels began to lose their appeal, and he found himself spending more time alone in his quarters. The walks no longer provided the solace he needed, and he began to experience violent outbursts. In the grip of these tantrums, he would lash out at his surroundings, throwing and breaking things, kicking and punching the walls until they crumbled and his fists bled. After each outburst, he would collapse onto his bed, utterly spent and hollow, lying in the wreckage of his own making for hours. It was a perfect mirror image of what his life had become—desiccated, incapable even of shedding a tear. *Like the husk of a dead animal.*

He kept deteriorating, and eventually, he stopped maintaining his living space. He ceased making his bed, stopped cleaning up, doing laundry, or even showering. He continued to avoid Scott and Dai, hiding whenever they came to check on him. He closed the blinds on his only window to conceal the chaos inside, ensuring he would be left alone. They knew him well, recognized his introverted nature, and respected his need for privacy. When they came by, they would knock on his door for a few minutes before leaving him to his solitude.

With a resolve born of desperation, he turned inward, seeking the keys to the forbidden berths of his mind, hoping against hope to find a sliver of the past untouched by the present. Aki decided to break the rules and attempt to retrieve some of his locked-away memory engrams of Saya. However, the Rothbard techies had done too good a job, and his efforts were in vain. He could only conclude that those memories were lost forever.

He turned instead to his braid's logical functions, instructing the AI to recreate a digital image of her using only his natural memories. The image that slowly coalesced on his lens was undeniably her, but like his own face in the mirror, it was somehow not quite right, with every detail just slightly askew, leaving him with the inescapable conclusion that she was now truly lost.

And so he took once more to wandering the endless halls of Rothbard, forever trapped in a loop, reliving the same day over and over.

Until one day when he reached his breaking point.

Scott

"You're still my handsome man," Dai remarked as she settled beside Scott on the bed of their cramped quarters, "even if it is a little creepy." Scott gazed at his reflection in the mirror. The swelling was settling down, and his new visage was taking shape—a bizarre sensation, seeing someone else emerge beneath the puffiness. *Creepy certainly is the right word for it.* Nevertheless, warmth spread through Scott at the comment, a reassurance that they might be okay after all. He looked the same but not quite, a delicate balancing act the surgeon had assured him was optimal for foolproof subterfuge against would-be cameras and scans, AI and human alike, that inevitably awaited them once they left.

The scent of their shared quarters, a mix of antiseptic rubbing alcohol and the underlying musk of their prolonged stay, hung in the air, mostly unnoticed but deeply familiar. Dai's altered appearance was equally disconcerting yet familiar.

"Your transformation, however, is an upgrade," he teased, grinning.

She swatted his arm in mock annoyance, and they shared a moment of levity, briefly forgetting their precarious situation. They had managed to find joy amidst the chaos, spending their days much like a retired couple—taking leisurely strolls, dining out, completing household chores, and grocery shopping at the

Rothbard market. The taste of the mostly reconstituted meals they shared, though bland, had become a comforting routine, each bite a small reminder they were still alive. But they couldn't rely on Rothbard's hospitality indefinitely and would need to seek employment sooner or later.

If we're going to stay, that is. Scott let the thought linger, a fragile bubble in an ocean of doubt. The simple pleasures of life here could be enough, however much draped in the shadow of their predicament. The prospect of staying put had increasingly crept into their collective mind over the last few days. *Why not?* They had accommodation, they had food, they had a friend in Tress, their lone ally, but Scott didn't see any reason why they couldn't expand their circle of trust with time. Staying underground provided a degree of protection, and their surgical modifications offered an added advantage when venturing above ground.

However, life had a way of complicating matters. The grim reality remained that a thorough genetic scan would unmask their identities, rendering their efforts moot. Simple scans and facial recognition software could be duped, but not the genuine article. Perhaps they could avoid the need for a perilous excursion to China if they exercised caution.

But on the other hand, living out your entire life in Rothbard? Or places like it? Or living in constant fear that someday a deep scan would out you? What kind of life is that?

Yes, the prospect of a life in hiding was unappealing, a sentiment Dai and Aki certainly shared. "We might look different, but we'll live," she reassured him. He caught her eye in the mirror, finding an echo of his own fears reflected back at him. Nevertheless, in that glance, a silent promise was exchanged—a vow to face whatever came their way, together.

"I know. But damn, I really miss my old jawline," he quipped, drawing a subtle smile from Dai.

"How's the pain?" she asked. He noticed the subtle shifts in her posture, the way she moved with a careful grace to avoid discomfort. It was a routine they both had learned, new movement patterns dictated by their healing bodies. Like the others, Scott and Dai had a patch attached to their medports, delivering measured doses of morphine every four hours. For

Scott, the initial bout of nausea had subsided as his body adjusted to the drug, but he was still drowsy and disoriented. Dai too, apparently. Fortunately, the morphine patch was a temporary measure, set to be phased out in favor of a less potent analgesic, such as tramadol, or, if they were fortunate, even a non-opioid. Over time, the pain would fade into the background, becoming a minor presence in their lives, like with other chronic pain sufferers. They would learn to manage it, and there was still a good chance it would eventually dissipate entirely.

"It's okay," he reassured her. The first two days after the procedure had been excruciating, even with the morphine patches, but the healing gel packs they had applied to their faces had made a significant difference. Now, the pain was more manageable, and they were both coping reasonably well.

"You?" he asked.

"Same," she replied, cuddling up next to him on the bed.

"I hope Aki's holding up," she mused. They hadn't seen him since their transformation. Scott couldn't fault him for avoiding them. Scott suspected Aki's psyche profile was less robust than his or Dai's. He was a tech specialist, after all, not a soldier. *Neither is Dai. But she is who she is.*

He suspected Aki harbored some misgivings about involving him in their scheme. Perhaps even resentment. Or was he projecting his own insecurities onto him? Nevertheless, he had to admit to himself that he grappled with guilt over dragging others into the fray, with the justification that he couldn't have succeeded alone. *Am I justifying or rationalizing?* He knew their actions might have saved countless lives, but it did little to soothe his conscience.

"I'll ask him tonight," Scott said. They had dinner plans later, marking their first night out since the surgeries. Excitement fluttered in Scott's chest, a rare sensation now. The prospect of something as normal as dinner out was a lifeline, a glimpse of the life they were fighting to reclaim. *Even if the dinner isn't exactly "out" when you're trapped in Rothbard.*

"He loves us," Dai reassured him. "He's a loyal friend, and he would do anything for us, as we would for him."

But would I? He couldn't say for certain. Did Aki join their insurrection against Alixha out of love? *Or did I draft him?*

Dark thoughts flickered in his mind like unwelcome specters, impossible to excise. The weight of leadership pressed down on him, having steered their course and exacted its toll on them. Aki was clearly unhappy with the idea of staying in Rothbard for an extended period, and Scott couldn't blame him; he and Dai were just as eager to move on, if he were being honest. The notion of settling down here was nothing more than a fleeting thought. *If I'm being completely honest.*

It was a temporary solution until the heat died down, nothing more. Of course, no one knew how long that would be. Alixha was tenacious, fueled by pure hatred toward those who betrayed her. Scott wasn't overly concerned about other parties searching for them, like Legacy or the contractors they employed. They lacked the necessary resources to locate them, as had been clearly evidenced by the past year following the London incident.

But Alixha—she would never give up.

A chill crept up Scott's spine as he thought of Alixha, her determination a vile predator, hunting them every step of the way. The safety of Rothbard was an illusion, a temporary haven from an inescapable confrontation.

It wasn't only Aki who was struggling. Scott grappled with Rothbard himself, continually reminding himself of the impermanence of their underground sanctuary—a pit stop on the road toward freedom. *Maybe the human mind can't tell the difference between a long-lasting but temporary arrangement and a permanent one? You can rationalize it, but they both feel the same.*

"Well," Dai interjected, "a nice meal and, more importantly, alcohol will lift our spirits."

He concurred, "Thank goodness the doc approved drinking." He wasn't merely paying lip service. Despite the pain medication, the discomfort was intense. A few shots of whiskey would indeed take the edge off.

"We need to lighten the mood," Dai said. "Tell me, after all of this is behind us, where should we go? To live, I mean?"

It was a good question, one he hadn't considered. He was too consumed with surviving the present to ponder the future. What would life entail once they escaped Alixha's grasp? His mind reeled at the enormity of that question. *Look at it this way, our future is a blank page, brimming with the potential for new beginnings! We just need to slip through her fingers. And the government's. And the privateers'. And whoever else is after us.*

Would they share a home, the three of them? Where would that be? Would they need jobs, or could they rely on Universal Basic Income or government benefits? Or would they resort to crime to make ends meet? *It's not like we have much to offer the world with our backgrounds.*

What would they do in their free time? Dine out? Grocery shop? Tend to a small garden? Perhaps in one of the new orbital habitats currently under construction?

"I don't know," he finally confessed. "But I'd like to get the fuck out of Asia, that's for sure."

Dai nodded in agreement.

"What about the south of France?" Scott proposed, unsure if it was a genuine desire. It was a popular place, albeit expensive. "The Riviera has nice domes with much of the natural environment preserved."

As long as we're dreaming, we might as well dream big.

Dai countered, "Scandinavia. Like Yossarian, let's go to Sweden. I've always wanted to see Stockholm."

"Yossarian?"

"It's from an old book. *Catch-22*, by Joseph Heller."

Scott's braid AI retrieved information on the book, displaying its cover and a synopsis from an offline memory cache. "I'll add it to my reading list," he promised, and swiped it away with a subtle eye movement.

But Sweden is not bad. And not entirely unrealistic. It was socially progressive, welcoming to immigrants once more after the mid-century clampdowns, and prosperous. The Outside was still tolerable, and the domes were open. Compared to Rothbard, it was a paradise.

"Stockholm it is," Scott agreed, and Dai beamed. "Let's fetch Aki."

The chill of the underground air brushed against Scott's skin as they moved through dimly lit corridors, a constant reminder of their subterranean existence. In the depths of their habitat, Aki occupied a different tunnel. Theirs was a corridor of double-room accommodations, kept separate from others, while Aki's tunnel was single occupancy, affectionately dubbed the "bachelor's corridor." Theirs was known as "The Tunnel of Love," but this moniker was somewhat misleading, as it housed not only romantic couples but also platonic pairings. A heaviness lingered in the air as he contemplated the solitude that Aki had embraced, a stark contrast to their own shared existence. It was unfair.

And he and Dai? Were they a couple? As for his own relationship status with his roommate, it was ambiguous at best. They had a longstanding fondness for each other and had even shared a bed on multiple occasions, including the present one. But were they a true couple? Probably not. More a couple of circumstance. They had never broached the topic, and he wasn't going to, so he resigned himself to the uncertainty.

What's a real couple, anyway? Was it sexual exclusivity? Plans for the future? A cozy apartment on the third level in one of the sprawling city sub-domes? A baby on the way? Perhaps a co-signed mortgage, if they were lucky enough to secure a private ownership opportunity? But these things were not in the cards for them, and they had made peace with that fact. *Well, there is hope for sexual exclusivity, I suppose.*

In Rothbard, being classified as a couple had its perks, one of which was eligibility for double-room accommodations. These rooms were not only more spacious but also boasted a higher standard, at least according to Aki. But they didn't have much choice in the matter, as there was no option for a three-person apartment. It was probably for the best, given the circumstances. *With Dai's and my burgeoning coupledom, it would be pretty awkward with the three of us.*

Space was at a premium in the facility, and Aki had been fortunate to have secured a place of his own, a minor miracle according to Treston, who had pulled some strings to make it happen. So no complaining.

As they made their way to Tunnel B, they passed through the East Market. The area was always bustling with activity, twenty-four hours a day. The eateries that lined the market were constantly cooking up a storm, causing a perpetual fog that the air vent system struggled to clear. In the midst of the bustling market, a moment of reflection. The thought of Aki, isolated yet so integral to their group, sparked a guilt and a desire to bridge the gap that had grown between them.

"I think we should get something nice for Aki," Dai suggested, as if reading his mind. It was a thoughtful gesture, though their meager allowance meant they couldn't afford anything extravagant. Despite the limitations, the supply of goods down here was surprisingly abundant, even if it couldn't compare to topside. Inside or Out. Down here, there were obvious limitations on choice. Nevertheless, Scott was impressed by the range of products available. Food was plentiful. Even fresh goods like vegetables and synthetic beef were readily available, and electronics, sporting goods, and other essential quality-of-life items were obtainable, albeit in limited quantities. It was possible to live here permanently.

Thanks to Treston's interventions, they had been allocated a modest allowance. Lux Aeterna wasn't highly regarded in Rothbard, so Treston had convinced the steering committee to offer them something as a reward for the blow they had dealt the organization. *And for the millions of lives, we hopefully saved.*

"You go ahead with that," Scott said, nodding in agreement with Dai's suggestion. "I think I'll check out the newsstand and see if there's anything worth reading."

Given the lack of braids down here, newsstands were the go-to place for those wanting to stay informed about the world above. The large screens played casts recorded off the Net, though they could be a bit outdated by the time they made their way to Rothbard. But they were current enough to report on the insurgencies happening in several major domes in The Neo-West. Tokyo, Singapore, Hong Kong, London, and New York were all mentioned, among a few others.

The news reported that a woman working for Aegis had been kidnapped by Outies right in the heart of the Frankfurt central dome, despite the heavy surveillance and the presence of a police escort in the area. The incident had caused collateral damage, with a family and some police officers held hostage too. The story was all over every channel.

Scott guessed that most of the incidents reported weren't directly linked to Alixha's operations. They were more like a ripple effect of her destabilizing tactics. Ever since the London bombing, the number of incidents had steadily increased. Some newscasters even proclaimed that "stability" was over, unwittingly playing right into Alixha's hands and feeding the sense of impending doom and panic. *This is what she wanted. Instability. Discontent. Dissent. Chaos. To destabilize the system.*

As she had written in her *Manifesto of Light*, stability and security were the enemies of revolution. She wasn't there yet, but she was well on her way.

Dai came up behind him, palm caressing his neck, her fingers running through his hair. "I found a cheap whiskey," she said. "It's not the best they had, but we can't afford anything else."

It was a Chinese brand with no English on the label. Nevertheless, Scott felt warmth spread through him at the thought of sharing a drink in the spirit of camaraderie, a rarity since their escape from overground Tokyo. "I'm sure he'll love it," Scott replied. *It will take the edge off just as well as the fancy stuff.*

They left the market and made their way to Aki's place, still having half an hour before they were due at the Lion, one of the only three restaurants in Rothbard with actual table service. They could get a taste of that whiskey before they left.

Aki's tunnel was strikingly different from theirs. The walls were lined with multilevel barracks, with the occasional shop at the bottom. These were old, discarded workers' accommodations, and everything about them seemed ancient and rotten. It was a stark reminder of the time before robots took over the jobs where workers would require dwellings of this kind.

People left without proper accommodations cohabited in tents along the passageway beside the building, with the occasional person inhabiting nothing but a sleeping bag. Scott and Dai didn't see any such signs of destitution and poverty in their corridor. Inequality existed everywhere. This place was no exception.

At least the three of them had access to outside money if they needed it. However, they would have to venture topside to move beyond the braid exclusion zone, inevitably leaving digital footprints all over the place. Even with Aki's crypto magic.

They ascended the stairs attached to the outer walls, heading for Aki's apartment at the top. Having no neighbors above him could be a blessing, especially if kids were involved. But when they knocked on the door, there was no answer. Dai went to the kitchen window to try to catch a glimpse of the inside.

"See anything?" Scott asked.

"Not sure. My eyes need to adjust to the light," Dai replied. She cupped her hands around her eyes, shutting out the ambient light. But then her expression turned to one of horror. Time slowed down as Scott watched, the air thickening.

"Oh God," she said, urging Scott to break down the door.

Scott began kicking near the lock. The wood was partially rotten, and the door itself thin, so it didn't take more than a few kicks to send it flying open.

Inside, they found Aki slumped over the tiny corner workbench, dark discolorations marring the skin of his right cheek, hair burnt, and eyes lifeless. Dai covered her mouth in horror, tears forming on her lower eyelids. Scott stood frozen, but soon roused himself and checked for a pulse. "He's gone," Scott whispered. "He overloaded his braid."

Aki had found his way out, leaving the two of them behind to face the darkness without his light.

In the bowels of Rothbard, a dimly lit basement incinerator room lay hidden behind the morgue. Scott, Dai, and Treston had gathered around the cold slab that bore Aki's body, now wrapped in a pristine white shroud. Scott noticed the mortician's hands—steady and respectful. Professional. Detached. The mortician, whose name had momentarily escaped Scott, wasted no time and initiated the gurney's agonizingly slow advance into the furnace's gaping maw. As the mechanism hummed, Scott held Dai close, seeking solace in their mutual grief.

Scott's gaze drifted to Treston, searching for some shared sense of loss in his stance, some mirror to his own disquiet. But Treston seemed carved from the very walls of Rothbard itself, stoic and impenetrable. *Why am I surprised? Or offended, for that matter. He didn't know Aki.* But he was offended, irrational as it seemed. Treston simply lingered at the room's edge, his back pressed against the far wall.

Scott had to admit he was unsettled by the lack of emotion in the room—his own in particular. He had expected to feel more—after all, a friend of over fifteen years now lay on the brink of immolation. Once the gurney locked into position within the incinerator, the mortician turned expectantly toward Treston, who, despite Aki being their friend, seemed to be perceived as the group's leader. They all stood in silence, and though it spanned no more than ten seconds, each tick of the clock echoed for an eternity in Scott's mind. In that silence, he found himself grappling with a tumult of memories, as if Aki's life, not his, flashed before his eyes. The quiet felt oppressive, laden with unspoken farewells and the weight of unshed tears.

Scott didn't doubt he was grieving, but from behind a veil of disturbing detachment. It was as if he had reached a limit, and further emotion simply registered, but was not felt.

"Anybody wanna say anything?" Treston asked, but was met only with more silence.

"Just get it over with," Dai finally said, her voice barely above a whisper, cracked with the strain of carefully contained emotion. Scott felt her lean into him slightly, and he reciprocated, a shared acceptance of the pain they felt.

Acknowledging the mortician with a nod, Treston watched as the man pressed another button. Behind the hatch, the incinerator roared to life, its flames devouring Aki's body. And just like that, he was gone. Treston expressed his gratitude to the mortician with a second nod before the group retreated back through the tunnels, emerging into the main habitat area.

As the flames took Aki, Scott's thoughts wandered. *Where does the smoke go? Was Rothbard a closed system?* He had never thought about it. *How was air circulated? How was CO2 scrubbed? How was heat exchanged?* An open system would be vulnerable to external influence. *My friend is dead, and this is what I'm thinking about.* He chalked it up to a defense mechanism, a momentary refuge from the reality playing out before him.

Grieving had never been Scott's strong suit. When his father passed years ago, everyone had warned him that the pain would eventually strike. But it never did, at least not in the way they said. Now the absence of sadness left him feeling hollow and angry. His life with Alixha had been a constant exposure to death, leaving little room for humanity. He had witnessed it, skirted it, and he had caused it. In time, the heart must numb itself, a defense mechanism against the unbearable weight of loss. To grieve repeatedly would be a death sentence—or worse, a descent into madness.

Dai had suggested once, when he had opened up about it, that perhaps people just grieve in different ways. *Perhaps. Or maybe I'm just a cold-hearted bastard.*

Under the glistening veil of the food court's neon lights, the trio gathered for a meal, honoring the memory of their fallen friend. The buzz of conversation and the clatter of utensils against plates filled the air, a cacophony of life both alien and precious in the shadow of their loss. In the artificial twilight, Scott found a surreal sense of camaraderie enveloping them. Each laugh and shared memory of Aki was a defiant spark against the loss, a collective refusal to let darkness consume them. As they partook, they reminisced about his life and braveries, about his deft navigation of the treacherous pitfalls of technology that he had made his domain. Laughter and joy filled the air as they sang rousing drinking songs and raised their glasses to Aki.

The bubble of their temporary joy, fragile and precious, seemed to Scott a rare treasure. He savored the moment, aware of how fleeting such reprieve could be in the future. Their revelry, however, was presciently interrupted by the chirp of Treston's comm. Raising a finger to his lips, Treston motioned for quiet as he answered the call. Treston's face went blank as he stared into his lens.

"We've got company," he said urgently, his voice suddenly serious. "Intruders on the premises."

A chill ran down Scott's spine, the sudden shift from warmth to dread a jarring plunge back into reality. He tightened his grip around Dai's hand, a silent promise to protect her in the face of whatever hell now awaited. The trio hastily settled their account and retreated to the administrative sector, taking care to conceal their movements as they navigated the main concourse.

Their fears were confirmed when they spotted the intruders. Scott's trained eye kicked into gear, grief momentarily forgotten. A group of heavily armed men was forcing their way through the checkpoint, scanning faces, clearly searching for someone.

"They found you," Treston said grimly. "I don't know how they did it, but they did."

With a subtle gesture, Treston directed them back down the tunnels.

"Alixha?" Dai inquired.

"I can't be certain," Treston replied. "But the sheer force and firepower they've brought suggests so, whoever they may be."

Scott managed a fleeting glance at the intruders as they advanced through the main concourse, edging closer to the administrative section. *Definitely bounty hunters,* that much was clear. *The question is, who hired them?*

At this juncture, their pursuers could be anyone. A plethora of individuals and organizations sought to apprehend them. Or kill them. If it wasn't Alixha, it could be law enforcement or freelancers roaming the world in search of their mark.

"Regardless, we must assume that your cover has been blown," declared Treston, urging them to hasten their pace. "We need to extract you promptly."

Surveillance of civilians was stringently regulated, and the technology required for such scans was scarce. While Legacy and their licensed subcontractors might be deterred by contraband instruments and bureaucratic statutes, such trifles meant little to Alixha. That revelation confirmed their suspicions: she had found them. As much as Scott detested admitting it, Treston's assessment was likely accurate.

"Aren't we heading the wrong way?" Dai inquired as Treston motioned them further into the tunnels. Scott too was curious; he had presumed they would try to circumvent their pursuers and come out behind them, but Treston kept leading them the other way.

"There are alternative escape routes that we can utilize, albeit they may not be the most comfortable. There's an emergency armory on the way where you can stack up. We want to avoid a direct confrontation, but should one materialize, it doesn't hurt to be able to respond."

Rothbard's ancillary entry points were few and far between, a fact not lost on Scott, who had experience being on the other side of similar raids. He assumed all known entry points would be covered, both above and below ground, meaning Treston was leading them toward an obscure, abandoned network of tunnels or a maintenance grid that was not charted on any maps. Perhaps a ventilation or drainage system.

They stopped in front of a heavily fortified steel door with a code lock. Treston tapped in the code and pulled the creaking door open, revealing the armory.

"Hello, my beauties," Treston greeted the weapons fondly. "We have tucked these little treasures away in various locations for situations like these." He gestured grandly, presenting the weapons like a waiter at a fine dining establishment. "Please, indulge yourselves," he said, grinning.

In the dimly lit armory, surrounded by the cold steel of death and destruction, Scott felt a surge of resolve. Treston's display of weapons wasn't just preparation; it was a declaration of their will to survive, to fight. *To our last breath, if so required.*

Treston handed Scott a shotgun. "They will deploy drones," Treston said. "Just point it in their general direction, and boom! Problem solved. It's going to be close quarters, but with this baby, you'll be alright."

Not sure about 'being alright', Scott mused. But he agreed; hitting a mil-spec drone with a bullet was virtually impossible, but a blast from a sawed-off even they couldn't dodge. However, one had to be in close proximity to make it count, and that would be well within the drone's own effective range.

Their armaments would be limited by what they could carry, but the armory was a renegade's paradise. Treston provided them with holsters and sidearms, grenades, EMP charges, extra ammo, and a knife. *Not sure how much use a knife will be, but what the hell. Can't hurt.*

"Alright, let's get moving," Treston said, pushing the heavy armory door shut.

Treston led them back into the main tunnel and further into the depths of Rothbard. After navigating through a maze of lefts and rights, they arrived at a dead end. A grate obstructed their path, leading to a smaller tunnel.

"Here, take this," Treston beckoned as they approached. He pulled out an old plaque and projected a map onto the screen, revealing a scan of a hand-drawn set of routes with one marked by a vibrant red hue.

"Don't worry," he said reassuringly. "It will be like a child's treasure hunt, and the reward at the end of the rainbow is your freedom. I'll stay behind and do my best to divert them. The tunnel system ends with a small climb up a vertical maintenance shaft. It's nothing major. The exit is near the old Haneda airport's international terminal, which should be mostly deserted these days, aside from a few strays and hoboes. Just outside the main entrance is an old Starbucks. Wait there until I arrive. Go!"

With a forceful tug, he removed the grate and ushered them into the tunnel. It was not precisely a crawl space, but neither was it a proper tunnel. They would need to stoop, but at least they wouldn't be required to crawl on all fours.

"What's that smell?" Dai inquired.

"Sewage," Treston replied matter-of-factly.

"Wonderful. More shit. Only this time the literal variety," Dai grumbled.

"Don't worry, the poop has been cleaned out, for the most part. The smell, not so much," Treston said as he guided them inside and replaced the grate. He retrieved a handheld welder and began sealing it in place behind them.

"This will stall them a bit further," he said. "What are you waiting for? I know the sparks are pretty, but for heaven's sake, go!"

As they set off along the highlighted path, holding their noses, Treston shouted after them over the din of welding sparks. "They'll come for you, but at least you have a head start. And guns."

Dai led the way with a flashlight illuminating the cramped tunnel as they crouched their way toward survival. The tight confines of the tunnel felt stifling, the path ahead pitch black outside Dai's narrow light cone. The old pad was backlit, sparing them the need to pause every few meters to shine the light on it and avoid getting lost in the literal maze of shit. Scott brought up the rear, ready to open up with the shotgun at the first sign of drones closing in. So far, so good.

"Next one, right," he directed, acutely aware that one wrong turn and they'd be trapped down here forever. *Well, not forever.*

Eventually, they would be captured and executed on the spot—best-case scenario. Worst-case, they'd be held captive for days, tortured in one of Alixha's dungeons until they divulged what she wanted, and then killed. A happy middle ground, he supposed, would be to become lost, wander for a few days, and die from dehydration. *Was there no water cache in the armory?* In all likelihood, there was not. Even if there were, this would be a brief conflict, regardless of the outcome. They'd be dead or free before needing it.

His braid notified him that it was rebooting.

"We're emerging from Rothbard's suppression zone," Dai informed him, noting the return of their braid's connectivity. *About time.* Cloud access would grant them unfettered utilization of their AI tacticals, as well as access to online databases and computational resources. He swiftly conducted a diagnostic scan, confirming that all systems were operational, albeit with intermittent net access due to their deep subterranean location. Nevertheless, it was a relief to be back in the age of modern technology. How people in the past managed without braids was beyond him.

A full combat suit and a squito complement would've been nice. If he had those, they could have deployed a swarm to map the entire tunnel network, perhaps discovering alternate routes and splitting up while still maintaining contact. This would provide them with a tactical advantage. However, one thing he could do even now was scan the map and allow the tactical to extrapolate a 3D visualization of their route, which could then be projected onto his lens. He did so and forwarded a copy to Dai.

"What do we do with the tablet?" she asked.

"Leave it on," Scott directed. "Toss it in one of the side corridors. If they pick it up, it might lead them down the wrong path for a few minutes. It might buy us some time."

She hurled the device into the next available corridor.

"Keep moving," Scott urged, pulling her along. Now, they both had the route they needed to take plastered over their line of sight, arrows floating before their eyes, consistently pointing them in the right direction. There was no need to halt every few seconds to look at the map. They were advancing much faster now.

Dai continued to lead while he fell back, constantly surveying the surroundings, scanning for any indications of drones tracking them through the tunnels. Thus far, no target reticles had materialized in the dimness behind them, although their tactical's range was restricted without squitos to probe further afield, relaying information back via the net. While his lens would still detect anomalies long before the naked eye, by the time a target reticle appeared, it might already be too late. Moreover, their braids could detect audio traces—voices, and whirring noises emanating from drone engines. These aural cues would likely alert them earlier than any visual cues, especially in the tunnels' confined spaces, with their limited lighting and obscured sightlines.

"A hundred and fifty meters to destination," Dai announced.

He confirmed her estimate on his display, although the tunnel's convoluted path would add an additional hundred meters due to all the twists and turns. *Which is good.* If the tunnel had been perfectly straight, they would have been utterly exposed without any cover to conceal themselves. *We would be dead, for certain.*

I wish Aki was here. If he were, he could have made the necessary adjustments, identified shortcuts, or found other ways to improve their chances of survival.

Just as he finished that thought, his braid detected and translated the first auditory cues, imperceptible to unaided human ears. It was the faint whirring sound of drone motors. Adrenaline surged, fear and anticipation mingling in a familiar manner. The grief, the warmth, the sense of camaraderie or desperation Scott had felt in the confines of Rothbard were drowned out in the whisper of the drone motors.

It was the sound of the hunt, and while they were the prey, he preferred it over despair. "They're coming," he alerted Dai.

They hastened their pace, seeking a hiding place. His lens painted target reticles over twelve targets descending the tunnel. Scott lobbed an EMP grenade as far down the tunnel as possible. The farther it detonated from their position, the less likely it was to disrupt their own electronics.

After the device activated, the number of targeting reticles dropped to four. The approaching squitos had been neutralized, but the larger drones remained—the ones equipped with firearms. The metallic taste of fear in Scott's mouth as he prepared to face the coming onslaught was all too familiar, a bitter yet electrifying reminder of the stakes. There could be no doubt that part of him preferred direct confrontation to fleeing and sneaking around.

He waited until they drew nearer before pivoting around the corner and unleashing a barrage from his shotgun, pumping out shells one after another until the chamber emptied. There was no time to reload. He slung the weapon across his back and produced his sidearm, ready to open fire. Yet, it proved unnecessary. The drones lay defeated, and the tally of targeting reticles was now zero.

"Go!" he shouted, urging Dai ahead of him while reloading the shotgun. Another salvo would soon be upon them, and they had only purchased a brief reprieve—a few minutes at most. That time they needed to scale the shaft.

They arrived at the ascent without further incident. The cool dampness of the tunnel walls, the musty smell of earth, and the faint odor of sewage that had been their constant companion throughout gave way to fresh air as open sky broached. The expansive shaft towered above them, daylight streaming in from the pinnacle. As Scott gazed upward, his tactical notified him that the shaft's depth measured seventy meters, with only a slippery and corroded ladder affixed to the wall, and no safety railing.

"No biggie, right?" Dai quipped, craning her neck to peer toward the sky. As Scott did the same, he felt a moment of vertigo, similar to when he had jumped from the London dome emergency vent. But the daylight at the top was freedom, the ascent before them a stairway to heaven.

"Let's go," Scott said. "We need to keep moving. We'll be defenseless if they capture us mid-climb."

Dai acknowledged him with a nod and began the ascent, with Scott trailing close behind. As they scaled the rungs, his tactical once more detected the whirring sounds of drone motors resonating within the tunnels.

Jarod

"There's something in there with you," Riley's voice crackled over the comm. Reflexively, Jarod pressed his finger into his ear, as if he had an old-style earbud like before he had himself braided. Although he knew her voice couldn't penetrate his skull into the air duct he was traversing and reveal his position, some habits were hard to break. A shiver squirmed its way down his spine, the sudden potential for danger sparking a rush of adrenaline. He was, of course, used to risks, but the immediacy of Riley's warning, her voice booming inside his head, took him by surprise.

"How do you know?" he whispered, mindful of the potential for his voice to carry out into the duct. He made a mental note to switch to texting from now on.

"I'm detecting radio transmissions. Squito control communication, by the looks of it. Encrypted. Advanced shit."

Jarod used his lens' tactical display to scan the area ahead of him. Nothing was in sight. Adriel had bestowed upon him a special gift for this mission—a full combat suit equipped with a large squito pouch. He had motion tracking, enhanced audio-visual, infrared, all available with extended range provided by the squitos, ready to pick up cues in the dark recesses of the shaft ahead. The suit's electronics relayed all this information to his braid through a direct link. Riley had access to the same through remote comms. *The question is, why is she seeing something I'm not?*

Jarod's pulse quickened, the sterile air of the ducts feeling suddenly thick with tension. The silence around him felt heavier, charged with the potential of unseen threats lurking just beyond his reach.

[Are you sure?] he texted, eyes flying deftly across the virtual keyboard, with the suit and braid AI collaborating, picking up his intentions as if they read his mind. Never had virtual typing been this easy.

"Ninety-six percent confidence level," Riley replied.

Perhaps it was her more advanced AI back at the safe house that could process information faster than his braid. Nevertheless, Jarod still checked his surroundings the old-fashioned way by physically turning his head and scanning the area with his naked eye. He minimized the tactical display and toggled the night vision and flashlight on and off, but still, he could see nothing.

[Relay information, please.]

Riley complied, and yes, the data suggested there was indeed an unknown presence lurking within the elaborate ductwork. The signal was weak, making it impossible to pinpoint, but nonetheless, it was there with a high degree of certainty. The tactical display indicated, though, that it was not immediately adjacent to his position. *Safe for now.*

[Keep me posted.]

"Aye, Sir," she replied, her usual sarcasm unmistakable, as if he had implied she wouldn't otherwise. "Stay frosty." He smiled to himself. She meant well, and he didn't mind.

The duct was a tight squeeze, even for someone as lithe as Jarod. Even something as simple as turning his head to spot a potential threat was nearly impossible. *I hate crawling through vents. It's such an uncomfortable and ineffective way to stalk a target.*

But Nyal Bahno—first name pronounced "Niel," despite the spelling—was no ordinary target. *Fucking modern parents. Always have to spell their kids' names in weird ways. I'll just call him Bahno, then.*

He had access to advanced counter-espionage gear, rendering the lazy approach of using a squito controlled from the safe house ineffective. What's more, he seemed to possess technology that even Kale—whom Jarod believed had seen it all—had never encountered.

Yes, Bahno had devised a formidable defense mechanism—an energy field, for lack of a better term—that spanned a twenty-meter radius around his location, blocking any kind of squito access. This incredible feat was something straight out of TwenCen science fiction, a concept described countless times but, to Jarod's (and Kale's) knowledge, never truly realized within the limitations of real-world technology. At least not one that lasted for more than a few seconds, or was so weak that it couldn't repel a fly.

But evidently, someone had managed to create one. The emitters that surrounded Nyal Bahno emitted a field, cleverly arranged in a way that created a barrier akin to a moat around a castle. Jarod couldn't help but marvel at the ingenuity of the design. The emitters were strategically placed throughout the building, engaging and disengaging as Bahno moved through the premises. This made the field mobile, allowing Bahno to carry it with him wherever he went—at least inside the building. He could operate his own squitos within the moat, which meant it wasn't a disruptive electronic warfare technology or an electromagnetic pulse, which would have rendered all electronics in the area useless. *All very clever.*

The protective barrier surrounding Bahno was only a few meters wide and nowhere near strong enough to repel anything remotely massive. A human would have little difficulty penetrating the field, most likely passing through it without even feeling a slight disturbance. Jarod marveled at the technological work of art Bahno had implemented, its sophistication a reminder of the lengths their targets would go to protect themselves. Both impressive and daunting, it was a challenge Jarod couldn't help but respect. It was clear that Bahno had designed this technology to prevent precisely what they had originally planned to do—fly a squito up close to execute the hit.

Access to the shield's operating system was blocked by some

of the most complex encryption that Kale had ever encountered. It would take weeks, if not months, to cut through it all, leaving any potential intruder or assassin with no other option but to physically cross the electronic barrier before being able to utilize any squitos against him.

I wonder how expensive this shit is? Jarod couldn't help but feel a pang of piqued interest amidst his operational focus. The cost and complexity of Bahno's setup sparked legitimate questions about the resources at their adversaries' disposal. *The man definitely has cash to splash. More so than any of the other targets we've encountered so far.*

And I'm just now realizing, isn't Bahno's last name the same as the singer from that old TwenCen rock band? The Irish ones who always went on about politics? Jarod struggled to remember the band's name. *Was it The Rolling Stones?* He didn't want to search for it using his braid, not in this vulnerable position. He made a mental note to look it up later when he was back at base—and to ask Adriel for more tech, the suit notwithstanding.

A larger drone would probably be massive enough to breach the barrier but couldn't navigate a narrow vent without bumbling around, potentially alerting Bahno to their approach. They couldn't just send one in through the main entrance either without triggering a flurry of alerts. Consequently, here he was, crawling through a vent.

The claustrophobic reality of this method grated against Jarod's preferences for direct confrontation, and theoretically threatened to trigger his PTSD. As much as he hated admitting it, that was the reality he faced. *So far, so good,* though. The suit's medical app had countermeasures to offer should an episode transpire. In the end, the physical discomfort of navigating the cramped space was nothing—not compared to the limitations it imposed on his effectiveness.

You're a lucky fuck, Wyatt. Human-on-human confrontations were his forte, and normally, he would be the one taking the lead on an op like this. But he was too bulky for vent crawling, and so were Dembwe and any of his team members, jacked as they all were. Jarod supposed they could have opted for a full frontal assault—Dembwe and his men certainly would've loved that—

but the building was located right at the heart of the City-State of Shanghai. Such a charge would not go unnoticed. *Not to mention, we'd all likely be killed if we did.*

Riley and Kale, on the other hand, could probably squeeze into a vent, he realized. He smiled inwardly at the notion—for they had never before taken another's life. *I mean, truly taken a life.* Not merely obliterating someone to smithereens with a drone strike or injecting toxic compounds from a distance via a stealthy squito attack, or even with a good old-fashioned sniper rifle. *No, what I'm talking about is standing up close and personal, using a handgun with a silencer, a blade, or even your bare hands to snuff out their life force, witnessing the spark literally fade from their eyes.*

Naturally, he was pleased for them. *After all, having killed someone like that isn't exactly a feather in one's cap.*

"One more junction, and you're inside the field," Riley said.

[Check. Got the junction. Right up ahead.]

One final push. He felt his chest tighten in anticipation and resolve, game time now imminently afoot. While he passed through the mote, there would be a brief moment of radio silence, and then he would be in business, provided Bahno stayed put in the conference room he currently occupied.

The vent narrowed considerably at the junction, requiring him to wriggle through, all the while ensuring he did so quietly. Right below him was a kitchen, and to the left of that, a security station. He was right in the middle of the proverbial hornet's nest, and at this point, any inadvertent noise could trigger alarms, flooding the vent with hostile squitos, ending the operation—and probably his life—prematurely.

The suit would provide some aid. The skin-tight materials would turn slippery at the activation of a command from his braid, allowing him to slip through more easily. *This suit is so cool!* He had worn similar exosuits during his active duty days, but that was a long time ago. The technology had come a long way since then. This suit had everything. Besides the full squito complement, it had stealth tech, shock absorption, augmented fibers acting like a bulletproof vest, and a palm and feet short-burst thruster setup for enhanced movement. However, the most impressive feature was the suit's interface. Back in his war days, he had to control the suit through menus and buttons, which made it difficult, especially in fast-paced situations. But this suit was different; it was as though the suit could read his mind. He had only to think of something, and the suit would execute the command. It was a remarkable experience, from the command to the braid, braid to interface, and interface to suit function.

He activated the slippery materials and started wiggling. *Adriel sure spoils us with all these cool gadgets.* Jarod couldn't help but wonder how the man managed to acquire them. It was no surprise that someone with Adriel's connections—working for Aegis and being close to the inner circle of Gibson himself—could get his hands on just about anything. *But how?* Kale was pretty resourceful with procuring tech, but something like this was beyond even him. Jarod was sure that a suit like this was illegal for civilian use, but he knew better than to look a gift horse in the mouth. *It's not like any of this is legal.* Without this tech—the suit, the squitos, and the comms—the mission would have failed before it even began.

He made one final push and wriggled his way through the narrow vent. The metal edges grazed his suit, emitting a soft screech reminiscent of silverware against porcelain. The confined space amplified every sound, turning his controlled breaths into a loud, echoing presence in the tight corridor. The squeeze hurt like hell, and he couldn't help but let out a quiet grunt.

"Quit your whining," Riley teased over the comms. "You know the chance of someone hearing that inside the vents may be slim, but it's still possible. Besides, I can hear you, and you're bumming me out."

Nag. The cold metal of the vent pressed against him through the suit, a constant reminder of how claustrophobia lurked around every corner. Every movement was a calculation, balancing silence against the need for speed.

[Ok. In position.]

Inside the mote, his squitos were once again free to roam. Jarod commanded the suit to release three of them—an audio-visual spy, a signal amplifier, and a pathfinder to clear any countermeasures Bahno's bots may have deployed. He kept the kill squito in his pouch for now, ready to deploy it when the time was right. *I love my little illegal Israeli squitos. They may be a pain in the ass, but nobody beats them in an all-out e-war battle.*

It didn't take long for the tiny little bots to feed back telemetry. *And voila!* There he was—Nyal Bahno, tech and surveillance expert, a known criminal and murderer—right where he was supposed to be.

"Jarod," Riley's voice cut through his thoughts before he could execute the kill. "I have some information."

The comms went silent, and Jarod cursed internally. *Perfect timing, Riley.* But the silence stretched on, and he knew that the news was likely not good.

[I'm waiting.]

"It's Dana," Riley said, her tone serious. "Apparently, she's been... kidnapped."

Kidnapped? What the hell was going on? This was no time for jokes. But he knew Riley—she would never crack a joke during an active op. Sarcasm, maybe. Tasteless pranks, definitely not.

"It's all over the news," she continued. "There's a whole situation outside Frankfurt. The police are there. There are protests, riots. It's a mess."

The world seemed to stop at the news, a cold dread washing over Jarod as the mission's immediacy and importance paled in his mind. The mental image of Dana, caught in danger, overshadowed the risks facing him and instantly recalibrated his priorities. Riley patched through the news footage, which he watched with utter disbelief. There she was, his Dana, her beautiful face plastered all over the scene of the hostage situation. Violent protests, pickets, tents, and barriers, all crowding an old, beaten-up high-rise in Niederrad outside Frankfurt Central's southern frontier.

"Jarod?" Riley said, her voice concerned. "Your heart rate is elevated."

Right. I forgot the suit has biometrics. But there was more. The newscast showed the faces of the three police officers who had accompanied her, two of whom were dead, and another in serious condition.

"How the hell did this happen?" he muttered aloud, not

thinking about the noise he was making.

"Do you want to abort?" Riley asked. "Just say the word, and I'll activate the contingency plan. Wyatt can rendezvous at the extraction point."

He closed his eyes. *I just need a moment to think. Just a moment.* Despite a lifetime of training, he was still human. When someone you love is in distress, all you want to do is drop everything and run to their rescue. He wanted nothing more than to do just that, but he knew that he couldn't, even if he aborted the mission. What good would it do? Should he run past the barricades, guns blazing? Attempt a risky extraction? This wasn't some action flick. Like everyone else, he would be glued to a newscast, waiting for the police to handle the situation.

[No.] At least he remembered to text his reply, keeping the noise to zero. **[We continue. I'll deal with it later.]**

It was the best decision, but he couldn't help but feel callous. *When a loved one is in trouble, aren't you supposed to sit and worry?* But this was likely their only opportunity to get to Bahno, and it had to be done now.

[I'm moving on.]

He started crawling, with the target in his sight but Dana on his mind.

"Head's up," Riley said, not thirty seconds later. "I'm reading something again, up ahead in the vent."

Goddamnit! "What?" Jarod said, again forgetting he was supposed to text. A spike of frustration, laced with adrenaline, shot through him as he cursed his lapse in discipline. *I'm so rusty. This is what I get for letting Wyatt and Dembwe do the dirty work all these years.*

"Shhh!" Riley hissed. "A probe... a squito, I think. It might be miked, so shut up!"

His tactical wasn't picking anything up, but he knew better than to doubt Riley's instincts. *If for nothing else than to avoid being nagged to death when she's inevitably proven right.* But also because she was the best at what she did. Out of everyone on his team, Riley was unmatched in her particular field. *Out of all eleven billion people on the planet, few—if any—could match her. God knows I can't.* With her raw data feeds and adept human eyes, she could occasionally see things even before the braid's AI. If she said she saw something, she did.

Squitos were small, and the best ones were challenging to detect even for an advanced tactical system. Thankfully, their relative tininess meant both limited sensor range and specialization. Most squitos were either search or destroy, not both. There just wasn't room to fit all that gear into a bug-sized machine and still have it remain bug-sized. *Good thing, or I'd be dead already.* Hopefully, he could remain undetected until it got closer.

Jarod's heart rate spiked, the suit sounding a warning and displaying a pop-up in the corner of his lens. He quickly minimized it, focusing on the path ahead, the darkness of the duct pulsing with potential danger. Each shadow was a hiding place for the unseen threat. Then he saw it—not the squito itself, but rather a shimmer from one of its guidance lasers about five meters ahead. As it passed by a grate, light and dust from the other side briefly illuminated the thin greenish beam. A fraction of a second later, his braid picked it up and put a target reticle on it.

[Check. Got it.] He didn't say anything out loud this time. *I'm getting the hang of it.*

The probe was approaching his position, and now data was flowing in.

"Okay," Riley said. "It appears to be alone and doesn't seem to have audio sensors. You can talk, but don't move too much. Signature indicates it might be of HKEC make. Heat-seeking, most likely, but it might also have motion sensors."

Hong Kong Electronics Corporation, his braid informed him. Annoyed, he swept the popup aside. *As if I don't know what that is.* He made a mental note to fine-tune the popup algorithm after the op was over. *Can't have it bug me with stuff I already know.*

The probe was of equal sophistication to his suit, and of equally questionable legality. His tactical system didn't recognize the make, but a quick analysis showed that it was designed to detect the presence of life signs. These types of probes were used for everything from pest control in civil society to military and corporate espionage, depending on the sophistication of the device. When someone in this line of work used one of these, they weren't interested in hearing what you said or seeing what you looked like. They just wanted to confirm your presence and then send in the guns, which would be mounted on a different bug. Riley would be able to do a wider search using the suit's telemetry and properly identify it.

Jarod whispered, deliberately not bothering with texting, "You got a read on it yet?" He needed to focus his eyes on the target reticle on his lens and couldn't waste time gesture typing.

"Yes. Confirmed. It's a heat seeker. No offensive weaponry. Just search and report. It's moving closer and will detect you in less than a minute. You have to hibernate."

Jarod was skeptical. "Hibernate? Isn't that a bit extreme?" He switched back to texting. **[What about a heat sink? Lead the body heat away from the sensors?]**

"I don't think that will be enough against this model," she said. "At least I don't want to take that chance."

The suit's hibernation function was designed as a survival strategy. It would drop your body temperature, slow your metabolism, and keep your breathing shallow while waiting for a rescue.

[Not a stealth mode. Will pass out.]

"Not if you reverse in time," Riley assured him. "But it will be close if you want the probe to miss you. Don't worry. I'll monitor your vitals."

Oh! Okay! No biggie, then. He refrained from typing that snide remark. Or saying it out loud. This squito was unlike any he had encountered before, so if Riley advised hibernation, then that must be the course of action to take. He had employed this method before, several times back in the war. He knew it could be effective, but it was risky. The key was to administer the counteragent at the right time, before the process progressed beyond the possibility of recovery. Failure to do so would render him completely incapacitated and defenseless against the squito and the little buddies it would call once he had been marked. *Defenseless and dead.*

He activated the suit's medical AI via his braid interface and commanded it to initiate the injection process. A protective helmet unfolded from his collar, its faceplate turning transparent, granting him an unobstructed view of his surroundings. Now encased head to toe, the suit acted like an insulating cocoon, his body emitting less detectable heat. The hibernation agent took hold, the dual compound keeping his mind alert for a few precious moments, while his body temperature rapidly dropped. All he had to do now was wait for the probe to pass, then administer the counteragent. Simple enough, yet a shiver ran down his spine at the thought of it. After all, it was a leap into the unknown and a loss of control to put your faith in tech this way.

As the probe drew closer, its guidance lasers shimmered again, cutting through the dusty air. Jarod watched intently. It paused right in front of his faceplate, rotating slowly as its sensors detected the subtle heat signature emanating from his head—the area most recently exposed. *It's sensing something, that's for sure.* He could see its body, feel its presence mere inches from his face. The slightest movement would betray his position and trigger the bug's defenses.

Riley's voice crackled over the comm, reminding him to remain still. *Well, duh.* Behind the protective barrier of the faceplate, he monitored his vital signs as the probe hovered and probed. 34 degrees Celsius, heart rate dropping, breathing steadying. So far, so good.

But the probe showed no signs of departing, its sensors undoubtedly confused by the presence of something indeterminable. He braced himself, knowing that in seven minutes, he would have to take action.

"A few more degrees, and it will leave," Riley said. He hoped she was right.

As the hibernation compound further asserted itself, he felt his body grow drowsy and numb. Though the formula was impressive, it couldn't completely eliminate the sensation of cold. Still, he couldn't complain—the science geeks had done well.

Riley's voice cut through his haze. "Your body temperature is 31 degrees. The probe is still there, sensing you or something. It hasn't sounded the alarm yet, but it's trying to determine what it's reading."

It should have moved on by now. No tech is this good.

"I have to take it out," he said. "A few more minutes, and I won't come back."

"Combat squito?" Riley guessed.

"Yeah, what else? It's not like I brought a fly swatter or anything."

Riley's point was valid, though. The squito would have electronic defenses and could potentially survive long enough to sound the alarm. But if he didn't act soon, he'd be compromised. He considered his options. "What if I fry it with my palm thruster?"

He hesitated, knowing that using his palm thruster this way could have consequences. The suit's fuel tanks were compact and lightweight, leaving little room for significant capacity. It was a trade-off between mobility and firepower—a few blasts to get him out of hot spots, and then it would be back to base for a reload. But desperate times called for desperate measures. The thruster would certainly be powerful enough to take out the squito, and he had other gadgets to rely on in case of future emergencies.

But Riley burst that bubble. "You'd have to move your arm to aim the burst," she said. *And there's that, naturally. I knew that.*

"I'd suggest a double launch of a combat and an e-war squito," she proposed. "The e-war blocks its comms, and the combat squito takes it out. Easy as pie."

"Sounds good to me."

He triggered the signal to launch, and the squitos sprang into action from his pouch. Their objective had already been transferred via his braid.

The miniature air battle that ensued was brief but nothing short of spectacular. Jarod watched, almost in awe, as the tiny automaton bees whirled and dodged, attacking and evading each other with lightning-fast moves. There was a surreal beauty in the efficiency of their movements, a stark contrast to the brutality of their purpose. The e-war squito successfully cut off the probe's communication, and the combat squito delivered the fatal blow with bursts of electrical charges. It was all over in a matter of seconds. The squito probe lay lifeless, and the combat and e-war squitos automatically returned to his pouch to be refurbished for future use.

Jarod exhaled slowly, the tension in his shoulders easing as he watched the return of his squitos on his lens, their mission completed. *Was that quick enough?* he asked.

There was a tense silence as Riley checked the logs. Unfortunately, the probe had managed to send a short transmission, likely incomplete but enough to alert its operator.

"I don't think so," Riley said. "Sorry, but we have to assume the operative controlling it has been alerted."

He injected the counter-agent, reversing the hibernation state. In just a minute, he would be even more alert than before, with no residual pain or fatigue, all thanks to hyper-advanced chemical engineering. *At least that's what Adriel assured me when he walked me through the suit specs.* But he couldn't help but wonder about the long-term effects. *What were the undisclosed ingredients in the drug, and what price would I ultimately pay for using it?* The science geeks always kept some secrets.

Have I lost valuable life span every time I've done this? I suppose if you have to spend it crawling through vents, it might not be such a bad trade.

"Feel better?" Riley asked.

"Getting there," he replied, feeling the effects of the counter-agent starting to take hold.

"What do you want to do? I can call in the extraction team," she offered.

Should I abort? He paused, considering his options. They had Bahno cornered, and despite recent events, they still had the element of surprise. *I can't do anything about Dana. And I'm pretty confident I can manage the threat up ahead, whatever it is.*

All they really had to worry about was a single squito that had possibly transmitted a garbled, partial message. It was nothing to get too worked up about, and it was entirely possible that the message was so garbled that it couldn't even be deciphered.

"Let's push ahead," he decided. "If things get dicey, we'll just back off. It's that simple."

He instructed the suit to pull back the faceplate, feeling a wave of relief at the sudden sense of space. The vent's stale air rushed against his skin and filled his nostrils, a minor but appreciated freedom after the constrictive presence of the plate. He launched a recon squito to scout ahead, crawling on hands and knees as it stayed a few meters in front of him, scanning for any hidden dangers. They had come too far to back down now. It was time to see this through to the end.

As he slithered forward, his body navigating the duct with a sinewy grace, Riley once more made herself heard.

"I have some new intel on the squito tech," she said. "It doesn't match what we know about Bahno or Lux. They don't seem to use this make."

He paused. *Hmm,* he murmured out loud, before remembering to maintain absolute silence. [I knoq!] he typed. *Damn. Misspelled. Who cares about such noises. The crawling is probably louder than the murmurs anyway.* The suit's design minimized friction, but not entirely; anyone below them could potentially hear him progressing. The ventilation system might dampen the sound further, but there was certainly no guarantee. He shook his head, refocusing his efforts on the task at hand.

[Someone is crashing the party?]

"Most likely, yes," Riley confirmed.

[Okay. Any other data to share with me?]

"Not at the moment."

He pondered his next move but ultimately decided that it was immaterial. It could be anyone—building security, another bounty hunter, or even Lux Aeterna themselves. Nevertheless, this was still their best opportunity to get to Bahno. He was confident he could handle whatever obstacles lay in his path, and he was determined to see the job through. And so, he pressed on.

"The four-way junction is up ahead," Riley said. "Proceed left, and you have five meters to the conference room vent."

His lens overlay confirmed her instructions as the recon squito swept the area. It was all clear.

"Do not turn right," Riley added with a light-hearted chuckle. "You might end up in the garbage chute."

[Haha. Funny.]

He couldn't help but laugh at that inside joke, a reference to a previous mission long ago when he had nearly fallen into a trash compactor due to a similar wrong turn. Back then, he had no braid or visual aids to guide him, relying solely on his wits to navigate through that particular maze of ducts. Ah, the good ol' days.

As he turned the corner, he caught only a quick glimpse of the duct ahead before a pipe exploded, releasing a torrent of scorching hot steam that enveloped him. *What the…* The recon had shown the path to be clear. The squito showed no…

But there he was—their mysterious interloper. The party crasher, equipped with the latest and most advanced model of squitos, was blocking his path to Bahno. They had waited too long to neutralize the probe after all, and it had managed to transmit his location.

Adrenaline surged, narrowing Jarod's world to the immediate threat. The suddenness of the attack, the steam obscuring his vision—it all condensed time, making each second stretch, filled with the potential for death. His training kicked in, but so did the stark realization of his vulnerability. The next few moments unfolded in a blur, his instincts flaring just a little too late. A boot to his face sent him tumbling backward, past the four-way junction and toward the maintenance bot storage area. His suit's AI had automatically switched to combat mode and deployed the helmet and faceplate, just narrowly protecting his face from the attacker's foot.

The suit's medical system pumped additional adrenaline into his system, catapulting him into a controlled fight-or-flight response, but the party crasher was lightning fast, striking again before Jarod could fully recover. Another kick sent him crashing through the vent grate, plummeting to the floor of the bot storage room, his head slamming against the ground. He heard Riley shout over the radio, cut short by static as the electronics took a hit from slamming into the ground.

A quick scan around him revealed the room was spacious—much larger than he had hoped. The walls were lined with rows of inactive maintenance bots, while at the far end, a vertical shaft provided access for the bots to move between floors. To the right of that was an airlock, used for servicing the building's exterior—window washing, and such.

The center of the room was dominated by a vast, open space, providing ample room for maneuvering. But that also meant that if his mystery opponent was armed, he'd be a sitting duck in the middle of it all. To Jarod's relief, he found a plethora of equipment and miscellany scattered around the corners of the room, providing an abundance of hiding spots. There were spare parts for the bots, repair tool kits, diagnostic equipment, and a handful of small scooters for the bots' human carers, all of which would provide adequate cover.

The operative rose to his feet, and his eyes locked onto the black silhouette of their intruder, who had now appeared in the opening above. It was too late to find cover, and before he could react, the shadowy figure lunged, knocking him off his feet again.

His tactical lit up, indicating the assailant had launched an attack with combat squitos. The suit AI responded automatically, deploying a defensive volley. The man charged at him, and while Jarod managed to block and parry, he lost his sidearm in the process. Training and instincts kicked in, with the artificial muscle fibers in the suit providing him with the strength and agility to evade. Seizing his opponent around the waist, he activated his foot thrusters, lifting him off the ground. A swift head-butt and a knee to the groin followed, before he released the man, who plummeted toward the edge of the shaft. Jarod watched as the intruder grasped the edge but failed to hold on, tumbling down the shaft. He caught a glimpse of three small parachutes deploying and disappearing into the darkness. *Damn. This one's got cool toys too.* Falling down a shaft wouldn't stop him for long. Even if the man was slow to deploy the chutes, he'd most likely walk away from the fall unscathed.

"Jarod, sound off!" Riley's voice boomed over the radio.

"I'm okay," he replied, not bothering to text. "It was him. Tough son of a bitch. If it wasn't for the suit, I'd be dead."

"Why didn't the recon pick him up?" Riley asked.

"Don't know."

"Status now, then?" Riley pressed.

"He's down for the count," Jarod responded. "I sent him tumbling down the maintenance shaft, but he had chutes to break the fall."

"Yeah, I got the shaft on the map," Riley replied. "It's a five-level drop. It'll take him some time to get back up. We can still use that time and get it done. Or do you want to withdraw?"

[No. We go on.]

Damned if he was going to quit now. If anything, he was even more motivated. *I'm not letting another bounty hunter steal our kill.* With renewed vigor, he reconnected to all the squitos in the field. Their target was still in the conference room, and the op was still a go. "That must be some conference," he mused to himself. "Probably immersive VR."

If Bahno was fully immersed in virtual reality, it would explain his lack of awareness of the commotion caused by their earlier fight. While Bahno may have remained oblivious, he knew he wasn't alone in the building. Others would soon come to investigate, and their window of opportunity was closing fast.

He started making his way back toward the vents. Rather than using what was left of his thrusters, he used a bot parked nearby to climb up the wall. He had a nagging feeling he'd need them again soon. More work, but hey, they say exercise is still good for you.

As he drew closer to the vent, his tactical AI sounded a warning, alerting him once again to the presence of their uninvited guest. There was a noise behind him, and he spun around just in time to see the glint of a gun barrel. It was too late to dodge, and the bullet struck him squarely in the chest, sending him reeling backward. The suit's defenses sprang into action, enhancing his every move and guiding his decisions through the seamless merger of mind and AI, doing its best to preserve his life. Alas, it wasn't enough. The sharp crack of the gun echoed in the room, the impact knocking the wind out of him. The lens displayed the damage to both the lightly armored combat suit and his own brittle bones. He was bleeding, and the pain was intense. *How could he be back so quickly?*

The suit's medical app sprang into action, injecting a potent cocktail of adrenaline and vasoconstrictors into his bloodstream. The rush of chemicals provided him with an instant burst of energy while simultaneously constricting the blood vessels around his wound to slow the bleeding.

The Party Crasher approached him, her face mask folded back, revealing the face of a woman. Defeat settled heavily over Jarod; the bitter taste of it, mingling with the metallic tang of blood, was sharp in his mouth as he lay incapacitated. The proximity of his adversary, her features now revealed, added a personal dimension to the confrontation. A strand of fiery red hair dangled from her bangs, her brown eyes holding a mixture of determination and what seemed like regret. Or pity. Regardless, this was no longer an abstract battle of wits and technology, but an unfurnished human moment of defeat and acknowledgment. She knelt down beside him, her face close to his, and for a moment, he entertained the idea of putting up a fight, but he was paralyzed, unable to move.

"I'm Elena," she said. "This was fun, but I can't let you have my kill."

The woman transmitted a message to his braid, then caressed his cheek before standing up. Jarod couldn't even lift his head to watch her leave. He sent out a distress call to Riley, hoping the interference had cleared enough for it to go through. As he waited for a response, he opened the message that Elena had sent him. It was a simple offer to team up and join forces, with no additional information provided.

The offer hung in the air, a tantalizing *what-if* against the backdrop of this new development. They were no longer alone in their pursuit. Yet, as intriguing as this offer might have been under normal circumstances, his thoughts went to Dana. The thought of her alone in the wild, with a gun to her head, was unbearable. He called up her picture on his lens, wanting her face to be the last thing he saw before losing consciousness. The cool floor beneath him leached the warmth from his body, each breath a labored effort. The room spun slightly, a disorienting effect of the blood loss and the chemicals coursing through his veins, blurring the lines between consciousness and the encroaching darkness. With a deep breath, he allowed his body to relax, the pain and fatigue washing over him. He held on to her delicate features for as long as he could, before it all faded to black.

Osawa

Hideshi Osawa stood spread-eagled, arms and legs wide in full surrender, while Alixha's human security guard patted him down. This physical scrutiny constituted the second tier in a convoluted security apparatus leading up to her penthouse suite, the first being a bullet-style scan. *Please, please, please let there be no cavity search*, he thought, utterly devoid of envy for Scott, who had endured this rigorous protocol upon each visit. The irony of his situation was not lost on him; appointed as the successor to a betrayer, Alixha had thrust upon him this unenviable mantle. Now, he was to navigate the twin gauntlets of this exhaustive ritual—and not only that—be the bearer of bad news. The search for the traitor had hit a snag.

Despite his efforts, the reason behind his selection for this dubious honor remained an enigma to him—he was merely the communications director. A showman, his craft was weaving grand narratives for oblivious audiences about Lux Aeterna's myriad undertakings, tasked with obfuscation, misdirection, and the artful execution of sleight of hand. He served as the preliminary spectacle to Alixha's increasingly scarce public unveilings. For these tasks, he excelled, but the organization teemed with more aptly suited people for the role of her confidant. *Yet here I stand, subject to the invasive scrutiny of armed muscle in body armor, summoned to the queen's lair.* They did go way back, Alixha and he, and he was one of the few who occasionally got to enjoy her physical presence. *Maybe that's why?* Trust was paramount to Alixha, and he did enjoy the dubious perk of inner-circle membership. He was well aware of Scott's "other duties," and he dearly hoped those would not transfer to him.

The security guards concluded their inspection, handed back his possessions, and disengaged the biometric lock on the front door. With his old-style analog watch secured on his wrist and his shoes and belt back in place, Osawa strode inside. A guard led him across the entryway into the dimly lit living room, dominated by the infamous wall of screens that continuously showcased humanity's most grievous atrocities, the volume cranked up to an almost unbearable level. Alixha sat reclined in the heart of the room, immovable, the broadcasts throwing fleeting shadows around her. As he drew closer, she lifted a hand, signaling him to halt, and with another gesture, silenced the tumult.

Uncertain of what was expected next, Osawa remained quietly stationary. In the sudden silence, his own breathing seemed deafening, the air in the room thick like sludge. *Should I speak now?* he wondered, feeling an anxious knot tighten in his stomach. The moment stretched on, beads of sweat emerging on his forehead, and he could quite literally feel every camera eye in the room fixed on him.

"Well?" she finally spoke.

"Uh…" he faltered, then steadied his voice. "We haven't located him. We believe a bounty hunter team contracted by Aegis found him in Rothbard, one of Tokyo's underground sanctuaries, but he escaped them."

Alixha stayed quiet, her gaze fixed on the now-silent screens. Osawa awaited a response, but none came. "There's more," he ventured, met with continued silence. "Aki Sato was found dead at the scene, apparently by his own hand."

She stood and glided toward him, her presence ghostly, as if existing in a separate quantum state. As she moved toward him, the room seemed to chill, Alixha's presence an invisible force that pushed the air away from him. Being well aware of Alixha's genetic experimentation, he couldn't rule out the possibility that the effect was more than merely psychological. At this very moment, his amygdala might well be flooding with fear-inducing neurotransmitters and hormones.

Drawing near, her breath caressed his face, her blank stare piercing him sharply, yet she remained wordless. Osawa's heart thudded in his chest, his mind urging him to retreat, but his feet were as if glued to the parquet floor, his eyes involuntarily shying away from her intense gaze.

"The codes are irretrievable with the death of Sato," Osawa announced. "Should we then abandon the pursuit of Scott?"

At the mention of Scott's name, Alixha's demeanor transformed; her previously distant gaze sharpened, now ablaze with anger and a palpable sense of betrayal. The treachery had deeply affected her, yet there was something more beneath the surface. *Grief?*

Scott had been more than just another operative. His relationship with Alixha was common knowledge among their peers. It had perhaps not just been a liaison of convenience and carnal pleasure but something more profound.

"No," she responded softly, yet with the weight of an unyielding command. "Continue the pursuit. And remember, I want him alive." With that, she retreated to her lounge chair. A single gesture restored the cacophony of the screens, another summoned the guard, who promptly ushered Osawa back through the hallway.

As Osawa departed, he carried with him a clear understanding: failing to capture the traitor would have dire consequences. He dared not contemplate the specifics.

Brett

"Go now," Brett said to her, his voice low, as Cali left the apartment for his usual perimeter check. Tension settled like a lump of lead in his stomach as he watched Dana rise from the couch. The stillness of the apartment seemed to amplify the sound of her footsteps, each one echoing across the room. Brett could almost feel the tension in the air—electric and tingling against his skin, as if the apartment itself was holding its breath, waiting for the outcome of their little operation. The plan was risky, but it nevertheless offered a sliver of hope.

Dana disappeared into the bedroom, shutting the door softly behind her. They had both agreed that approaching Daemon without Cali's presence would be more likely to succeed, so they were waiting for their chance when he was out for his walks. They could only attempt this once, maybe twice. However, this little "divide-and-conquer" ploy was not without its obstacles.

Daemon was a wildcard, and it was uncertain how he would react if he uncovered their strategy. They were gambling on him agreeing that Cali's unstable disposition made him a liability. The past day had shown signs that Daemon was getting tired of his partner in crime, regretful of what they had done, and seeking a way out. They needed to seize this opportunity to form a united front against Cali. Nevertheless, everything would be for naught if Cali caught them in the act.

That's where Brett came in, partially immobile as he was. His duty was to keep a watchful eye, ensuring the paranoid young man would not interrupt their conversation. He couldn't help but surrender to a pang of helplessness, his usually active role reduced to that of a mere lookout. Immobility frustrated him, a constant reminder of his, and the others', present vulnerability. The strategy they'd worked out was for him to feign a coughing fit once he heard Cali ascend the stairwell, hopefully providing enough time for Dana to conclude her discussion and emerge from the room in a seamless manner, returning to the couch and pretending it was a rainy day. Brett would have felt more at ease if he could be there to assist her. Once Dana went into that bedroom, she was on her own. *Perhaps it is for the best.*

He was not well-versed in the art of negotiation. Dana, on the other hand, was an expert. Despite her lack of experience in this particular flavor of deliberations, she was a shrewd negotiator. Brett, by any definition of the word, was not. He would only get in the way, intimidating the boy and undermining their efforts. A rueful smile touched Brett's lips at this realization, a moment of self-awareness that stung with the bitter taste of humility.

The gel packs were doing their job with his leg. He glanced down at the translucent, bulky pack strapped to his thigh, its cool liquid seeping through his skin, providing both relief and repair. The pain had transitioned from a sharp, burning sensation to a dull, pulsing throb. And it itched—a symptom he perceived as a sign of progress. He was no doctor, but his body was definitely recuperating. Another few hours of gel therapy, and he could bear weight on his leg once more. *And that will come in handy.*

Sooner or later, they would have to move, and he loathed the idea of being what hindered their escape. Brett's gaze drifted toward the hallway, where the front door hid behind the corner. Beyond it lay their uncertain path to freedom. The thought of being a burden, an anchor dragging them down, filled him with silent despair. He despised failure. And he had failed—there was no denying that. In that moment, in the quiet of the apartment, the echo of his failures seemed to grow louder, a chorus of missteps and missed opportunities that played relentlessly in his mind. His complacency had led him into a false sense of security, deluding him into thinking that they were safe within the dome. He had allowed his assignment to be compromised. The fact that his tactical, obviously having human biases built into its logic, had not detected any threats and had been caught off guard was of little consolation. Two comrades and a young boy had died. Blaming the braid was not an acceptable excuse.

Outwardly, he carried the burden with silent resignation, but inside, guilt wrapped its cold fingers around Brett's heart. The shadows of the past loomed large in his mind, failure having been a constant companion throughout his life. Twice divorced, and two grown children, estranged. He had been passed over for promotion multiple times, hence why he found himself in his mid-fifties relegated to tasks like escort duty, while his peers had advanced to the rank of captain or, at the very least, detective. *I'm such a police cliché.* At least he didn't drink. Well, not excessively, anyway. That realization offered a small consolation, a fragile barrier against a tide of regret.

Now, once again, he found himself teetering on the precipice of defeat, if not entirely there just yet. For if Dana, Aea, Tabayah, and their captors remained alive from here on, there was still a chance for a happy ending. That was something, he reminded himself.

He groaned as the itching beneath the gel pack resurfaced. The itch was a maddening distraction, a persistent annoyance that sapped his ability to focus. He shifted uncomfortably, seeking a moment's peace from the relentless irritation, but alas, the irritation endured. He adjusted the pack cautiously, ensuring that it remained firmly affixed to his thigh. Moving it around slightly offered relief, but only temporarily.

Satisfied for the time being, he settled himself as calmly as possible to minimize any noise, straining to hear the conversation emanating through the drywall. Though only murmurs penetrated, it provided him with insight into their emotional state and how things were progressing. *No angry shouting. That's a good sign.* A flicker of hope in the midnight of his anxiety. Perhaps, just perhaps, their gamble would pay off.

He wished his braid was equipped with audio enhancers, but German Legacy Police hadn't seen fit to equip a man who primarily worked escort duty with such functionality. *Why not?* It was a modest expense compared to the tactical AI they had deemed essential. For a second, he allowed himself to wallow in frustration at the bureaucracy and shortsightedness that permeated the department. Governmental priorities never ceased to baffle him. So much hinged on the small stuff, the details overlooked in the grand scheme of things. For instance, lacking such enhancements meant he had to rely on his natural hearing when attempting to discern what was transpiring in the bedroom while simultaneously monitoring for any indications that Cali was returning from his walk of paranoia. With the proper equipment, he could have outsourced one of those tasks. *Or both!* He closed his eyes, concentrating on the faint sounds from the bedroom, trying to amplify them in his mind's eye. Each muffled word was a puzzle piece, a fragmentary clue to the conversation he was desperate to comprehend.

"How are you, Mr. Brett?" Tabayah said, smiling from the hallway, holding a glass of water. The sudden interruption of Tabayah's voice was a gentle reminder that life existed outside the immediate scheme they were working. Brett returned her smile.

"I'm okay, sweetie."

"I thought you might be thirsty?" she explained, extending the glass to him.

Such a sweet kid. Warmth briefly chased the cold from Brett's thoughts as he accepted the glass, the brief irritation he had instinctively felt from being interrupted instantly gone. In Tabayah's simple act of kindness, he found a moment of solace, a reminder of the innocence they were fighting to protect. Though he wasn't particularly thirsty, he downed the water and requested another. "And a sandwich?" he added.

"Sure, Mr. Brett," she replied gleefully before scampering back to the kitchen.

That should keep her busy for a while. He watched Tabayah's retreating back, her youthful energy now returned, as if she had adapted to being held captive, as if she no longer realized the danger. Her willingness to help, however small the task, was certainly a ray of light in the gloom that had settled over them, but her cheerfulness was an illusion. The danger was undoubtedly still present, and he didn't want her nearby when Cali returned, in case something were to go down. Sudden terror washed over him, scenarios playing out in his mind. Each one was more catastrophic than the last. The need to shield the two girls from any potential fallout with the unstable boy added an unmistakable layer of urgency to his already overstretched vigil.

He strained his ears once more, attempting to discern what was being said. Instead, footfalls resonated through the stairwell outside, unmistakably those of Cali. He had returned earlier than Brett had hoped, cutting his perimeter walk short for whatever reason. Time had run out. It was time to send the signal.

He took a deep breath, steadying himself for the act. The knot in his stomach tightened further as he held off to the very last moment before coughing. Then he coughed as loudly as possible, hoping dearly that Dana would recognize it in time and realize she had to depart.

Dana

Dana trailed closely behind Aea and Tabayah as they descended the stairwell toward the apartment building's main exit, ready to deliver the younger girl to the authorities—a handover agreed to by all parties. Cali followed, keeping a watchful eye, gun surreptitiously tucked away in his jeans behind his back. Dana could feel the weight of Cali's gaze on the back of her neck as if that gun were literally pressed against it, a precarious reminder of how catastrophically wrong this could go. Each step of her heels echoed ominously in the stairwell, compounding her anxiety with every floor they descended. *And the fluorescent lights flicker,* she thought, *as if some movie director had set the scene.* But it was obviously just the standard lack of maintenance that plagued so much of the Outside. *That they work at all is a small miracle.* The boy had warned them not to make any sudden moves, threatening to use the weapon at the slightest provocation. *I'm not entirely sure he actually would,* she thought, finger twitching nervously at her side, *but I can't rule it out either.*

A tiny flame of hope had sparked within Dana when she brokered the agreement to move the girl to safety, yet that hope was tinged with the stark reality of an increasingly unstable Cali watching their every move. Despite the risks, they had made progress. Cali and Daemon had agreed to give up one hostage, and one only. The plan was for the police to meet them downstairs by the door, grab Tabayah, and then the two of them would head back upstairs. Simple enough on paper, but it was hardly the perfect solution they all desired. However, it was a step in the right direction. *I guess I can add hostage negotiations to my résumé.* Although technically, she had merely been the intermediary between Daemon, Cali, and the police hostage negotiator. The real hostage negotiator.

It was vital that they got at least Tabayah out of harm's way. Once they were in the tunnels, they had to move quickly. Tabayah wouldn't be able to keep up. The police wouldn't listen to reason with Aea. Brett was probably right about that, but Tabayah was still considered a hostage—a victim, not a perpetrator. It made no sense to endanger her with their risky escape plan back through the tunnels.

She had proposed a plan to negotiate Brett's release too, so he could receive proper medical attention for his wounds. However, Brett had quickly quashed that idea before it could gain any traction. *It was a noble gesture*, she thought, *but ultimately foolish.* Instead, they had settled for replenishing his supply of healing gel packs and additional painkillers.

Dana knew that Brett was in it for the long haul. She empathized with his sense of duty and understood why he wouldn't want to abandon two scared civilians with two armed and equally frightened little boys. For Brett, Dana was his mission, and people like him didn't abandon their missions once they had been assigned. He insisted that he would be able to move once the time came. The healing gel was doing its job, albeit slowly and incompletely, and every glance she threw in his direction revealed an uncomfortable grimace across his features—a silent testament to both his pain and stoicism. But in that stillness lay an unspoken resilience, a quiet strength that gave Dana some hope they'd make it.

"Slowly," Cali reminded them as they neared the last bend before the ground floor. *We know, little boy. We know.*

Brett was confident that the police had been primed to storm the building for at least a day. Her intervention as a mediator had stalled things, and she hoped that their successful negotiation to release Tabayah would further postpone their plans. With every moment that passed, Brett's leg had more time to recuperate, the healing gel more time to work its magic.

Dana's gaze drifted to the SWAT team outside, their figures blurred through the glass. The sight was surreal, like a scene from a movie none of them had ever asked to star in. Her stomach churned with terror and anticipation at the view, the reality of their predicament crystallizing with painful clarity. As they reached the entrance on the ground floor, Dana saw the SWAT team gearing up. There were three officers, with one poised at the door, ready to grab Tabayah the moment they emerged. The other two were positioned on either side, weapons at the ready but not yet aimed at them. Brett had warned that snipers would be on standby, ready to take action if necessary. It was a sobering thought, but it made sense. *But what the hell do I know? It's my first hostage drama.* Brett might have just said that to keep her calm, to instill a sense of comfort that backup was available if things went wrong. It didn't do much to soothe her frazzled nerves, her heart pounding, threatening to burst out of her chest at any moment. *What good will it do if they have to invoke that contingency? More bloodshed.*

Dana turned to face Cali only to see his right hand sneaking toward his concealed firearm. Her breath stopped dead in her throat, and the space between her heartbeats stretched to an eternity. "Don't do that," she warned him, forcing sound through her vocal cords.

"Eyes forward," Cali retorted.

Dana wasn't going to let it go. "No, seriously, you don't want to make any sudden moves. If they suspect you're going for a weapon, they might open fire."

Cali seemed to grasp the gravity of the situation and withdrew his hand. Relief washed over Dana, leaving her knees weak and her heart racing in its aftermath. She did her best to conceal her trembling hands, adrenaline coursing through her veins. The brief standoff with Cali had peeled back the veneer of control she laboriously maintained, revealing the raw fear beneath. She couldn't believe that she had actually spoken up to a man with a gun who could have been prepared to kill her at any moment.

They had reached the door, with Tabayah clutched tightly in Aea's arms as Dana held them both.

"Go ahead and open the door," Cali instructed.

Dana undid her right arm from the embrace and pushed the door outwards, taking care to observe Brett's instructions to proceed slowly, as if in slow motion, to avoid provoking aggression from their captors—or from the police, for that matter.

As soon as the door was ajar, the closest officer swiftly moved forward and plucked Tabayah from Aea's arms. Tabayah screamed and reached out for her protectors. Dana's heart contorted at the sound, a visceral pull resonating with the instinct to protect she'd felt earlier with Aea. The girl's cries were the cost of this entire catastrophe laid bare.

"You'll be safe with them," Aea cried. "Don't worry. Dad is waiting for you. I'll see you soon."

Dana followed protocol and pulled Aea back inside the doorway, while the police carried Tabayah away from the building and toward the barricade.

"Back upstairs," Cali ordered, taking up the rear as they made their way back up to Brett. The entire exchange had taken just a few minutes from start to finish. Dana's mind raced, replaying the interaction over and over as they ascended the stairs back to their prison—Tabayah's cries, Aea's promise—a tumultuous mix of relief, sadness, and terror simmering within her.

"Look," Brett said, pointing toward the rapidly approaching hurricane outside—the kind of storm that would necessitate a curfew or even evacuation to shelters. The police would be incapable of operating in such extreme weather conditions, the wind now howling like an injured beast. On the horizon, trees were bending, their silhouettes warping against the darkening sky. The police would have to retreat and regroup until the hurricane had passed. Or make their move now. Brett leaned in closer. "Whatever time we bought ourselves with the kid's release is gone. The police will have to act before the storm hits us."

Which forces our hand as well, Dana thought, a surge of urgency sweeping through her as she stared at the building front.

"How much time?" she asked. Their braids were still blocked, and the TV forecasts were significantly delayed, which meant they wouldn't be able to obtain an accurate update.

"Not long," Brett said, his voice tense. "We have to act now."

Dana's heart raced, adrenaline pumping through her veins as the weight of Brett's words settled in. They would have no choice but to confront Cali. *Force his hand too.* Dana had hoped to let him come to his senses gradually, but that was no longer an option. The thought of taking such decisive action ignited a fierce determination within her, even as panic gnawed at the edges of her resolve. She felt some relief to finally put their plan into action, risks be damned. Hastily, they moved away from the window before their captors spotted them.

"Daemon seems to be the one with the weaker resolve," Brett said. "We'll continue to go through him. Get him to convince the other one to lay down the guns."

Dana agreed, but she couldn't shake the feeling that Cali would rather shoot it out with the police than surrender. She shuddered at the thought of it. Daemon, on the other hand, had shown some hesitation and obviously cared for Aea. Like before, they approached Daemon while Cali was out scouting, giving them only a few precious minutes to act. Brett played to Daemon's rational side, while Dana appealed to his emotions. *Like good-cop-bad-cop from a crappy crime show.*

As they faced off, she could see the conflict etched in his eyes, the young man torn between loyalty and logic. Her plea was earnest, every word infused with a desperate hope to break through to him, to appeal to the sliver of reason she believed still resided within. Brett added weight to the argument, trying to reason with him that escaping in the tunnels was their only option, that a firefight with a SWAT team was unwinnable, and that Aea's life would be in grave danger if they resisted. They urged Daemon to come to his senses and accept that prison was a better outcome than death, and that freedom was better than both.

"You have to believe us," Dana implored, her voice steady, belying the inner turmoil and doubts threatening to overwhelm her. "When the police come, it's over. We'll all likely be killed if you resist. There's a good chance we'll be even if you don't. We have to go."

Aea snuggled up to Daemon, gazing at him without a word. Dana couldn't quite decipher her expression, but it seemed to be a mixture of terror, support for her loved one, and an unspoken plea for him to see reason.

Brett spoke calmly and rationally, "Listen, kid, they'll shoot first and ask questions later. This is the world we live in since London."

Daemon looked back at Aea, and Dana could see that he was giving in, a fragile hope that their words were finally penetrating the fortress of fear and defiance he had built. She felt like he was about to break when Cali barged into the room. "No," he declared, a tangible tension settling over everyone like a shroud. "We're not leaving, and we're not surrendering," he went on, "even if this bitch ends up dead or in a fucking hole for the rest of her life."

The room seemed to constrict around Dana, the air thickening as Cali's refusal obliterated the fragile hope they had fought hard to nurture. As reality settled, her stomach clenched, her pulse hammered in her ears. "Cali, please," she reasoned, but he wasn't having it.

"We wouldn't be running," Daemon interjected, coming around at last. "We're just living to fight another day. We'll take the tunnels like they say. The cops won't be able to find us down there. We'll get new IDs and wait for the right time to strike again." Daemon, now wholly on board with the plan, kept explaining, reminding Cali about the extension through the basement, the shelters, and the tunnel leading into the dome. But Cali wouldn't listen.

"It won't work," Cali insisted. "Making our stand here is the only option. We're not running like cowards. Let them come."

"No, we're not," Daemon asserted. "I'm in charge. I decide."

"You always were a coward." Cali drew his gun from the back of his jeans, holding it in his hand but not yet pointing it at anyone. His eyes were bloodshot from lack of sleep, his desperation approaching a fever pitch. One small prick, and the balloon would burst. Daemon stepped forward until he was face to face with Cali, the two of them locked in a staring match. "The game is over, Cali. You know it is," Daemon said.

"Fuck you. Gabriel will kill you when we report back in."

"You still don't get it, do you? We're never seeing him again. We die here, go to prison, or we run. Those are the options. Gabriel's gone," Daemon said.

Cali didn't say anything, stubbornly refusing to accept the situation.

"You think you're going to take a fuckin' SEK team with a few peashooters? You'll be dead before you get a shot off," Daemon said, holding out his hand, motioning for Cali to hand over the weapon.

Dana started to move toward them, but Brett held her back, shaking his head to signal her not to intervene. Their best chance was to let Daemon talk Cali down.

Cali pushed Daemon away and pointed the gun toward the couch. "I won't be shooting at the police. I'll be shooting at them," he said, his aim finally settling on Aea. "Maybe I'll shoot your bitch."

Dana's blood ran cold as Cali's aim shifted. Time seemed to stop, each second stretching endlessly as the violence they had feared threatened to burst into devastating reality. Daemon, face now twisted with rage, lunged forward and grabbed for the gun, causing it to go off, the bullet ricocheting into the ceiling. Brett reacted instantly, exploding up from the couch, lightning-fast. Despite his injured condition, he pulled Daemon away, tackled Cali, knocking the gun out of his hand, and placed him in a chokehold.

"Relax, kid," Brett said. But Cali wouldn't give up. He kicked and heaved, even attempting to headbutt Brett as he tightened his grip.

"Don't make me kill you," Brett pleaded, but Cali continued

to resist. The boy pulled a knife from somewhere and plunged it into Brett's already injured thigh. Brett screamed in agony and tightened his chokehold before Cali could strike again. Blood oozed from Brett's leg, and Dana prayed that the femoral artery was not hit.

As Dana watched the struggle, emotions roiled within her—fear for Brett's safety, horror at the escalating violence, and a deep, aching sorrow for the tragic trajectory that had led them all to this moment. And while Cali was slowly losing the fight, he refused to give up. The young man continued to reach for the knife lodged in Brett's thigh, desperate to cause more harm. Brett knew he had no choice but to take drastic action. "I'm sorry, kid," he said, tightening his grip until Cali's air was completely cut off. Eventually, Cali stopped moving and went limp. Brett loosened his grip, and both of them slumped to the floor. A heavy silence fell over the room, the aftermath of the confrontation hanging between them like a dense fog. Dana's heart ached as she moved to assist Brett, the reality of what had just occurred crushing her. Aea and Daemon were frozen, unsure of what to do as Dana helped Brett. She rolled the limp Cali off of him, and in the background, the police comm line started beeping.

"They heard the gun go off," Brett said, "or at least they saw the muzzle flash through the curtain. We don't have long."

Dana rushed to grab the first aid kit that the police had delivered earlier and pulled out the last gel pack and gauze for Brett's leg. He instructed her to slap the pack right over the wound, as there was no time to clean it. As he tied off his leg with the gauze, he ordered someone to check on Cali.

Daemon, still in shock, moved over to Cali's body and checked for a pulse. "Nothing," he said.

Once Brett had finished tying off his leg, he dragged himself over to Cali's body to confirm. He slumped over and momentarily rested his forehead on the child's chest. *Brett is a good man,* Dana thought to herself. Much like Jarod, all those years ago when he had escorted her back to the States for one of her first negotiations. Like Jarod, Brett was obviously scarred by the past, but despite the trauma, he remained a man of integrity—one willing to risk his life for the sake of others.

Daemon held Aea tight, shielding her from the sight of Cali's lifeless body. Brett, despite his injuries, rose to his feet and limped toward the window, his eyes darting behind the curtain.

"There's movement," he said grimly. "We don't have much time."

Outside, with the storm now imminent and the situation rapidly spiraling beyond their control, Dana felt a rising sense of desperation. She suggested answering the comm and trying to talk the police down—a last-ditch attempt at de-escalation—but Brett shook his head.

"It's too late for that," he said. "The hurricane, combined with the gunshots inside the apartment, has pushed the situation beyond the point of negotiation. The police will be coming, and there's nothing we can do to stop it now."

"What about Cali?" Aea asked quietly. "Are we just going to leave him there?"

"Sweetie," Brett said, his voice soft, "I'd really like to do something for him, but we gotta go. Now."

He turned to Dana and instructed her to grab the weapons, then looked back to Daemon and Aea.

"Kids, you're up. Take us to the tunnels."

Journal

...Berlin, Kyoto, Paris, Doha, Warsaw, Bonn, Sharm El-Sheikh, Lima, Guangzhou, St. Petersburg, Wellington, Kyiv... Agreements aimed at reducing the emission of greenhouse gases were plentiful. The early twenty-first century was characterized by good intentions but ultimately fell short in delivering meaningful results...

...the convergence of political resistance and opposing economic interests contributed to a lack of decisive action, ultimately leading to the emergence of the perfect storm that the global community had hoped to avoid. Despite the presence of compelling scientific evidence, a significant portion of the public, along with some political leaders, remained skeptical of the gravity of the threat, even as mid-century approached. As a result, several critical tipping points were reached, unnoticed by many, with severe consequences...

...characterized by a multitude of alarming phenomena, including the melting of Greenland and Arctic ice, Amazon deforestation, irreversible permafrost melt, methane release, the expansion of desert areas, and the increasing frequency of extreme weather events...

...As the reality of the situation became apparent, with the Intergovernmental Panel on Climate Change's (IPCC) dire projections of a potential five-degree Celsius temperature increase and sea level rise exceeding five meters by the end of the twenty-first century becoming unavoidable, many nations withdrew from emission reduction agreements. Instead, their attention shifted toward the management of the inevitable consequences of climate change...

...Climate models projected additional temperature and sea

level rises, and by the conclusion of the twenty-second century, the planet's climate would be unable to sustain civilized life. In fact, "life as we know it" would truly become a thing of the past...

...The period spanning from the 2030s to the 2060s was marked by significant political upheaval, food shortages, a substantial rise in global migration, mass extinction of animal species, and unprecedented human casualties...

...In a pivotal chapter of climate science, Dr. Elinor Vasquez introduced the world to her eponymous model, a synthesis of complex variables like technological transformation, political resistance to change, and societal willingness to adopt new behaviors, all set against the backdrop of Earth's dwindling resilience. The Vasquez model, encapsulated by the deceptively simple formula **T = f(T_tech, P_inertia, S_behavior, E_resilience)**, starkly outlined the timeframe humanity had missed to avert irreversible climate catastrophe. "We're beyond prevention, beyond 'T'; our focus now is on adaptation," Dr. Vasquez remarked. Her model became a cornerstone in understanding the new era of human existence under the domes...

...significant advances in material sciences, quantum computing, artificial intelligence (AI), self-replicating smart robots, fusion power, synthetic biology, and the reduced marginal cost of manufacturing numerous consumer goods facilitated the mass production of biomes protected by domed megastructures. The UN's DomeEX program, established to oversee the construction of these arcologies, enabled human societies to persist in the face of catastrophic...

...Numerous city domes were constructed using existing levees that were initially designed to protect against rising sea levels...

...for many coastal cities, particularly those in developing nations, the construction of domes came too late. These cities now experience significant flooding and are often referred to as "Venetian." Some countries, such as Barbados and the Maldives, have yet to be reclaimed from the sea...

...While we cannot definitively state that humanity completely abandoned efforts to prevent climate change with the introduction of Singapore's dome concept, the sense of urgency diminished significantly. The development of this solution was viewed as a major breakthrough, leading many to believe that there was no longer an imperative to pursue alternative...

Aea

"How is your leg, Mr. Brett?" Aea asked as they proceeded down the tunnels, their steps muted against the packed dirt floor. She took a deep breath as she finished the sentence, the air cool and damp, the scent of earth and a faint hint of mold in the labyrinth beneath Niederrad all too familiar. The silence in the corridors was broken only by their footsteps, the occasional drip of water from the ceiling, and their labored breathing as they scurried toward safety. They had now managed past the buildings and were heading into the subterranean maze for Daemon's passage into the Frankfurt dome.

Aea watched Brett limping and grimacing in pain, the gauze around his upper thigh tightly wrapped, digging deep into his flesh. The dim beams from their flashlights cast ghostly shadows over his face, highlighting the strain around his eyes and the set of his jaw. Aea clenched at the sight, a mix of admiration and worry churning within her. They may have a head start, but she feared it wouldn't be enough. Brett turned to face her as he hobbled along, correcting her, "Stefan, sweetie. It's Stefan." A faint smile tugged at the corners of his mouth. "And it's okay."

Aea returned the smile, though she had her doubts about the

true condition of his leg. She held on to whatever confidence she could muster—she had played in these tunnels every day when she was a little girl and knew them like the back of her hand. She was still unbeatable at hide and seek, and knew every nook and cranny of the underground labyrinth, at least until they ventured further into the underbelly of Niederrad. Daemon too seemed certain. They had simply asked the police to count to a hundred and slipped away undetected. For all their training, tech, and access to data, the authorities were clueless about the tunnels underneath. All they knew were the maps in their braids, and these passages weren't in any official plans. The Innies simply did not know anything about the Outside.

It's been ages since I played hide and seek, she thought, momentarily distracted from the urgency of their escape. *Einfach eine Ewigkeit.* She still occasionally indulged with Tabayah, keeping the skills alive. It was their little secret, though. Of course, one could not admit to partaking in such immature endeavors once you're in high school, lest you suffer the harsh judgment of your peers.

As they proceeded, the flashlight beams danced across rough walls, occasionally revealing patches of graffiti from years long gone and the occasional scuttle of a rat fleeing the intrusion of light into its domain. "Which way?" Dana asked, pulling Aea back to reality. They were approaching a fork in the tunnel, and Aea indicated to the right. Brett moved up ahead, peeking around the corner. Daemon followed closely—so close that Brett gestured for him to take a step back.

"They won't be there," Daemon reassured them. "They're all behind us."

"Even so," Brett countered, his tone unwavering. A gun was now firmly clasped in Brett's hand, as was one in Daemon's. However, Brett had said they would be of little use, a statement Aea took at face value, having next to no knowledge about guns.

"Let's keep moving," Brett urged, gesturing for Dana to take the lead. "I'll cover our rear. Now that we're out of the police exclusion zone, my braid is working again. I can use enhanced imaging to spot them when they come. Still no connection to the Net, though. Maybe we're too deep."

A sense of unease now tore at her confidence as they forged ahead. The deeper they went, the more the reality of their situation weighed on Aea. *For some reason, I'd forgotten about drones.* Or had she repressed the idea as some sort of psychological defense? The tunnels were a maze, and with each step, the weight of the earth above seemed to press down on her, the line between safety and entrapment thinner than she had thought. She became acutely aware of the sound of their collective breathing, strained to the limit from trying to keep pace. It was now impossibly loud and oppressive in the dark.

"When will we know they're coming?" Daemon asked.

"When they're already upon us," Brett replied grimly, his words hanging in the air. A chill crept down Aea's spine. The police, so far removed from the world Outside, yet so dangerously close, was a paradox unresolved. "I wish I had a shotgun," Brett added wistfully. Turning to Dana, he said, "Have you ever tried to hit a drone, much less a squito, with one of these?" He gestured to his firearm. Dana nodded her understanding. Aea wasn't entirely sure what all that meant, but she understood enough to know that if the police caught up, it was over.

"Are there any corridors up ahead that aren't this wide and straight?" Brett asked Daemon.

Daemon nodded and replied, "In a few hundred meters or so, there are some smaller corridors. It's like a labyrinth, easy to get lost in. But I know them inside out."

"I do too," Aea interjected, feeling a twinge of disappointment that Brett hadn't asked for her input.

"Alright," Brett said decisively. "Lead the way. We need to move quickly. We're too exposed here. If they catch up to us now, we're dead."

"We'll be sitting geese," Aea said, glancing back at Stefan, his silhouette a steadfast presence against the ever-encroaching darkness. His determination, even in the face of great pain, lent her courage.

"Ducks, sweetie," Brett corrected her. "The expression is 'sitting ducks.'"

Aea smiled back and nodded in acknowledgment. Daemon

grabbed her hand and gave it a reassuring squeeze, and she squeezed back. His touch made her feel safe and protected.

Brett urged them up front to show the way, while he fell behind. *Stefan,* Aea reminded herself. *He wants me to call him Stefan.* She couldn't help but notice how Stefan kept glancing over his shoulder, likely monitoring readouts on his lens, enhancing his view down the dark tunnel. She could also see Stefan increasingly struggling to keep pace as Daemon pulled her along, his injuries worsening by the minute. Aea was now seriously worried that he might not make it all the way.

"Come on," Daemon urged, pulling her as they approached a large container in the distance, abandoned long ago by the former tenants of this underground sanctuary. Beyond that, the passages would branch off in different directions.

Stefan's voice echoed from behind them, "Drones incoming. They're coming."

Daemon and Dana stopped in their tracks, but Brett urged them to keep moving. Daemon released Aea's hand and hurried back to assist Stefan. Suddenly, a drone materialized out of the darkness, hurtling toward them. The appearance of the machine shattered the silence like breaking glass, its motors a high-pitched shriek reverberating in the tunnel. Aea's heart skipped a beat, fear seizing her as the drone attacked.

"Stay back!" Stefan yelled. But it was too late. The drone emitted a flashing light and a resounding thump. Daemon crumpled to the ground, his body seeming to slump in slow motion. He hit the ground with a protracted thud. Aea screamed and lunged for him in desperation, but Dana held her back. The boy groaned in agony, and all Aea wanted in that moment was to defy death and be close to him. She pulled with all her might, but Dana's hands were too strong.

"Get behind the container!" Stefan barked. "It'll give you some cover."

With fierce determination, Stefan opened fire on the drone, unleashing several rapid shots and adjusting his aim with lightning-fast reflexes as the nimble machine dodged and weaved. Aea could barely keep up with the frenzied exchange, the gunfire booming like thunder in the enclosed space of the tunnels. After a few more shots, the drone finally plummeted to the ground in defeat. Stefan limped over to Daemon and checked on him, signaling to Aea that he was still alive. She breathed a sigh of relief as they pulled him behind the container.

"He's just tased. That's good news. It means they may not shoot to kill," Stefan said.

"The bad news?" Dana added.

"The bad news is that this was just a scout. A mapper, basically. It found us, and now they know where we are. The rest will be here in a few minutes at most."

Stefan turned to Dana with stoic resolve. "Daemon isn't going anywhere. Go now, take her with you. Find my contact, tell him I sent you. I'll stay behind with the kid and buy you some time."

Dana began to pull Aea away, but she screamed in protest. "No! We can't leave him!"

"He'll make it, sweetie," Stefan reassured her, "but you've got to go. Now."

Every instinct within her urged her to stay by Daemon's side, to protect him from the impending danger that loomed down the tunnel. But she also knew it would all be for nothing if they didn't escape. Perhaps Stefan was right, and Daemon would be taken into custody rather than killed. Aea turned to Daemon for a final glance.

"Bye, love," she whispered.

Then she leaned in and kissed Stefan on the cheek, grateful for his bravery and determination. "When the police come," she declared, "they'll be the ones who are sitting ducks."

"Geese," he said and winked. "The expression is 'sitting geese.' Go now."

Dana pulled Aea along into the smaller corridors, Aea guiding them toward the illicit underground entrance to the dome. Her mind raced, every turn a step away from Daemon but closer to safety—opposites impossible for her to reconcile. In the distance, she could hear loud, cracking sounds echoing through the tunnels. These were no mere thumps of tasers discharging, but the unmistakable sounds of gunshots.

...neo-feudalism, while often characterized as a contemporary phenomenon, spans more than a century in its evolution [...] the ascendance of these massive corporations has led to CEOs and board chairpersons being likened to feudal lords, rather than traditional business executives...

...significant population decline, poor adoption of automation in the workforce, and subsequent economic collapse in Russia and China led to a weakening of their state apparatus in the mid-twenty-first century. These events served as a catalyst for a new world order, with affluent Western nation-states standing in opposition to global corporate interests rather than...

...the term "legacy" has been used to describe governments, implying that they are outdated and no longer relevant...

...the exorbitant cost of dome construction subsidies has imposed a substantial financial strain on governments, particularly in the first few decades when costs were highest. As a result, they have ceded ground to...

...the decline of wars of conquest, underscored by the collapse of the Russian and Sino regimes—both of which attempted such endeavors on a significant scale in Ukraine and Taiwan, respectively—led to a reduction in military spending. It wasn't until London that military budgets again underwent a sharp increase...

...the void left by the dismantling of centralized power structures presented an opening for private interests to assert themselves...

...the nature of organizations like Lux Aeterna presents unique challenges that cannot be resolved through conventional means. Alixha Rahena's domain does not align with a traditional nation-state that can be defeated by military means or weakened through economic sanctions. Consequently, it is unclear whether governments and law enforcement agencies possess the necessary capabilities to counter this threat effectively...

Part Three: Resurrection

Elena

The domes were no place for someone like Elena. Too many prying oculi, both human and artificial, constantly on the lookout. Microphones, cameras, spyware, law enforcement intrusion—the ever-present hum of drones patrolling the domes' inner skies. Inside posed a constant reminder of the presence of eyes that never blink, the risk of imprisonment or even death always looming. *If you don't wanna do the time, don't do the crime*, as the expression goes. Eight o'clock in the morning and she was already quoting clichés to herself. *Get a grip.*

As the early morning light seeped through the curtains, a fleeting sense of vulnerability swept over Elena. In a world of glaring surveillance, she was a shadow, a rebel heart beating against the cold, calculated rhythm of a captive world. She needed to constantly remind herself she was just a hair away from a more literal incarceration. Or death. Even here, in her sanctuary up north.

With a sigh, Elena threw off her covers and donned her robe. The chill of the floor beneath her feet was a daily reminder of the simple life she chose to live—no AI, no environmental controls, no luxurious floor heating, just plain old solar-powered electrical radiators. The cold bit into the soles of her feet, a sharp contrast to the warmth of the bed, drawing a shiver as she made her way across the room. She had a pair of moccasins somewhere, but they were probably kicked off and forgotten somewhere in the house, as per usual. In the living room, probably. Or in the study.

Doing the time, in her case, meant living the considerably harsher life of an Outie, despite having the resources of an Innie. The flamboyant lifestyle of the wealthy would put her in the crosshairs of those she sought to avoid, so she resigned herself to a life of minimalism and anonymity—except when working a target, when venturing Inside was often unavoidable. *At least I'm not a tunnel dweller.*

Living on the fringes was a balancing act, a constant tête-à-tête with danger that kept her heart racing even in moments of stillness. The stark contrast between her sparse lifestyle and the opulence she could afford highlighted a defiance that was as much a part of her as her own skin. It was a choice that carried the weight of isolation, a price she paid willingly, but not without its ghosts—the longing for peace of mind and human connection alike, both lost to the darkness of her profession.

Killing was a profitable business venture, especially when it came to inside hits. Those jobs paid a premium, but they came with their own set of challenges—cameras and various scanners, advanced AI-powered defenses, braid-equipped scum, and an endless array of paranoid detective and defensive squitos or larger drones. If you could navigate those obstacles, you had struck gold. But when off the job, it was best to stay out of sight. Yes, life Outside was tough, but with resources and know-how, you could make it comfortable.

And then there was the raw, almost primal satisfaction in outsmarting the labyrinth of security that cocooned her targets. Each successful hit was a testament to her skill, a silent scream against the oppression she felt from a world that had never welcomed her. Yet, in the quiet aftermath, when the adrenaline faded, Elena often found herself wrestling with a solitude that clawed at her—an emptiness those victories could not quite fill.

She had found her sweet spot a decade ago in the desolate snowscape of northern Sweden, just outside Kiruna—a former mining town. She was off the grid, but still only a few hours away by scooter from the European bullet network, which provided access to the world and her targets. Her home was under a small, private, unregistered dome—a haven from the elements and the world's prying eyes, ears, and electronics. But not the cold! Here, she could rest and plan her next move without the constant threat of detection looming over her.

It had been a while since Elena had been back to this place. The hit on Nyal Bahno had been a complete disaster, physically and emotionally exhausting. Weeks of surveillance had been necessary just to get close to the agoraphobic Bahno, and then the run-in with Jarod Lima had almost killed her. To top it off, after disposing of that threat, Bahno had escaped her clutches. It had made her question everything. Was it still worth it? She had enough money to retire for life, to live a simple but comfortable existence under a new identity in a domed city of her choosing. *It won't be a rich life, but it would be enough.* She could travel, paint, jog, and never work again. *Still sounds terrible.* Maybe she just liked killing too much. *Does that make me a psychopath?*

To Elena, the thought of retirement was like gazing into a nebula of possibilities, each more foreign and unsettling than the last. The idea of stepping into the light, of living without the veil of anonymity, was a horizon too distant, too alien. It stirred a restlessness in her—a fear not of death, but of irrelevance, of a life devoid of the shadows that had become her refuge, her identity.

She had always told herself it was a job. The only excitement it brought was the money. Possibly—just possibly—she also experienced that vague sense of satisfaction people with normal jobs felt. A sense of purpose and all that crap. *Or am I deluding myself?* She had to admit, maybe she didn't want to put the machinery of death away because she secretly enjoyed it. The moments when she was in close proximity to the target were the most thrilling, even more so than when the deed was done and the operation was complete. She got a rush when she was up close and could see or hear life fade away. Killing someone from an impromptu operations center with the help of a remotely controlled squito was, by comparison, unsatisfying. Blowing someone up with remotely detonated explosives or shooting someone from a distance with a sniper rifle felt equally detached and unfulfilling. *What does that say about someone?*

Fully acknowledging the thrill of the hunt, the exhilaration of being the harbinger of death, was like staring into the abyss and finding it staring back—familiar and inviting. This dark revelation was a mirror to her soul, threatening to reveal facets of her being she had dared not examine too closely. It was a dance with the devil that lent a grotesque beauty to her existence, a secret embrace of her darkest self that continued to both horrify and compel her. In the end, she didn't know what to think, but she did know that she wasn't ready to hang up the holster just yet.

Today, her doubts were cast aside when she saw the new additions to the job boards—Scott and his accomplices were on there, now along with their would-be hunters: Jarod Lima, Dean Kale, Riley Mack, and Wyatt Bruford. The bounties were high, almost as much as Scott himself. *Oh, the temptation...* The names on the job board, displayed virtually on her lens, were like a siren's call, pulling her back into the tempest with promises of gold and glory. Yes, beneath the excitement, a shadow of doubt lingered—it always would—but it was a fleeting thought, quickly crushed under the weight of ambition and the thrill of the chase.

She ran her fingers over the text hovering in front of her eyes, stopping at Jarod Lima. Blood surged through her veins as her fingertips pierced the virtual letters. She had offered to work with him, but the offer was rejected. That was fine—if they wanted to be adversaries, she could work with that. *Especially now that you're all over the wanted list.* Yes, there could be synergies here. She could hang back and let Jarod do the work, then hit the entire team at once. What a glorious job that would be! She'd be the hitman that everyone in the industry envied, but she had to admit that such an operation would be beyond even her skills. *Unless I go against my principles and use explosives. Get them all in one place, and kaboom.*

No, hitting them all at once was too risky. She'd have to start with one of them, as a trial run. If it went well, she could revisit the idea of hitting the rest of them in a bunch. *But how?* She had some intelligence gathered on all of them. They occasionally had downtime, private moments when they were more vulnerable. Bruford had a taste for the ladies of the night, Mack liked to hit the treadmills at local gyms, and Kale frequented bars, drinking shots alone. Lima was a wildcard and had mostly stayed off the grid since the Aegis job had started.

It wouldn't be easy, but Elena knew that if she wanted to hit them, she'd have to be patient and pick her targets carefully. She couldn't get reckless or let her desire for fame and glory cloud her judgment. These were trained killers, and they wouldn't allow themselves to be taken out easily. She had to be smart and careful, just like she always had been.

Starting with Mack or Kale seemed like the most logical choice, the other two being combat-trained. But the real challenge was *how* to hit them. Their defenses would make the use of killer squitos virtually impossible. Their AIs would be running defensive tactical algorithms around the clock, and their electronic warfare squitos would prevent her killers from gaining access. The electronics would also likely alert the city defenses, leading to a police presence. She would be caught in a matter of minutes. That meant a physical hit, and although she normally reveled in those, with these targets it was risky.

Elena needed to get them under a privacy shield—a forsaken back alley on the ground level or a high-class hotel room that provided such services. There, her killers could work without drawing attention. *They don't live in hotels, though.* On the job, they would rent apartments or squat in abandoned or empty ones Outside, where their presence wouldn't leave a trail. It made them practically impossible to locate. Logic pointed to Kale. He liked to drink, and on occasion, he visited not only dives and other dumps but fancy hotel bars. She could put a tail on him and strike when he least expected it. *But what method of execution?*

Elena ran her fingers through her hair, twirling a strand for a moment. *He's a man. I'm an attractive female.* She smiled to herself, realizing that Mr. Dean Kale might just be vulnerable to one of the oldest traps in the hitman game: the honey trap.

Jarod, Scott, and Adriel

Eleven whole minutes had elapsed since Dembwe's notification that they had spotted Scott, but it was their best lead yet in their pursuit. The man stubbornly continued to evade them, even now, a mere kilometer from their current location. Dembwe's exhaustive raids of Tokyo's underground sanctuaries had borne fruit at last. They had tracked Scott to Haneda, the old defunct Tokyo airport. However, the drone tracking him had caught only a fleeting glimpse before losing him in the adjacent part of the city with the same name.

Eleven minutes. A lot can happen in eleven minutes. Jarod's heart was pumping with that familiar blend of anticipation and dread, his palms working up a sweat as he briefly recalled how past operations had spiraled out of control in less time. But they finally had Scott on the ropes, with Dembwe's team canvassing the area now while Jarod and his crew were arriving on a screamer out of Singapore. Riley was already setting up comms, Kale was running surveillance via braid, and Jarod was studying Dembwe's briefing. Wyatt was sleeping, as usual. But they were ready. They were going to catch Scott, and they were going to do it now.

Fifteen minutes until deboarding, another forty to reach

Haneda Ota—an area still outside the Tokyo dome network—which added a layer of complexity. But that was to be expected. Even someone with Scott's talents would have trouble disappearing Inside, so seeking refuge in the concrete wilderness of the Outside was a logical step. Haneda was still a bustling hub, making it easy to blend in with the crowds. The inclement weather would add additional challenges. His weather app painted a picture of heavy clouds hanging low over Tokyo, with real-time aerials showing the central domes encumbered under a leaden blanket. The rain, an incessant drizzle, blurred the boundaries between sky and ground and painted the city in shades of gray. Nevertheless, such conditions worked both ways, and there was now a fair chance that Scott wouldn't be able to evade them again, with both teams bearing down on him.

To further increase their odds, Jarod would have preferred to bring in another contract team, but they were already pushing the limits—even for an operation Outside. Any additional drones or ground support would surely attract unwanted attention from the Japanese authorities. They had to tread carefully as it was to avoid raising suspicion.

He opened a new window and began following Dembwe's drone coverage of the city. Next to it, another window, another city—Frankfurt, where Dana was. The news reports suggested that the situation had slipped out of the police's control. The hostages and their captors alike had vanished through a tunnel system beneath the city.

I know you're still alive. I can feel it. It was an irrational feeling, of course—he knew one couldn't literally feel such things. But he allowed himself a moment of comfort in the thought. Nevertheless, images of Dana's face, strong yet so vulnerable, played in his mind, igniting a storm of helplessness and rage within him. *That, I can feel.* But as long as there was no confirmation of her death, he could hold onto hope. Amidst the chaos of the situation, the news reports confirmed that two police officers and one of the male hostage-takers had been killed in the crossfire within the tunnels. But there was still no news on Dana or the young girl. So, he held on, refusing to give in to despair until there was confirmation of their fate.

The media otherwise focused on the police's mishandling of the crisis. The hostage-takers were children, and two of them were among the casualties. The fact that they were Outies didn't change that they were just kids. The world would take notice, even if just a little, and accountability for the screw-up would be exerted.

The screamer touched down at Narita, and after clearing immigration, they boarded the Tokyo bullet headed into the city. As they arrived at Tokyo Station, one of Dembwe's men met them at the platform and briefed them on their next move. They had established an operations center in an old apartment in Haneda, just northeast of the old airport but south of the central domes. It was standard operating procedure—even the apartment was customarily damp and moldy. Wyatt shrugged off the news, remarking, "Same as always, then."

Upon arrival at the apartment, Riley and Kale immediately set up their equipment, preparing to monitor the drone footage from the safety of the apartment. Jarod and Wyatt, however, were eager to get out into the field, where they were normally more effective. This time, though, they already had plenty of flying eyes covering the area to the fullest extent of the operation's parameters. Their presence was mostly symbolic, but Jarod couldn't help feeling useless just sitting in the apartment, twiddling his thumbs until Kale and Riley got a hit. *Everyone needs to feel useful, including me.*

The only way for Jarod and Wyatt to make a real difference at this point was if they practically stumbled upon Scott. They had no cars at their disposal, so they were consigned to moving around on foot. They could have acquired one, but that would undoubtedly draw unwanted attention from the Tokyo authorities, even outside the central domes. The paperwork required for visitors to use a vehicle legally would leave a trail they couldn't risk.

This operation, like all the others before it, was not officially sanctioned. The less bureaucracy involved, the better, and illegally procuring a vehicle was out of the question, which meant walking. They were at most ten minutes away from the farthest points of the defined operating theater. If the drones spotted Scott more than five minutes away from either Jarod, Wyatt, or any of Dembwe's team, they would simply track and report until someone arrived. It wasn't the most efficient strategy, but it was the reality of conducting a covert operation in a sprawling metropolis like Tokyo. *I guess we can always hop on the bus.* Haneda still had some public transportation available, but it would likely take longer than traveling on foot.

The wind howled, and rain pelted his face, making Jarod feel as though he were being washed away. He had hoped the initial surge of anxiety upon Scott's sighting would subside, but his heart was still pounding, his palms damp with perspiration. The meteorological conditions were borderline for an op like this. Many things could go wrong, and he couldn't shake the awareness of that fact. His tactical was working overtime to filter out the worst of the noise as his drones continued to feed him real-time images from all corners of the theater. The wind was too strong for squitos, but the larger drones were holding up fine. They were doing everything they could to ensure success, but nevertheless, he couldn't help but feel uneasy.

The Frankfurt news feeds were minimized in the bottom right-hand corner of his visual field. He knew he should disable them. They were an unwarranted distraction, and it was antithetical to every fundamental operating protocol in existence to deliberately allow anything to divert attention from the mission at hand. But he didn't. Instead, he had created bespoke searches and alerts in case there were any references to Dana or the young girl. The alerts made a real-time feed redundant, so there was that, but he couldn't bring himself to terminate the feed altogether. *I just can't.* At least he muted the sound.

As the rain intensified, he sought shelter beneath the arch of an abandoned hotel entrance. The archway provided scant cover from the downpour, with raindrops splattering against the concrete and his waterproof gear. Watching the pulsating life of Tokyo move around him, Jarod felt like a ghost among the living. Each person's dull, everyday routine was a stark contrast to the limbo he inhabited, caught between the living and the dead, the past and the future. They were close to the prize, but Adriel had more than implied this would not be the end. *How do we get out of this? This... suicide machine I've put us in.*

He dug deep and pushed the doubts aside, forcing himself to focus on the task at hand. *Now is certainly not the time to brood.* His tactical said Wyatt had taken cover one street over, near the Ota Market, which had closed for the day. Down the thoroughfare, the imposing edifice of Tokyo's Dome One South loomed large, obstructing the vista entirely. From where he stood, Jarod could see nothing of Tokyo—only people rushing by, defying the horrible weather to go about their daily routines. They were going to and from work, grocery shopping, picking up their kids, getting a haircut. The hustle and bustle of everyday life went on, no matter the circumstances.

His braid had told him that Haneda used to be an average-income area before the domes. But now, it was a hub for the poor and disenfranchised. Its proximity to the dome border ensured that it remained as busy as ever, if not more so. People from all over Outside flocked here to find work or score a permit to go Inside.

Amidst the vast sea of people, it would be a futile endeavor for the naked eye to identify a particular individual—but not for state-of-the-art facial recognition software. He and Wyatt had it, Dembwe's team had it, the drones had it—all of it working tirelessly and relentlessly in the background. He could have brought up the targeting reticle on his retina display to watch it jump rapidly from face to face, scanning, extrapolating, and comparing faces against vast databases, but instead, he opted to turn off the entire HUD and take in the natural view. *No need to know everything it does.*

If he chose to, he could have just sat down, indulged in a good book, or taken a nap, allowing the drones to perform their duties. But the innate desire to feel useful refused to let him succumb to idleness. *It's the caveman principle. We don't leave everything to machines, not because they're incapable, but because we simply don't want to.*

"Hey," Wyatt interjected over the comm, echoing his sentiment, "we need to keep moving if we hope to score a hit out here. Otherwise, we might as well return to our apartment."

Fine. Jarod called up the itinerary that the braid's tactical had meticulously constructed based on the most probable locations where someone in Scott's predicament would seek refuge: weapon outlets, food sources, medical professionals, and various criminal elements that could aid in evasion and concealment. The tactical had even calculated a thirty percent likelihood that Scott would take extreme measures and alter his appearance to avoid detection, utilizing the latest in cosmetic surgery or genetic engineering. Haneda, according to the tactical, was the prime location for such activities, including the illegal ones. *Especially* the illegal ones. The task of finding these elusive venues, however, was another matter entirely, but the tactical was hard at work on the problem. In the interim, it would direct them to the more conventional options.

First on the list were hairdressers, followed by clothing stores and even novelty costume vendors. The mere mention of the latter elicited a chuckle from Jarod, but it was a box that needed ticking nonetheless.

The variety of businesses was impressive. The mere existence of novelty stores in the Outside implied that life beyond the safety of the Inside was not the abject misery many believed it to be. There was still room for some luxury and entertainment, beyond the bare necessities required for survival. Of course, Jarod was well aware of the dangers and misery that often plagued the Outside—he had seen more of it than most. However, even in the most miserable places, some pockets of civilization still managed to offer a degree of comfort and quality of life.

He reminded himself to focus, not to drift off as usual. Returning his attention to the itinerary, he investigated Scott's other options. Beyond the novelty stores, there were other possibilities. Beauticians, the cosmetic sections of supermarkets—any place that could aid in altering one's appearance, even through small means.

"All right, let's move," Jarod said to Wyatt, almost forgetting he was on the comm. He peered upwards at the deluge pouring from the heavens, resembling nothing short of a cascading waterfall. He gritted his teeth and marched onward toward their next destination, a nagging thought tugging at the back of his mind. *This is madness.*

Perhaps it was the relentless downpour, but a wave of melancholy suddenly threatened to overwhelm him. *What if they actually found Scott? What if they killed him?* Kale had posed this question only the other day.

"So what? What would it change?" he had said.

What indeed? The thought continued to plague him. *Had all of this been for nothing?* And to make matters worse, Dana was still missing.

"Partial hit on the female companion," Wyatt said over the comm, pulling him back to reality. Jarod swore under his breath, reminding himself not to indulge in any more distracting ruminations. "Forty percent probability it's her," Wyatt continued, promptly forwarding the location, a mere five-minute sprint away from their current position.

"You wanna check it out?" Jarod asked. Forty percent confidence wasn't great, but it wasn't like they had much else to do. Except indulge in more distracting ruminations.

Gazing at the picture of the woman, Jarod's braid instantly determined that she had likely undergone extensive cosmetic work, with changes made to her skin tone, facial symmetry, and even her bone structure. Factoring in these alterations, the AI's confidence level rose to a respectable seventy-one percent, making it worth investigating. They set off toward the rendezvous point suggested by the tactical.

Sometimes, Jarod couldn't help but wonder if they were becoming too reliant on all these AI applications. As he pulled his hood up and braved the relentless downpour, he tried to recall the last time he made a decision for himself, without the aid of any kind of decision-making software. *Hell, I can't even decide what to have for lunch without asking the damn braid.*

As they closed in on the location, the drones were able to

provide more accurate readings, confirming the woman's identity. Just before they reached the rendezvous point, the drones also identified Scott with over ninety percent confidence, taking into account the physical changes he had likely undergone. He was here, no longer able to elude them. Slippery as he may have been, nobody could hide forever.

"Activity?" he asked.

"They're just talking," Dembwe said over the comms. "Waiting for something. Or someone."

Dembwe promptly streamed the footage, revealing that Scott and the woman were waiting at a street corner outside a robonoodle place. They weren't eating, confirming Wyatt's earlier suspicion that they were there to meet someone. *Or they've just finished?* But if they were done with their business, why were they still loitering around the robovendor? *Nobody hangs around a vending machine just for the ambiance.*

"Privacy screens?" he asked.

"Of course. The best money can buy. We're working on getting through, but it'll take at least twenty minutes," Dembwe replied.

He instructed Dembwe to stream the footage to Kale as well, knowing that the added computing power might shave off a few precious seconds.

Although, do we need to hear what they're saying? After all, their mission was to take him out, nothing more. But at this moment, he simply couldn't resist the curiosity. Scott was just a pawn in a larger game, a mere lieutenant in the grand scheme of things. His death was clearly important to his employer, but hardly the endgame, and Jarod wanted to know what it was. The world was burning after London, and Jarod was pouring gasoline on the fire. *So, should I be? And shouldn't I at least know why?*

Dembwe's voice cut through the silence, interrupting his thoughts. "We have a shot," he said, awaiting the order to strike. *No. I should just carry out my orders and move on.*

"Any sign of them moving?" Jarod asked, hoping for more time to consider his options.

Dembwe replied in the negative, and Jarod made a decision.

"Hold off until we get there. Keep working on the crypto. We're five minutes out. Let me know if there's any change." He wanted to know what the targets were discussing, to see if he could get the inside scoop on the motivations of his employer. After all, Adriel had subtly threatened him the last time they spoke, and he couldn't afford to be caught off guard again. Staying informed was a sound strategy.

Wyatt must have sensed his hesitation and switched to a private channel. "Are you sure about this?" he asked.

"No," Jarod admitted.

But Wyatt didn't press the issue. He knew Jarod better than anyone and trusted his instincts. They fell into a tense silence as they made their way toward the rendezvous point.

Arriving at the site, the status quo still prevailed. They took cover in a small courtyard located approximately fifty meters away from Scott's location, concealing themselves from his view but maintaining close enough proximity to intervene when the time came. Dembwe was perched on a nearby rooftop, keeping a watchful eye on the target's movements, sniper rifle at the ready. Jarod, meanwhile, projected the gun sight's perspective onto his lens, granting him the same view. Before long, a third, unknown person materialized.

"Run facial recognition," he ordered and took it upon himself to do the same. Regrettably, their efforts proved fruitless—the individual in question did not appear in any database.

"Intriguing," he mused, the words, meant primarily for his ears alone, escaping his lips.

"Do we engage?" Dembwe interjected again, this time his tone carrying the weight of impatience. However, Jarod remained silent, his desire to hear the conversation now surpassing his desire to bring the mission to a close. It eclipsed the lure of the promised financial reward and even his fear of Aegis's reprisal if he failed.

In that fleeting moment, his curiosity metamorphosed into an all-consuming obsession. He couldn't shake it off, no matter how much he willed it to vanish. As despair engulfed him once more, the same despair he had felt after the assassination of

Fiscal/Siscal in New York, he froze. He had remained steadfast since then—devoid of emotions, able and professional—but now those emotions were resurfacing, and with greater intensity. *Like a clean drug addict, relapsing.*

He was overwhelmed by a profound sense of remorse as he remembered what he had devolved into—a cold-blooded killer. A part of him was repulsed by his own actions, and a sense of disgust surged within him. The irony was palpable. He was in a position to extinguish a life with a mere utterance, and it was a man he should have felt nothing for, but instead of animosity toward Scott, his loathing was directed inward. *This wasn't how it was meant to be.* Although, if he were truthful with himself, he knew the inevitable had been set in motion the moment he accepted Henry James Gibson's proposal in that towering London skyscraper. But he had let himself be dragged down that path regardless.

Just then, in the midst of his breakdown, a fourth figure materialized before their eyes. His tactical equipment identified the newcomer as Chinese with over ninety percent accuracy. The third individual introduced the fourth to Scott and Dai, and an exchange of pleasantries ensued with handshakes, nods, and bows, indicating that they were meeting for the first time.

"They're making a move," Dembwe cautioned.

Indeed they were. "It's now or never," Wyatt said, urgency rising in his voice.

Yet at that moment, Jarod's conscience still waged its battle. No part of him wanted to give the order to take the shot, and he no longer had a desire to know more about Scott and his machinations. All he wanted was to head to Frankfurt, locate Dana, get the hell out of Europe, and leave it all behind.

"Jarod!" Dembwe's voice broke through the silence, but Jarod was incapable of replying. The moment stretched on, the battlefield within him encroaching ever more on the one before him, threatening to take over completely. His finger gently tapped the side of his pistol, still at his side. The cold metal brought back memories of past kills—faces blurred and long forgotten. They welled up inside him, whispering, imploring him to run away. But with a momentous effort, he managed to snap out of it. "Engage," he commanded. The sniper rifle went off, but the target had moved.

"Miss," he heard over the comm.

Another shot followed. "Miss."

Then a third. "Hit."

He watched as one of the figures fell—not Scott, but the third unknown person. The rest took cover, seeking refuge from the attack, as Dembwe, in a last-ditch attempt at success, continued firing, but his efforts proved futile. "Target no longer in sight," Dembwe was forced to report.

The others sought his approval to pursue. He authorized it but remained still, opting not to follow. The sounds of the city, muffled by the rain, receded into the background, leaving Jarod isolated, enveloped in a bubble. The echo of the gunfire that followed brought him out of it. They hit like a gavel, condemning him for his failure. The adrenaline rush faded, leaving behind a hollow emptiness, another addition to his list of defeats. The missed shots were not just a tactical error, but a damning exposé on his mental state.

"What the hell just happened?" Wyatt's voice crackled over the comms, breathless from the pursuit and laced with anger. But Jarod had no desire to engage in a heated exchange. He was exhausted—mentally and physically drained—and didn't have the strength to further deal with the situation. All he wanted was to retreat from the chaos and find solace in a hotel room, complete with a relaxing soak in the bath, a generous dose of opiates, and a bottle of fine Scotch to help him disappear into oblivion.

"Shut it, Wyatt," he barked into the comms. "And get to work."

Robertson Quay, that venerable haunt of the Singaporean affluent, lay uncharacteristically quiet this morning—more so than Jarod had anticipated. The tranquility of the quay, with its muted conversations and the soft lap of water against the concrete pier, seemed to amplify the chaos in Jarod's mind. The quiet served as an unfavorable backdrop to the worry he felt for Dana, and the frustration of recent failures.

Only a handful of patrons occupied tables at Coffee Pod, the chosen rendezvous for his next check-in with Adriel. The café sported a rustic, albeit artificial charm that usually drew quite the morning crowd. Today, it whispered of solitude and secrets. Jarod chose a secluded table near the back, where the murmur of the quay's water could still be heard. *I will barely need to use the privacy screen.* He did, of course, taking no chances with uninvited listeners, whether human or silicon-based. Adriel's penchant for face-to-face meetings was somewhat bewildering—Jarod failed to see the need to involve human ears in the already complex equation. *Old school? Or a Luddite, stubbornly clinging to old ways.*

It was true, of course, that remote communication and cryptography had their vulnerabilities, but Adriel's disposition was perhaps a tad excessive. Moreover, Jarod was more than a little annoyed at the time spent on a screamer from Tokyo. While those supersonic, LEO-skimming jets were the fastest in the world, it was still a solid two and a quarter hours of his life he would never get back, including time spent on bullets getting to and from airports. *All time that could've been spent more profitably, in the service of our mutual employer, or in the pursuit of other activities. Such as ruminating over life choices and drinking Scotch?* Each minute on that plane had felt like a theft, a robbery not just of time but of possibilities—of moments that could have been spent unraveling Dana's whereabouts or at least seeking solace in those vices of his. *Speaking of which, time to get to work.*

The repercussions of his botched assassination attempts on Bahno, and most recently Scott in Tokyo, were waiting. The elusive nature of these men made it unlikely they'd get another shot at them, and failure to neutralize their targets would not sit well with Aegis—a legitimate and respectable corporation, perhaps, but one with a less-than-legitimate reputation in certain circumstances. It was clear to Jarod that they were the sort of employers who expected nothing but success from their operatives.

While the sting of failure was familiar and should have bothered him more, it didn't. Jarod's thoughts were preoccupied with Dana, and any repercussions from Aegis paled in comparison. The gnawing anxiety over her safety was eating away at him. The authorities had yet to locate either her or the young girl. But on the other hand, they hadn't uncovered any bodies either. *She's safe. She has to be.*

According to the news reports, she was likely making her way toward the dome but hadn't surfaced at any border control stations. *Had she made it through undetected?* If so, why hadn't she contacted him? *Because she's clever.* She may not have been trained like him, but she was too shrewd to risk exposing herself with any communication within the confines of the dome. To get in touch with him without revealing herself, she would need access to high-level crypto-tech, far beyond what any normal citizen would have. *Legacy or any private contractor worth a damn would easily dismantle any commercially available privacy screen—she knows this. She'll find a way to reach me. Or vice versa.*

But he didn't have the luxury of time for a side gig at the moment. Dembwe and Wyatt were still hot on the trail of Scott and his female companion, and Riley and Kale were diligently tracing their digital footprint. He had little to contribute in this regard, he realized. Dembwe and Wyatt could handle the fieldwork without his assistance. After the last operation, one could argue they might even perform better without him. *So, maybe I can afford a side gig?*

Jarod couldn't help but ponder what was truly the main gig and what was the side gig. He loved Dana more than anything else, and the mere thought of losing her was unbearable. She was far more important to him than any job or contract. She was anything but a side gig—his concern for her was an undercurrent to everything he did. Her safety was the beacon that guided him, especially in the murky waters of his profession. In these moments of quiet reflection, she was both his anchor and his compass.

Jarod was so lost in thought, he didn't even notice when

Adriel took a seat across from him. There was no exchange of pleasantries between them. For a good thirty seconds, neither of them spoke. The silence stretched, filled with the unsaid, tension building like the electric charge before rain. *If you're Outside, that is.* The clink of cups and the low hum of conversation from the other patrons seemed to fade into the background, leaving just the two of them in a bubble around their table. Finally, Adriel broke the silence.

"You're unhappy," he stated matter-of-factly. "You have doubts." He didn't pose these as questions. "And you're preoccupied with your wife's safety."

"Wow. You read me like an open book."

Adriel didn't seem fazed. "Ah, sarcasm. I see you're still good at that."

"Gee, thanks."

Adriel turned to the waiter and placed an order for an Americano. "Okay," he said. "Let's address these issues. Shall we start with your doubts?"

As good a place as any, Jarod thought. He briefly contemplated broaching the subject that weighed most heavily on his mind—could Aegis help him locate Dana? They had unimaginable resources that could aid in the search, but at what cost? He decided against bringing it up, at least not yet. Not until Riley and Kale came up empty. Instead, he asked Adriel about their recent targets.

"The men we killed," he began. "Are they guilty of what you say they are?"

Adriel chuckled. "They're guilty of *something.*"

Before arriving, Jarod had gone against his better judgment and asked Kale to delve deeper into their targets—not just to locate them but to verify their involvement in the London attack. He had even requested Kale perform retrospective checks on the individuals they had already eliminated. None of them had proven to be saints, but Kale couldn't verify Adriel's claims about their complicity. *Not unsurprisingly.*

Jarod was well aware there was nothing to find—at least nothing that would hold up in court. They were all hired to do a job, to eliminate targets without the burden of proof that Legacy would have to provide in a legitimate legal system. Adriel took a sip of his coffee and said, "We tell you who to hit, you hit them, and you get paid. That's how this works."

"So we're really just murderers?" Jarod said.

Adriel didn't reply. The silence that followed his question was a void, swallowing any semblance of justification Jarod had clung to. In its absence, he was left with a raw, unfiltered reflection of what he had become—or perhaps, what he had always been, except when they tracked Outies illegally trespassing in the domes. At least then, they hadn't killed anyone. *Why did I bother asking?* He already knew Adriel didn't have answers.

Adriel changed the subject, asking about Jarod's concerns for his wife. He gave Jarod a pathetic spin about how eliminating targets like Scott and Bahno would make the world a safer place—not only for her but for everyone. Then he transferred a file containing a new list of targets. The columns of names glowing in bright terminal-green font on his lens were another tangible manifestation of the cycle of violence they perpetuated—a never-ending loop that promised action but no resolution, engagement but no satisfaction. Each name was another life to be erased, a potential echo of past burdens and future regrets.

"What's this?" Jarod asked, despite knowing exactly what it was.

Adriel smiled. "Surely, you're not naive? You don't think that because you clear out a bit of weed, the lawn stays pristine forever?"

Jarod skimmed through the list of targets, realizing that they were Lux Aeterna's replacements for the ones they had already eliminated.

"So, for every man we eliminate, someone else takes their place," Jarod said. "Why bother?" *A world of peace and stability, my ass.*

"Why bother taking a shower?" Adriel replied. "You'll just be dirty again the next day."

"I may not understand the endgame here," Jarod said, "but

you and I both know that whatever's on the other side of this isn't what you think."

Adriel patted Jarod's forearm. "Keep tracking Scott and start on the new list. We'll see what we can do about locating your wife and the girl, if you wish. If they're still alive."

Adriel paid the bill, got up to leave, then sat back down, re-engaging the privacy screen. "And one more thing. The woman you've been having trouble with is Elena Petrova. A freelancer like yourself. We don't know who contracted her. It could be Alixha, it could be someone else. Regardless, you're authorized to hit her. Get her out of the way."

Jarod exhaled, tired of the conversation.

"Don't be like that," Adriel said. "We knew there was a distinct possibility of you becoming a target yourself. It was unavoidable, even. Well, now it's happened, so you may want to put your tech nerds on the case. Find her, and get rid of her. Okay?"

Jarod didn't reply as Adriel left. He finished his coffee and started heading back to the Changi train, before boarding a screamer to Tokyo.

Anya Pacula and Henry James Gibson

Anya Pacula cautiously peered around the corner into the executive dining hall. Henry, a glass in hand, was seated on the couch by the panoramic window, likely sipping Scotch. Meanwhile, the serving staff busily cleared the room's table. Her pulse quickened, each tiny step toward the entrance feeling heavier. A lump formed in her throat. *Why am I nervous?* she admonished herself. *All I want is to defect! To betray? To abandon?* The right word still eluded her, but she had tossed and turned over it for weeks. Nevertheless, it was time. In the end, every endeavor faces its own margin call—the moment when all debts come due, in more ways than one. And she wanted hers before that happened. *So, you're damned right, I'm nervous.*

She had been in business with Henry for over twenty-five years, and they had known each other for almost forty. As one of the most senior officers in the company, she ranked just below Chen and Warburton, but she and Henry were undoubtedly closer than anyone else. The C-suite might have been on equal footing formally, but the two of them shared a bond that transcended professional hierarchy. *At least I'd like to think so.* Maybe you're never really friends with colleagues, particularly with the likes of Gibson. Perhaps that was the question she was really about to ask—whether they indeed were friends. Or if they still would be after her request.

Well, there's no point in putting it off. She knew from experience that the best time to ask Gibson for anything was right after lunch, when he had his Scotch in front of the panorama. It was then that he was most content, his senses lulled by the alcohol, his belly full, and his attention drawn to the vista of lower Manhattan, toward the Hudson, toward the levee keeping the water at bay, toward the geodesic latticework of the dome built on top of it, towering over them, protecting them. His empire.

Anya straightened her dress and jacket, running her fingers through her hair to make sure she looked presentable. With a deep breath, she strode into the room, the click of heels on the polished floor marking a countdown to the moment of truth. She approached and took a seat next to Gibson on the couch.

"Anya," Gibson acknowledged her with a nod. "Beautiful day." He gestured toward the stunning view of Manhattan outside the window. "On paper, we don't own any of the buildings you see in front of you, but we still do, don't we?" It wasn't a question but a statement of fact.

Anya knew the story well. It was one of Gibson's favorite anecdotes, trotted out on occasions like this. *I can read you like an open book, old man.* She resisted the urge to roll her eyes. The familiarity of the anecdote did little to ease the tension knotted in her shoulders. *He can read me just as well*, she reminded herself. While Gibson's casual displays of power were tiresome, they still signified a critical gulf between their positions.

"Yes, sir. We own the only structure that really matters," she replied dutifully, following his finger as it pointed upwards, toward the gleaming dome.

Gibson leaned back against the couch, his eyes fixed on her. "I know you want something," he said, cutting straight to the chase. "You, Chen, and Warburton have been whispering in my ear for years, telling me you can get things from me after lunch. But I'm not stupid." He chuckled, but there was a hard edge to his voice. "Or maybe I am. Or maybe I've just let you think that all these years. Who knows?"

Anya felt the weight of his gaze—sharp, calculating—peeling back the layers of her composure. *It's time or I'll soon lose my nerve.*

"I want out," Anya said, blunt and direct. There was no point in sugar-coating it. Gibson didn't seem surprised by her request, nor did he appear angry or upset.

"I know," he replied calmly. "You always were the conscience of the group. I'm not surprised you're struggling."

Anya took a deep breath, trying to gather her thoughts. "I'm just not sure what we're doing anymore," she said finally. "I'm a businesswoman, not a warmonger."

"Warmonger," Gibson repeated, his voice contemplative. "War. Is that what you think we're doing?" He took a sip of his Scotch, and Anya remained silent. "I suppose you're right," he said after a few moments of awkward silence. "This really is a nice Scotch. Do you want one?"

Anya shook her head. She was never a fan of Scotch.

"Right, I forgot," Gibson said. He took another sip and then continued. "Well, it's the same thing in the end. War and business. Don't you agree?"

She had doubts. While any competition, struggle, or conflict could be described with the terminology of warfare, there lay a vast gulf between that and actually taking up arms—a full-fledged war on a colossal scale, no less. Nevertheless, that was the course they had taken. Aegis had chosen to retaliate against Alixha using her own methods. The repercussions of their actions were snowballing out of control. The attacks were incessant, directed at Aegis assets, with retribution forthcoming, both financially and physically. Private mercenaries, black ops, and sabotage—all of which were not typically part of the corporate handbook. In its aftermath, lives and livelihoods were obliterated, ordinary citizens becoming collateral damage in what could only be characterized as terror, if not a full-blown war. *Call it what you will, but it's too much.*

The planet was in turmoil, a state of utter chaos. Their scheme to weaken Alixha had proven to be a catastrophic miscalculation. The notion of fighting fire with fire had misfired. *And other such trite aphorisms,* Anya thought.

"I demand the immediate activation of my parachute," she declared. "I expect compensation as per the agreement, and I desire to depart."

Gibson shifted on the sofa, turning to face Anya partially. "I will release you, Anya. I promise. But I require your presence for another eighteen to twenty-four months, until this operation is complete." His words were a leash, tethering her to a future she no longer desired, but with enough slack to instill a sense of hope. *Better than an outright rejection,* she thought. *And make no mistake, he has the power to outright reject me.*

"Once that is accomplished," Gibson continued, "I will ensure that you are set for life. You can finally get that private bubble vineyard in the south of France, or whatever your dream was all about again. But not until we're finished."

Anya remained silent, knowing what was to follow. Gibson wouldn't lash out; he rarely did. He seldom raised his voice and always seemed to be in high spirits, even content. No, it was time for *the* speech.

"You believe that we've gone too far," he remarked, once again not posing a question.

Yep. Here we go.

"We fanned the flames, and as a result, we destroyed and claimed lives," he stated calmly, his tone condescending. "But let's be honest, what are we doing that hasn't been done countless times before? Look out there. People like us and people like them will always exist." He gestured toward the streets below their towering structure. "Perhaps you're correct. We're at war. This time, it's us. Next time, it will be someone else. It doesn't matter who is fighting or why. Be it in the name of democracy, freedom, equality, power, control, profit, or any other cause. State-sponsored warfare, terrorist-sponsored warfare, private or corporate—the specifics don't matter. We'll always be up here, and they'll be down there," he said, gesturing again toward the streets below. "Perhaps those of us up here are more untouchable now than ever before, but life will go on—for us and for them. And then the cycle will begin again. The players may change, but the game will remain the same. Europe in the twentieth century, 9/11, Hong Kong, Ukraine, Taiwan, Alphabet in 2047, Meta, Microsoft, and now it's our turn. We can't help ourselves; it's in our nature."

Anya listened as Gibson painted the world in shades of gray, his rhetoric weaving a tapestry of inevitability and resigned acceptance. His words were meant to soothe, to justify, but she didn't believe them. Not anymore. She nodded, rising from the sofa and approaching the panoramic window, placing her hand against the cool surface. The view was breathtaking—that much was undeniable. The authority and influence wielded by Aegis were equally remarkable. She pivoted to face Gibson.

"I'll do it," she said. "I'll stay, but not because your Machiavellian pseudo-philosophy convinced me, but because I need the cash." It was a concession, a white flag raised not in defeat but in pragmatism. Or at least, that's what she told herself. "You wouldn't believe that, would you?" she continued. "After all this time at the top of the earning spectrum, I still need it."

Gibson held her gaze for a moment. Another power play—one where the first to look away lost. He grinned. Anya tried to hold his gaze as long as possible, but it was a lost cause. She had already lost the moment their eyes met, possibly even before entering the dining room. *I lost ages ago,* she thought, as she broke eye contact and departed, hearing Gibson shift on the leather couch behind her, savoring another sip of his Scotch.

Dana

Brett had come through, the contact materializing as promised. *I hope you and Daemon are alright,* Dana thought as she and Aea navigated through the neon-soaked Bahnhofviertel, deep in the seedy underbelly of Frankfurt Central. The air was thick with the scent of overcooked food from nearby eateries, mixed with the tang of electronic miasma from ubiquitous vapes and the sharp stink of traditional tobacco. Sounds of dome life—muffled conversations, the distant whir of drones and public transport, and the hum of electric cars—melded into a constant urban soundtrack that enveloped them as they moved. It was a welcome contrast to the claustrophobic confines of both the apartment and the tunnels.

The man they sought was holed up in a back alley, in a building her braid told her once served as a bordello. Now a clock shop, it was wedged unobtrusively between a bustling robo-sushi joint and yet another bordello—this one, disturbingly, still active, as evidenced by the scantily clad girls loitering outside, smoking, vaping, sipping coffee. *I guess they're on a break.* They stood there, seeming bored and disinterested, not speaking. *Like they're counting down the minutes until their shift is over. Like any other boring job.*

At this establishment, the women loitering outside were real—that much was clear, even to a casual observer. This was in contrast to many other places in the Bahnhofviertel where synths were commonplace. Unlike most robo-sex toys, these women had all the physical imperfections inherent to those of flesh and blood. Still, they seemed just as disinterested in their surroundings as their synthetic counterparts in power-saving mode. *Perhaps,* Dana mused, *they were synths with top-of-the-line models equipped with advanced AIs, designed to mimic the very real human behavior of boredom? Maybe even custom models with physical flaws deliberately incorporated into their appearance, catering to specific preferences or fetishes?*

No, Dana decided. *These were real. No dolls or genetic engineering here.* The dim glow of a blinking neon sign spelling S-E-X threw flickering shadows over their faces, revealing tales of weariness and resilience. One woman had a visible C-section scar on her bare stomach, while others sported love handles, sagging skin, cellulite, and other imperfections common in people without the benefits of genetic engineering. Sometimes still while young. *Clearly not top of the range—human or synth.* Immediately, a pang of guilt hit her. *These are people, Dana! Don't be mean.* Judgment was easy; understanding, not so much, she reminded herself. *But in the end, we all navigate the same waters of life, just in different boats.*

In truth, the women outside the bordello were not unattractive. One or two of them might even be considered pretty, in the right light. But the contrast with the perfect, synthetic dolls so prevalent in other parts of the Bahnhofviertel was hard to ignore. *I'm paying way too much attention to this.*

Dana noticed Aea's gaze linger too, and couldn't help but feel a tinge of annoyance. She didn't want to draw any unnecessary attention to themselves, and staring at the women like they were some kind of spectacle was a surefire way to do just that.

"Don't look," she said, her tone firm but not unkind. Aea quickly averted her gaze, looking a little embarrassed.

She paused for a moment, taking in the shop's quaint facade, a stark contrast to its brightly lit neighbors. Dana approached the door of the clock shop and knocked, but there was no answer.

She tried again, and again, not giving up, just as Brett had instructed. The man they were looking for was something of a recluse, so she knew he had to be in there somewhere. She kept knocking harder until finally, a shadowy figure appeared behind the curtain covering the glass door. *Everything certainly fits the description Brett gave: clock shop, brothels, wild-eyed looney. We've got the right place, at least. That's something.*

The man pointed angrily to the closed sign on the door, as if they couldn't read. "We're closed!" he shouted, swiftly pulling the curtain shut again, disappearing as abruptly as he had appeared. *Damn.*

Dana took a deep breath and called out to him. "Mr. Fernis!" she said, knocking again. And again. And again. Each time she knocked harder, until her knuckles were sore and she thought she might break the glass pane. Finally, the man reappeared, looking even more irritable than before. He fiddled with the locks for a moment, then tore the door open. "What!?" he barked.

"Stefan Brett sent us," Dana said, hoping to diffuse the situation. The man's expression changed in an instant.

"Brett, huh?" he said after a moment of surprise. "That old fucker. Well, why didn't you just say so?" He scoffed and slammed the door shut, causing the window pane to rattle alarmingly. The sound startled the girls next door, who briefly looked up from their coffees, vapes, and cigarettes before returning to their apathetic haze.

Undeterred, Dana knocked again and again, until the man reappeared. Now, even the girls seemed to take proper notice of the commotion, their boredom temporarily interrupted by the activity. The man swung the door open violently, his impatience growing by the second. "What?" he demanded once more.

"We need your help," Dana said, determined not to be intimidated.

Fernis was about to speak, but before he had a chance, she added, "Brett told us to tell you that you owe him. I'm not sure what that means, but he's calling in his favor."

Fernis froze at Dana's mention of Brett's favor, visibly taken aback. The air seemed to thicken, the balance of power shifting. The man stared at them, Dana's heart racing as she wondered if he would keep ignoring their plight. But after a moment of hesitation, he relented.

"Fuck! Fine. Come on in," he grumbled, stepping aside to let them enter the shop. The girls outside the bordello stirred, their interest piqued by the commotion. "Oh, what are you looking at?" he shouted at them, before slamming the door shut even harder. The glass held, but just barely.

"Clocks, huh?" Aea tentatively said as Fernis led them toward the back of the shop. She looked anxiously at Dana as if asking for permission to speak. *Go ahead, girl. I'm just grateful I don't have to carry all the conversation here.*

Aea took the hint and continued. "My dad has one. A mechanical one, I mean. Around his wrist. He's the only one in our house who does," she said, a note of pride in her voice. Dana watched as a nostalgic spark lit in Aea's eyes, offering a rare glimpse into the person she truly was before her world turned upside down—someone with interests, desires, and dreams. It was a moment of innocence and pride amidst the chaos, a reminder of what they were fighting for.

Fernis chuckled. "Listen," he said, motioning toward the clocks surrounding them.

"What? I don't hear anything," Aea responded.

"Exactly! No ticking of the clocks here. All broken, turned off, or fake. It's just a front, young lady. Shhhh. Don't tell anyone," he said with a sly grin. His demeanor had changed entirely, from irritable to almost jovial, as soon as the favor was mentioned. *Though he hasn't said what that favor might be. Probably better that I don't know,* Dana thought.

She looked around the cramped little shop, taking in the rows of grandfather clocks and analog wristwatches. "Must be some nice value here," she said, trying to make conversation.

Fernis scoffed. "It's all fake. Cheap knock-offs. Like I said, a front. Come on back," he said, gesturing for them to follow. Clearly, there was more to this fake clockmaker than met the eye. *He sure as hell isn't a cop.* Someone Brett knew from the underworld, no doubt.

As they followed Fernis into the back of the shop, Dana couldn't help but notice the man's disheveled appearance. He looked like a complete mess, with a crumpled white shirt, unbuttoned at the top and covered in what looked like spaghetti sauce—or blood. *Not sure which would be worse,* she mused. His eyes were wild and jumpy, and he had the shakes. *Drug use?* Whatever the cause, Dana saw a man dancing on the edge of something. *Whatever your cliff edge is, please wait to fall off it until we're gone.*

The back room was even messier. The threshold between the shop's front and its hidden depths felt like crossing into another realm. Dana's senses heightened—the air now charged with the tang of metal and an undercurrent of desperation. Every step felt like a descent deeper into the shadows they were trying to escape. For a moment she couldn't believe she what she was pursuing, as if she had stepped into a spy flick, far removed from the mundane negotiations and administration that normally filled her days. But here they were.

It was clear that the back was host to a different kind of operation altogether. The room was cluttered with all sorts of equipment—imagers, servers, medical devices of various kinds. And then there was the dental chair, which Dana suspected wasn't used for any kind of dental work. *Braid modifications,* Dana guessed. *Illegal ones.*

Aea looked horrified, and Dana couldn't blame her. This was clearly not what either of them had expected. Fernis seemed to pick up on their discomfort and attempted to make a joke. "Oh, don't worry," he said with a forced laugh. "I'm not Dr. Mengele or anything."

The attempt at humor fell flat, and when Fernis noticed, the contrived laugh trailed off into an embarrassed chuckle before finally giving way to silence. Aea looked confused, perhaps clueless as to who Dr. Mengele was.

Fernis leaned back in his creaky lounge chair, seemingly unfazed by his faux pas. He looked at Dana and Aea with a hint of amusement in his eyes. "Anyway," he said, "I work for people who have no options on the open market. Like yourselves, I'm guessing. I mean, why else would Brett send you?"

Dana started to explain—how they needed to stay low until they could contact help, how Aea was an Outie with no permit to reside or even visit the Inside, and how finding her, even though Dana herself was legal, could lead to Aea being discovered.

"The good news is, I can help," Fernis said with a grin.

Dana felt a surge of relief. "How much?" she asked cautiously.

Fernis chuckled. "If Brett sent you, I better not charge you. Not that I don't *want* to, mind you. But if I do, Brett will kill me. Figuratively speaking, of course. No, he wouldn't do something like that. He'd throw me in the slammer, and there, someone else would kill me. Not because of Brett, you know. No, no. Just generally. But the end result would be the same, wouldn't it? Me dead."

Relief now coursed through Dana, mixed with gratitude. Brett's unseen hand had guided them to this odd man, who had turned out to be a lifeline in their darkest hour. Outwardly, she just nodded, still content to remain oblivious to the details of Brett's and Fernis's relationship. It was obviously tangled in old alliances and debts, something to remain cautious about.

"Okay," Fernis said, "down to business."

He rose from his creaky chair and strode over to a nearby table covered in medical equipment. Dana had no clue what most of the instruments were for, but she was strangely relieved when Fernis's twitchy hand passed over a neat row of scalpels and instead landed on two syringes. Aea, nevertheless, looked on in horror. That now-familiar protective instinct surged in Dana, her resolve hardening as she watched Aea brace herself. The girl looked terrified as Fernis approached, the needles trembling in his hands. This young girl, thrust into a whirlwind of danger, was about to pay yet another price—to live with the weight of a new identity and a positively uncomfortable procedure. But the clockmaker's words were reassuring, if a bit cryptic.

"Don't worry, little lady," he said, motioning toward his trembling hand. "I know. That's what the left one is for." With that, he plunged the second needle into his own thigh and groaned as he pushed down on the plunger. "At least, I *hope* it's the left one," he muttered, before his hand steadied and a smile spread across his face. "There we go. Just a little cocktail to temporarily put a stop to the shaky nonsense."

Aea seemed to relax, if only slightly. Fernis went on to insert the needle into Aea's left shoulder, explaining as he did so, "This will last for a week or so. It's a marker that will trick the city identity scans. Nanobots. It will fade after a few weeks once the body absorbs them. But for now, it will allow the girl to move about any dome without being flagged. Mmm, okay?"

Dana nodded, relieved that there was indeed a solution to their problem. She glanced at Aea to make sure she was okay. Aea gave her a thumbs-up.

"You'll have to get her a braid," Fernis continued. "I don't have any. I just do mods. Any commercial variant will do. The marker will make sure she isn't flagged when they install it. You'll have to use the identities I'll provide, though. From now on."

Aea's face fell. "Like, forever?" she asked.

Fernis nodded, his wild eyes confirming the finality of their new reality. "But what about my sister? My dad?" Aea asked, desperation creeping into her voice. Dana ached for the girl—for the dreams lost and the connections severed. Fernis looked at a loss, clearly unsure of what to say. Dana held Aea's hand, offering reassurance. "Don't worry," she said. "We'll figure something out. But right now, we need to stay hidden until we contact Jarod, okay? He'll know what to do."

Aea looked scared out of her wits, yet Dana saw a flicker of resilience in her eyes, an echo of her own determination to weather this storm. They both shared the resolve to push through, but Dana couldn't blame the girl for wavering. The situation was deeply unfair, but they had no choice but to make the best of it.

"Now for your identity spoofs," Fernis said. "Another injection for the girl to complement the marker. For you, I'll just upload some code to your braid."

Dana raised an eyebrow skeptically. "That simple, huh?"

Fernis chuckled. "No, not really," he said, explaining the complexities of the process as he prepared the second injection for Aea. Dana didn't understand most of it, but all she could do was hope that Fernis knew what he was doing. She hoped that Jarod and the rest of their team were safe and that they'd be reunited soon. Kale and Riley would be able to shed some light on things.

Fernis administered the second injection to Aea. This time, the girl barely flinched. Dana breathed a sigh of relief. "All good?" she asked, her concern thinly veiled.

Aea gave her a thumbs-up. "Didn't even sting this time," she said with a smile.

Dana gently patted Aea on the back and brushed a strand of hair out of her eyes. *Good girl.* She had held up remarkably well through all this. Most people would have crumbled under the weight of such circumstances, but Aea had proven herself tough as nails. Or maybe it was all a facade. Maybe she was in shock, on the verge of breaking down. There was no way to tell.

"What about me?" Dana asked Fernis.

"Already done," Fernis replied calmly. "Check your Basic."

Dana accessed her Basic and confirmed that all of her identity information had been changed. She was now Dana Limon, not Dana Lima. It was a simple change, but it meant everything for their survival.

"Like I said, yours will stick," Fernis continued, satisfaction evident in his voice. "The girl's won't. After you get her a braid, I've left the code for her identity in your inventory for you to upload. It comes with instructions, but it's easy. Once you upload it, she'll be Anna Limon. You're mother and daughter. Just remember—these identities are only skin-deep. Anyone who digs a little will see through them, but it's the best I can do on short notice. They'll last you a while, at least until you can take more permanent measures."

Once she made contact with Jarod, everything would fall into place. Kale and Riley were experts at their craft and would ensure they remained undetected.

"Just be careful with cameras," Fernis warned. "The handshake and markers won't protect you from facial recognition scans, but as far as I can see, there's no alert out on you inside."

Safe for now. Their pursuers likely assumed they were still outside. It would be some time before anyone realized they had managed to sneak past the dome frontier, evading the checkpoint through the tunnel. There was still hope. *Thank God for old, obsolete infrastructure—and for engineers being human and occasionally overlooking things.*

Aea expressed her approval of her new identity. "Limon," she said with a smile. "I like that better than my old name, Lamonte. So lame. My friends used to tease me about it, called me Lame-o and such, but that was a long time ago now."

"What about my first name?" she asked. "Is it really safe to keep it the same?"

Fernis responded, "Rule number one when you lie is to lie as little as possible. Easier to remember that way. You'll blend in enough. There are a hundred and seventeen Danas in Frankfurt and six Dana Limons. There are nine Anna Limons. Not common enough for your would-be pursuers to run through search algorithms, but not uncommon enough to raise suspicion during everyday life—shopping, traveling, checking in and out of places, etcetera. And it's not similar enough to your real name to be flagged. Aeona or Aea won't work, though. Too uncommon. Trust me. I ran it through the AI. It'll work."

Fernis strode over to his desk and retrieved a burner pad, handing it to Aea. "Speaking of lies, here are your backstories. Practice them. Your credibility as your new selves depends on how well you apply these. Use them only if you need to. Don't volunteer information. If nobody asks you, don't say anything. Simple, yes?" He then turned to Dana, "Yours is uploaded as a file. Check your inventory to make sure it's there."

Dana quickly checked her inventory and found the file. They had some reading to do.

"You have to leave now," Fernis stated bluntly. "I may owe Brett, but I don't owe him enough to risk my entire livelihood. And I'm too pretty for prison." He chuckled.

Dana had hoped for more assistance from Fernis, but she knew they had already asked for too much. "What about accommodation for the night?" she asked anyway.

"You won't need my help for that," Fernis replied confidently. "Just get a hotel with your new identity. You'll be safe. Hide in plain sight." With that, Fernis all but pushed them out onto the streets of Bahnhofviertel, where the anonymity of the crowded street would provide a paradoxical comfort.

"Okay," Dana said, turning to Aea, her new 'daughter.' At that moment, she felt a rush of determination, a flicker of hope that maybe they'd be okay after all. "Let's see how these new fake identities work, then, shall we?"

...cultural expression has branched out, giving rise to the emergence of "Innie" and "Outie" cultures. Although similar at their inception, they have diverged significantly over time...

...cultural divergence is manifested in various forms of expression, including music, film, entertainment, sports, drug use, and sexual practices, among others. These domains of cultural expression exhibit discernible differences that reflect the unique features of the "Innie" and "Outie" cultures...

...the practice of "domescaling" is on the rise, and with it, the occurrence of related accidents. Despite being illegal, policing this dangerous and illicit extreme sport has proven to be a challenging task...

...the increasing availability of personal and medical technologies has facilitated a broader scope of individual expression. This phenomenon is more prominent among Inside residents in the West, where higher levels of wealth and greater tolerance for such liberties prevail. Sexual expression is a prime example, with advancements in gene therapy enabling the realization of gynandromorphism and sequential hermaphroditism. Nonetheless, it is essential to emphasize that information on these practices remains scarce...

..."Inside personal freedom is mostly an illusion," says Huxley in an interview for a BBC documentary recorded last year. "Domes are essentially hermetically sealed machines where every part plays a crucial role. Any activity that could potentially endanger the integrity of the machine itself must, by default, be subject to strict regulation or even prohibited altogether." True freedom, he insists, can only be achieved Outside. Huxley continues to list... [Pink Floyd's *Welcome to the Machine* plays in the background]...

...an emerging trend among Hollywood celebrities is the use of exowombs to carry and birth children, forgoing natural pregnancy and childbirth. Exowombs are artificial devices that simulate the intrauterine environment, providing a controlled and tailored experience for both the parent and the developing fetus. While controversial, proponents argue that exowombs offer numerous advantages, including increased safety, greater control over the birthing process, and the ability to balance career demands with family planning...

Aea

Just around the bend from the hotel, another garish neon spectacle lit up the façade, featuring a scantily clad female figure. Admittedly, the woman wasn't entirely disrobed—she was sporting neon lingerie. Regardless, Aea was unaccustomed to this sort of exhibitionism, something she had never encountered in dreary old Niederrad, where excitement came in the form of a thunderstorm. Here, neon underwear was like a beacon from another world—garish and unapologetic. *Cool, in a way*, she thought, unable to avoid sneaking peeks. She was sure such things existed elsewhere Outside, though. *It's not like poor people like us get to travel the world or anything.* "Don't look at it," Dana cautioned.

"I'm almost 17. I know what sex is, duh!"

"I'm sure."

"Daemon and I have done it like a hundred tim—"

"Okay, I believe you. But I don't need to know *everything*," Dana interrupted, tugging Aea along. Dana seemed anxious to escape the Bahnhofviertel. Aea had heard stories about the area but had never visited. Well, *obviously*! Aea had never journeyed Inside, lacking the requisite Permit. *Outie can't go Innie without Permie*, as the adage went. Wait—*is that a rhyme? Or more like just an expression? Innie, Outie, Permie*—all ending on the same syllable. *Ah well, what does it matter?*

Her mind sprawled, reaching in every direction all at once. The Inside was a spectacle unlike anything she had ever seen. Aea had caught glimpses of it on her pad or through her VR glasses, but the real thing was more chaotic and brilliantly illuminated than she could have imagined. Lights were everywhere—self-driving cars, trams, drones for every purpose, from transport and delivery to surveillance. It was nothing like the images or flicks she had seen on her pad or even her VR visor. The real thing was louder, brighter, and overwhelming. Her heart and mind were flipping in weird ways, like she was in a real-life version of a VR game. The city pulsed and vibrated with its own energy, and she felt like a character inside it. Tiny, terrified, yet fascinated and exhilarated.

And then, of course, there was the massive dome looming high above her head, with its glass-like panes and sturdy beams holding it in place. Its sheer height was something that couldn't be conveyed through pictures or streams. *Glass panes?*, she wondered. Were they glass? Probably not—glass would break. She vaguely recalled reading about dome construction materials in school, but she couldn't quite remember any of the names. There were a few different ones. Still, the sight of the dome's massive beams—the same kind that terrorists destroyed in London, causing everything to collapse—coupled with the storm raging outside, was unsettling. The entire structure groaned as the wind pummeled it, making eerie sounds she had never heard before. *Is 'groan' the right word?* It was like the wind battering an old house, but also distinctly different. Maybe it was the echoes bouncing around?

Fascinating as it was, the wonder she felt was tinged with anxiety. The dome's grandeur clashed with the visceral reminders of nature's fury she knew from Outside. The dome's resilience was awe-inspiring and unnervingly alien. *This is how the other half lives,* she thought, with a mix of wonder and a pinch of resentment. Outside, storms meant huddling in a dark basement, hoping there was something left once it passed.

Dana appeared unfazed by the noise, leading Aea along with the ease of a true Innie, someone so accustomed to the phenomenon that they didn't notice it. Dana walked the dome like it was just another day, completely at ease with the eerie sounds of the storm battering the glass. Totally chill! Aea watched her, trying to borrow some of that calmness. If Dana wasn't worried about the dome crashing down on them, then maybe Aea shouldn't be either. Still, Aea knew that outside, people would be seeking shelter as the storm raged, causing severe damage and claiming lives. *I hope Tabayah is okay,* she thought. She would be with Dad now, hopefully out of harm's way. *They'll all be alright,* she reassured herself. *I'm sure of it.*

"Don't stop," Dana urged, tugging at Aea's arm whenever she paused to gaze up at the transparent panes of the dome ceiling. Despite their clarity, she couldn't see anything beyond them. The storm had blotted out everything, the night sky a chaotic mishmash of red and dark gray hues as dusk settled in.

"What's the name of this street?" Aea asked, her inquisitive nature getting the best of her. The onslaught of new experiences was overwhelming. She was in Frankfurt, a place she had always longed to visit! Her senses were bombarded by the new sights—the imposing dome, the raging storm, the novelty of a new place.

Frau Gerhling had always admired Aea's inquisitiveness, even if it sometimes made her seem like a goody-two-shoes in front of her classmates, especially Jema and Kaliyah. Frau Gerhling had encouraged Aea to ask questions, no matter how silly they seemed, so she did.

"Where are we going?" Aea asked eagerly, her mind ablaze with curiosity, each unfamiliar sight and sound a puzzle piece of the Inside she was eager to piece together. Her curiosity was an ember refusing to be smothered by the trauma she'd just survived.

"To Zeil," Dana replied.

Aea beamed. *The shopping street. Yes!* She had always dreamed of visiting. The abundance of shops, bots scurrying about, and adverts popping up in front of your eyes. It was so exhilarating! Just like the flicks and VR worlds she'd seen through her visor.

"Don't get too excited," Dana interrupted Aea's rambling. "The ads get old very quickly, and you won't be able to see any until we get you a braid."

Oh, right! Aea had almost forgotten. Dana was treating her to a braid. She had always wanted one. *Duh! Like everyone else!*

Aea couldn't wait to tell Jema, Kaliyah, her dad, and Tabayahh everything when she got home. She found herself in the strangest of moods, oscillating between sadness, worry, guilt, and excitement. She missed Daemon, her dad, and Tabayahh desperately, but the city mesmerized her. The towering buildings, the trams, the affluent people everywhere, the calmness, and the lack of wind and rain—it was all blowing her away. She would forget about her loved ones for a while, caught up in the moment, but then the guilt and sadness returned just as quickly.

The news had not mentioned Daemon or Stefan, but Aea knew that didn't mean much. Outie events were often overlooked by Innie media, so the absence of news didn't necessarily mean anything. Still, she clung to the hope that the lack of coverage was a good sign—as long as she didn't hear anything, maybe they were alive.

Everything felt surreal, like a dream she couldn't quite shake off. It seemed like only yesterday that she and Daemon were walking around the dome construction site or the park, but it also felt like ages ago. *How could it feel like both at the same time?*

They passed another robovendor, a hole-in-the-wall shop selling an array of goods—food, toys, medicines, electronics. *A pharmacy, maybe?* But there was no recognizable pharmacy cross. A convenience store, then. Outside, they had similar stores, but they were all manned by humans. *Did humans do anything here?* Aea recalled her father's complaints about Innies on UBI, idly passing their time without working.

As they turned a corner, a massive square unfolded before them. "What's this place?" Aea asked.

"Hauptwache," Dana replied.

Aea had heard of it before, from school or streams, of course. The square bustled with activity, teeming with people dining at outdoor restaurants, browsing shops, and just lingering, soaking up the ambiance. There were so many people around. Outside, people spent a lot of time indoors due to the storms. *Outies stay inside. Hehe. That's kinda funny.*

"We'll head to My Zeil," Dana informed her. "I'm sure they have a surgery there."

My Zeil turned out to be a colossal shopping mall, with several floors of stores—clothing, electronics, cafés, fast food—all under one roof. There was nothing like it in Niederrad, at least not in her neighborhood. The floors spiraled around a central atrium, offering a clear view of the glass ceiling, which resembled undulating ocean waves. *Undoubtedly cool.*

The richness of My Zeil was overwhelming. There was nothing like it Outside. Each step further into the mall felt like a step further away from her past life, a journey into a world as dazzling as it was alien. It was like she'd stepped into a fairytale. Aea had grown up hearing her father say that while Innies may have more, Outies weren't dirt poor. But after today, she wasn't so sure she believed that anymore.

Nevertheless, they were all supposed to become Innies at some point, when the domes around the world expanded to accommodate everyone. Her family had never paid much attention to the protesters and... what was the word?

Demagogues! Those preachers who claimed the Outside could survive without a dome or that Innies didn't actually want to expand the domes and secretly wanted all the Outies to perish as the world deteriorated. Daemon had been one of the former, believing they could manage without the Innies. He despised them and everything they stood for. If Aea had ever shared his sentiments, she wasn't so sure now. *Why wouldn't anyone want to live here?* Inside these walls, one could do or have anything they desired. Perhaps Dad was right—Outies weren't starving, but life was unquestionably better here.

They rode the escalators to the top floor, where electronic stores clustered together. Dana mentioned that there were several to choose from but that they'd go to the shop where she had bought her first kit years ago. *Yeah, like a hundred years ago,* Aea thought, studying Dana. She didn't seem that old. *Do Innies age better?* Maybe it was the absence of harsh weather. Her father always claimed wind and rain aged him.

Dana pulled her into a store abruptly, and Aea stumbled slightly before regaining her balance. The store gleamed in white, everything sleek and sterile. Glass shelves displayed electronics with holographic images hovering above them. One showed a human head with a cutaway revealing brain structures, pop-ups providing information. Aea wanted to get closer to read them, but Dana kept her close, looking tense. *Is she afraid of the surgery?* Aea wondered.

It probably wasn't the procedure itself that scared Dana, but the fact that they were out in public, surrounded by people. The risk of being caught gnawed at Aea, too. Still, the allure of the store's Aegis products was hard to resist. The logo was everywhere, and it suddenly hit her—her old pad back home had that same logo.

Aea turned to Dana. "Why's it called a surgery?"

Dana, searching for a salesperson, responded absentmindedly, "I don't know."

"Will it hurt?" Aea asked.

Before Dana could reply, a youthful voice answered, "It won't hurt." A tall, stunning girl had approached them, her voice melodic. She was dressed in white, perfectly matching the store's pristine aesthetic. "It's called a surgery because, a long time ago, braid installations required actual surgery. Now, it's just a painless injection."

Aea grinned—not just because of the reassurance, but because of the girl herself. She was the most beautiful person Aea had ever seen, her skin flawless, almost blending into the white background. *Perfect,* Aea thought, feeling a pang of envy.

"I'm Maria," the girl said, flashing a sales-perfect smile. "What can I do for you today?"

Aea was surprised to see a human working at the store. She had heard it was uncommon Inside. For a second, she even wondered if Maria was a robot—a synth, like the girls they'd seen in the Bahnhofviertel. The thought intrigued her so much that she interrupted Dana, blurting, "Are you human?"

Dana shot her a look, quickly apologizing on her behalf, but Maria laughed it off. "It's fine," she said warmly. "Yes, I'm human."

God, I want to be pretty like her. Aea had so many questions bubbling up—how could someone be that flawless? But remembering Dana's earlier reprimand, she held back. *Probably an inappropriate question,* she thought.

Still, her curiosity got the better of her. "Why don't you have a synth?" she asked. "I hear they do everything Inside."

Dana immediately corrected her again. "Don't say 'Inside.' It makes it sound like we're in prison."

Damn. Got it wrong again. Aea made a mental note not to repeat the mistake.

Maria seemed unbothered, though. "Where are you from?" she asked, clearly catching on that they weren't locals.

"She's adopted through one of the EU migration programs," Dana said smoothly, steering the conversation away from anything personal. "We want to get her a braid."

"Excellent," Maria beamed. "We have anything you need. Follow me."

She led them toward a curtained entryway at the back of the store. A holographic image of a girl with virtual icons floating around her—films, music notes, documents—was projected onto the curtain. Aea realized it represented the contact lenses she was about to get. *I can't believe it!*

They stepped through the curtain into a room lined with reclining chairs. Two of them were occupied, robot arms hovering over the customers' heads, performing mysterious tasks. Maria explained that the process was fully automated. One robot would inject nanobots to build the braid, while another would form the visual screens and install the auditory implants. Aea could barely focus on the explanation, too mesmerized by the other customers. *So cool.*

Aea was in awe as she watched the robots working on the other customers. The salesgirl further reassured her that the injection wouldn't hurt, though some people found the fitting of the screens a bit uncomfortable. Aea wasn't listening, engrossed in her schemes to put her new gift to use. "They are molded directly over the cornea," Maria continued, explaining that the whole process would take about half an hour, during which Aea would just sit while the robots did their work. Once they finished, she'd go through some basic tutorials for her new braid. Aea couldn't contain her excitement. *This is so cool!*

As Maria prepared the robots, Dana said she would try to track Jarod down. Aea nodded absentmindedly, her attention fully focused on the procedure.

Aea turned to the salesgirl, who had now prepared the robots. As Maria droned on about the procedure, Aea's excitement was close to bursting. *Get on with it already!* The promise of becoming more connected, more a part of this new, wonderful world, was electrifying. Only a tiny part of her felt any trepidation—about the procedure, about the change itself. To be connected to the world, that was the prize. Price be damned. It could only get better.

"Ready?" Maria asked.

"I've been ready all my life!" Aea replied eagerly.

"Well then, here we go," Maria said, initiating the procedure.

The administration of the injections and the installation of the lenses were completed in a matter of minutes. *It wasn't that bad,* Aea thought. She felt slight pressure on her eyes as the injectors settled on her corneas, but nothing more. Despite her unease, she managed to suppress the urge to blink. It was like having a robot affixing old-style contact lenses, she mused. The other injections felt like minor stings, akin to flu shots. She had braced herself for discomfort, tightness coiling in her stomach, but was pleasantly surprised at the minimal intrusion.

After fifteen minutes of waiting, Aea suddenly saw a flicker before a woman's face appeared in front of her, welcoming her to the tutorial for her new braid. The woman's face was slightly translucent, and Aea could see the ceiling behind her. She listened to the soothing AI voice coming from this translucent woman's mouth, her first guide into a future she had only dreamed of—literally bridging the gap between reality and what had previously been fantasy. The woman explained that this translucency was intentional, meant to ease Aea into the idea of having graphics projected in front of her eyes. She also clarified that the graphics didn't have to be translucent; they could be made to look as solid as anything in the real world, indistinguishable from it if desired.

The tutorial progressed to control interfaces. Aea learned that she could use voice commands, hand and finger gestures, and, with greater difficulty, subtle eye movements to browse, manipulate objects, and select items, much like she would on a touchpad.

Aea found that using eye movements was by far the most exciting method of control, but also the most challenging. The AI reassured her that she would improve with time and that apps were available to help train and enhance her abilities. The AI also explained that most people preferred using eye movements, as they were discreet and didn't draw attention, unlike waving around and talking to oneself. *Okay, I've seen people wave about and talk to themselves, but the lady has a point. It does look a bit weird.* The fire of a challenge lit in Aea's mind. She was determined to master this discreet art of using her eyes. It would be like silently commanding the digital realm—a form of magic, a secret power she could wield unnoticed! It wasn't, of course. Countless others had mastered it before her, but that only made her more determined. She wasn't going to be some second-rate Innie!

Moving on to content, the AI explained that Aea could stream news, music, movies, and games, as well as work and overlay virtual elements onto real-life environments—like directions to locations or even adding clown makeup to someone's face. The promise of escaping into flicks or enhancing mundane reality with overlays tickled her imagination. Her visor back home could do something similar, but it was never truly convincing. The tutorial even demonstrated this by adding a large, fantastical bunny rabbit into the room with Aea, perfectly integrated into the environment. The bunny stood next to her chair, waving. *This is sooo cool!*

Aea's heart leapt with joy, a giggle escaping her. It was as if the virtual creation stood tangibly beside her; the level of intricacy in its design was breathtaking. The texture of its fur was so meticulously detailed that every strand seemed drawn with pinpoint precision. This was clearly beyond what her own virtual reality visor back home could achieve. She instinctively reached out to touch the digital creature, only to discover her hand passed through it. As the demo went on, Aea was already dreaming up ways to use it—messing with her friends, streaming music and flicks anytime, directly into her head, maybe even overlaying her boring chores with something epic. The bunny demo was just the start. *I'm going to be a wizard,* she thought, a grin spreading across her face. *No, an astronaut. No, a professor at Frankfurt Uni! No, wait! That's boring. What's wrong with me? How can I go from wizard and astronaut to professor?* Either way, forget about blending in; she wanted to explore every trick and tweak this tech offered.

The tutorial then progressed to complete virtual environments, generating an entirely rendered version of *The Wizard of Oz* around her. Aea held her breath as the fantasy world enveloped her, taken aback once again by the fidelity of the image. It felt utterly real, not like a rendition with obvious computer graphics. The vibrant yellow brick road lay before her, and she could see the familiar forms of the Lion, Scarecrow, Tinman, and Dorothy. The physical room she occupied seemed to evaporate, and for a moment, she was no longer a fugitive but a wide-eyed adventurer on the yellow brick road to somewhere wonderful.

The AI demonstrated how to interact with objects from the real world, such as vendors, doors, cars, public transport, and home appliances. It was an overwhelming amount of information to assimilate at once, but at least she wasn't utterly lost. After all, The Outside had most of these items; they just weren't integrated into one's mind like this.

"Everything okay in here?" a voice inquired. A targeting reticle immediately honed in on the source of the sound, revealing Maria, the salesgirl. A pang of disappointment briefly washed over Aea as she was unceremoniously yanked back to mundane reality. Looking around, she was reminded that this mundane reality was still *Inside*, not old Niederrad. The disappointment abated quickly after that, but she was left with an unmistakable impression of how powerful braid-powered fantasy could be. *No wonder addiction is a problem.*

A pop-up message explained to Aea how to minimize and hide the tutorial. It also revealed that anything in her visual range could be hidden using the same technique. Aea mimicked the tutorial's hand gesture and minimized it. *The eye movement thing will have to wait.*

"Yes," Aea replied, turning her attention to Maria. "Everything is fine."

As she resumed the tutorial, Aea was promptly interrupted again—this time by Dana.

Aea had nearly finished working through the tutorials when Dana reappeared.

"I haven't been able to reach Jarod," Dana said, her words a cold shower on Aea's exuberance. She was reminded of their predicament, her bubble of excitement bursting, her mind racing again with fears of what lay ahead. They were still on the run, still hiding. The awesome tech in her head suddenly felt heavy—a reminder that the real price paid wasn't the discomfort of installing it, like Maria had described, or the money Dana had so graciously provided, but the danger they were in, and the lives lost.

The medical app in her new braid detected the change in her mood, and a pop-up immediately suggested ways to cheer her up. *Well, there's that,* she thought, attempting to sweep it away with an eye movement like the tutorial had taught. The bubble stubbornly remained. Finally, she gave up and closed it with a hand gesture. *I see what they mean. I need to practice.* She managed to instruct the braid to halt everything for now, as reality encroached. She'd get back to it later, when they found some respite.

After Dana paid, they quickly left the shopping mall. Aea was soon back to exploring the braid and everything it could do, pushing her dark thoughts firmly and deliberately into a distant corner of her mind. However, the urgency in Dana's step as they hurried down the bustling Kaiser Strasse kept reminding her of the reality of their situation. It was too risky to be out in the open with their current identities. They needed to keep a low profile and hide in a hotel room for now. Aea felt a pang of disappointment but knew Dana was right. They couldn't afford to get caught or attract unwanted attention. She wondered how long they could keep this up. How long could they hide and stay safe? The thought made her anxious, but she pushed it away, focusing on the present moment. They would have to deal with the future when it came.

"What should we do, then?" Aea asked.

"Until I get a hold of Jarod, I...uh...I don't know."

Kale

"You got this?" Kale asked Riley as he rose from his workstation, tucked away in the cramped Tokyo apartment, where the cluttered walls, flickering screens, and the stale stench of burnt coffee and sweat had begun to feel more like a prison than a base of operations. "I need a break."

Riley replied with a weary nod, a slump of the shoulders rather than a gesture of assurance. The hours in front of the screens—lenses or physical—were long, and they were both exhausted. Jarod was out scouting, and Wyatt napped, which meant Kale could abscond for an hour, perhaps two or three, before anyone noticed he was gone. The first few times he had snuck out, he'd worried about getting caught, but over time he'd grown indifferent. *So what if I'm caught? All I'm doing is having a few drinks.* He needed it to cope with the stress. Coping with the stress was necessary for all of them, except for Wyatt, who seemed annoyingly impervious to any kind of adverse conditions. Riley relied on antidepressants—something only Kale knew. He didn't know what coping mechanism Jarod preferred, but he was sure Jarod had one. *And as for me, I like the sauce.*

He was certain Jarod harbored suspicions. Ever since New York with Fiscal-Siscal, he'd been aware. Kale relied on stimulants to counteract his inebriation, and most people would have been deceived by the ruse, but not Jarod. He knew Kale too well. However, Jarod had refrained from pressing the matter and hadn't mentioned it since, allowing Kale to continue his behavior.

He took the stairs down; the elevator in the dilapidated but not entirely abandoned building was out of order. The evening sky was awash with light rain, an insignificant drizzle that posed no real threat, and the wind was relatively tame. The drizzle felt like whispers against his skin, each drop a muted echo of the world's relentless indifference—its own crawling demise. Kale paused, letting the moment wash over him, a rare instance of peace amidst the chaos he inhabited. The cool air brushed against his face, a stark contrast to the stifling waft of the apartment. The neon lights of Tokyo flickered gently through his closed eyelids, much like the stroboscopic effect of the screens, but the scent of rain offset any lingering feeling of claustrophobia. He was outdoors.

In Outside Tokyo, a mere drizzle like this constituted a good evening. The sun was descending, casting brilliant rays that pierced the crimson, almost violet clouds on the horizon. The Tokyo nightlife was reaching its apex, and they weren't far from bustling downtown Haneda. It was only a matter of time before he found a watering hole—hopefully a quiet place where he could knock back a few shots of vodka in relative calm, surrounded by normal people. People living mundane, everyday lives. People who had never taken another's. That's how he coped—getting inebriated on both alcohol and observing life's regular ebb and flow. It was a stark contrast to his day job of operating tiny machines that ended such lives.

He strode north, toward the towering dome, its western facade bathed in the glow of dusk. As darkness set in, the dome's night lights would illuminate, accentuating the structure's grandeur. Inside, a bustling, safe, and prosperous Innie city life thrived. Outside, bright red positioning lights adorned the dome's exterior. It was a towering wall of affluence that stretched out in all directions, a constant insult to those on the outside. Kale's eyes traced the curve of the immense structure, feeling a mix of awe and guilt. Yes, for the Outies, the dome's presence was a taunt, a daily reminder of their lot in life. *I only work Outside,* he reminded himself.

Most places of interest Outside—whether commercial, nightlife, or other indulgent activities—tended to amass near the dome frontiers, near the checkpoints. It was as if people assumed they were closer to heaven if they stayed near its gates. But in truth, they were no closer than anyone else. Physical proximity had nothing to do with it. However, if you wanted to drown your sorrows, that was the spot to do it.

Outie places near the checkpoints were popular, both with Outies and adventurous Innies who wanted to go 'slumming.' Being near the checkpoint was safer. It wasn't quite the *real* Outside, or at least, so it was perceived. Arguably, such places were tourist traps, but they boasted better security, and if the weather turned, the checkpoint remained within quick reach. *So the Innies can scurry back into the safety of their bubbles.*

Kale never believed the Outside was as horrendous as it was portrayed. Yes, you were vulnerable to the elements, but there were solutions beyond spending a lifetime in a bubble. Crime wasn't as prevalent as Innie news made it seem. Life was bearable, at least for most people, especially in the West and here in Japan.

These days, China was pretty much off-limits to Westerners, and so was Russia—for different reasons. Regardless, no one wanted to go there, particularly not Russia. Not even wanted criminals went there anymore since the Russian legacy government had lost the interest and capacity to safeguard them. It had been that way since the end of the Ukraine war and the downfall of the Putin regime in the first half of the twenty-first century.

Anyway, back to the task at hand. Kale found the perfect spot, a hotel bar on the periphery of the action yet still close to the apartment. One of the finer establishments the Outside had to offer: reasonably stylish and calm, with a moderate crowd—not too sparse, not too suffocating. Perfect. The bar's ambiance was a cocoon of dim lighting and soft jazz, a gentle hum of conversations providing a backdrop. The air carried a blend of aged wood and spiced aromas from the kitchen, creating a sense of warmth and anonymity. It was the perfect escape, a place where his story could intersect without ever really touching.

He took a seat in the far corner and ordered three shots at once. When the waitress arrived with the drinks, he placed them in a neat row and gazed at them for a while before knocking them back in quick succession. He did that every time, unsure why he felt compelled to. He watched the bartender with a practiced eye, noting the precise movements, the elegant pour that ended each shot with a delicate swirl. The clink of glass as the shots were set before him was familiar, marking the beginning of his brief respite from reality.

His mouth watered at the sight. As the shots lined up before him, Kale saw them not as mere drinks but as markers of his descent—each one a step further from the man he wished to be. The bitter taste of each shot gradually blurred the faces and places he tried to drown out. Once they were all down, his mind would be void of any particular thoughts—an effective way of managing guilt. Temporarily, at least.

He knew that his need to dull the pain made him vulnerable and weak, and he was well aware that Jarod wouldn't approve. He had let Jarod down, and perhaps more painfully, Riley, who, unlike the others, was privy to his indiscretions yet chose to keep it to herself. He had never explicitly asked her to cover for his transgressions, but he still felt like he had made her a liar, and that hurt the most. He snapped out of his thoughts, downing all three shots in rapid succession before ordering another three.

The second batch he imbibed at a leisurely pace, savoring the experience after getting his initial fix. *If one can actually savor vodka. It tastes like shit.* It wasn't the taste he liked, he guessed—it was the ritual. He typically limited himself to six shots since any more than that would possibly impair his ability to perform his job, even with the aid of stims. *Possibly impair? Yeah, you keep telling yourself that, pal.*

As he sat there, something caught his attention—a woman. She sat at the bar, eyeing him. Such a thing wasn't commonplace during his little getaways. Women showing him interest had occurred before, obviously, but it was never a typical part of his life. *Intriguing,* he thought as his heart skipped slightly. Her interest, foreign and unexpected, cut through his usual facade of indifference. *Someone sees me.*

Her dark hair contrasted beautifully with her pale skin, but he could tell from across the room that she wasn't Japanese. Dressed in an elegant black dress and heels, her long earrings sparkled in the hotel bar's lights as she shifted her head. It was expensive-looking jewelry, the kind of luxury rarely seen Outside. She flashed him a warm smile, toying with her hair and dangling her shoe from her toes. *A bit obvious, isn't it?*

His thoughts went straight to the possibility that she might be a working girl. However, this wasn't the sort of place where such individuals usually plied their trade. It wasn't posh enough for someone of her stature—not like the places he frequented when in the mood for such a thing. *Perhaps an Innie out slumming?* She rose from her seat and began making her way toward him.

The light caught in her hair, casting an ethereal glow around her, making her seem like a specter from a world far removed from his own. *Maybe it's the booze talking.* Her movement toward him was graceful, almost as though she hovered an inch above the floor. Each step was measured and deliberate, drawing not only his eyes but the eyes of those around them. As she neared, he observed that she looked vaguely Eastern European, perhaps Russian—light skin, high cheekbones. At first, he wondered if she was looking at someone behind him until he remembered he was seated in a corner, and there was no one else around. She pulled out a chair and sat down opposite him, putting all doubts to rest.

"What's a handsome man like you doing in a place like this?" she quipped, grinning. It was a tongue-in-cheek remark, a playful jab at the cheesy pickup lines men often used on women. He found himself blushing a bit, a novel experience—he had never encountered anything like this before. The only women who gave him the time of day were prostitutes, and she was certainly not one.

"I don't know," he stammered.

"Well," she continued, "why don't we find out?"

Kale nodded. "Yes, why don't we?" He summoned the waiter and ordered more drinks.

Osawa

Hideshi Osawa stood spread-eagled once more, subjected to the meticulous pat-down by Alixha's guard before being granted entrance to her penthouse. The routine was familiar by now, yet the atmosphere this time bristled with a tension far thicker than he remembered. In the normally stoic guard's eyes, Osawa discerned fear—and something else, something deeper. A shiver coursed down his spine.

As the lock disengaged and the door swung open, Osawa was assaulted by an acrid, indescribable stench—a mélange of rotting flesh, the metallic tang of blood, and something antiseptic. The guard met his gaze with a silent warning, as if to say *I told you so.* Osawa's stomach both turned and knotted, his heart pounding in his rib cage as he was escorted through the hallway leading to the living room. They stopped just short of the corner, the guard gesturing for him to proceed alone. *He's never done that before,* Osawa thought, sensing a palpable fear of what lay beyond.

Rounding the bend, Osawa was confronted with a sight beyond imagination. At the room's heart, Alixha floated, her form reminiscent of a Westerner's Jesus on the Cross, ensnared by a network of tubes that fed into her like the limbs of a grotesque beast. She was the queen in her hive, a spider at the web's center. The tubes, invading her skull, nose, mouth, and groin, pulsed rhythmically, a ghastly mimicry of breathing. Her eyes, rolled back to show only whites, presented Osawa with a vision that would haunt him for life.

The room itself had succumbed to a biomechanical growth that sprawled across every surface, including the now-inert wall of screens. This growth, with its throbbing veins crawling across its surface, appeared organic yet followed a starkly inorganic, mechanical pattern. Like circuitry. Bubbles and holes spread symmetrically, eliciting both visceral fear and revulsion. The more Osawa observed it, the more he felt an instinctual dread, a primal reaction to something that challenged the very essence of what was natural and right. *Is this the supercomputer I've heard so much about?*

"Osawa," Alixha's voice filled the space around him, not emanating from her lips but from the air itself. "Update me."

Gathering his composure, Osawa began, "The search for Scott remains inconclusive." The response from the entity that was Alixha was nonverbal but unmistakable—the room's biomechanical tendrils and wall growth vibrated with irritation, the holes and bubbles undulating.

Osawa swallowed hard. "Perhaps focusing on cracking the codes would be more productive—"

"The codes," she announced, her voice resonating from everywhere and nowhere simultaneously, "are of no concern now. The liaison has yielded results. We proceed as planned."

The revelation left Osawa both relieved and bewildered. The cryptos applied by Aki Sato were deemed unbreakable but had succumbed to this...thing. *Whatever it is.*

"And Scott," he whispered, the question barely leaving his lips before the living machine stirred. The patterns on the wall rippled, the energy in the room palpably shifting. Abruptly, he was lifted off the ground by an unseen force, his heart seized by a spectral grip, as if Alixha had literally reached into his chest and caught it. His consciousness slipping, black spots spreading across his vision, he floated up to Alixha, his face inches from hers. The whites of her eyes bore into him as she tightened her grip on his very life force.

"I want him," she commanded.

"We know he's still here in Tokyo," Osawa gasped, fighting his slipping consciousness. Alixha remained silent. Osawa couldn't help but wonder, as he faded away, why she couldn't locate the man herself, her abilities apparently omnipotent.

Released suddenly, Osawa crumpled to the floor, gasping as lifeblood surged through his veins. He staggered to his feet, meeting the gaze of the transformed Alixha. Escorted back by the guard, Osawa pondered the paradox of power and desire. Alixha's reach now extended into the realm of gods, yet the simple affection of Scott, a mere human, remained out of her grasp. And if Osawa failed to locate the man, he knew nothing could save him from her wrath.

Jema and Kaliyah

"Gimme that," Jema demanded, snatching at Kaliyah's bottle. "Mine tastes like ass." She grimaced and spat. *It really does taste like ass!*

"It's not my fault your parents have terrible taste in alcohol," Kaliyah retorted with a smirk. Jema made a face and hurled a rock at the dome wall, provoking a hollow thud against the material. *I wonder what it's actually made of?*

Sure, they'd been taught all about it in school, but Jema had never been one for paying attention. Neither had Kaliyah, for that matter. It was always Aea who excelled at that—the brainiac, the geek. *And yet she's the one all the boys want. I wonder why. She's not prettier. Not than Kaliyah, anyway.*

Jema took another swig of the tepid beer she'd pilfered from her dad's shoddy stash out back by their Crescent dwelling.

Kaliyah chucked a stone of her own, producing the same hollow resonance. The material looked like concrete, but it wasn't. Frau Gerhling had taught them all about dome construction—how the material was fabricated by bots without human intervention, a testament to modern engineering, a safeguard against environmental ravages. *Blah, blah, blah.*

The desolate town to the south of Frankfurt, and south of

The Crescent, was infamous for its abandoned dome construction. The project had been scrapped, the city sealed off, and its residents relocated to other Innie settlements—some to Frankfurt, some to Offenbach, Mainz, and Wiesbaden. Now, Neu Isenberg was a ghost town, its perimeter marked by checkpoints that had been boarded up to prevent unauthorized entry. The dome itself was only partially erected, looming over the small settlement's western side like a colossal tidal wave about to engulf everything in its path. *A tsunami! Ha! I remembered. A tidal wave is called a tsunami. Who's the dumb one now?*

She, Aea, and Kaliyah often met here to sneak cigarettes and booze. Well, not Aea. Aea was the good girl in the group, content to merely engage in conversation. That was before Daemon, however. After they hooked up, Aea had practically vanished, lost in a haze of canoodling, constantly smooching the boy's ugly face. Too infatuated to spend time with her old friends. Jema still wondered how she was doing, though. The events of recent times had been harrowing. Daemon and that fool Cali had kidnapped an Innie woman, resulting in the deaths of numerous people. And now, they were missing. *Poof! Just gone, like a magic trick.*

A weird mix of sadness and fear tugged at her. Aea's absence definitely left a void, irrevocably altering the dynamic of their trio. Memories of laughter and shared secrets hung heavily in the air. Kaliyah was great—it wasn't that—but it wasn't the same with just the two of them.

Their friends' whereabouts remained a mystery. Jema couldn't help but feel a sense of longing for Aea—her infectious smile, boundless curiosity, and razor-sharp intellect. Aea wouldn't hurl rocks at the dome foundation. She'd be up there touching it, examining it, and offering insightful commentary on its composition. She would definitely know what it was made of.

"Do you think she's okay?" Jema voiced her concerns, her voice cracking uncharacteristically. The question lingered, heavy with unspoken worry. It was a moment of vulnerability, a stark departure from Jema's usual carefree banter, but Kaliyah merely shrugged dismissively, taking another gulp of her beer. Jema watched her friend with both frustration and understanding. It was an uncomfortable question, and they had both become adept at dodging reality—an act that was consoling but was wearing thin.

"Want another cigarette?" Kaliyah offered, choosing to deflect the issue once again. Jema let it go and accepted the offer, having failed to pilfer any from her father this time. Kaliyah had come prepared, though, managing to snag a whole pack. The flicker of the lighter and the soft glow of the cigarette end punctuated the twilight—an act of defiance in the shadow of the unfinished dome to the south and the magnificence of the fully erected one to the north. She drew a puff and exhaled, watching the smoke twist in the air before a gust of wind dispersed it. *I love smoking, even if that too tastes like ass. Thank God for Kali.*

Again, Jema couldn't help but wonder how Kaliyah had acquired them. If she took an entire pack from her father, he'd undoubtedly notice. No, she had to make do with one or two at most when she worked up the courage to sneak some. Maybe Kaliyah's parents didn't care? Or perhaps Kaliyah had a fake ID? It wasn't hard to get one Outside, and many vendors didn't bother to check. But Jema had never been brave enough to try. If Kaliyah had one, she'd say. *Nevermind. Who cares? Kali has smokes, and she's willing to share. That's all that matters. And they're real smokes. Real tobacco and shit. Not synth stuff without all the bad stuff in it. Hardcore!*

She threw another rock. *Thump!* It was a strangely soothing sound, though Jema couldn't explain why. She loved this place—Neu Isenberg, the old abandoned road that led up to it, and The Wasteland in between. These places were largely uninhabited, and they almost never encountered anyone here. And on the rare occasion they did, those individuals left them be. No adults with prying eyes telling them what to do, no one shooing them away or warning them about the weather. It was too far from Frankfurt for the Innies to bother monitoring, so there were no drones either—well, hardly any. It was nothing like the areas near the checkpoints or just north of The Crescent. Here, in the deep south, they could do as they pleased. *Not that we actually do much. Except drink and smoke. And throw rocks at the dome.*

"Do you think the Innie kids smoke?" Jema mused aloud.

"I dunno," Kaliyah replied, shrugging.

Jema pondered the notion. Was smoking even allowed Inside? She had no clue. *Mom always yells at Dad when he smokes indoors.*

Inside was like one enormous *indoors*, she reckoned. Maybe smoking was forbidden, like it was inside houses? She had no frame of reference—she'd never been Inside.

"We should start making our way back," Kaliyah suggested.

Jema shot her a disgruntled look. "Already?" She wasn't eager to return home just yet.

"It's getting dark," Kaliyah pointed out.

Indeed, the sun was rapidly descending toward the horizon. While there were scarcely any people out here, it wasn't wise to linger after dark. *Even I know that!*

"Don't worry," Jema reassured her. "We can cut through The Wasteland instead of taking the road. We can stay for another beer, and we'll still make it back before dark." It was another act of defiance against the encroaching night and whatever drudgery awaited back home. *Homework. Chores. Blah!*

Kaliyah agreed, albeit somewhat reluctantly. "We can pass through the clearing," she suggested. It was their way of savoring the last vestiges of freedom. The setting sun, with its deepening hues of red, formed the backdrop to their youthful insistence on seizing the moment. *Yes, the clearing,* Jema thought. She knew exactly the spot—one of their old haunts they hadn't visited in a while. It was more enjoyable in the summertime, on rare mild days. However, it hardly mattered what season it was anymore—the weather was always dreadful in some way.

The Wasteland had once been teeming with trees, but they were long gone. Since before Jema was born—maybe even before her parents were born. *Der Stadtwald—that's what it was called. I think.* Now it was called The Wasteland. Well, not *officially*.

They'd studied it in school, learning about the lake and the various trees that once stood tall. Most of it had been cleared to build the domes in Frankfurt and Neu Isenberg, and what remained had been ravaged by storms or plundered by Crescent residents in the days before the shanty had electricity. Nowadays, the area was under government protection to prevent further deforestation.

Nevertheless, most of the vegetation had disappeared over time, with only a few clearings remaining in shallow valleys where the surrounding hills sheltered the plants from the fiercest winds. In one of these clearings, there were several weather-beaten benches where one could rest. It was situated between the Neu Isenberg dome and the southern border of The Crescent.

Jema and Kaliyah lit another cigarette and finished off their beer before chewing some gum to conceal the smell from their parents. *Not that it matters. They probably wouldn't care that much.*

Once they'd wrapped up, they set off for home.

As they drew nearer to the clearing, Jema and Kaliyah noticed lights flickering in the distance. Dusk had arrived, leaving them exposed and visible from afar. As they got closer, they heard murmurs and voices. There was never anyone here, and certainly never any lights. Jema was eager to investigate, but Kaliyah hesitated.

"We should take a look," Jema insisted, pulling Kaliyah along. "We'll be careful."

Cautiously, they crept toward the clearing, keeping low behind the hilltop to avoid being detected. Eventually, they saw several men gathered there, some of whom Jema recognized from town. They were Gabriel's men, and they had erected a massive cylindrical tent nestled among the trees on the hillside. *Like a hangar or something.*

Then they spotted Gabriel himself, conversing with the other members of the group. The distance made it difficult to discern what they were saying, but Jema thought she overheard Gabriel asking if everything had been completed in Neu Isenberg, to which one of the men replied in the affirmative. Gabriel then asked whether they were certain nobody would discover it—whatever "it" was. The man shook his head and said it was only for a few days until they could dispose of it.

Both girls exchanged a nervous glance as they slowly realized the gravity of the situation. The activity in the clearing was clearly not intended for their prying eyes, especially with Gabriel present in person. Fear and curiosity warred inside Jema—the sweet thrill of discovering something off-limits marred by the potential danger. The sight of the cylindrical tent, alien and out of place among the barren trees, along with the men scurrying around, sent a shiver down her spine. Her heart pounded in her chest, adrenaline coursing as the potential consequences of their inadvertent espionage began to dawn on her.

She discreetly motioned for the two of them to leave, and they were just about to when the ground trembled, prompting the men in the clearing to retreat. The trembling intensified, evolving into a low rumble that rapidly grew louder. The shaking beneath their feet escalated, and suddenly the ground in the clearing began to rise.

With a deafening crack, a colossal drill head emerged from the earth. Jema immediately recognized it as one of the tunneling bots used for constructing the domes' underground structures. The noise was overwhelming, but it only lasted a few seconds before the drill shut down. The bot remained still for a moment before breaking free from the rails and tunnel structure behind it, then headed toward the hangar-like structure. Once the drill had ceased, the massive machine was surprisingly quiet.

"Oh my God," Kaliyah exclaimed, a little too loudly.

Jema quickly covered Kaliyah's mouth with her hand to silence her. But it was too late. One of Gabriel's men had spotted them, and he shouted to his companions, "Hey! Over there!"

"Run!" Jema shouted, pushing Kaliyah ahead of her. Panic surged as they turned to flee, the instinct to escape overtaking all else. With the ground beneath their feet unsteady from the tremors, they bolted as fast as they could. Jema's heart thumped, almost overpowering the sound of rushing blood in her ears. Their footsteps pounded against damp soil as they sprinted for their lives, every shadow turning into a potential pursuer. The once-familiar wasteland had turned into a nightmare as they dashed madly toward the uncertain safety of the night.

Adriel

Adriel could recall the days before the Tel Aviv dome with vivid clarity—a time when scorching heat waves relentlessly assaulted his homeland. A time of climate terror that spanned his childhood, adolescence, and early adulthood. He couldn't quite reach back to the days before that, a time when hope still lingered and average global temperatures seemed achievable at a modest 1.5 degrees, revised upward to 2 degrees, then 2.5, then 3 degrees... until Aegis Corporation constructed the world's first city dome in Singapore. Then... the world soon forgot about global temperature goals. Well, the *Innie* world forgot.

Adriel, however, didn't pine for the days of old. The mere thought of them brought a sheen of sweat to his brow, a physical memory so imposing he momentarily wanted to adjust the aircon. He reveled in the dome's climate-controlled environment, devoid of natural elements like wind, rain, clouds, and fog that his forebears had experienced—or perhaps merely tolerated. Now, the blistering heat, the unbearable humidity juxtaposed with parched dryness of the past were nothing but fading memories. Those who were even older than him may lament the sterility of their environment, feeling trapped under the unrelenting care of what was tantamount to a massive office air conditioner, but Adriel had no complaints. *We're all a product of the times we live in.*

He loved his luxurious beachfront apartment, perched high in the Ben Gurion building, a token of appreciation bestowed upon him by Aegis for long and faithful service. Currently, he sat on the balcony enjoying his breakfast. In this moment, everything was as it should be. The breakfast—a plethora of flavors as he dug in, the warmth of the sun (simulated, yet convincing) kissing his skin. The distant sound of ocean waves provided a serene yet artificial backdrop, and the meticulously engineered orange juice, all a celebration of technology's ultimate triumph over nature. He took another bite. The texture of the flatbread—perfectly crisp yet tender—the olives' briny tang, and the delicate, lab-cultured fish's imitation of freshness were marvels of science that played deliciously upon his senses. The balcony offered a panoramic view of Tel Aviv, its dome-covered skyline another testament to human ingenuity, a sight that never failed to fill Adriel with a sense of pride.

All other aspects of reality were blocked. His braid was set to receive only essential notifications, and his audio filters blocked out the noise from the trams roaming the streets below. Not that they made much noise in the first place. The cars cruising the streets of Tel Aviv were equally quiet, with any residual noise efficiently filtered by the algorithm before it reached his inner ear. *Oh, yes! The good ol' days. Who needs them?*

Having a few days off was a rare pleasure, one that he intended to savor to the fullest. He had completed his meeting with Jarod and addressed the setback they encountered with Scott—the nastiest part of his job—and the other two teams were delivering as expected. He had informed Pacula that he preferred not to be disturbed, and she usually respected such requests. Now, he was as much at peace as he ever was.

He took a sip of his orange juice, relishing the full spread he'd ordered from the deli around the corner. It was an enormous feast, more than he could ever finish: yogurts, peppers, flatbread, olives, and even fish, though he wasn't particularly fond of the latter for breakfast.

He wouldn't usually go for the classic spread. He wasn't *that* kind of Jew. The kind who rigorously observed tradition. He didn't observe kashrut. Or kosher. And he ate pork. Did it matter? His food was all lab-grown anyway, printed and reassembled at a molecular level, far from the natural production methods of the past. He didn't know what tradition said about synth food, but he was of the opinion that no one could really taste the difference anyway. Those who claimed they could were nothing but clueless fundamentalists or elitist snobs—all of whom would be thoroughly embarrassed in a blind taste test.

Down at the beach, the wave machines were on, although calm seas were simulated today, so the waves weren't particularly exciting. He never went anyway, except to the boardwalk. He hated sand, but he appreciated the efforts of Aegis and the Tel Aviv authorities for building the dome frontier out to sea, preserving the beautiful beaches. He had heard the wave machines were automated, running on an algorithm simulating weather patterns of the past, before the tipping points. Though he was too young to remember those days before the collapse, he loved the unpredictability of it all. The algorithm was available to the public, along with weekly forecasts that could be subscribed to, just like people did in the past. He didn't, though. But the general idea of it appealed to him.

The artificiality of the beach, with its meticulously engineered waves, was both a marvel and a mirage. Adriel's gaze often lingered on the horizon where the dome met the sea, a boundary between two worlds—one real, the other a facsimile of nature's past beauty. The salty tang of the sea air was just another detail in the dome's illusion, leaving him to wonder about—but not long for—the authentic experiences of wind, rain, and the unpredictable sea that his forebears had known. *I suppose I could venture Outside, but it wouldn't be the same as it was back then.*

For many, the semblance of continuity with the past provided a sense of comfort, even though everyone knew it was merely a simulation. Young people born and raised inside the dome, who knew nothing else, seemed to appreciate it as well. *Our connection to nature runs deep, beyond our conscious thoughts, memories, experiences, and senses. It's in our genes, or something like that. What the hell do I know?*

He took a final piece of bread to balance out the acidity from the yogurt and milk, feeling stuffed and ready to embark on his day's plans. He had a full itinerary: a visit to the Tel Aviv Museum of Art, followed by shopping at Dizengoff for new shirts, and finally dinner on the boardwalk. *Meat or fish?* He glanced down at the half-finished breakfast spread. *I can't believe I'm already thinking about food again,* he thought, eyeing his belly. Still flat. *Well, flat-ish.* Aegis had kindly provided him with extensive genetic reconfiguration therapy, but one still had to be cautious. *There's no substitute for exercise*, and ever since Gibson enlisted him in his little private war, he hadn't been able to hit the gym as much as he used to. *Not so little anymore, that war. Is it?* He was hoping Gibson would ease off a bit once they eliminated Scott. *Come on, Jarod. I know it hurts, but it's just one more. Then I'll let you have a break.*

He rose from his seat and headed for the shower, but his plans were abruptly halted when an alert from Pacula arrived. It was of the highest priority. *Damn.*

The message was succinct: **[Turn on the news.]**

Speaking of usually respecting do-not-disturb notices. A flicker of annoyance surfaced, a wrinkle in an otherwise smooth morning. The seamless integration of tech—his braid and its wondrous audio filters, its tactical capabilities, all the characteristics he so admired—suddenly seemed like an intrusion. And unlike him, the weight of duty—his role in the machinations of Aegis and the world—never had a day off.

Nevertheless, he decided to be a little rebellious and not comply with Pacula's request, at least for the time being. He continued to dress leisurely, putting on his shoes and jacket as more people called and were diverted by his do-not-disturb notice, sending urgent notifications in response. He obstinately disregarded them all until Gibson himself sent a message.

Alright, alright. Better get this one, then, he thought, switching on his lens and bringing up Keshet. The news was dire. There had been a massive explosion in Quito, Ecuador, with casualties on a scale that made the London bombing seem like a New Year's Eve firecracker incident. The Aegis space elevator construction site had been destroyed, along with a substantial portion of the city. A nuclear weapon was suspected to have been used.

The news hit him like a literal blow to the gut, the words on the screen searing his retinas with the intensity of an old-school branding iron. The images of destruction—the scale of the tragedy unfolding in Quito—did not compute. The fire, smoke, and rubble where once stood a city would be forever etched in his mind. It was a reminder of the fragile state of the world, a looming shadow of the coming war. *Coming? It's here!* For a moment, Adriel felt the apartment shrink, the walls closing in as the reality of the situation pierced his bubble of constructed reality.

The gravity of the situation couldn't be underestimated. Yes, this was indeed the next stage of the war—the escalation he had hoped would never come. Gibson would go completely apeshit. He stood frozen, staring at the news projected on his lens, garbed in his dress shirt, jacket, and good shoes, ready to head out to the museum. "Oh, shit," he finally muttered aloud, still trying to process the magnitude of what had just happened. *I guess my day off just got canceled,* he thought as he ordered his braid to dial up Pacula.

Scott and Dai

"I think it passed straight through. Keep pressure on it," Dai said to Scott, inspecting the wound in his side. Scott's jaw clenched at her touch, but the panic in her eyes was worse than the pain. "Come on. We gotta keep moving," she added. Scott pressed his hand against the gash, blood seeping through his fingers. He had endured his fair share of bullet wounds, but this one was gnarly. The sting as he pressed was excruciating, as if molten metal had pierced his flesh. A little higher, and it would have shattered ribs. It would slow them down, but it wasn't fatal.

Yet, as bad as his injury was, he was luckier than Treston—their comrade lay lifeless in a pool of his own blood, and the Chinese contact, hired to help them access DNA resequencing services in Shanghai, was also gone, along with their hopes of eluding capture. Scott felt a wave of guilt wash over him. Treston, who had sacrificed himself to help, who had fought alongside them, was now silenced forever. *And all I can think of is the resequencing.*

The alleyway where they sought refuge was a deathtrap. Even with their scramblers working overtime, their pursuers' squitos would quickly sniff them out. They needed to create distance and throw off their scent, or else find shelter indoors, where walls, furniture, and possibly electronics and machinery could obscure their signals and make them less visible to prying eyes. *None of that will save us, probably, but why make it easy for them.*

"Stay still," Dai commanded, holding the injector steady against Scott's bullet wound. With a sharp hiss, the sealant gel surged through the nozzle and into his flesh. Scott grimaced, feeling the chemical burn as it sealed the entry wound shut. Dai turned him around and repeated the process for the exit wound, her hands steady despite the urgency.

"That's all we've got for now," she said. "It won't last long. We need to find a safe spot to hole up, and I'll make a run to the pharmacy for some healing patches."

Scott nodded, gritting his teeth against the fierce pain in his side as he got to his feet with Dai's support. They needed to move quickly, but also blend in with the crowds on the street. Scott tried to keep an eye on the few squitos Tres had been able to provide while limping alongside Dai, but it was a struggle to focus on both at once.

As they emerged from the alleyway, Scott withdrew his arm from Dai's shoulder, determined to appear as unremarkable as possible. The last thing they needed was to attract the attention of the city's—or their pursuers'—surveillance systems. The cool air and drizzle brushed against Scott's face, a brief respite quickly overshadowed by the sharp stab in his side with each step. The city's pulse around them felt alien, a rhythm out of sync with what he could muster. They continued on, Scott gritting his teeth, with Dai steady beside him.

"I think I'm okay to walk on my own," he said, "but I won't be able to run."

However, the data on Scott's lens made it clear that they would need to run—and soon. They were surrounded, unless, of course, his tactical was giving him false positives. It was entirely possible; their pursuers were running pervasive interference, making it difficult to get a clean reading. Regardless, the situation demanded the same immediate action: finding a place to hide. His tactical displayed several routes, but they all required them to move quickly and cover long distances in a short amount of time. Given Scott's injury, the odds of doing so undetected were slim. When the tactical factored that in, hiding quickly became their best bet. *Well, duh! AIs can be so obvious sometimes.*

His mind raced, processing the tactical data. The city around them, once an avenue to get lost in anonymity, now felt like a tightening noose.

"Shit," Dai cursed as Scott shared the data with her. "The abandoned building behind us is our only option."

According to the tactical, it wasn't ideal, but it was their only choice. Ideally, they needed a location further from ground zero. Historically, the bounty hunters had shown concern for collateral damage, so staying central with people around might prevent them from resorting to dramatic measures. *Like carpet-bombing our asses with drones.*

Scott did a quick search for the apartment building's blueprints in public databases and cursed under his breath when it came back nil. They'd have to improvise, but it was still their best bet at survival. Returning to the back of the alley, they blasted the padlock on the basement door and made their way inside. The darkness of the basement enveloped them, a stark contrast to the deceptive brightness of the city outside. The air was stale, thick with the dust of abandonment. As they moved through the concrete labyrinth, Scott was acutely aware of the echoes of their footsteps, a reminder of their intrusion into this forgotten fragment of the world—and of their vulnerability. *One probe with audio receptors...*

He dispatched a volley of squitos to assess the situation ahead, hoping to find a defensible position. *Defensible position, right!* If it came down to a direct confrontation, it would be over before it even began. Scott checked his inventory—seven rounds left in his handgun's magazine, one extra clip, and no offensive squitos remaining in his launch pouch. Dai wasn't much better off.

The basement was a maze of concrete hallways and abandoned utility rooms. The compact walls provided some protection against squito scans, but there was nothing of use down here. Worse yet, it was a dead end with no escape route if they were cornered, so they moved upwards.

The apartment building's dilapidated stairwell loomed ahead, a reminder of how far the Outside had fallen into disrepair. The harsh elements—heat and thunderstorms over the last few decades—had ravaged the structure, leaving it barely standing. It was a minor miracle that any windows remained intact at all. *Clearly, this has been abandoned for ages, maybe even since before the domes were erected.* When the world was still livable without the cages. As he surveyed the interior, he noted the lack of structural reinforcements that were commonplace in buildings beyond the safety of the domes. It was clear this building had received no such upgrades.

Scott launched a few scouts to assess the situation. There were biosignatures present in the building—six or seven scattered throughout different areas.

"Good," Scott replied, nodding. "If we're still here when our enemies arrive, it'll take them a few minutes to figure out which biosignatures are ours."

He activated his e-war squitos, ready to create false signatures and buy them more time if they were discovered. But as useful as the squitos were, they were no substitute for a solid escape plan. *We just better not be here when the show starts.*

Scott grimaced, the pain from his wounds becoming increasingly unbearable. Escaping the building was a long shot, but if they could dress his wounds and stem the bleeding, they might just stand a chance.

The hallways were cluttered with abandoned belongings—cartons, blankets, and moldy food littered the ground. It was clear someone had lived in these stairwells, but they were nowhere to be found now. That was a small blessing, at least.

"The stairwell is too open," Scott said. "We need a place that offers cover." After surveying their surroundings, they agreed that the penthouse apartment was their best bet. It was large, with plenty of rooms and abandoned furniture that could be used to obscure their presence. And, perhaps most importantly, it had multiple exits and a fire escape, meaning they wouldn't be trapped. *Hopefully*.

The penthouse, with its layers of dust and decay, was an eerie testament to a life paused. The light filtering through the cracked windows painted shadows across the walls, a canvas of ruin. Scott's eyes drifted over the remnants of domesticity, each item a ghost of the everyday, long estranged from the warmth of human touch. Their presence in this place was a juxtaposition—a blend of urgency in the present and a forgotten past. Dai gently set Scott down on an abandoned couch covered in dusty sheets. The former owners had certainly left in a hurry, but had still taken the time to cover things up, perhaps hoping to one day return. Scott couldn't help but wonder what their story might have been.

Dai dug out a pillow from under the sheet, smacked it a few times to get rid of the dust, and placed it under Scott's head. "Wait here," she said. "I'll be back from the pharmacy in no time. Try not to move around too much. You'll rip the wound."

Scott nodded, a smile playing at the corner of his lips. "Stay frosty," he added.

As Dai left, Scott checked the net for news, something he hadn't done in a while. He was met with a frenzy of reports about a massive explosion in Quito that had leveled the city and left an unimaginable death toll. He knew what this was—something he had tried to stop, but had clearly failed. *How had Alixha broken through Aki's decryption?* It wasn't supposed to be possible, yet she had done it. *This could only be her doing.*

As Scott shifted to a more comfortable position on the dusty couch, he groaned in pain. He needed to focus on his wounds, not the news. He shut off the net, his eyes growing heavy as he fought off the dizziness. But a few moments later, he passed out from his injuries, still bleeding.

Dawn broke through the cracked window in the living room, casting prismatic rays of light throughout. It was beautiful—

Scott took it as a symbol of hope amidst the forgotten ruins of the apartment building. He had managed to get a few hours of sleep after Dai returned with the med kit. The patches were working their magic, healing his wound, controlling inflammation, and preventing infection. His braid had informed him that he had briefly been running a fever, but the patches had quickly resolved that. He felt stronger now. But strong enough to move?

Time was running out, and the longer they stayed in the penthouse, the higher the risk. They couldn't hope to remain hidden here forever. Their pursuers were competent and hot on their trail. Scott's scouts had reported that the penthouse was still empty, and he noted that the front door was now barricaded with loose junk—a set of drawers, an old couch, and a partly blocking bookshelf. *It's more symbolic than anything else,* he thought. *It wouldn't keep anyone out. Dai must have done that while I was passed out.*

The penthouse apartment was surprisingly intact, Scott observed as he surveyed the place once again. The dining room had a sturdy table and chairs that were mostly intact, and the kitchen still had furniture. The bedroom had a bedframe, but the mattress was missing. It was a big place, especially for Tokyo.

He set his scouts to keep watch over the entire building, not just the apartment, in case he dozed off again. If any new biosignatures showed up, he would be alerted. He set the braid to notify Dai as well, just in case he was too out of it to hear the alarm.

Dai's voice interrupted his thoughts. "We've been through worse, right?" She sat down next to him and ran her fingers through his hair. That simple act gave Scott a quiet strength, a shared resolve that spoke louder than words. Her touch, the comfort she offered, was a bright light in the turmoil of his thoughts. The weight of their past, the losses they had endured, the challenges ahead—were all lifted, but only momentarily.

"We have. I just can't remember when," he said with a smile. *Have we been through worse?* Aki was gone, and so was Tres. The rendezvous Tres had set up for them was no longer an option, leaving them with nowhere to hide. Even if they managed to evade their pursuers now, their situation was far from ideal. Alixha was out there somewhere, and so were Aegis, Legacy, and a scourge of independent bounty hunters waiting to strike. And in the end, Alixha set off her bomb anyway. It had all been for nothing.

"Remember the Indonesia raid," Dai said. "We were backed up inside that apartment, just like now. Only I was the one with a bullet wound."

Scott nodded. "That time, we had the cavalry waiting around the corner, as I recall."

Dai sighed. "It's a shame it will end like this. I would have liked to see Stockholm."

Scott took her hand. "It's not over yet."

Dai didn't say anything in response. She lay down next to him on the sheet-covered couch and snuggled up. After a few minutes, he dozed off again, dreaming about Stockholm.

A jarring beep resonated inside his cranium, yanking him from slumber. "How long was I out?" he grunted, trying to shake off the residual dizziness from the nap. The beep that pulled him from the depths of his feverish sleep left a lingering echo in his mind, a harsh reminder of the world insisting upon them. As he sat up, the room swayed slightly, the edges of his vision blurring as if resisting the abrupt return to consciousness.

"About an hour and a half," Dai said.

He gingerly touched the medical patch covering his wound. The fabric felt cold and alien to the touch, its edges frayed from constant movement, but the soreness underneath was a positive sign. The wound was healing.

The notification that roused him was a message from the Chinese. The message on his lens pulsed like a translucent beacon against the dimly lit room. Astonishingly, Treston had still come through somehow, and the meeting was still a go. A new contact had been dispatched, and they were advised to wait patiently for further instructions. The Chinese, as expected, delivered a first-rate service, but it also came with the heftiest of price tags.

A befuddled frown spread across his face as he perused the message. Dai noticed, her features tense with what seemed like a mix of concern and anticipation. "What's wrong?" she inquired. "Has the Bolivian army arrived already?"

He arched an eyebrow, confused by the reference. "It's a line from *Butch Cassidy and the Sundance Kid*, remember? I watched it with Aki some time ago, and you declined the invitation."

"Ah, yes, I recall," Scott replied, smiling. Dai's expression relaxed. "So, what is it then?" she asked.

"It's the genetic engineering specialist," he replied. "Tres came through, and the meeting is still on in three hours."

Dai inhaled deeply, her face shedding its anxiety in an instant. "Excellent," she breathed. "You had me worried for a moment there."

He forwarded the time and location to Dai. "By the way, nice reference," he remarked.

A smile crept onto her lips.

Scott savored the glimmer of hope flickering in Dai's eyes. He hadn't deceived her. Despite the perilous predicament they found themselves in, there was still a chance, however slim. Rebuilding their identities from the ground up, incorporating new identities into the very fabric of their physiology, could still bestow upon them the gift of unrestricted movement. They would never be entirely unfettered or entirely secure, but that hopeful whisper—that they could settle in Stockholm and live out their lives—remained. However, before they could enjoy that future, they had to extricate themselves from their present quagmire.

"We need to go," he declared.

The wound had yet to heal entirely. It was too soon to mobilize, a fact they both acknowledged. Nevertheless, they had no choice but to move. The therapeutic gel patch was working swiftly, but not swiftly enough. He could barely put pressure on the wound without exacerbating the injury. Scott figured he had a few hours before it was safe to move without tearing it open again. Even then, it would be at least a day or two before it healed completely. However, if they didn't have to run or engage in combat, he might manage to strain it a little without risking his life. They also had another patch to use later if the current one tore.

As he began to stand up, Dai stepped in to assist him. "On your feet, soldier," she said. "On your feet!" Scott grunted, the act of standing a rebellion against his body, each tiny movement a negotiation with the pain. It wasn't terrible, but it wasn't easy either. *It can work,* he thought. *Just switch it off.*

As they advanced toward the exit, his braid beeped. He checked—it was indeed the notification they had hoped would not yet come: new biosignatures in the building. Downstairs, infiltrating the lobby.

"Shit," he swore, his pulse instantly hammering in his ears, adrenaline rushing.

"What is it?" Dai inquired.

"The Bolivian army."

Jarod

"We search in pairs and cut him off," Dembwe declared, already in the middle of the briefing. Jarod and Wyatt had arrived late to the scene, leaving Dembwe's team waiting outside the back of the building for several minutes as they zeroed in on Scott's location. As Jarod stepped into the alleyway, the weight of grief bore down heavily upon him. He caught a glimpse of Wyatt—his eyes a mirror of his own—and for a moment, he saw some humanity in the normally stoic man.

The news of Kale's death had hit the team hard. Jarod, in particular, now struggled even more to maintain focus on the task at hand than before. The gruesome image of Kale's lifeless form sprawled on the bed in that hotel room lingered unmercifully, like a persistent projection on his lens that he couldn't close. This line of work was never meant for him. Nor for Riley. They weren't former special forces like Wyatt and himself, accustomed to the harsh realities of this profession. It was this burden that had driven Kale to his breaking point, and someone had taken advantage of his vulnerability. *Adriel warned us. But I didn't listen.* He hadn't taken the necessary precautions. No, he had been too preoccupied with his own guilt to notice the needs of his team. And now, they were once again on the brink of repeating the very actions that had ultimately cost Kale his life.

He vigorously shook his head, attempting to banish thoughts of Kale. Dembwe's voice droned on in the background, a necessary distraction in Jarod's current state of mind. He saw a brief flicker of impatience on Wyatt's face—eagerness to redirect his pain into action. Jarod let out a wild grin and slapped himself on the cheeks, the only way to purge himself of the mental intrusion and regain focus. He must have appeared unhinged to anyone watching, but no one commented. Dembwe continued with the briefing, swiftly bringing Jarod and Wyatt up to date before sending tactical data to their braids.

Jarod hastily checked his ammunition, realizing with a jolt that he had forgotten to restock. It was just another indication that he wasn't fully committed to the mission. But he had three spare magazines, which would have to suffice.

Without formal jurisdiction, they couldn't bring any of Dembwe's heavier weapons. They were limited to 3D-printed, unregistered, and easily concealed handguns, which, should they be careless, could still raise suspicions in the highly monitored streets of Tokyo, where even the Outside was covered by state-of-the-art surveillance—at least near the frontiers.

"Enough," Wyatt interjected, now bored and annoyed. "Six of us, two of them. Got it. Let's go."

"Easy there, big guy." Jarod patted him on the shoulder, knowing that Wyatt's impatience and thirst for revenge were his ways of coping with Kale's death. Jarod made a mental note to keep an eye on him this time. If he thought it would help, he would've reminded Wyatt to respect Scott's capabilities. Injured and outgunned, the stubbornly resourceful young man might still find a way out. However, Wyatt was the type of person who relied on instincts and reflexes. Jarod knew the former were seldom wrong, and the latter were as swift as lightning. He glanced over at Dembwe's two teammates but couldn't remember their names.

Hicks and Hudson? Did it matter? They were merely hired

guns, mercenaries with no loyalty or connection beyond the contract, bound by an honor system rather than personal ties. In fact, Jarod realized that, in this very moment, he couldn't even recall Dembwe's first name, even after working with him for years. *Jana. Jana Dembwe. That's it. Funny. After all this time, I still struggle.*

He had never taken the time to get to know Dembwe beyond the parameters of their contracted jobs. They had never gone out for drinks or dinner, nor had he ever inquired about Dembwe's personal life—like whether he had a wife or children. All that mattered was that Dembwe showed up, did his job, and sent a bill for his services afterward. Beyond that, there was no need for further interaction. *Just as well, probably.*

Dembwe finished the briefing. "The area is rife with false positives. We'll need to eliminate his defense squitos before we can get a clear reading."

Scott knew they were coming and was undoubtedly prepared for their arrival. "Riley," Jarod said over the comm, "you got us on your HUD?"

"Got you. All feeds and vitals on display," Riley confirmed. "Don't worry, boys, I'll hold your hands through this."

"Very funny," Wyatt said.

Jarod gave the order, and they entered the building, each releasing a swarm of scout and electronic warfare squitos to disrupt and take down Scott's defenses. Jarod minimized the lens display to prevent information overload, relying on Riley to provide him with the most pertinent details.

"Okay," she said as the squitos left their pouch. "Bugs on the loose. Let's see what we can see."

The team dispersed, systematically progressing through the building section by section, adhering to Dembwe's tactical recommendation to start with a quick sweep of the basement. According to the analysis, Scott was unlikely to hide there, given the lack of viable exit strategies in the event of detection. The analysis was correct; the basement was clear. The team then proceeded to the ground floor, clearing it methodically.

Despite decades of merciless weather taking a toll on the old building, leaving it in a deplorable state, most of the windows were still intact, with some storm shutters either up or down. The presence of open shutters and intact windows suggested that someone was using the building. *Derelicts seeking cover? Squatters? Or maybe there's some automation involved—an AI operating them as if the building's tenants still lived here. Probably not. The building predates such tech.*

Although AIs were unlikely, there could be other types of automation in use, such as dumb-bots—window washers and the like, or even automated doors, although none seemed to be present.

It's a ghost house, for sure. Jarod speculated that perhaps the owner would occasionally check on the run-down building—too dilapidated to fix and too worthless to sell.

One of the team members detected third-party signatures, which meant they had to be careful with their targeting. The last thing they needed was to mistake a squatter for Scott and cause needless harm.

"Yeah, well..." Wyatt whispered, "better them than me."

Jarod understood the sentiment but also knew that a fraction of a second's hesitation could be the difference between life and death, especially with someone as skilled as Scott, who probably wouldn't bother with the same level of caution.

"Okay, Dembwe, take the upper levels. We'll clear the ground floor," Jarod ordered, reluctantly splitting the team to cover more ground. He warned everyone to be careful, emphasizing again that Scott was a slippery target.

Wyatt winked at him and smiled. "If you're scared, boss, you can take Dembwe and the team, and I'll go solo."

"Hilarious," Jarod replied, deadpan. "Riley, give me a reading. What's the status upstairs?"

"I'm on it. Give me a minute," Riley replied, and Jarod checked the lens for her feed. The first floor had several signatures. *So, what are you, my little friends? Decoys? People? Or targets?*

As he observed the swarm of bugs in action, he was reminded that Scott also had access to high-tech equipment, which meant he might still have a line to Alixha, and their previous intel on Scott's attempts to break free from the organization was likely false—or he had alternative connections.

"I'm having difficulty getting a clear reading," Riley reported. "But the tac says it's eighty percent confident that these signatures are false positives."

"That's good enough for me," Wyatt responded, though Jarod was uncertain whether Wyatt truly understood the concept of confidence levels. He had a habit of saying "good enough for me" regardless. A few moments later, Riley confirmed that the second floor was also riddled with similar false signatures. Jarod signaled to Dembwe to proceed.

"Best we can do for now," Riley said. "Stay alert while I work on the third floor."

"Copy," Jarod replied. An eighty percent confidence level meant that the tactical would suggest a manual sweep, confirming the accuracy of the readings with human eyes. Wyatt likely knew this and probably hoped the confidence levels would stay in that range so he could justify going in—*guns blazing too, if he gets to decide.*

As Dembwe's team headed upstairs, Jarod and Wyatt began sweeping the ground floor, apartment by apartment. Some of the units didn't even have doors, while others had old, abandoned furniture and boxes of personal belongings left behind long ago, probably when the tenants were granted dome residency through one of the programs or lotteries. Some chose to leave their old stuff behind or were forced to when they hit their allocation limits.

Things were different back in those days. When these buildings were cleared, the domes were smaller, and you couldn't bring all your belongings with you as you can now. The apartments inside the dome were tiny compared to what people had left behind. *But free from perpetual wind and rain.* In a few decades, none of these old buildings would remain unless the dome expanded. Jarod quickly checked his braid and discovered that Haneda Ota would eventually be included in the expansion, but it was still ten years away if they kept to the schedule. *Come on! Focus!*

He had never been interested in dome expansions or social programs aimed at helping the Outies; that was Dana's thing. Why he felt compelled to mull over such things now, during a life-and-death operation, was beyond him. He forced himself to focus on the task at hand and took in the hallway with its broken light, Wyatt's swift movements, and the sound of the mercenaries clearing the apartments above them one by one. He listened intently to the outside world—the wind, the rain, the elements battering the building—all to keep his head focused on the task at hand.

Wyatt's voice broke the silence. "Clear," he announced as they moved to the next apartment. Riley's voice came over the comms, confirming another false positive. Dembwe reported in, clearing the apartments on the second floor. "Second floor is clear," he said. "Starting on the third."

Only the third floor left, then.

Soon. Don't get ahead of yourself.

Jarod shook his head once more, trying to clear the distracting thoughts before regrouping with Dembwe by the stairwell leading to the third floor. If Scott was in the building, he would be up there somewhere. Jarod checked the last room on his list, and there he saw the sun shining through a pair of sheer curtains, casting rays of warm light across the walls. It reminded him of their bedroom back home, on those mornings when they slept in, and his thoughts drifted to Dana.

Why wasn't he with her? Why hadn't he abandoned the job and set off for Frankfurt as soon as he heard that she was missing? Or after she had escaped? Or was she dead? *Am I completely insane?* He took a deep breath and moved through the rest of the apartment.

He had been holding on to the idea that he was dispensing some form of justice. Fighting fire with fire, perhaps, but doing what legacy law enforcement or the world's militaries could not. But it was all just a revenge mission ordered by a conglomerate of the super-rich to exact revenge against the people who destroyed their precious dome. *It sure as hell isn't about the lives lost.* And now Quito, with hundreds of thousands dead. Innies and

Outies alike.

The whole conflict had been a sham, a false dichotomy propagated by both Gibson and Alixha Rahena. They spun the narrative that the world's present strife was solely about the Outies' fight against the Innies, and vice versa. But was it? The crimes he was supposedly reacting to, in Aegis's name, were not even committed by Outies. Scott, Bahno, Sicscal, Alixha herself, as well as Gibson and Adriel, were all Innies, killing other Innies and Outies alike. *Neither was the root cause.* It was crystal clear that neither party was the cause of the world's tensions, and neither Gibson nor Alixha's actions were saving anyone. He knew deep down that he wasn't saving anyone either. If anyone was working to save the world, it was Dana. *His job should be to support and defend people like her, not participate in whatever this is.*

Despite his distracting thoughts, Jarod had finished sweeping his section and was fairly confident it was clear. Wyatt joined him. "My section is clear," he reported.

The ground-floor apartments were barely cleared when the shooting began. Dembwe's voice boomed through the comms, "Contact!"

Without hesitation, Wyatt—ever the cowboy—raced toward the third floor. Jarod ordered him to hold at the stairwell's bottom, but Wyatt was already halfway up, completely zoned out.

"Damn it, Wyatt," Jarod muttered under his breath, frustrated with his teammate's incessant recklessness. He knew Wyatt was unstoppable when he was in kill mode, now relying solely on his instincts. Jarod started climbing the stairs cautiously but at a brisk pace. He pulled up the tactical display on his lens and monitored his team's life signs. One of Dembwe's men had already flatlined. He was gone.

The gunshots thundered through the stairwell, and even his inner ear noise cancellation struggled to filter out the deafening noise. He quickened his pace, adrenaline coursing through his veins.

As he climbed the stairs, another one of Dembwe's men flatlined. His tactical display flickered, and more life signs appeared. *More false positives? Or had we missed legitimate targets during the initial analysis of the building?*

"Riley," he barked over the comm. "Talk to me. What's going on?"

"I'm working on it," Riley replied calmly. "Be careful."

Be careful! Gee, thanks! Hadn't thought about that.

He held his gun firmly, scanning the level above him as he climbed the stairs. The electromagnetic interference in the building simmered, frying his electronics one by one. With aim assist off, he now had to rely solely on his own skills as he reached the third floor.

But there was nothing.

Wyatt had vanished, no longer visible in the stairwell. A second later, the sound of gunshots resumed, reverberating like a cavalcade of fireworks.

"Wyatt!" he yelled into the comm.

Dembwe flatlined. *Goddammit!*

He approached the second apartment, from where the gunshots had originated. As he entered, Wyatt screamed, followed by more gunfire. Then, silence. A second later, Wyatt's life sign flatlined too.

"What the hell is going on?" Riley's voice crackled over the comm, her tone now panic-stricken.

He texted her to maintain radio silence, unable to handle any distractions. The comms were breaking up, and he could barely hear her anyway. He needed to focus on what was in front of him.

He clung to the hope that Wyatt might still be alive, reassuring himself that a flatline on the monitor didn't always mean death. It could be that Wyatt's braid had been damaged or that his life signs were simply too weak to register. *You keep telling yourself that.*

All these deaths! It's pointless, and now I know it. There was no peace to be found in this bloodbath—no justice. Even if Scott was guilty of something, this had nothing to do with dispensing justice or filling in the gaps left by impotent Legacy law enforcement agencies. It was just a corporation waging war against its enemies, and Jarod was nothing more than the tool they used to accomplish their objectives. *It has to stop.*

Jarod's heart raced, not just from adrenaline but from the sudden, piercing clarity that this endless cycle of violence offered no real closure, no peace.

"Scott!" he yelled. "Hold your fire. I'm coming out."

He lowered his gun and made his way through the apartment hallway toward the living room. "I just want to talk," he said, holstering his weapon. "Guns down."

As he entered the living room, he saw Wyatt and one of Dembwe's men on the floor, lifeless. In the corner, he saw Scott and a girl. They were both alive, with the girl holding an injured Scott. They both looked at Jarod, their eyes showing a mix of terror and surprise. It was neither the look of triumph nor defeat he had expected.

Riley was pinging him furiously on the emergency channel. "Finally!" she exclaimed. "One of the life signs we thought were ghosts is the real deal. Looks like a party crasher."

"What?" Whoever it was must have used some advanced technology to hide their life sign so well, making it difficult for their squitos to detect anything. No heat signatures, no blips indicating the presence of anyone.

Jarod had no time to figure out who the party crasher was. He heard a sound behind him and swiftly turned. It was a slender shape—a woman. The same operative who had almost killed him in the skyscraper while he was going after Bahno.

"You?" he said, shocked.

The woman had a handgun trained on him, while Jarod's own weapon dangled uselessly in its holster by his side.

The woman said nothing.

He remembered her name—Elena—and knew she was here for more than just Scott. Everything happened in a split second. He ducked and brought his gun to bear, displaying catlike reflexes he didn't think were possible without a full combat suit. But it wasn't enough. Elena fired—twice—hitting him in the left shoulder and the side. The impact of the bullets tore through him, knocking him backward but not all the way down. The sharp report of the gunfire was shockingly loud, the smell of the discharge acrid in his nostrils. Pain flared hot and bright, but Jarod gritted his teeth and pulled the trigger, firing blindly until Elena, too, fell to her knees, injured. His actions weren't driven by training or even anger but the raw, primal urge to survive. He fired again and again until she toppled over.

As he fell to the ground, bleeding, he barely caught a glimpse of Elena as she dragged herself away and disappeared around a corner. *That will have to do,* he thought. *If she comes back, she's won.*

"Riley," he said urgently over the comm. "Medical. Now."

Riley confirmed that help was on the way.

With a Herculean effort, he rolled over to get a glimpse of Scott and the girl. "Go now," he said, his voice strained. "It's over. For us, anyway. We won't come after you anymore."

Scott nodded, and the girl helped him up as they both limped out of the apartment. It was the last time Jarod would see them. "Good luck," he called out after them.

As he lay there, bleeding and in pain, he had a moment of absolute clarity. He knew what he needed to do—what he had needed to do for a while now.

"Dana. I'm coming, my love," he whispered to himself, once more bringing up her picture on the lens. And then darkness embraced him as he blacked out.

Dana, Jarod and Aea

Dana and Aea languished in their relatively confined quarters within the Herman Messe Hotel, a room nestled midway up the towering pencil-scraper in Frankfurt's Messe district. They remained as inconspicuous as possible, avoiding public appearances to evade the ever-watchful gaze of city surveillance cameras. They frequented the hotel's more discreet restaurant on the third floor, rather than the flashy establishment at the top or the ground-floor breakfast room. Fewer people, fewer braids, and fewer lenses meant less risk.

Dana occupied herself with reading and watching flicks on the room's flatscreen, while Aea explored the bounties that lay within her newfound braid. Three days had elapsed since their arrival in Frankfurt Central, and Dana was now growing increasingly restless. The vibrant cityscape beckoned from just beyond the hotel window, its tantalizing allure taunting her. She would periodically steal a glance outside, careful to obscure her face from potential prying eyes. One facial recognition data point captured by a passing drone or a surveillance camera mounted on the scraper opposite could spell the end of their freedom—of Aea's freedom in particular. Nonetheless, she couldn't resist the occasional glimpse; the monotonous view of the curtains offered little in the way of respite.

Aea, being an Outie, fared better in these cloistered conditions. Accustomed to avoiding the harsh outside environment, she found solace indoors. Her new braid, a constant source of fascination, provided ample distraction. Dana respected Aea's privacy and took care to remain ignorant of the content with which she immersed herself. It was just as well that Aea kept busy, Dana reasoned. Aea had endured so much; any diversion from thoughts of her family, Daemon, and Stefan was probably a welcome reprieve.

Dana's fingers traced the cold glass of the hotel window, the protective barrier between her and the vibrant life of Frankfurt's central dome. The city blurred before her eyes, each neon twinkle a reminder of a world moving on without them. But she had to protect Aea, even if it meant doing so from this gilded cage. Jarod's continued absence weighed heavily on her mind. She recalled his caution before all this began—that his mission was dangerous and would often require him to go dark. Despite this warning, concern gnawed at her. Surely, he couldn't be so deeply entrenched that he remained oblivious to the widely publicized abduction of the Innie woman? Her name saturated the news; it was inescapable. Yet Jarod had made no contact. What did it mean?

Each passing day stretched into an agonizing eternity. Dana found herself lost in mental images of Jarod's reassuring smiles, the warmth of his touch. The flicks and books that filled her days couldn't dispel her worry, a constant, gnawing presence that refused to be ignored. The artificial glow from the hotel flatscreen cast fleeting shadows, sometimes playing tricks on her eyes—shadows that never materialized into the figure she so desperately wanted to see. The tactile memory of their last embrace, that morning before she departed for this place, lingered on her skin with a ghostly sensation, both comforting and torturous.

And now, the explosion in Quito had claimed the lives of hundreds of thousands, pushing the world to the brink of catastrophe. Thus far, no one had retaliated, and nuclear annihilation remained at bay. Dana mused on the improbability of the situation. She was skeptical that the world's superpowers had truly relinquished their nuclear arsenals, despite their claims.

Undoubtedly, the US, Russia, and China retained a secret stash, hidden from the eyes of the UN's Nuclear Weapons watchdog. For now, it seemed they lived on borrowed time, as Chile, bereft of such destructive capabilities, was unable to strike back. Dana couldn't help but wonder what the result would have been if the United States or England had been the target.

Their dwindling funds added to Dana's mounting anxiety. The hotel was a costly refuge, and while Mr. Fernis' digital acrobatics granted her access to her accounts, the ever-growing bill loomed ominously. Relocation would soon become a necessity, but Dana delayed the inevitable, fearing exposure during the transition. Her heart skipped a beat every time she reviewed their finances, the numbers on her lens dwindling all too swiftly. Every click on the Net was a microtransaction, eating away at their financial safety net. But she rationalized that staying put would make it easier for Jarod to find them, should he, against all odds, be out there trying to locate them. That thought provided a small measure of comfort in their increasingly dire circumstances.

Oh, Jarod. My love. Where are you? Are you lost to me, my dear? Or are you under the surface, unable to rise and make contact? Are you injured, lying lifeless in some distant hospital bed?

Dana tried hard to suppress her worries, aware that fretting would not alter the outcome. Outside, twilight had ebbed away, ushering in the end of another day. Another day, confined within their cramped sanctuary, prisoners to circumstances beyond their control. *At the very least, we're no longer at gunpoint.*

At night, they shared the bed, choosing to conserve funds rather than splurge on a double room. If they had opted for the latter, their resources would have been depleted by now, and staying stationary and concealed was the priority.

In the depths of the night, Aea would sometimes seek out Dana's hand for solace. She accepted the gesture gladly, providing comfort to the young girl while finding reassurance in their shared touch. Those moments of quiet solidarity were their silent rebellion against a world tearing at the seams. Come morning, they readied themselves, showered, dressed, and had breakfast delivered to their room. Dana occasionally pondered what the hotel staff might think of their unconventional arrangement—a young girl and an older woman, secluded in their room, never venturing out. Yet, their bond was more akin to that of mother and daughter than anything illicit. *Likely, they haven't even noticed,* she told herself. *It's a big hotel.*

Two more days passed, without any news. Dana cautiously probed the Net, utilizing the limited encryption capabilities her commercial-grade braid afforded her, but Jarod remained elusive. By the fifth day, they had all but surrendered hope and were prepared to risk relocating. Dana contacted Chaboney, her old mentor, and arranged transportation for the following day, steeling herself for the move. The decision to relocate was a storm cloud looming on the horizon, each day drawing it closer until it could no longer be ignored. *No dome will protect us from this hurricane.* Dana packed their belongings with mechanical precision, each item a choice between necessity and sentimentality. *Not that we have much, anyway. But we still need to travel light.* She felt as prepared as she could be.

However, that night, her slumber was disrupted by an encrypted notification. It was him. Finally. Jarod had located them and made preparations for a rendezvous. His instructions were succinct and purposeful: Prepare to move.

An hour later, they stood fully dressed, their sparse belongings either packed or discarded as circumstances dictated. A knock resounded at the door. When she opened it, Jarod stood before her—bruised, disheveled, bandaged. The moment Jarod's battered form appeared, the sterile, recycled air of the hotel corridor rushed in. Gel packs swelled beneath his shirt at his shoulder and side.

Dana flung herself into his embrace, the floodgates of relief opening within her. Her touch elicited a pained groan.

"What happened?" she asked, her fingers brushing the cold surface of the packs. His familiar scent, mixed with the unmistakable tang of gel antiseptics, filled her with a tumultuous blend of comfort and fear. However concerned she was, in his embrace, the world's chaos momentarily receded, replaced by an overwhelming surge of love.

"I'm fine," he responded, cutting straight to the point. "We need to go."

Jarod acknowledged Aea, but the pair exchanged no words. There would be ample opportunity for them to become better acquainted later, assuming they survived. He guided them toward the elevator, clarifying their predicament as they moved. Not only were they being pursued, but Jarod himself was also a target. Legacy, bounty hunters, and perhaps even Aegis, his erstwhile employer, were on his trail. They had not taken kindly to his failures and subsequent abandonment of his mission.

Continuously glancing over his shoulder, he ushered them into the elevator.

As the elevator doors slid shut, they ventured forth into the wilderness.

Epilogue: Aea

In the seat opposite Aea, Dana rested against the slow-train window, with Jarod leaning on her shoulder. Their eyes were shut, but recent events had taken a toll on their bodies and souls, leaving all three with precious little sleep. Looming ahead was the checkpoint at Gare du Nord, a chokepoint that would make or break their new identities.

Aea gazed out of the train window, watching as the suburbs of Paris slid by in a blur. *The world has gone mad,* she thought. The bomb in Quito had been catastrophic, setting off a chain reaction of chaos and confusion. If the world was crazy after London, the madness had now gone into overdrive, ripples spreading far and wide. Her two substitute parents were on edge—she could tell—though they kept their worries to themselves. They were afraid of being exposed, and rightly so. Aea knew that if they were discovered, the consequences would be horrific—perhaps most of all for her.

The warning they had received from the weirdo in Frankfurt still rang in her ears—their new identities were only a thin veneer, easily peeled away by a more determined search. She was still wanted, hunted by the German police and Interpol, while her companions were pursued by Aegis and bounty hunters.

The events of the past few days had plunged the world into darkness. Communications were down, borders sealed, and cities under lockdown. The entire planet had ground to a halt, as people cowered in their homes, afraid to venture out. And as the train slowed down, Aea knew they were approaching crunch time. What awaited them at Gare du Nord was anyone's guess. But one thing was certain: they were not safe. The world had become a dangerous place, and they were trapped in the eye of the storm.

As the train decelerated, the reality of their approach to Gare du Nord gripped Aea with a tangible urgency. The mix of anticipation and fear was a bitter concoction that clouded her thoughts. She watched as Paris's outskirts gave way to denser, more imposing structures, all domed as they passed the frontier. Each kilometer now brought them closer to a moment of truth she wasn't sure they were ready for. Dana had managed to secure a safe haven for them with an old mentor in Caen, though Aea couldn't quite recall his name. *Chardonnay, was it? No, that's a type of wine.* But it didn't matter. What mattered was that they would be switching to a local train in Paris and heading there to wait out the storm.

Dana's friend had connections and resources that would keep them hidden from the police. And once things cooled down, they would make their way to North America—either the United States or Canada—where Jarod's companion Riley had made further arrangements. Yes, Europe was in shambles, and South America was no better after the bomb in Quito. Asia was also a mess, with Alixha—what's-her-name—wreaking havoc.

But the United States had managed to stay out of the fray—at least on the East Coast. Getting there would require a plane—a *screamer,* as Jarod called it. Dana had never flown before, and the thought made her uneasy. It wouldn't be like taking a bullet tunnel under the Atlantic. Planes had to avoid the weather, and delays were always a possibility. *It's not as smooth as taking a bullet,* she thought. *But what do I know? I've never been on one of those, either.* She had technically been on a plane before, but only as a small child when her parents fled Africa for Germany. She had no memory of it. So the prospect of flying was just another new experience to add to the list.

Despite all the loss and tragedy that had befallen her, Dana couldn't help but feel a glimmer of excitement about the future. It made her feel guilty, of course, knowing that others had suffered far more than she had. This anticipation of something new was often overshadowed by a deep-seated sorrow for the life she had left behind—the family and friends who were now but a whisper of a past she could no longer return to. She prayed that her loved ones were safe, that they would all be reunited someday. *Dad. Tabayah. They're all safe.* She could feel it. *Daemon and Stefan too. Even Jema and Kaliyah. Yes, they're all safe, out there somewhere, waiting for me.*

As the slow train pulled into the station, Dana felt a sense of awe at the grandeur of Paris Central. The dome overhead, the Eiffel Tower, the Arc de Triomphe, and the Champs-Élysées nearby—it was exhilarating. Frau Gerhling had told her that the Eiffel Tower, when it was first built, was the tallest structure humanity had ever created since the pyramids. It had taken three thousand years for mankind to surpass that record. Aea found it fascinating, wondering if she would ever get to see it up close. But she knew that was unlikely given their current circumstances. *Not this time, anyway.* They had to keep moving, keep running.

Dana had assured her that the police would eventually stop looking for her once they realized she had nothing to do with the kidnappings. The bomb in Quito had forced the authorities to reprioritize their efforts, and they wouldn't have time to waste searching for a teenage girl on the run. Aea would be safe again, free to live her life as she pleased.

As the first light of dawn crept into the compartment, dimmed somewhat by the dome, Dana stirred and asked if she was okay. Aea nodded and smiled, feeling a sense of calm wash over her despite everything that had happened.

She watched as Gare du Nord loomed into view, a sprawling station even bigger than Frankfurt Hauptbahnhof. But she knew that it was nothing compared to the grandeur of what she would see in America. New York City, with its towering skyscrapers and massive domes, was a world away from the quiet suburbs of Niederrad, on the Outside.

As the train came to a stop at the platform, Aea, Dana, and Jarod gathered their belongings and stepped off. Dana's hand on Aea's cheek offered a sense of comfort and reassurance, and Aea smiled gratefully, knowing that she had friends who would always have her back.

"Don't worry, we'll be fine," Dana said, her voice soft and soothing.

Aea thought of her little sister Tabayah, with her boundless curiosity and infectious energy. She wished that Tabayah could be there with her, experiencing all of this for herself. *Oh, Tabayah. How I miss you.* But she knew that one day they would be reunited, and they would have all the time in the world to explore the wonders together.

They made their way down the platform, and there in the distance, the Paris checkpoint loomed.

2032: The "Great North American Heatwave" kills over 100,000 people and sparks mass migration from southern U.S. states to Canada.

2035: The Arctic becomes ice-free during summer months for the first time in recorded history. Shipping routes open, but geopolitical tensions over resource extraction escalate.

2038: Widespread crop failures in sub-Saharan Africa lead to a global food crisis. Climate refugees surge, overwhelming existing aid structures in Europe.

2041: The Amazon rainforest reaches a critical tipping point, transitioning from a carbon sink to a carbon source. Global CO2 levels spike, accelerating warming.

2042: Singapore begins construction of the first environmental dome to combat rising sea levels and extreme weather events. This initiative comes in response to catastrophic flooding that submerges one-third of the city-state's landmass.

2045: Aegis introduces its first successful neural braid interface.

2049: A nuclear exchange between India and Pakistan devastates Chennai and Faisalabad.

2050: Global sea levels rise by an average of 1.2 meters, displacing millions in coastal regions. Entire islands in the Pacific and Indian Ocean disappear, and nations like the Maldives relocate their populations.

2055: A category 7 hurricane devastates the eastern seaboard of the U.S., leading to the first discussions of doming cities like Miami and New York.

2057: Aegis Corporation begins construction of city domes *en masse* in rich Western countries and soon dominates the market.

2062: The Thwaites Glacier in Antarctica collapses, accelerating sea-level rise and inundating coastal cities across Asia and the Americas.

2063: Nuclear weapons are banned globally and remaining stock placed under UN control.

2065: An Outie rebellion near Paris coincides with Europe's hottest summer on record, further stressing agriculture and water supplies.

2070: Mass coral bleaching events wipe out the remaining Great Barrier Reef, devastating marine biodiversity and local economies.

2071: The UN DomeEx program is formed to aid in dome construction in less affluent countries.

2075: Alixha Rahena publishes the *Manifesto of Light*, emphasizing the role of corporate greed in exacerbating climate-related destruction and inequality.

2078: A megadrought spanning 15 years cripples much of western North America. Water becomes the most contested resource across the region.

2082: Dead zones expand in the oceans, reducing global fish stocks by 60%. Dome governments increase food imports from Outie-controlled territories, straining relations further.

2085: Outie migrations surge as record-breaking wildfires consume millions of acres in Siberia, California, and Australia.

2090: Lux Aeterna operatives begin sabotaging water purification systems within domes to expose vulnerabilities and highlight resource inequities.

2093: Heatwaves in Europe reach unprecedented levels, killing thousands. This accelerates the exodus to domes, with waiting lists for entry stretching for decades. The Crescent is formed outside Frankfurt am Main.

2098: A methane eruption from melting permafrost in the Arctic Circle disrupts weather patterns globally, leading to erratic monsoons and flash flooding.

2102: Lux Aeterna successfully hacks the Paris central dome's AI, exposing critical resource mismanagement tied to corporate corruption.

2104: Protests erupt inside the London Dome over water rationing policies after new desalination technology promised relief but was instead monetized by Aegis.

2105: Alixha Rahena coordinates a covert meeting of revolutionary leaders from across Europe, using recent climate disasters as a rallying cry for unity.

2106: An attack by Lux Aeterna devastates the London central dome.

Cast of Characters

Main Characters

Aeona (Aea) Lamonte: Aea is a resourceful young Outie living in Niederrad, a settlement outside Frankfurt's dome. She dreams of escaping the hardships of Outie life and yearns for a better future Inside.

Jarod Lima: A hardened contractor for Legacy Law Enforcement charged with locating and detaining Outie trespassers in the London dome network. A former PTSD-afflicted combat veteran, he walks a fine line between duty and disillusionment with his work.

Dana Lima: Jarod's wife, a negotiator for the disenfranchised during dome-related projects. She has keen sense of right and wrong, and struggles with her husband's dangerous, and ethically dubious work.

Scott Davies: A senior operative in Lux Aeterna and close confidant of Alixa Rahena. Scott suffers from doubts about the road taken by his organization.

Supporting Characters

Alixha Rahena: The visionary and calculating leader of Lux Aeterna. She is both a symbol of revolution for the disenfranchised and a controversial figure known for her radical methods.

Henry James Gibson: The enigmatic and recluse CEO of Aegis, a corporate giant controlling domes across the world.

Riley: A savvy member of Jarod's team. A key player in managing field operations and tech coordination.

Wyatt: A member of Jarod's team, known for his brash personality and combat prowess.

Kale: A quiet and analytical member of Jarod's team, who prefers working from behind the scenes. Tech-savvy drone operator.

Simian: A trusted operative in Scott's team.

Adriel: Jarod's handler who works off the books for Aegis.

Anya Pacula: The Chief Risk Officer of Aegis Corporation.

Lee Chen: The Chief Operating Officer of Aegis.

Dembwe: Leader of a private security team subcontracted for sensitive missions.

Tari: Dana Lima's personal assistant.

Gabriel: An enigmatic business leader in Niederrad, connected to the Outie resistance. His actions and network of contacts play a pivotal role in undermining dome negotiations.

Tabayah: Aea's younger sister.

Daemon: Ambitious young man tied to Gabriel's Niederrad crime syndicate resistance. He has a strong influence over Aea, intertwining their personal relationship with his revolutionary goals.

Ameer: Quiet and thoughtful friend of Daemon

Cali: A volatile and aggressive member of the Niederrad crime syndicate who often clashes with his comrades over strategy.

Kaliyah: A childhood friend of Aea.

Jema: A childhood friend of Aea.

Brett: Police escort assigned to protect Dana Lima.

Remy: Police escort assigned to protect Dana Lima.

Treston: An administrative member of the governing body of Rothbard, a Tokyo underground sanctuary, and old friend of Scott Davies

Tatum: Narcissistic middle-manager and Dana's boss heading the Niederrad dome expansion project.

Dai: Level-headed companion to Scott Davies.

Aki: Tech-specialist and close friend to Scott Davies.

Garrick: Friend to Davies and former combatant, loyal to Lux Aeterna.

Osawa: Communications director at Lux Aeterna.

Author Acknowledgements

The author would like to thank Kaare Hansson and Dorota Gorna for their indispensable contributions to this work. Special thanks go to Valentin Nordstroem for all the wine and late-night discussions about science, philosophy, and religion—many of which made it into the book in one form or another.

About the Author

André Hansson is a Swedish-British author, born in 1976. He debuted in 2014 with *The Jacket Trick* and currently lives in London. *Dome* is his second novel.

Printed in Great Britain
by Amazon

59749100R00290